# A Thin Bright Line

# Also by Lucy Jane Bledsoe

## Fiction

*The Big Bang Symphony: A Novel of Antarctica*
*Biting the Apple*
*This Wild Silence*
*Working Parts*
*Sweat: Stories and a Novella*

## Nonfiction

*The Ice Cave: A Woman's Adventures from the Mojave to the Antarctic*

## Childrens

*How to Survive in Antarctica*
*The Antarctic Scoop*
*Hoop Girlz*
*Cougar Canyon*
*Tracks in the Snow*
*The Big Bike Race*

# A Thin Bright Line

Lucy Jane Bledsoe

The University of Wisconsin Press

The University of Wisconsin Press
1930 Monroe Street, 3rd Floor
Madison, Wisconsin 53711-2059
uwpress.wisc.edu

3 Henrietta Street, Covent Garden
London WC2E 8LU, United Kingdom
eurospanbookstore.com

Printed in the United States of America

This book may be available in a digital edition.

Library of Congress Cataloging-in-Publication Data
Names: Bledsoe, Lucy Jane, author.
Title: A thin bright line / Lucy Jane Bledsoe.
Description: Madison, Wisconsin: The University of Wisconsin Press, [2017]
Identifiers: LCCN 2016013572 | ISBN 9780299309305 (cloth: alk. paper)
Subjects: LCSH: Bledsoe, Lucybelle, 1923–1966—Fiction.
Classification: LCC PS3552.L418 T47 2016 | DDC 813/.54—dc23
LC record available at https://lccn.loc.gov/2016013572

This is a work of fiction. While, as in all fiction, the literary perceptions and insights are based on experience and research, names, characters, places, and incidents are either products of the author's imagination or are used fictitiously.

For
Lucybelle Bledsoe
August 16, 1923–September 29, 1966


Also for
Rachel Carson, Lorraine Hansberry, and Willa Cather

I lost two cities, lovely ones. And, vaster,
some realms I owned, two rivers, a continent.
I miss them, but it wasn't a disaster.

**Elizabeth Bishop**

Snowflakes fall to earth and leave a message.

**Henri Bader**

A Thin Bright Line

## Author's Note

I'm named for my father's sister, Lucybelle Bledsoe. They grew up in Pocahontas, Arkansas, their mother a devout Christian homemaker and their
father both a farmer and a county judge. Lucybelle died in a fire in 1966,
when I was nine years old. Time and again I've imagined the horror of that
death.

She lived in a one-room apartment atop a detached garage. She would
have been asleep at the time of the fire, so she must have awakened coughing, her apartment filled with smoke, her brain already sluggish from the
carbon monoxide poisoning, her arms and legs aching. I imagine her un-
tangling her limbs and setting her bare feet on the hot scorched rug. They
say her bed was on fire. Perhaps, with the lethal thickening in her brain
preventing her from thinking clearly, she tried to fight the fire with pans of
water. A hot roar filled her ears as the flames leapt from the bed to the
curtains on the window facing the street. She might have tried hoisting the
sill of the other window—the one I now know looks out on an elm tree—
but didn't have the strength.

And yet her will to survive, that animal imperative, drove her weighted
legs. She shoved her way through the dense smoke, stepped through the

flames, tripped on some burnt shoes, and made it to the door. Opening it, she entered what she thought was the stairwell. A flight of stairs and she'd be at the door to the outside.

But she miscalculated the geography of her studio. She opened the closet door, rather than the entry door, and stepped inside that closed dark place. Her arms were empty. Her brain was saturated with carbon monoxide. She slumped to the floor of the closet and that's where she died. She was forty-three years old.

Over the years I asked my parents so many questions about my namesake, but I was never able to gather much information. My father told me that Lucybelle had wanted to be a lawyer, but that my grandfather told her it wasn't a proper profession for women. Without going to law school, she studied for and passed the bar exam anyway. My father also told me that she could read twice as fast as he could, and that Lucybelle and Judge Bledsoe, as my grandfather was called even by my grandmother, were the only two people who checked out Gibbon's *The History of the Decline and Fall of the Roman Empire* from the Randolph County Library.

My mother told me that Lucybelle was extremely independent, that even in the forties and fifties she wouldn't let men hold doors open for her. She never married. My sister, who is six years older than me, remembers a companion named Vera. For years I wondered about Vera, who might have been still alive, who possibly had grieved my aunt. I couldn't fathom any way of finding her.

My own memories of Lucybelle are slim: a woman of extreme kindness and much humor, a giver of perfect presents. I have a photo of her, taken in the forties, wearing trousers, her knees apart, staring stormily into the camera. On the back of the photo she, or someone else, had written the word "Showdown."

The above bits were the sum total of what I knew about my aunt and namesake, until one day a few years ago a friend suggested I Google her. The idea, frankly, seemed ridiculous to me. She died in 1966, a time when for most people computers were the stuff of science fiction. And anyway, Lucybelle—just a farm girl from Arkansas—had died in a fire, leaving no traces of the life she had lived. Even so, I went home that night and did exactly what my friend suggested.

What I discovered was astonishing. So began my journey through public records, historical documents, and interviews with her old friends and coworkers. Here is her story.

# Part One

## New York City, 1956

## Thursday, May 3, 1956

The grand steps leading down into Morningside Park were a one-block walk from Lucybelle's office at the Geological Society of America, where she was an assistant editor. She took her bagged lunch into the park nearly every day, even during the snow weeks in the winter. She loved the winding promenade, the rugged schist walls, big rocky outcroppings right in New York City, and the way the park formed a boundary between Morningside Heights and Harlem, a geographic zone of transition. She enjoyed the rub, the thin region of mixing, as if the park itself resisted a defining identity.

"That's Harlem, you know," the typist at the GSA told her at least weekly, as if they toiled on the border of a hostile foreign country.

"Yes," Lucybelle responded emphatically every time. They worked for geologists, for god's sake; she knew the ground upon which she walked. She enjoyed pretending that she didn't take the typist's meaning and would add a comment on the park's history, how it had been developed because city planners didn't think they could build streets and housing on the steep cliffs, or on the characteristics of the rock itself, or how she enjoyed watching children play ball or young mothers push their babies in carriages as she ate her lunch.

Finally, to shut the girl up, Lucybelle told her that her attorney brother, out in Oregon, had prepared that state's comparison of public school education for whites and Negroes, which fed into the national study resulting in *Brown v. Board of Education*. The look on the girl's pale face was a mix of distaste and chastisement. She never mentioned Harlem again.

On that warm spring day in early May, as Lucybelle reached the top of the steps, she paused to admire the clean rays of sunlight finding their ways through the iridescent green leaves of the trees. At home in Arkansas the light was warm and spongy, but here even sunlight took on a purposeful task, shooting down into the park where it lit a young woman's fresh walk and warmed the wooden bench where Lucybelle would sit. She liked reading the *New Yorker* while she ate her sandwich. Sometimes during lunch she took notes for her novel.

As she began her descent toward the inviting spot, a tall skinny man with thick, messy black hair and a matching goatee fell into step beside her. He said, "Washburn says you're first rate. A real hotshot."

She picked up her pace, intending to lose the creep, and then registered the famous geologist's name. She respected Link Washburn enormously.

7

No one understood the Arctic better than he did. She stopped and looked up at the man who waited a few steps above her, grinning as if all of life were a joke. His eyes were a dark blue under striking black eyebrows, and his face bony, like Abraham Lincoln's, only much more handsome. He wore too-short blue jeans and an unironed short-sleeved plaid shirt.

"The very best, Washburn says." The man spoke with a European accent. Maybe French. Had he followed her?

"Who are you?"

"Henri Bader."

She scanned her memory for the name. But no, they'd never published a paper by an Henri Bader.

"I don't know you." He'd jogged down the stairs to stand next to her, but she still had to look up at least a foot to tell him that.

"But you know Washburn," he said.

"Not personally."

"He knows your work."

Why was this man waylaying her? She wasn't sure she liked the mocking look in his eyes. She would never turn away from Washburn himself, but this wasn't Washburn himself. She looked over her shoulder, down into the sunlit park, and then without another word, headed for her bench.

"Give me five minutes," Henri Bader said to her back, following. "I have a proposal for you."

The word proposal hit home. The heft of it, the way it pointed into the future. She couldn't resist the combination of his connection to the legendary geologist and a proposal. She sat on her bench and turned to him when he sat on the other end.

"Assistant editor for the Geological Society of America. For ten years already. You read at about three times the pace most college-educated people read. You studied for the Arkansas bar and passed—without going to law school."

Astonished, she asked, "How do you know that?"

He grinned, revealing crooked teeth and a dark-red tongue. "Graduated top in your high school class, valedictorian of Pocahontas High." He paused and laughed at the dubiousness of that distinction. "University of Arkansas. Phi Beta Kappa. Smart girl! Masters degree in literature from Columbia, after which you mysteriously dropped your studies—you were a shoe-in for a PhD and university teaching job, what happened?—and went to work as an assistant for the GSA. It doesn't add up."

A chill prickled her skin. She made herself look this Henri Bader in the eye. "You said you had a proposal."

Bader laughed. "I like that: a girl who gets right to the point."

She pulled her bologna sandwich out of her brown paper sack, peeled back the waxed paper, and took a bite.

"It's a job offer with the Army Corps of Engineers. Between you and me, I don't give a rat's ass for the military side of this thing. I'm in it for the research dollars, plain and simple. However, a little finesse in that regard will be required. Washburn says you do speak your mind, but that you can be discreet. That's going to be necessary on several fronts." Bader pointed at the other half of her sandwich. "May I?"

Before she could say no, Bader picked up the remaining half of her bologna sandwich and devoured it in two bites.

"You want half of this too?" She held up her apple and meant the question sarcastically.

He grabbed the apple, took a big bite, and handed it back. With juice squirting out the sides of his mouth, he said, "Of course they care mostly about the military applications of the research. You know that boy scout who went to Antarctica with Byrd? He's convinced everyone in Washington that the Russians are coming for us, as we speak. They're on their way, crawling across Siberia and . . . who knows, are they coming via Greenland or Alaska? Either way, we've got to be ready. We've got to understand snow and ice." Bader roared his big laugh. "I can work with that scenario. You've heard about the International Geophysical Year? That's my baby. And it's phenomenal what we've got funding to do."

Henri Bader paused. He lowered his chin and looked at her through those dark-blue eyes. They made her think of Washburn's photographs of glaciers: translucent, cerulean, futuristic. She'd stared and stared at those photographs, aching to experience the intensity of the pure polar light shining through ice crystals.

"The Russians are coming," Bader said in a low quiet voice, and then he threw up his hands, wagged his fingers, and chortled a ghost laugh, ending with "Ha!"

Lucybelle smiled.

"Just as an aside, I've been to Russia. I *speak* Russian, along with five other languages, and sugar, those people are smart and they fund their scientists, but cold is cold and ice is ice. They'd be fools to come for us on sleds, but well, policy isn't my job, and I'd shoot myself in the foot if I convinced anyone this research isn't necessary for political purposes. So suffice it to say, the Russians are coming, and we need to stop them, and to do so, we need to understand everything there is to know about ice. This is where you and I come in. I have no time for niceties, for modesty, so I'm going to give you the facts. I'm Swiss, the preeminent ice scientist in Europe. America doesn't *have* an ice scientist, so they've brought me over. Let me tell you what we have planned." He paused again and looked out in the distance. "The most exotic project I can't tell you about because it's classified. Enticing, no? More on that later. For now: we'll be building roads and runways that can stand up to permafrost. That's the dull part. But listen here, the best of all: we're going to find a way to pull ice cores. Think, Miss Lucybelle: the snow falls year after year, throughout the millennia, and in the far Arctic and Antarctic, none melts because it's too cold. It just piles up. Each year's new snowfall tells a story. A story of earth's climate, for one. But other stories too, depending on what gets embedded in the layers of ice. Leaves, bones, shells, volcanic ash, meteorites, spores, bacteria. Treasure troves. Preserved, perfectly preserved, for thousands of years. We could look at that, if only we could pull up a core of ice without breaking or melting it." He clapped his hands. "Got a cookie or something?"

"No. The job. What is it?"

"You'll run the editorial department. You'll have assistants working for *you*."

She concentrated on looking disinterested. She wadded her paper sack, shoved it in her purse, and pulled the *New Yorker* onto her lap, as if she were about to start reading.

"You're interested," he said. "How could you not be? A promotion. More money. Much more exciting work."

For ten years she'd read the papers of world-renowned scientists who wrote about the making of mountains and the habits of prehistoric insects, who measured the depths of the seas and the travel patterns of sand dunes. She'd felt lucky to get so close to the frontiers of knowledge, but Bader's offer projected her into an unknown beyond all that. The poles. The Arctic and the Antarctic. The lucidity of ice.

For a moment, the possibilities transported her. But only for a moment. She knew what he was hinting at when he said it didn't add up. *You were a shoe-in for a PhD and university teaching job, what happened?* Her advisor, Joseph Wood Krutch, had been so angry when she quit the graduate program after getting her master's degree. He was convinced she had a brilliant academic career awaiting her. But by then she'd moved into the apartment on West 12th Street in Greenwich Village, discovered the attendant pleasures of that neighborhood, and wasn't willing to give them up. If she were to teach at a college or university, she would have no privacy. She'd be expected to participate in the social life of the faculty, probably in some small town.

The military would be ever so much worse than a college or university. She'd heard stories of exposure, of people's families receiving unpleasant letters. The thought of such a letter in Daddy's hands curdled any bit of enthusiasm she had for this offer.

"No," she said. "I'm not interested."

"We *know*, you know."

She didn't lower her eyes.

"This is a classified position," he said. "Highest level, actually. We've already done a security check on you. We know everything."

"Meaning what?" She hated the way her voice broke, and she cleared her throat loudly to correct the appearance of uneasiness. She slid her hands under her thighs so he wouldn't see the tremor.

"Meaning McCarthy would not approve." That roar of a laugh again and then the same abrupt halt to it.

Had they actually followed her? Someone must have. How could they know that about her?

"Yeah," Bader grinned. "*That.*"

He wasn't laughing at her. He was laughing at the absurdity of them, whoever they were. She saw that. But she'd taken enough risks for a lifetime and she had everything she needed. She'd come so very far from there, the farm in Arkansas, to here, a job in New York, an apartment in the Village, filled with Phyllis's theater friends. She had so much more than she ever thought she could have. Greenland and Antarctica? Not necessary.

"You're smart as a whip," he said. "You have the exact skills we need. There really would be no sacrifice on your part. Just stay out of the bars. Don't get arrested."

She stood and straightened her skirt, shoved the handle of her purse up her arm. Looking down at him, she said, "No, thank you."

"No one else finds out," he continued. "You have my word. It won't be discussed at work, between anyone. You'll have my full support."

She looked beyond Henri Bader to the rocky outcroppings of Morningside Park, her lunchtime cliffs. She longed to explain to this arrogant man exactly what he was asking. To give up friends. Her dream of writing a true novel. She wanted more sunlight, not less.

"Look. I only brought it up so you would know you don't have to worry about any surprising, uh, revelations getting in your way. We'll all be scientists in our division, and scientists are a whole other breed of animal. You know this. You've worked with us for ten years at the GSA. No one would care, even if they did find out, but they won't."

Lucybelle shook her head. "No, thank you."

"You're going to be an assistant editor for the rest of your life because you're afraid?"

How dare he. She'd never had this conversation with someone who wasn't. He had no right. *His* entire career wasn't on the line. His reputation. The lease on his apartment. The love of his family.

"Besides," he said, "Chicago is America's best-kept secret. You'll love it there."

"What's Chicago got to do with it?"

"That's where we'll be. Wilmette, actually, but close enough."

She left him on the bench and walked briskly down the promenade, letting her heels hammer the pavement. The steps leading up to Morningside Heights felt as challenging as a mountainside, but she pushed her pace. She was sure he watched her the entire climb up the dozens of stone steps. When she crested the top, she turned and looked down. He sat with his knees spread, long arms across the back of the bench, his face tipped toward her, basking in the sunshine. He raised a flattened hand to his brow and gave her a little military salute.

Lucybelle turned her back and tried to retrieve the pleasure she'd gotten, just a few minutes earlier, from the May sunshine, but the feeling of the day had been ruined.


## Monday, June 11, 1956

Lucybelle got off the train at 14th Street, walked down 8th Avenue, and took a left on West 12th. It still pleased her, all these years later, that she'd landed an apartment just one block away from where Willa Cather and

Edith Lewis had lived. Cather had walked these same routes home. She'd lived under the same patch of sky.

The air was light with an early summer freshness, not yet too hot. She hoped to work on her novel tonight. Maybe Phyllis would go out with friends. Or maybe she'd already had a few drinks this afternoon, which meant she'd go to bed early. Though Lucybelle had complained back then, she now missed the years when Phyllis had been in shows, out every night at rehearsals and performances. She knew she shouldn't think of Phyllis like that, shouldn't be glad when she was gone, but didn't everyone feel that way after a few years together?

She did love Phyllis. How could she not? Phyllis was everything she'd come to New York to find. They were like Willa Cather characters, both punching through the dull expectations of their small hometowns, making their way to New York, Phyllis the gifted and radiant one, finding her way on stage, and Lucybelle content to hold a hand up to the glare of stage lighting, watching from the shadows, devoted. At first, just being there was enough.

Lucybelle had felt guilty about slipping away from the farm during the war, when her family was busy worrying about John Perry on a ship in the Pacific, when the eyes of the entire country were focused overseas. What right did she have to do just what she pleased when so many were sacrificing so much? And yet, all kinds of girls were fleeing farms, and she took her chance too. Oh, but what a moment that had been, getting the acceptance letter from the graduate program in literature at Columbia University. Even Daddy conceded that in literature a woman might be able to claim what he called "a life of the mind." She'd moved quickly, before Daddy or the university could revoke approval, and took a room near Columbia. Within weeks Krutch hired her to ghostwrite his theater reviews for the *Nation*. He invited her to all the parties, where she met actors and actresses, lighting designers, producers, directors, and stagehands. It had been enough to simply witness the dazzle, to bask in the spilled light.

Phyllis Dove had black hair, red lips, and far-reaching gray eyes, capable of pinning back-row audiences to their seats. Blood flushed to her cheeks and throat with little provocation, and she used that volatility to her advantage. She was desperate for approval, all actresses are, that's the primary goal of their trade, to win people to their characters, and at first that desperation caused her to work very hard. She won a couple of good roles early on, but then her career fizzled. It was possibly just bad luck, poor timing. Not everyone can make it. But it was all the more painful because she'd been on the brink of making it, so close. Everything soured after her performance in Ibsen's *Doll House*. The reviews were good, some quite good, but Phyllis had been angered by a couple of critical remarks. One reviewer said she'd never make it on Broadway, and in her fury, she'd thrown a vase full of water and red roses against the wall. Her hair was dyed blond for the part, making her look especially sinister in that moment of passion, the red of her lips and eyelids harsh against the yellow hair. The criticism snaked into Phyllis's consciousness, took up residence, began to fester. She had the thinnest skin.

Lucybelle implored her to ignore the reviews, to keep on working, to develop her voice, to forget what the critics said. Anyway, one called her "a bright new talent," and another said, "Phyllis Dove embodies the role of Kristine with sensitive perfection." It didn't matter. She wanted Broadway. She wanted the leads. One day, when one of their friends got tired of her whining and said, "You can't sing, Phyllis. You aren't going to get a Broadway show," she slapped him so hard the café owner called the police. How many times had Lucybelle argued that there were lots of good roles she *could* have? It was true: she was a character actress, not a lead. She needed to listen to their friends. Though she was lovely enough for a lead, she had far too much personality. Phyllis was very funny when she wanted to be, and once Lucybelle made the mistake of suggesting she look for comic roles. It was the morning after a particularly humiliating—Phyllis's word—audition, and they were in the kitchen making coffee. Lucybelle was late for work and exasperated by Phyllis's lengthy description of the director's idiocy. But it was also a funny description, and so Lucybelle made the suggestion. Phyllis, who was putting a piece of bread in the toaster, froze in place as if she'd been stunned. She blanched to the color of skim milk, then quietly left the apartment, with the piece of bread in her hand, and didn't return for forty-eight hours.

Occasionally, if they were both in good moods, maybe on a Friday night after a couple of martinis, just the two of them alone, Lucybelle still tried to convince Phyllis that it wasn't over. If only she could impart even a tiny fraction of the substance of her conversations with Krutch about the meaning of art, the bedrock of human creativity. Making meaningful words and objects created lifeblood that held people together. Our stories.

14

Our visions of beauty. A life in the theater, Lucybelle would tell Phyllis, holding her hands too tightly, didn't mean stardom. It meant devotion to the work, love of the work.

Phyllis's eyes would fill with tears. "I know. I *know*. I can be so shallow. That's why I need you."

"You don't need me. You need to act. No one is going to hand you anything, ever. You need to do what you love, not just wish for it."

"You're right. You're always right."

Sometimes it seemed as if Phyllis kissed her to stop the talking. It always worked. Phyllis's mouth was an epic poem all on its own, an unfolding story. The striving and anger fell away when Phyllis kissed, and her longing took over, as if she was trying to get at something, but couldn't. They bedeviled Lucybelle, these kisses, the way they supplanted language. Their lovemaking always felt unfinished, as if there was more to say, or *something* to say, but they had failed. As if, just beyond the kisses were all the answers. Lucybelle tried to ignore that incomplete feeling, her desire like a hand reaching down her throat, grasping for something that it had not yet found.

They lived on the third and top floor of the brick building at 277 West 12th. She loved the cobblestoned street, the five-step stoop with iron railings, the windows' stone lintels, and at the top, the bracketed stone cornice in a soothing gray to contrast the warm red bricks. She climbed the stairs tonight, happy to be home, looking forward to taking L'Forte out for a walk in the still-warm evening. She checked the door; it was locked and so she used her key. As she stepped inside, she heard the tenor of a man's voice. A scenario she'd been foolish enough to not consider: Phyllis had brought her friends home to drink tonight.

"Hello," Lucybelle called out.

L'Forte came skittering around the corner on his short legs. He always made the turn too fast when Lucybelle came home, and his toenails had scored a thicket of scratches in the hardwood floor. She scooped the brown dachshund up into her arms and kissed both black eyebrow patches. He licked her face as she stroked his long silky ears.

There had been no human answer, so she called out again. She heard the sound of a chair scraping on the floor and something akin to a whimper. She entered the room to find Phyllis standing in front of the refrigerator, nearly at attention, and Fred Higgins, a newish member in Phyllis's crowd, maybe an actor, she couldn't remember, sitting at the kitchen table. A slight man with a handsome enough face, a bit winnowed and tense, but with a quick and eager smile, Fred was the exact sort of person Lucybelle preferred to avoid: intelligent, probably quite intelligent, but possessing a viral fear, a timidity that would stop any forward movement of his intellect in its tracks. Daddy loved to laugh at her impatience with people and commented often and proudly that Lucybelle didn't suffer fools gladly. Now she raised her eyebrows, unable to disguise her displeasure.

"Lucy," Phyllis said.

The way Phyllis spoke her name felt like a reprimand, as if she could read Lucybelle's critical thoughts. She tried to correct her attitude by smiling at the insipid Fred and giving him a hearty hello.

Fred made circles on the Formica tabletop with his middle finger, as if he were stirring an imaginary pile of salt, and didn't answer. A yeasty unpleasantness thickened the air.

Lucybelle set L'Forte down on the floor, fished the pack of Chesterfields out of her purse, and lit one. She leaned back against the yellow countertop, her spine pressing into the edges of the tiles. A question dangled in the room, and she tried to focus, discern what it was asking. She believed in her ability to solve problems, but she needed to know what the question was.

"How was work?" Phyllis finally asked.

"Fine." She reached down and petted L'Forte, who sat on his haunches loyally right at her feet. She repeated, "Fine."

She used to ask about Phyllis's day too. Had the audition gone well? Had she learned of any new roles or met any helpful people? For a while anyway she'd bought the story that Phyllis needed to hang out in the cafés and bars in the Village, that her work required she meet people, lots of people. Even when Lucybelle stopped believing it, she liked the way Phyllis's charisma brought interesting people into their lives, people who loved books and plays and music, people who believed there were hundreds of different ways to live a life.

"Sit down, Lucy." Phyllis ran her hand, fingers spread, through her black hair. The color in her cheeks was high, nearly feverish. She wore a tight, gray pencil skirt and a yellow, short-sleeved sweater, as if she'd dressed to go well with their kitchen. Lucybelle still thought she was beautiful, sometimes even ravishing. But now, standing with her back against the refrigerator, with Fred Higgins at the table drawing imaginary circles with his finger, Lucybelle thought she looked unpleasantly puffy and jaundiced, as if the sweater and kitchen tiles reflected her skin tone. She felt disloyal by the thought. Was Phyllis unwell? Perhaps Fred had weaseled his way into her afternoon and she'd had more than she could take of his passively demanding presence. There was something dogged about Fred, a neediness that was partially disguised by his good looks.

She thought of a way to rescue Phyllis. "I'm going to go change," she announced. "Remember we're due at Harry and Wesley's in half an hour."

Instead of a grateful smile, Phyllis said "Lucy" again.

*Was* she ill?

"I need to talk to you. There's no easy way to say this. Fred and I have decided to marry."

Lucybelle waited for the punch line. She even coughed out a little laugh, so sure that this was a joke. Fred. *Fred.* That was funny.

L'Forte put his front paws up on her thighs, under her skirt, tearing her stockings. She lifted the dog and again tried to focus. Here was her kitchen. Her dachshund. The stove, refrigerator, and coffeepot. The narrow window looking out into the airshaft. And Phyllis. Here was Phyllis with whom she'd shared the last eight years of her life.

She snuffed the cigarette in the sink and carried L'Forte to her bedroom, passing Phyllis's on the way. Through the open door she saw the two suitcases sitting neatly side by side on the bed. Lucybelle set down L'Forte and entered Phyllis's room. She looked in the closet: empty. Oddly, numbly, she tried to remember what Fred did for work. She'd been supporting Phyllis for the last however many years. Would he do that now? She must be quite sure about this relationship—*married?*

Lucybelle pushed both suitcases off the bed, and they thudded onto the colorful oval rug her mother had made from old rags. It had been a gift for Phyllis's thirtieth birthday, and Phyllis had had a heyday with the symbolism. Lucybelle had tried for days to convince her that the rug represented affection and hours of labor, the weaving of one life into another. She'd been touched her mother had given Phyllis such a personal gift. Phyllis only ever saw the reworking of old rags, something to walk on. She insisted on keeping the rug central in her own bedroom, as a reminder, she liked to say, of what was in store for her. Even old rags had a use.

How many times had Phyllis started sentences with "If this acting thing doesn't work out . . ."? She'd move to San Francisco. She'd start a bakery. She'd adopt orphans. Lucybelle ignored these rants. She knew no one in San Francisco; she couldn't scramble an egg, let alone bake; and she didn't have the money to support herself, never mind orphans.

What a fool she'd been to not see that Phyllis truly had been searching for an escape route.

At least one thing was diamond clear: Lucybelle would not plead.

"Get out," she told Fred when she returned to the kitchen.

It would have been better, much better, if Phyllis had stayed resolute. But tears filled her beautiful gray eyes, rainwater wetting stone, and she looked at Fred, asking him—the far weaker personality—to make this fit. It didn't fit. It was as wrong as overalls in church, as wrong as anything Lucybelle had ever known. Fred stayed right where he was, though he remained mute.

"I can't," Phyllis said to Lucybelle, the tears streaming now, her hands working the air in front of her heart as if she were acting on stage. "I'm not you."

Ah yes: Lucybelle was the one. The dark sister. The odd girl.

But no, Phyllis didn't mean that. She wasn't making a point even half as sharp as that. She only meant that she had no integrity. Couldn't love. Couldn't live. Instead, she'd head down a long dark tunnel of marriage with Fred Higgins. Lucybelle saw the whole thing so clearly. Later she'd wonder if she *should* have pleaded, explained, described the hell for which they were headed. Later, during insomniac nights, she'd regret having given in so easily. Even Daddy, who knew nothing about the nature of her relationship with Phyllis, was disgusted at her easy acquiescence. "You just gave them the apartment?" he said. "It was yours. You found it before you even knew her."

But in those first moments, she lost herself. She felt nearly transparent in her slight, pale build. Her outsized intelligence felt like a crippled leg she had to drag about with her. She returned to Phyllis's bedroom, hefted the two suitcases, and clicked them open. She turned the contents out onto the oval rag rug. Then she took the suitcases to her own bedroom and stuffed clothes into them. She'd come back later for her books.

For now she just wanted out of this apartment, away from that pathetic scene in the kitchen. She carried the two suitcases to the entryway, set them down, and picked up L'Forte. Holding her dog, she stepped into the kitchen. Phyllis was sobbing into her hands, and Fred was comforting her, his arms around her shoulders, his mouth murmuring into her hair. Lucybelle grabbed the grocery basket from off the kitchen counter and dropped L'Forte into it. He barely fit and she had to push his hind end, but he must have sensed the gravity of the situation because he didn't make a sound.

Phyllis lifted her head, cast her gaze desperately about the room, as if she were the one being left, the ruby lips fishing open and closed, open and closed.

"Don't talk," Lucybelle said. "Not a single word."

It was almost impossible to walk carrying the two suitcases and dog-laden grocery basket, and anyway, she didn't need to drag her entire life down the streets of the Village, allowing her departure to be viewed by gawkers, so she hailed a taxicab. Once her suitcases were in the trunk, and she and L'Forte were in the backseat, she realized she had no idea where to go, so she gave the driver the address of the Geological Society of America on 117th Street. She used her key to let herself into the office and stowed the suitcases in a closet. She lay on the floor, with L'Forte in her arms, for the rest of the night. She still had her job, after all, the world on her desk every morning, literally. She edited the papers of men who explored the Amazon, mapped the Pyrenees, climbed Mount McKinley. She'd never expected a dark-haired Bohemian lover. It was almost a cliché, nothing she would have tolerated in a novel. No, not true. This, she thought, is exactly what Cather would have written. I'm to get on a train, move on with an ironic appreciation for the heart's beauty and wreckage.

In the morning she asked her boss for a week off, booked passage on the train to Little Rock, and went home.

## Thursday, June 14, 1956

Daddy drove to Little Rock in the blue Plymouth to meet her train so that they'd get a chance to catch up, just the two of them. As the soybean and rice fields flew by, and they talked about the price a hog could fetch this year, Lucybelle felt that disturbing mix of deep relief and acute irritation. Coming home always triggered a tug of war between two essential selves. She was this: the fields and hogs and easy banter. And she was something so different as well. As she listened to Daddy talk, she forced memories of parties in the Village, the library at Columbia, the walks through Harlem to pass like moving pictures through her thoughts. As if some day the seam between her past and her present would smooth out and her selves would

19

merge. How could she be this, so fundamentally this, and also that, mostly clearly and purely that?

She turned to check on L'Forte in the backseat. He'd climbed out of the grocery basket and stood with his front paws on the window's edge, head out in the air, brown ears flying. God, she wanted a cigarette.

"So what have you been reading?" Daddy asked his favorite question.

"I don't know. Nothing."

His eagle eyes, peering out from under overgrown eyebrows, turned on her with disapproval, and his thin-lipped mouth tightened into a pale line. He barely fit under the steering wheel with what her mother called his "prominent abdomen," as if it were a character asset.

She didn't need him following the scent of her despair, so she quickly changed her tune. "Phyllis and I have been reading *Macbeth* aloud."

"Ah ha." He was well pleased.

That had been over a year ago, but it wasn't a lie. She'd been trying to prompt Phyllis's deeper thespian, return her to a love of theater, the language, the depth of feeling in drama, to get her past the personal disappointments. For a while it seemed to almost work. They both loved those evenings.

Arriving at the house in the early afternoon, Daddy didn't rush her inside. He understood her need to stand in the front yard for a few moments while he carried in her suitcases so she could look at the scruffy grass, the fat-trunked oak tree, the exterior of the little blue house. Lucybelle walked away from the shade of the oak, to the far side of the front yard, and stood in the place where she'd lain for hours as a child. Her bookishness, her pale skin and bad eyes, and her reluctance to eat tagged her as "sickly." Dr. Wilson prescribed two hours of direct sunshine a day, weather permitting, and so Daddy had built a wooden pen where she could have privacy while lying naked under the sun. As she listened to the cheerful shouts of other children, comfortably clothed in overalls, playing freely in the surrounding yards and streets, she accepted that she was sickly—she was too young to know otherwise—and yet some deeper part of her knew that there was nothing at all wrong with her, that she just liked to read and fantasize about worlds far from this one. The pen did allow her hours of uninterrupted reading. Daydreaming too. She liked to lie on her back and look up at the black crows circling, their fingerlike wings spread open against the white-hot sky.

Why had she thought coming home a good idea in her condition? Pocahontas always seemed to comfort her brother, remind him of who he was, and she supposed it reminded her of who she was too, but it also showed her who she wasn't. Phyllis had left her, but it felt as if all of New York had left her, as if her entire life had been a figment of her imagination. *Poof.* Gone.

In the morning she rode to town with Daddy and while he went to the barbershop for a shave, she visited with people on the street. "New York!" they still said, all these years later, grasping her hand and shaking their heads slowly, neither admiring nor admonishing, simply perplexed. Only Edie, the editor of the *Pocahontas Star Herald*, looked directly into her eyes and said, "Lucky you." Later in the morning, Lucybelle sat in the courtroom and listened to Daddy preside. It was comforting the way he doled out justice, honoring the complexity of the issues before his bench even if they were about the placement of a fence or a woman's drunken rampage. As a child, she and John Perry thrilled at the occasional murder and along with everyone else in town they'd attend the entire trial.

In the woody confines of Daddy's small courtroom, Lucybelle saw herself too clearly: the slim, pale figure; the sandy hair, not quite curly, but unruly just the same; the deep-set eyes, the skin below too often pooled with bluish half-moons, obscured, in any case, by thick glasses; the expressive mouth, her mood broadcast in the set of her lips, parted or tightened, her pleasure or frustration. Wry and brainy, she was the perfect foil for vivacious Phyllis.

She hated Fred Higgins, and yet she felt almost grateful to him, as if he were a tornado whisking Phyllis away, quick and sudden, the pain acute but necessary. She might have held out a hand to pull her back, but she didn't. Deep down, past the raw heartbreak, she felt as if she were getting away with something, abandoning her post. She realized that what scared her most was the possibility that Phyllis would not actually, truly go away.

## Monday, June 25, 1956

She would never tell Henri Bader that he had rescued her. He'd like it too much. He sounded smug when she called him the week she returned to New York.

"So," he said, "that didn't take long."

"It's been well over a month."

"What makes you think we still have the position open?"

She remained silent until he suggested they meet at a diner on 7th Avenue. "That's in Harlem," he added, and she smiled, thinking of the frightened GSA secretary.

"When?"

"Right now. I leave for Chicago in the morning."

That suited Lucybelle just fine. An hour later she pulled out the diner chair across from Bader and folded her hands on the tabletop. She looked at the craggy, dark-haired man and they both smiled.

"I ordered you a burger, fries, and a chocolate shake," he said.

"I prefer to order my own lunches."

"Sure. I can understand that. Next time." He pushed a piece of paper across the table at her. "Salary offer. Just say you accept, and we'll move on to other details."

"You're asking me to move to Chicago. I'll need a thousand more." She could feel her heart thumping just below her exposed clavicle. She tucked a napkin into the top of her dress's scoop neck, as if that flimsy scrap could protect her.

"I can go up five hundred."

The sizzle of potatoes being lowered into a vat of hot oil made her flinch. This place smelled too much like home, sweet tea and frying meat, as if he'd intentionally picked a place that would weaken her. She girded herself and said, "A thousand."

"Okay, fine." Bader sat back in his chair and squinted at her. "There's one more thing we have to talk about. A little stipulation. With regard to your inclinations. I don't give a rat's ass, but this is a classified position. Basically, we have to ask you to not act on them. Agreed?"

Her inclinations. "I thought you said—"

"The documents will show you as widowed."

"But I'm not."

"You were only twenty. How tragic, losing your husband so young like that."

"I'm thirty-three."

"I mean when he was killed overseas. In the war."

Lucybelle stared at the crazy man. "I don't understand. That's a lie."

"In fact," Bader continued in a falsetto, "it's too tragic to even talk about. Please don't bring it up."

She couldn't help laughing and surprised herself by playing along. "I probably can't ever fall in love again. That's how heartbroken I am."

"That's the spirit," he said.

Lucybelle looked past his head of shaggy black hair, past the wooden tables and lunch counter, even past the people hurrying down 7th Avenue. She could see a small slice of the blue sky, like a cap on the city, as if it were part of a costume. In New York she could be anybody she wanted to be, and everything—the tall buildings and paved streets, even the sky—would go along with the ruse. But in the Midwest, the sky witnessed, reigned, demanded a certain plain truthfulness.

Yet, she said yes.

As she walked back across Morningside Park, she decided that it wouldn't really be a lie. It was actually true that she couldn't imagine falling in love again. She'd live a life of the mind, just like Daddy said. It would be a new kind of freedom.

## Wednesday, August 1, 1956

Her friend Harry showed up at five o'clock on her last day at the Geological Society of America. He had no idea she'd quit, that she was moving to Chicago; so far as he knew, it was just another Friday night.

"Where've you been?" he asked, walking right by the typist and stopping in front of her desk. "No one has seen you for weeks. I decided to investigate."

"Phyllis and I broke up." She laughed at his struggle to look like this was news. "It's okay. You don't have to pretend you don't know."

"I've been worried about you."

"You needn't have been. I'm fine." Could she tell Harry that a part of her was even relieved? She had loved Phyllis, she truly had, but what was left by now, after all these years and bottles, was the fantasy, the idea of the woman. If Lucybelle were truly a Willa Cather protagonist, she'd stay in that fantasy, be staunchly loyal, despite Phyllis's dissolution. But she wasn't a Willa Cather protagonist, and she would not ally herself with self-pity. Harry would probably laugh if she told him her plan for a life of the mind.

23

Harry had served in the Navy, like her brother, and now lived with Wesley, whom he met in the service. He had a thriving psychiatric practice and unlike the stereotype was one of the happiest people Lucybelle knew. She liked being with him, even if his conversation wasn't always scintillating, just for the relief he brought with his easygoing laughter and perennial kindness. Wesley too was a nice man, but much more quiet, even studious, perhaps a bit pedantic, a freelance scholar of Renaissance music. It was unclear if he had any actual employment, though he referred often to his "work," which she took to mean listening to old records and hunting down recordings in music stores.

"Let's go to the Bagatelle!" She could use a couple of strong drinks. Tomorrow she'd pack, which would take all of about a half an hour—she still didn't know what to do about the rest of her possessions at 12th Street—and the next day she and L'Forte would take the train to Chicago.

"But what if Phyllis is there?"

"What if she is?" Lucybelle took his big arm and smiled at the typist who, having long since written off Lucybelle as an old maid, literally dropped her jaw. Harry was handsome in a furred and chunky kind of way, his cube of a nose echoing a squared chin. He had a thick, muscled build, like a strongman in a circus. She fluttered her fingertips at the typist, a mocking gesture, and rode Harry's arm out the door. "Anyway, she won't be. She and Fred have gone straight, remember?"

Harry patted her hand on his bicep and pinned her with one of his bovine looks, all long lashes and syrupy pupils. "Thank god you've extracted yourself from the maw of that woman."

"Maw? She's not that bad, is she?"

"She used to be delightful."

"Well, thank you for that." It was painful to remember the delightful Phyllis, but reassuring to know that Lucybelle hadn't been crazy to be drawn in.

Wesley and Clare sat in one of the red leatherette booths at the Bagatelle. She and Harry slid in beside them.

"How *are* you?" Clare asked.

"Fine. I'm moving to Chicago."

"Moving?" Clare said. "Phyllis is hardly worth leaving the city over."

"We're not talking about Phyllis tonight," Wesley said sternly.

"Levity," Harry said, "and cocktails. What's everyone drinking?"

Lucybelle glanced at the burgundy velvet satchel sitting on the booth bench between herself and Clare. The woman's trademark accessory was a miniature homosexual library, always stuffed with pamphlets, newspaper clippings, and books. Clare chided anyone who wasn't as obvious as she was, which covered pretty much everyone else. She loved to talk openly about her love affairs, of which she had many, and she was always the first with gossip about famous members of the tribe.

"Don't worry," Clare said, seeing her glance at the satchel. "I'm not going to ask for it back again."

Over a year ago Clare had stopped Lucybelle on Greenwich Street. "You'll never guess what I've acquired."

Phyllis never wanted to be seen even pausing with Clare, but Lucybelle had been alone that day so she gratified the keen young woman by asking, "What?"

Clare pulled a glossy photograph from her over-the-shoulder collection and held it up for Lucybelle to see. It depicted Willa Cather with a brush cut, looking defiantly into the camera. A charge surged through Lucybelle as she took the picture and held it in her own hands. If the woman's eyes were expressive, her mouth was downright . . . kissable.

"How'd you get this?"

It was Clare's favorite question. It seemed to be her lifework to gain access to all things queer. She smiled broadly and shrugged. She wasn't telling.

"May I keep it for a few days?"

Clare smirked. "It's just a picture. You can't sleep with a photograph."

"I'll get it back to you."

Clare hesitated. She treated the items in her satchel as contraband and enjoyed the currency of possessing them. But she liked Lucybelle, and even more, she liked the way the Willa Cather picture was a hook. "A couple of days would be okay."

Lucybelle had intended to have a copy made, but she'd felt shy about taking the butch picture into a photography shop. If she'd had a camera she could have just shot the picture itself, but the result would have been a much fuzzier image, ruining Cather's bold transcendence. The third time Clare asked for the picture back, Lucybelle said that she'd misplaced it.

"I know you didn't lose the picture," Clare said now as she moved the burgundy velvet satchel to her other side, leaving the space between herself and Lucybelle open. "But if you want it bad enough to lie about it, I guess you should have it."

Thankfully she didn't have to answer Clare because Harry arrived with their drinks. He had Helen and Serena, whom he'd found at the bar, in tow. Here came Charles too, an overly talkative and effeminate man. Lucybelle sipped her martini and relaxed. Even if Phyllis came in the door, she'd leave immediately when she spotted either Clare or Charles. With seven now in the booth, Clare's hip and upper arm squeezed right up against Lucybelle's.

"Marriage!" Charles rang out, having not heard the prohibition on mentioning Phyllis. "It's pathetic. I mean, *Fred.*" He did a quick imitation of the simpering man.

Serena said, "That's not funny."

"Oh, come on, honey," Charles said. "Please. You have to laugh. What other response is there?"

Harry reached under the table and squeezed Lucybelle's hand. He asked, "Are you really moving to Chicago?"

Everyone quieted to listen. "I have a new job. Big pay raise."

"Is that a good idea?" Harry shifted into his intensely focused mode, the one she imagined he used with patients.

"It's a great idea," she said and polished off her martini.

"But do you know anyone there?"

"Holy cow, that's too close to the farmstead!" Charles cried. "It'll suck you back. A worse fate than a life with Phyllis, you'll be branding hogs within the year."

"No danger of that," Lucybelle said but wanted to change the subject off of the farmstead.

"Lucy will be fine," Clare announced. She grabbed the stem of Lucybelle's empty martini glass and pushed Serena and Helen out of the booth. She didn't ask the rest of the table for their drink orders, and Harry nudged Lucybelle with his knee under the table, meaning that he noticed Clare's attention to her.

Lucybelle lit a Chesterfield and watched the girl ordering her a fresh drink at the bar. Clare had light-blue eyes and messy shoulder-length blond hair. She dressed like a nature poet in unusual and richly colored fabrics. Tonight she wore a green, sleeveless top covered with loose threads, like a pelt of grass. Several years younger than Lucybelle, the girl was exuberant, baldly truthful in blurting whatever came into her head, and terribly earnest. Compared to Phyllis's nonstop subterfuge, that honesty was a balm. Clare was a walk on a mountain path. Why not?

Charles was saying that he might go home himself, just for a little while, to help out with the Montgomery bus boycott.

"Now there's a good idea," Helen said. "You sashay anywhere south of the Mason-Dixon Line, you'll be shot and killed."

"I come from Alabama, darling. I know what I'm doing."

"You got out of Alabama alive, and they don't want you back. Trust me."

"Harsh."

"You want harsh," Helen said, "you prance down to Montgomery."

Charles shrugged. "There's room for all of us. Rustin was arrested for lewd behavior a couple of years ago and—"

"Arrested. Exactly."

"Who's Rustin?"

"Bayard Rustin. He—"

"I don't like that word," Wesley said.

"What?" Charles asked. "Lewd?" He squirmed a tiny demonstration of the word and then blew a kiss across the table at Wesley.

"I have things to do." Wesley slid out of the booth.

Charles hummed a hearty and fictitious Renaissance tune, bobbing his head to the high-pitched musical parody.

"Coming with you," Harry said, following his boyfriend and winking at Lucybelle. "I'll miss you. We all will. Stay in touch. Come back and visit."

Clare returned with her martini just as Serena and Helen were saying their good-byes.

"I should go too," Lucybelle said. "L'Forte's been inside since lunch." But she didn't move. She took a swallow of the martini. She couldn't resist the urge to unmoor, to drift a bit, just for a few minutes.

"So no one's seen you since the middle of June," Clare said. She sipped her beer. "Where've you been staying?"

Lucybelle wished everyone hadn't left. She needed the swell of jokes.

"Are you really going to Chicago? Why?" Clare nudged Lucybelle. "You're running away."

"No. I'm not." How could she explain any of it to this young woman with her satchel of homosexual literature? She'd agreed to a new alliance, a strange and risky partnership with an ice scientist, with the snowcaps themselves. "I'm running *to*."

"To what?"

"Something unknown. That's the best part."

Clare nodded slowly, pleased that Lucybelle was answering her questions. She waved her hand at the bartender, and when she got his attention, held up two fingers. Then she thumped her satchel up onto the tabletop. "I want to show you something. It's brilliant." She pulled a piece of yellow construction paper out of her satchel and laid it on the table. A simple black line drawing depicted a ladder leading up into some clouds and off the page. Two women stood at the base of the ladder, and below them were the words "San Francisco, California." "The first issue of a new magazine. I have an ex who's working on it. This is the cover art."

"What kind of magazine?" Although Lucybelle thought she knew.

"A new group of gay ladies. They're calling themselves Daughters of Bilitis, though I have no idea why. They're all in San Francisco."

The waiter delivered the martini and beer, and Clare toasted Lucybelle. "To Chicago and new love."

"To Chicago," Lucybelle said, and she finished off half of the martini in one swallow.

"They're still working on the articles," Clare said. "I thought maybe you could write something."

"What would I write?"

"I don't know. What it's like to be a gay girl in New York?"

"That sounds like something *you* should write."

"I can't write. I can only talk." Clare smiled and took Lucybelle's hand. "I'm going to miss you."

"We hardly know each other."

"I've always wanted to know you better."

*Why not? Why not?* The words were so liberating. When she'd first come to New York, she'd been too green and too shy to go with girls like Clare. Then her life got consumed by Phyllis. But now she was entirely free to do as she pleased.

Except, of course, for the small matter of her agreement with Henri Bader. But she hadn't started her job yet. She wasn't in Chicago yet.

"I'll walk you home," Clare said. "Where are you staying?"

Home. Lucybelle pictured this hardy girl holding her hand, crossing the Appalachian Mountains on foot, braving the blowing winds of the prairie, and then dropping into the northeast corner of Arkansas. Home. That abrasive rub between her little blue house in Pocahontas and the streets of New York. It always made her dizzy, thinking of that distance, her journey so far. Then again, it was probably the three martinis making her dizzy.

"Come on," Clare said. "At least to the subway station."

Lucybelle scooted out of the booth and took Clare's arm. It felt good holding on to someone who felt so sure of herself. Below the grassy shirt Clare wore loose blue jeans cinched with a rough-hewn leather belt and a big brass buckle. Strapped to her feet were coarse leather sandals with thick black soles. All she needed was a staff to look like an urban shepherdess.

The gin made her feet clumsy and she leaned into Clare. It was a hot night and a sheen of sweat covered their joined arms.

"Tell me exactly where you'll be," Clare said. "I'm concerned."

"I took a job with the Snow, Ice, and Permafrost Research Establishment lab."

"The what?"

"It's a promotion. I'm happy."

"Do you miss Phyllis?"

Lucybelle pulled away from Clare and stopped next to a streetlamp. Of course she did. In spite of everything.

"How could you not? You were together forever."

"The first time I saw her she was on stage doing *A Midsummer's Night Dream*. She was so funny and sexy. Shakespeare's poetry in her mouth. Maybe it was just her mouth. Maybe that's all I loved."

Clare laughed, leaned in, and kissed her.

She'd had all that gin and no dinner. The air was hot and thick, the evening light too persistent. She stepped into a dark entryway and pressed her back against the cool stone wall. Clare followed her into the deep corner. "Are you okay?"

"Sure."

Clare pushed the damp curls off of Lucybelle's forehead.

Was desire a form of courage? Sometimes she thought it might kill her, this friction between the simple truth of what she wanted and the fear of getting it. How could they both exist, side by side? One day they'd combust.

"You don't need her," Clare said, her alpine eyes brightening the entryway. "You're a hundred times the woman she is." Her fingertips traced the vein running down Lucybelle's neck, the span of her clavicle. "She's always

29

acting, even when she's not on stage. Which I've noticed she hasn't been in some time."

Lucybelle snorted gently.

"Anyway, her cowardice is despicable. Marrying that man as a cover. Her soul will eat her from the inside out."

"Okay," Lucybelle said. "You've made your point."

She let Clare run a finger over her top lip and then along her bottom one. She gave in to the solid wall against her back and the soothing wrap of darkness. Why not? She was leaving New York in two days.

There had always been something a bit apologetic about Phyllis's kisses, but not Clare's. Lucybelle's life of the mind took flight, soared from the dark entryway and up into the twilit sky above the Village. She pulled Clare against her, gripping the back of her head with both hands. The hot night caused both women to sweat sheets of saltwater.

When, a few minutes later, Clare began to button up the front of Lucybelle's dress, she grabbed her wrists and said, "Not yet."

"Ho!" Clare said. "I'd never have taken you for a greedy girl."

The word greedy only scratched the surface of the longing she felt. She wanted Henri Bader's glaciers. Their clarity. Translucence. Boldly edging forward, they carved their own paths on this planet. After gasping against Clare's hand, she slid down the wall and sat in that dark corner while Clare stood over her asking, "Are you okay? Lucy? Are you okay?"

She realized she was crying, and she didn't want Clare to see this. She got to her feet and said, "I'm fine. I better go."

"I'll walk you."

"It's too far."

"I'll go with you in the cab." Clare did see the tears and wiped them with her fingertips, a bit brusquely, thankfully devoid of sympathy.

Lucybelle kissed her, right out in the open of the lit street. "I'm going to walk," she said, "and it's a long way." She wanted to feel the hot pavement of New York against the soles of her feet one last time.

Clare wouldn't go away. She chatted cheerfully at her side, the melody of her banter not unpleasant though Lucybelle hardly listened to the content of the words. They hiked uptown, past the theaters and then the park, the streets emptying and the light dimming. Her legs ached by the time they reached the guesthouse.

Clare said, "I think you'll be back."

"Thank you for walking with me." Poor L'Forte. By now he'd probably soiled the room's rug.

"I admire you a lot," Clare said. "Call me sometime, okay?"

Lucybelle stood on the guesthouse doorstep, hot and exhausted, unwilling to speak a lie, impatient now to rescue her sweet dachshund. She said good night, pushed open the glass door, and walked briskly across the lobby without looking over her shoulder. A few minutes later when she brought L'Forte back outside—the good boy had held his bladder all these hours—Clare was nowhere in sight. In fact, the street was entirely deserted.

Part Two

## Chicago, 1956–61

## Saturday, November 10, 1956

The Snow, Ice and Permafrost Research Establishment lab was in Wilmette, twenty miles north of Chicago, and so Lucybelle found an apartment in nearby Evanston, on Michigan Avenue, just a couple of blocks from the lake. The rooms were large, freshly painted a creamy yellow, and filled with light. She didn't know what she'd do with all that space but took the place in an expansive moment. The landlord said no dogs, so she was glad she'd left L'Forte tied to a tree. She signed the lease and smuggled him in. Luckily the elderly couple that occupied the apartment across from hers at the top of the outdoor stairway, Mr. and Mrs. Worthington, admired L'Forte and approved of her infraction. They themselves hid a basset hound in their rooms.

The first weeks passed in a satisfying pitch of nonstop work. She understood geology and was well versed in the vernacular of academia, but here at SIPRE she worked cheek by jowl with the scientists themselves, a heady crew of men who lived and breathed the language of water, ice, rock, and air. There were thrilling moments, when she understood, when the importance of their work shone through the veneer of bawdy humor and the deceptive office attire of blue jeans and rolled up shirtsleeves, as if everyone were on a camping trip rather than investigating the edges of human knowledge. Other moments she felt nearly crushed by the weight of her job, to make these explanations of earth itself comprehensible to the public. Editor-in-chief, wordsmith, report writer: they dumped their data on her desk and she was supposed to transform it into readable sentences. Worse, all of them to a man believed he'd already written up his data in the best way possible. She did not have a knack for massaging egos, nor did she want to develop that skill. It would be a waste of time. It confounded her the way her habit of speaking her mind plainly did not go over well in these circumstances.

"I changed your words because you hadn't written complete sentences, so—"

"Change it back to how I had it."

Or another time: "You've buried the conclusion in the middle of your paper. An opening paragraph stating what you will show and a concluding one summing up your results strengthens your case."

"Change it back to how I had it."

Even when she told a scientist, "I didn't change a word. I only corrected spelling and grammar," he insisted she, "Change it back to how I had it."

There were moments, rare ones, when the results of her hard work managed to drip through tiny crevices. "I checked the math. It doesn't add up. There's a mistake in your calculation about the pH levels."

"You're not a mathematician."

"And yet I checked the math and found an error."

An hour later, Peter Hauser returned to stop in front of her desk to say, merely, "So you did."

Russell Woo, for whom English was a second language, was particularly and inexplicably defensive about his writing, and yet almost furtively grateful at the same time. Within earshot of others, he'd adopt a gruff reluctance with her suggestions. In private, he met eyes with her and said, "Thank you."

In the middle of November she finally took off a Saturday and rode the train into Chicago. She spent most of the morning at the Art Institute, waiting until the very end to find Willa Cather's picture, or rather her character Thea Kronberg's picture, *The Song of the Lark*. "The flat country, the early morning light, the wet fields, the look in the girl's heavy face . . ." The girl in the picture might be barefoot, but she's holding a scythe and looking out to the far distance. Thea Kronberg felt a "boundless satisfaction" in looking at the picture, and so Willa Cather too must have felt the joy of recognition. What exactly did the girl with the scythe see on the horizon? Lucybelle looked at the picture for nearly an hour.

In the afternoon she braved Marshall Field's on State Street. Thankfully, an animated young salesgirl found her wandering among the racks and offered help. She bought three dresses, two pairs of trousers, heels that went with all the dresses, and tie oxfords for the pants. When the salesgirl asked if she needed anything else, Lucybelle had her fetch stockings for the dresses and a pair of Keds for L'Forte's walks. A new coat for winter? the girl suggested. Good idea. She bought the first one the girl showed her, plum wool with wide overlapping lapels and brass buttons. She was finished shopping in just over an hour.

Even with full shopping bags in both hands she didn't much feel like getting on the train back to Evanston. She ought to find a diner and get a bite to eat. She'd had coffee this morning, and maybe a glass of juice, but no breakfast or lunch. Sometimes she liked the light-headed feeling that came with not eating, but if she let it go too far, and she probably had today, she risked judgment impairment. Not that she had anything she had to decide or even think about today. She walked along the river, and when she came to the Michigan Avenue Bridge she stopped to investigate the bas-relief sculptures. She liked the woman with wings.

Lucybelle walked to the middle of the span and looked down into the water. Earlier in the day it'd been a lovely muted green, but the river was blackening with dusk. She looked up at the jagged skyline, the dark buildings geometrically friendly as if their purpose were to frame the sky. The winged woman in the bas-relief sculpture could sail right up through the dark city and into the purple beyond.

To be able to defy gravity! This bridge did just that, creating a pocket of space between the roadway, with her on it, and the slipping river. She looked down again at the flow. It was easier to avoid thinking about Phyllis and Fred on workdays. The backlog was tremendous and she usually stayed at the office long past quitting time, working on the reports and letters and other documents that needed her attention. Finally Bader told her to stop staying late and to stop coming in on Saturdays. It was the look on his face more than his words, as if he were studying her for signs of mental illness. He was a man who liked to have a good time, and while he'd hired her because of her reputation for hard work and precision, she could tell he didn't fully respect someone who didn't share his capacity for fun.

She did in fact have a capacity for fun. She and Phyllis had had loads of fun, especially at first. She couldn't imagine Phyllis having fun with worm-like Fred, or even having a laugh. Daddy was right: she should have kicked them out of the apartment even if she herself wasn't going to keep it. Having such an intimate knowledge of the rooms they occupied was unbearable. If she didn't know where they were she couldn't imagine their lives. But she did know. She could picture perfectly how Phyllis dropped bread into the toaster each morning and then leaned against the refrigerator with her arms crossed, scowling, groggy, waiting for it to pop up. How she poured too much heavy cream into her strong coffee. Did she ask Fred to rub her feet at night? Of course she did.

The Michigan Avenue Bridge was considered a wonder of engineering the way it held her suspended over the river. But she could overcome its defiance of gravity: she could jump. Would the shopping bags be heavy enough to pull her under? Of course she'd let go of the handles. How embarrassing: to jump from a bridge and survive, with new dresses, stockings, and heels floating about her body. Just the thought of facing her boss—tall, hale Henri Bader with his thicket of black hair, raspberry red lips, coarse sense of humor—after such a fiasco made her flush.

She did want to please him. The bald arrogance of his pitch at life refreshed her. He was like a smart Paul Bunyan, wielding a giant axe to clear the way for his vision of the future.

She ought to eat something. She hardly had the strength to heft her shopping bags and walk to the train station. She laid her cheek against her hands on the railing and closed her eyes, just a tiny nap here on the bridge. When she opened them again, she looked right into the lens of a camera, not ten feet away. *Click.*

The young man—no, it was a woman—lowered her camera.

"You took my picture."

"I took the bridge."

"With me on it."

About Lucybelle's height, but heftier, with dark brown skin and a man's haircut, the girl had a quick smile, perfectly straight teeth, and two big dimples in her cheeks. She wore a pair of tan trousers, a white button-down shirt, both pressed to perfection, and a woolen herringbone vest under an unbuttoned black wool overcoat. She had a big satchel slung over her shoulder, like Clare's only in a heavy tan canvas.

"You look so tired resting here. I like the contrast between the wisp of you and the grandeur of the bridge." Cradling the bottom of the camera in her left hand, she raised it a bit and gestured at Lucybelle. "Where're you from?"

"How do you know I'm not from here?"

She bunched her lips to one side and cocked her head. "You have an accent."

"Arkansas."

"Which part?"

Her brain was swimmy from lack of sustenance. She ought to pick up her shopping bags and leave. "Pocahontas. It's in the northeast."

"I know where Pocahontas is. I'm Stella."

Why wasn't Lucybelle walking away? Instead she stared at the girl. It was the camera, the way she held it, claimed it, a sure link between herself and the world.

"And you are?"

"Lucybelle." Most everyone just called her Lucy. Why had she offered her whole name?

"Very nice to meet you, Lucybelle." Stella hefted her camera, gesturing toward the purple sky and black river. "Don't worry. It's too dark. I didn't capture your image."

"It's getting late," Lucybelle said, unnerved by the word capture. "I better get home."

"I'll walk you."

"No, thank you. I'm fine on my own."

Stella smiled as if Lucybelle had answered correctly. What nice girl let a stranger walk with her in a big city?

"Hey," Stella said, "you look like a reader."

Lucybelle didn't walk away, but she looked away. And refrained from asking what the girl meant.

"Those glasses and eyebrows. The set of your mouth."

"Make me a reader?"

"Yeah." She opened the flap of her satchel and dug through the contents, reminding her again of Clare. She handed Lucybelle a small book called *HOWL*. "Do you know it?"

"Yes! I mean, no. Not the book. But I met Allen Ginsberg. He was in school with me at Columbia." She hadn't known he was publishing a book.

"Columbia? Fancy."

"No, just smart."

Stella laughed. "Must be. I don't think there's any fancy in Arkansas."

Lucybelle laughed too. "How do you know Pocahontas?"

"I come from a farming family myself. Well, back a generation. My parents are both teachers. But I still recognize country when I see it."

"My father is a judge."

"Oh. So you *are* fancy."

"In a tiny town. He's a farmer too. We have Herefords, hogs, rice. You weren't wrong." Lucybelle tried to hand back the book.

"Wait." Stella dug in her canvas satchel again and this time withdrew a pen. She took the volume of poetry from Lucybelle and opened it up to the first page. "Never write in books," she mumbled as she wrote. "I always write in books. It keeps them alive. Books aren't artifacts to let get dusty on a shelf." Stella handed the book back. "When you're finished you can return it to me. That's my telephone number."

She didn't give Lucybelle a chance to say no. Stella turned and strode away, the affected swagger a code, a comical one, and Lucybelle laughed. "Hey!" she called, but too quietly, and Stella kept going.

That night Lucybelle read *HOWL* four times, each time nearly losing her breath on the fifth stanza where Ginsberg had written, "who passed through universities with radiant eyes hallucinating Arkansas . . ."

## Tuesday, November 13, 1956

Bader didn't even stop at the open door of her office as he stomped by saying, "My office. Now."

She shook a cigarette from her pack and followed him to his office, where she stood in front of his desk. The unlit cigarette embarrassed her, as if she expected a chivalrous gesture from him.

"Where's your pad and pen?" he asked.

"What is it you need?"

"Dictation."

"I don't know shorthand. Ruthie is the secretary. I'm the editor."

"I'm leaving for Greenland tomorrow. I can't—"

"Tomorrow? You are?" She spoke with too much feeling, a wave of panic cresting. "But I—"

"But you what?"

"I don't know. I just, well, you're the only person I know here. I'm not sure how it'll go without—"

He smiled like a wolf. "Without me? I'm flattered, sugar, especially coming from you. But I spend more time in the field than in these human fortresses called cities and I can't wait to get the hell out of here. You have enough work to keep you busy until long after I get back."

"No, it's not that." She grasped for something reasonable to say. "It's November. No one goes to Greenland in November."

"Worried about me?"

"No."

"I didn't think so. In any case, I want to spend the winter there. So what *is* the problem?"

He looked impatient but also curious, as if he might really listen, but she realized that anything she said would work against her, would count as whining. She'd been at SIPRE for three months. She was exhausted already and didn't have any friends. The scientists barely looked at her when they dropped their papers on her desk. She bet they wouldn't be able to tell their wives whether she was blond or brunette. Bader was right: there was an enormous backlog of editing and even though she'd been working her way through the pile there was no end in sight. Of course no one thanked her for her work. Why should they? She was being paid money, not compliments. She could handle the reticence. But she was growing quite tired of putting in the long hours only to have the scientists change their sentences back to whatever ungrammatical mess they'd written in the first place. She'd been meaning to speak to Bader about this. He'd said when he hired her that she'd have his full support, but what exactly did that mean? Most of the scientists thought she was just another secretary, maybe a little smarter. Even he seemed to think that, asking her to take dictation.

"How long will you be gone?"

"Months." No smile when he said, "Really? You'll miss me?"

"No," she lied. "I won't miss you. But I'd like you to tell your scientists that I'm head of publications and an editor. I can't make them let me improve their prose, but they can at least know that's my job."

Bader nodded and then looked at his watch. "Damn," he said. "Okay, get Ruthie in here. And tell her that I can't tolerate a single snicker out of her, not one. That habit of hers irks the hell out of me."

As she turned to go, he added, "And Lucy, get the report from Ruthie as soon as she's finished typing it. I'll need it *edited* tonight. In my hands by tomorrow. Here's my address." He scratched it down on a matchbook and then before handing the book to her, he tore off a match and lit it. Lucybelle cupped her hands around the cigarette in her mouth and leaned gratefully toward the little flame. As she inhaled, Bader said, "Drop it off any time before eight o'clock tomorrow morning."

"Is it even possible to fly to Greenland this late in the season?"

"I meant to leave two months ago. So much damn work. I need to be there for a winter season, so I've convinced them to give it a go."

Lucybelle crossed an arm under her breasts and rested her other elbow on her wrist. She drew from her cigarette while examining his long face. His ferocity appealed to her. "And if you don't get there?"

"I'll dally in Paris or somewhere else civilized until I *can* get there. Lucy, please, get Ruthie."

Ruthie, the secretary, and Beverly, the office manager, both had desks in the open foyer. Lucybelle was glad to have an office with a door that closed so that she wasn't on permanent display as they were. She stopped in front of Ruthie's desk and told her that Bader wanted her in his office to take dictation. In her peripheral vision she saw Beverly waving her hand in the air about her head, something she'd never do in the presence of the scientists who smoked.

"Now?" Ruthie snickered, as if Lucybelle had suggested she go fornicate with Bader in his office. She did have an odd habit of laughing nervously and flinching at sudden movements. A few years older than Lucybelle, Ruthie had sensitive gray eyes, an upturned nose, and a delicate chin. She wore her black hair in a shoulder-length pageboy, the fringe of bangs softening her pointed features.

"Yes. Now."

Ruthie coughed. Lucybelle needn't have punched the word "now."

They both glanced at Beverly who didn't look up from the paperwork on her desk but who did lift a penciled eyebrow and shake her head, almost imperceptibly, but enough to make Ruthie hesitate. Beverly lacquered her bottle-auburn hair into hard waves that framed her heavily made-up face. A layer of foundation did little to conceal her pocked skin, and Lucybelle couldn't imagine why she plucked out and then drew back in her eyebrows. She went about every task, no matter how minor, with a raw and angry determination. On her first day at the lab, Peter Hauser told Lucybelle to look out for Beverly, that she was "a real martinet."

Lucybelle took a final pull on her cigarette and looked for an ashtray. The two women seemed to try extra hard to make her feel unwelcome. If the scientists were oblivious to her job as editor, these two were hyper-aware of it, resentful of her private office and perhaps even of her attempts to speak with the scientists as a peer. She wasn't *their* boss, the secretary and office manager found ways to make clear with every interaction. Bader had said she'd have a staff but she didn't yet and apparently wouldn't until he returned from Greenland, at the very earliest, and that was not going to be for months.

"Girls," Bader said coming out into the foyer. "Lucy is in charge of all documents, got it? If she needs something typed, type it. Ruthie, in my office now. Dictation."

When late that afternoon Bader dropped the sixteen-page report on her desk, Ruthie and Beverly were long gone for the day. Lucybelle stayed until two in the morning editing and then typing a clean copy. She took a taxicab to Bader's apartment on the north side of Chicago, planning to leave the document in his mailbox, but when she saw light along the edges of the window shade, she rang the bell. If it was so important that she finish it tonight, she'd better put it in his hands.

She expected a pajama-clad, sleepy-eyed Bader to open the door, grab the report, and growl something about being awakened.

"Lucy," he said. "Come in. Come in." He was fully dressed and wide awake. She stepped into an apartment strewn with clothing and dirty dishes and assorted oddities, including two huge earthen pots, nearly as tall as Lucybelle, and a hand-painted Japanese screen, and as she followed him into the kitchen, she encountered a stuffed jaguar. She managed to swallow her gasp just in time, and because she was behind him, he didn't see her recoil.

"Nerves of steel. I like that," Bader said. "Most girls scream."

She stopped in front of the jaguar and tried to look into the two marble eyes, not knowing whether to run or laugh.

"Drink?" Bader asked, lifting a bottle of gin off the kitchen counter.

Lucybelle nodded.

He poured a couple of fingers into two juice glasses, removed a metal ice cube tray from the freezer, and pounded it on the counter. Gin splashed out of the glasses as he dropped in the ice, and again as he swung one of the drinks in her direction.

He returned to the living room, sat on a wicker chair designed for a patio, and read the report, turning the pages quickly, until finally a smile cranked up one side of his face. "Washburn was right. Smart girl." With the grin that was more of a leer still in place, he added, "With nerves of steel." He went back to the kitchen, wrapped his arms around the midsection of the taxidermic jaguar, and brought him to the front room. "Like my cat?"

"Not really."

He roared his laugh and then said, "Help me pack."

"No. I have to get home."

"Not your job, right?"

"Right."

"I understand. But I don't see how I'm going to pull everything together for a couple of months in the Arctic in what—?" He consulted his watch. "Three hours."

"What are you going to do in Greenland?"

"What?" As if the question had an obvious answer.

43

No, that wasn't it. He was stalling. He wanted to talk but was curbing himself. His hesitation was so uncharacteristic it made her curious. "Drilling in the winter?"

As Bader stared at her, it was as if she could see, just below his skin, the gathering storm of some hidden enthusiasm. He said, "Classified."

She nodded. "Still, I'm interested."

"You're going to know soon enough. You'll be editing the plans, the feasibility reports."

"So tell me."

She saw him lose his battle with himself. He wasn't supposed to tell her. But he couldn't help himself. "State of the art research facility. One hundred percent manned. Year round."

"On the ice cap? But—"

"*Inside* the ice cap." He practically glowed as he watched for her reaction. She enjoyed teasing him by being blasé. "Inside. How is that possible?"

"A complete city under the ice."

"Just for the ice cores?"

Now he looked away and shook his head tightly, briefly. "You'll know more later. Much more. For now, do you mind?" He waved at the mess of his apartment and then looked at his watch.

Lucybelle finished the gin in her glass and as she picked her way through the detritus to the door, he began digging through a pile of clothes, seeming to have already forgotten her. She let herself out and walked toward downtown until she found an available taxicab. She got home just in time to walk and feed L'Forte, shower, and go back to work.

## Wednesday, November 14, 1956

The mail boy slouched into her office and dropped the fat packet of letters on her desk. She'd told him at least once a week that mail distribution was his job, not hers, but although he was a good ten years younger and was paid considerably less, he liked to think he could tell her what to do.

"You're documents," he would reply.

"Yes, and you're mail," she'd answer, noting the double entendre, though of course he did not.

On several occasions she'd considered dropping the pile of mail on one of the tables in the lunchroom and letting everyone find his own, but that would have backfired and made her, not him, look bad. She was new and would have to pay her dues.

Today she didn't have the energy to do anything other than walk around the lab offices and make the deliveries. As she flipped through the letters, sorting them, she found one addressed to her in purple ink and a familiar hand. The return address: 277 West 12th Street, New York. Lucybelle shoved the letter into her purse, snapped the clasp shut, and kicked the purse under her desk.

At home that evening she had a glass of gin and a cigarette for dinner and then carried the sealed envelope into her spare room. A fleeting optimism had caused her to take this large, two-bedroom apartment all for herself. Her typewriter sat on the floor, next to the boxes of books she'd asked Harry to pack up and ship, making him promise to not give Phyllis her address, not even the city or state. The typewriter squatted among the books, scabrous and skeletal, like a starving poet.

She stood hugging herself, hoping for an infusion of courage from the sight of what she hadn't yet allowed herself to call her "study," but the typewriter and books seemed to shrink away from her, their mistress who couldn't even provide them with a desk, chair, or shelves. She dropped the letter on the floor and dug through a box of papers until she found the picture of Willa Cather with a brush cut. She set Cather, face up, on top of the typewriter.

"I'll be back," she said.

Then she took Phyllis's letter to the living room, scoffed at the purple ink—always so dramatic—and tore it open.

*My Sweetest,*

How dare she begin with a term of endearment.

*I know you have no respect for what I've done, and how could you, being who you are, so committed to the Truth, in all its forms. You with your feet so securely in the soil of the Earth, your head filled with the Classics, your eyes trained on that new and amorphous Future that will hold you better than this Now.*

The capital letters! Lucybelle brandished the pages, considered tearing them to shreds, but her curiosity kept her reading.

45

*Fred and I got married. I know that sentence will fill you with . . .
what? Rage? Sadness? Disgust? I'm sorry. I'm truly sorry, though I'm
sure you'll never believe that. You'll always think I acted out of self-
interest, and nothing more.*

Was she really going to try to make a case for her actions being about
anything other than self-interest?

*Fred needs me. It's that simple. You don't. And I need to be needed.
You know how devastated I am about my Dead Career. I'm old
now, Lucy. Too old for this life of auditions and eyelash batting and
competing against girls far prettier than me.*

Pretty. If it were only about pretty. That was like settling for a thought
when you could have an epiphany.

*I can still have a family. There. I've said it. Yes, a family. And
why not? You could too, my sweetest. There are plenty of men out
there whom you might tolerate. I know, you don't suffer fools. And oh
so many men are fools. But really, don't you have to suffer them
anyway? At work? On the street? Why not get the goods too? I want
children.*

Lucybelle lowered the pages and stared at the black windowpane. The
goods: children.

*Please write me. I can't stand not having you in my Life. Fred is
here, yes, for the Duration. But he's not so bad, now is he? You and I
have too much together to let it drain away with this little storm.*

This little storm: Phyllis's marriage.

*You know my address. Write me. Better yet, call me.*
                                                    *Love always,*
                                                        *Phyllis*
*P.S. I'm keeping my stage name, just in case. But my legal name
is now Phyllis Higgins. It has a solid ring, don't you think? Can't you
just picture me at a PTA meeting?*

Lucybelle couldn't bring herself to make confetti out of the letter, and so she carried it back into the other room. She dug through the shipment of books until she found *Shakespeare: The Complete Works*. Daddy had given it to her on her twenty-first birthday, and she liked to keep the rich block of text close, like a talisman. She should have unpacked it right away. Now she considered the green marbled pattern on the edges of the pages, selected a place about one inch in from the front cover, and opened the book. She tucked Phyllis inside *The Merchant of Venice* and then lugged the doorstopper out to her living room. She set it on the floor next to her new wingback chair. Phyllis and Shakespeare. How the former paled next to the latter. It was comforting diminishing Phyllis that way.

Her head hurt. She found a box of Ritz crackers in the kitchen and sliced up some cheddar cheese. The sandwiches made her feel a little better.

She called Harry.

"Lucy! Oh, we've missed you."

"So much so that you gave Phyllis my address. My *work* address."

"What? Of course I didn't. You asked me not to. I don't even have your work address."

"So how did she get it?"

"How am I supposed to know? The telephone book maybe?"

"I didn't even tell her what city."

"I don't know, honey. It wasn't me."

"I miss you too," she said. "Why don't you come visit. You and Wesley would love Chicago."

"What fun! Tell me about the new friends you've made."

He was a psychiatrist, he was supposed to see and understand individuals, but his cheeriness, his need for everyone to be happy, only exacerbated her loneliness. She'd grown up in a place where everyone knew everyone else. They liked you or they didn't, but there was no work to do about it. You didn't "make" friends. You just existed. You were just you. Most people did like Lucybelle when they got to know her, but she'd never learned how to lure a friend. Since leaving home, she'd depended on the charisma of others, like Krutch or Phyllis. She'd never felt so alone as she did now.

"How are you? How's Wesley?"

"I'm well. A fascinating roster of patients at the moment. They keep me on my toes. And Wesley has discovered some obscure composer about whom he's terribly keen." She let herself sink into the husky warmth of Harry's voice. "How's L'Forte? I understand you abducted him."

47

"He's fine. We walk to the lake, if you can call that massive body of water a lake. There are actual waves. I can't yet get him to go in after a stick, but maybe in warmer weather."

"Smart fellow. If you wanted a swimmer, you should have gotten a spaniel, not a dachshund."

"I suppose so."

"Are the people friendly?"

She considered the question. Bader's social style had a voracious quality that took it several degrees beyond the word friendly, and this was perfectly balanced by Ruthie and Beverly's chilliness. "If you added them up and took an average," she said, "I would say yes, they're friendly enough."

"Good! Wonderful!"

Lucybelle pitied Harry's patients. Perhaps his obliviousness was useful, something they could do battle against.

"I'm bushed," she told him. "I've been working ridiculously long hours."

"Don't do that to yourself. You need to play. We all need play."

Lucybelle lit a cigarette. "I'll find a sandbox. I better go. It's nice to hear your voice." No point in reminding him to refrain from sharing information about her with Phyllis. She hadn't divulged anything new and what he did know he'd apparently already dispatched.

"Call again soon. Take care of yourself."

Lucybelle let L'Forte under the covers that night. Only women, according to her agreement with Bader, were disallowed. The dachshund settled in with a long shuddering sigh, as if he'd missed as much sleep as she had. In the few moments before the soporific effect of her warm bed sucked away her consciousness, Lucybelle took inventory of her life: thirty-three years old, single, tucked into the middle of the country, a dog and a woman, a difficult job, part of a team trying to understand the ice caps. Was that enough?

## Monday, December 31, 1956

In September the idea of that enormous lake just a few blocks away had entranced her—she'd moved to the seaside!—but now it felt more like an ominous and stormy presence splashing at her door. After a nightmare in which a tidal wave washed her off the apartment steps as she was leaving for work, L'Forte too grew afraid of the lake. It was as if he'd dreamed along with her; in the morning after her drowning dream, he refused to go outside at all. She had to carry him to his tree. Later in the week, when she coaxed him out on walks, he balked at the end of his leash when the water came into view, forcing her to take him on strolls through downtown Evanston instead. She supposed the crisp shops and populated sidewalks comforted him, though nothing about Evanston resembled the Village where the narrow streets embraced a person and the buttery aroma of warm pastries and the clinking of coffee cups on saucers softened the effects of winter.

Here in the Midwest, the winter air smelled metallic and knifed at Lucybelle's skin. She had a pair of prescription dark glasses made, but they did little to mitigate the icy brightness. She imagined that even Bader was more comfortable than she was, wintering-over in Greenland, hunkered down in some igloo, planning his city under the ice by candlelight.

Her brother in Oregon had invited her out there for Christmas, but Helen was very pregnant, and with their three other children, Lucybelle guessed they didn't need a houseguest. Instead she'd gone home to Pocahontas for a few days, returning to Illinois well before New Year's.

She resumed her regular work schedule even though most of the staff had taken that week off. Russell Woo came into the lab for an hour or so every day, and a couple of the other scientists stopped in to find things on their desks or get a bit of time away from their families, but for the most part she was able to work with gratifying concentration. By the end of the month, she'd reached the bottom of her piles.

Still, she went to work and sat in her office, sharpened pencils, and read scientific papers that had been published before her tenure at SIPRE. The lab library contained a wealth of geological information and by the start of 1957, she'd be better versed in the literature than some of the scientists. So far as she knew, Bader never did speak to any of them about her job title and attendant skills and duties. She'd have to earn their respect the hard way, with impeccable integrity, unflinching endurance of every joke and test, and by making them dependent upon her intelligence.

On New Year's Eve, at around eight in the evening, she slipped a fresh sheet of paper into the typewriter and typed, "Chapter One." She tried to think of the opening lines of her favorite novels but could only hear Ginsberg's lilting threat. *I saw the best minds of my generation destroyed by madness, starving hysterical naked, dragging themselves through the negro streets at dawn* . . . She wanted to eat those lines and spit them out at the same time. She had to find her own true, potent words. She reached into that place just in front of her coccyx, perhaps it was at the base of her uterus, where she felt the truest story she knew. She must transport the words of that story from there, concentrated in her viscera, up to her brain, where they could be organized into sentences and sent back down through her neck, across her shoulders, along her arms, and pop out of her fingertips onto the typewriter keys.

As she sat trying to do this, she experienced a calm expansion, as if a hundred doors opened up inside her. It was a lovely feeling, that sense of possibility, until too many minutes had passed without the feeling producing a single good paragraph. She ripped the sheet of paper from the typewriter, the roller gears stuttering, and tossed it in the wastepaper basket. She fed in another sheet of paper and again typed, "Chapter One."

It was after nine o'clock when she rose from her desk. Even Russell Woo wouldn't come into the lab this late, and certainly not on New Year's Eve. Everyone would be at parties by now. Peter Hauser's wife, Emily, had invited her to one they were having and she should have gone. She had planned on going. She could still go. She could take the train home, put on her burgundy dress and black heels, and call a taxicab. She'd be there well before the celebratory moment.

Instead she found herself trying the door to Bader's office. It was unlocked of course. That man probably had never locked a door in his life. Two filing cabinets towered in the corner behind his desk, a total of eight drawers. Perhaps, she told herself, she could organize these for him.

Even without an audience, standing there in the lab offices completely alone, she embarrassed herself with the false pretense. She had no intention of becoming a filing clerk, as she'd made very clear, nor was she willing to lie to herself. What she wanted was to see what kind of information about her he'd accumulated and squirreled away.

Actually, what she really wanted was to find out what Ruthie and Beverly might have discovered about her.

A few weeks before Christmas, on a day too snowy for leaving the building, Lucybelle had tried to join them in the lunchroom. Usually Ruthie and Beverly took their lunches off premises, sometimes with Dorothy Shipwright the SIPRE librarian. When they did eat in the lunchroom,

50

they came in late, after Lucybelle was already seated, and took places at the other table, as far from her as they could get. This time Lucybelle re-wrapped her bologna and mustard sandwich in its waxed paper and moved to their table.

"Mind if I join you?"

Beverly's face pruned up and she looked away. Ruthie giggled nervously and then coughed into her hands, hiding her entire face with the gesture. Dorothy smiled at her with what Lucybelle thought might be relief and gestured toward an empty chair. "Please."

"We'd better get back to work," Beverly said wadding up her own waxed paper.

"You've only eaten half your sandwich," Lucybelle pointed out.

The office manager and secretary stood up and pushed in their chairs. Dorothy hesitated as Beverly and Ruthie left the lunchroom. She leaned across the table and said, "I'm sorry," but then she too walked away.

On the Friday night before the start of everyone's holiday, Lucybelle was in her own office, with the door open, when she heard the three women making plans in the foyer.

Dorothy said, "Eight o'clock? Your place?"

"Oh good. You got Sally to stay with your mother."

"Yes, thank god. I need a break."

"Bring those eggrolls," Ruthie said and then snickered. "With the dipping sauce."

"Don't I always?"

Lucybelle stepped into the foyer. "What are you all doing tonight?" she asked. It was humiliating, hinting at an invitation.

"I'm going to clean house," Beverly said.

"I guess I'll visit my folks," Ruthie said.

"Look, I overheard you making plans just now."

Everyone froze in a diorama of office life: Beverly's hand on the door-knob, Ruthie's coat pulled on just one shoulder, Dorothy gripping the handset of the telephone. The dial tone buzz rasped against the silence.

"I'm sorry," Dorothy finally said. "It's a difficult time."

"I don't understand."

"Good night, Miss Bledsoe." Beverly pulled open the door. As many times as Lucybelle had asked her to use her first name, Beverly made a point of being especially formal in her presence.

"Your sergeant is leaving," Lucybelle said to the other two who gaped at her angry outburst.

"Actually," Beverly turned swiftly to face Lucybelle again. "I *am* a sergeant. I served my country in the war. What about you?"

"No rank," Lucybelle said. "Just a civilian editor trying to make friends."

Dorothy reached out a hand and squeezed Lucybelle's forearm before following the other two out the door.

She was pretty sure Bader wouldn't have gossiped about her romantic proclivities, but as the office manager Beverly might have access to personnel files. All three of the other female SIPRE employees were unmarried, so perhaps they feared what any kind of association with her might suggest about themselves. Or perhaps it was she herself they feared: the predatory habits of gay girls were well known. That was almost funny. Me, Lucybelle thought, with my thick cat-eye glasses and too deeply set eyes, my twig-snapping limbs, on the hunt.

Well, she'd find out what her security clearance papers said and maybe that would explain the ladies' behavior. If it did, she'd find a way to move forward with them, beyond whatever crude notions they nursed. The current chill was unacceptable.

She located her slim file and pulled out the manila folder. Her application papers were there, and a glowing letter from Link Washburn, the one recommending her to Bader in the first place. An official looking but nearly indecipherable document from the State Department, stamped with an affirmation of her security clearance, lurked behind the letter. She found nothing damning whatsoever, no mention of Phyllis Dove, nor any murky photographs of her with a blond girl in a dark entryway. The skinniness of her file disappointed her, a reaction she recognized as laughable. She should be relieved, but instead she felt erased, or at best, inconsequential. She read through the application papers until she came to the part where Bader had insisted she write, "Widowed." In the four months she'd been at SIPRE, no one had asked her about the husband killed in the war, no one had asked her any personal questions at all, so she hadn't had to lie, not yet. She slipped the flimsy file into its place among the B's and flipped back to the T's. There she withdrew Beverly Turnbull's file, which, perhaps the office manager would be pleased to note, was much thicker than Lucybelle's.

A good hour passed as she read with great interest the details of Beverly's employment history. The woman had indeed served her country in the war and had received an honorable discharge, only to be fired from a secretarial position in the State Department in 1952. A document outlining the details of her dismissal made the cause quite clear without using any overt language. A quick check of Ruthie Underwood's file revealed that she and Beverly lived together in Evanston. Lucybelle and the two women were practically neighbors, though she'd not once seen them in the grocery store, drugstore, or anywhere at all in public. Each morning they arrived at work in separate cars.

Lucybelle pushed the file cabinet drawer slowly and silently back into its housing, as if she might set off another round of dismissals if she made even the tiniest sound, and crept out of Bader's office. She sat again at her own desk and stared at the words "Chapter One" typed on the sheet of paper in her typewriter. That well of calm she'd felt earlier in the evening, the possibility of a story, was gone. Instead a thick, muzzy curtain closed on her imagination. How tired she'd grown of Phyllis's weakness, the constant maneuverings to conceal. Now here were Beverly and Ruthie, sneaking about, afraid of their own lives.

A charge of contempt bolted through her, followed quickly by a sinking feeling of shame. How hypocritical of her to judge. She'd agreed to "widowed." Worse, she'd agreed to be permanently single. Beverly had lost her job, been exposed to the entire world, and still she lived with Ruthie. Their personalities may have warped under the pressure, and yet they were undoubtedly having cocktails, maybe even eggrolls with dipping sauce, together tonight.

While she, Lucybelle Bledsoe, thirty-three years old, was still typing the words "Chapter One" followed by blank pages.

She rose from her desk, and as if she were the night watchman, climbed the stairs to the cold labs on the top floor. She stepped into one of the refrigerated rooms and let the chill suck away her body heat. Lined with insulating aluminum-coated cork, these labs were cooled by chemicals circulated from huge tanks on the roof. It was Bader's dream to not only drill ice cores in both Greenland and Antarctica, but to keep them intact and frozen, which he did by having them packed in six-foot aluminum rods and shipped by refrigerated airplanes and trucks all the way to here, Wilmette, Illinois. Already they were studying the structure of ice crystals, and even some partial cores, but an entire core of ice, that would be like reading the rings in trees, only the record would reveal not just hundreds of years, but thousands of years. The dust, mold, bacteria, and ancient air trapped in these ice cores would tell a story of epic proportion about our planet.

Lucybelle wondered what Bader saw when he stepped out of his igloo in Greenland. There would be no sunlight up there in the Arctic for weeks to come, and yet the moon on all that ice would be luminous. She imagined a soft and transcendent blue reflected on his pale skin, the big roughness of the man diminished to a speck in the vista-busting space surrounding him. It must feel so good to see far enough at last, to experience such vast illumination. Sometimes she almost thought she loved him, but it wasn't love and it wasn't him. She ached for the companionship of someone who had such grand vision.

She supposed she ought to feel some kind of satisfaction in her discoveries about the office staff, but what she'd learned about them only made her feel more rather than less lonely. The endless subterfuge—driving to work separately when the powers that be knew, or at least could know by a careful reading of their files, that they lived together!—was like being buried alive. She looked at the thick door of the refrigeration room. Another few minutes and hypothermia would take her quite painlessly. She'd slip to the floor and fall unconscious. The moment reminded her of the one on the bridge, when she considered what it would be like to jump.

That woman had come along, the one with the camera. Stella. She really ought to return the Ginsberg poems. *With radiant eyes hallucinating Arkansas.* Had he written that line about her? It was absurdly egotistical to think so. They'd met only briefly before he left Columbia for his travels, and yet she was the only student in the graduate program from that state. They'd talked just that once, at a party, but he'd laughed at Arkansas and said her eyes were like little caves with candles burning deep within.

Yes, she ought to return Stella's book. She'd brought it in to work weeks ago, intending to make the call, get an address, and send it out with the office mail, but found she couldn't quite part with the poems. For goodness' sake, she could buy herself a copy. She needn't steal Stella's. And stealing is what it would be if she didn't call the girl and get the book back to her. The Willa Cather picture was one aberrant incident, with extenuating circumstances—she was a Cather devotee—but if she did it again it would be a pattern. A pattern of thievery. This made Lucybelle smile. In fact, the entire train of thought reversed her mood. She left the cold lab and ran down the flight of stairs.

In her office she put on her plum wool coat and sat at her desk shivering. It was New Year's Eve. Stella would be out like everyone else. This could be a practice call. Lucybelle lifted the handset and dialed.

"Acme Transport. Happy New Year. May I help you?" The voice on the other end of the line was melodious, southern, a lazy float on warm water.

Stella had given her a false number, written any old string of digits inside the book cover, just to play with Lucybelle, a tease, like the exaggerated swagger. She began to hang up but stopped midair. The woman's voice sounded like home and she wanted to hear her say something else, so Lucybelle said, "Yes, thank you. This is a taxicab service?"

"Yes, ma'am. Where do you need to go?"

"Into Chicago." Why not? The holiday lights would be lovely. She could get a drink at the Drake Hotel. Her wool coat and the lush voice had warmed her, and she suddenly craved a cold martini.

After a long pause, the woman said, "Into Chicago? But where are you?"

How foolish of her. The transport company was already in Chicago. "I'm in Wilmette. 1215 Washington Avenue."

"I'm sorry, ma'am, but we're not able to service Wilmette. Especially not on New Year's Eve. Truth be told, we don't have a driver available until well after two in the morning anyway."

"Oh. Well, thank you. Happy New Year."

"You too, baby," said the woman in her cushiony voice. "Good night."

Lucybelle gently set the handset back in its cradle. She closed her eyes and tried to picture where a girl like Stella celebrated New Year's Eve. She imagined Bader lifting a glass of whatever the Inuits drank. Phyllis and Fred were no doubt into their second or third bottle of champagne.

## Friday, February 1, 1957

The Western Union delivery boy pushed past Lucybelle as she picked her way down the icy path along the side of her apartment building. The dirty slush from yesterday's warming trend had frozen hard overnight, and she wondered how she'd make it to the train station without slipping and breaking her neck. She turned to see the delivery boy dive into her own entryway and take the steps two at a time.

"Western Union!" he shouted, his voice echoing in the stairwell. She heard the heel of his hand pounding on wood, either her door or the Worthingtons'.

She skated back to her stairwell. The boy flattened her against the railing as he flew down the stairs.

"Who's the telegram for?" she yelled at his retreating back.

"Apartment 814," he hollered over his shoulder and then cursed as he took a long slide on the ice, arms flailing.

"That's me!"

She grabbed the telegram, climbed the stairs, and keyed open her apartment. The flimsy slip of paper depicted a long-legged stork flying across the top with a baby dangling from its beak. Pink ribbons and white baby shoes embellished the margins of the telegram. "Female Bledsoe born at 4 a.m. on February first. Name Lucy Jane contingent upon Aunt Lucy assuming burden of clothing, education, special gifts, and general obligations of sponsorship. Mother and daughter well. Love, John Bledsoe."

She would miss her train, but she was too stunned to move. A baby Lucy. She felt delighted, a rush of pleasure, as if the fresh start were her own. Then, just as quickly, she deflated. Her brother was joking, of course, when he wrote about assuming a burden of material support, but he wouldn't be able to conceive of the hidden burdens, the subjective ones. Having a namesake felt like too big of a responsibility. This new Lucy would be looking to her for . . . something . . . someday.

By lunchtime it was snowing hard, preventing the unfriendly trio from leaving the building. Lucybelle waited until they'd taken their seats in the lunchroom and gotten halfway through their sandwiches before pulling a chair up to their table.

"My brother and his wife had a baby this morning," she said. She wouldn't mention it being named for her. Beverly would think she was bragging.

"How nice!" Dorothy said with too much gusto, as if babies were something one must admire.

"I've six nieces and nephews," Beverly said dismissively.

"Well, you win. I've only got four so far." Lucybelle took a chance on teasing Beverly about her competitive tone.

Ruthie laughed, but mirthlessly. Dorothy guffawed with genuine amusement.

Lucybelle decided to go for broke. "I'm sorry to barge in on the three of you like this, but it's hard getting to know people. I lived in New York for twelve years."

"Well, la-dee-da." Beverly, of course.

"Where in New York?" Dorothy asked.

"The Village."

Ruthie giggled, the very mention of the bohemian neighborhood triggering her nerves.

Lucybelle wanted so badly to just blurt what she knew, but instead she followed protocol by making an indirect reference. "I once got Djuna Barnes to speak to me."

All three women stared like prisoners at gunpoint. Perhaps she should have chosen a less provocative reference.

"Never heard of her," Beverly said.

"You did not," Dorothy said, her eyes now gleaming with interest.

"You don't know who she is either," Beverly said to Dorothy.

"We spotted her at a big party, and my friends dared me to approach her. So I did, and to everyone's amazement—since she has a reputation for being a complete recluse—she chatted with me for about ten minutes."

"And it was your charm that brought her out?"

Lucybelle tossed down her sandwich. "Look, I—"

"Beverly didn't mean to be rude. It's been a difficult time," Dorothy said, her comment similar to the one she'd made at the beginning of December. "Beverly's good friend—"

Beverly emitted something like the letter "n" with a great deal of emphasis, as if saying the word "no" would be too revealing.

"Oh, come on, Bev," Dorothy said, but already Ruthie was packing up both her and Beverly's lunch things.

Dorothy stayed for about five minutes after the other two left, and they talked about a radio show Lucybelle had never heard, the weather, and some new books Dorothy had purchased for the library. Despite the boring topics, everything about the woman, including the silvery streaks in her otherwise light-brown hair, her large mouth with the wide gap between her two front teeth, and especially her prominent, globe-like dark-green eyes, seemed to announce a suppressed zeal. Lucybelle thought she could like Dorothy quite well, if that zeal were freed.

57

## Monday–Friday, April 22–26, 1957

Bader returned in March, much to her relief, and he invited Lucybelle, along with all the scientists, out on his first Friday night back in town. They took the train into Chicago—Wilmette and Evanston were both dry cities—and spent the evening being entertained by Bader's Greenland stories. The night he and some other scientists puked their brains out, thinking they'd eaten some bad food, only to eventually realize they'd developed carbon monoxide poisoning in their airtight ice cave. The twenty-foot-tall snowwoman they'd made one night, complete with breasts and vulva, and then lamented they'd made her standing rather than in repose where they might enjoy her offerings. The time Klaas, a Dutch scientist, came shouting into camp, after a trip to the loo, announcing that he'd seen airplanes on the horizon. "The Russians!" he'd screamed, really he had, Bader insisted, howling himself with laughter. Poor Klaas had hallucinated the invasion; the planes never arrived, nor did anyone else see them at all. That would be the Dutchman's last chance at fieldwork.

Lucybelle hadn't laughed so hard in months. The next morning her stomach muscles actually hurt from the workout. Even better, her enjoyment of the stories brought her, finally, into the visible landscape of the scientists. Lights blinked on behind their eyes. They saw her: this woman who would laugh at bawdy jokes, who didn't flinch at coarse language, and who, they slowly began to realize, made them look a lot better with her marks on their papers. She became bolder in drawing lines through entire paragraphs, circling others and sending them forward or backward in the text. Peter Hauser began sharing stories with her about his fieldwork, and Russell Woo told her about his parents, who were still in China. Friday night trips into Chicago for drinks with the scientists became the highlight of her week.

On a Monday morning, late in April, upon her return from a trip to Portland where she met—and couldn't help but delight in—her infant namesake, Lucybelle found a small brown paper package on her desk. She cut the twine and ripped away the wrapping. There was no letter, or even a note, just a paperback novel entitled *Whisper Their Love*, by Valerie Taylor. The cover depicted two women, one in pants of course, with short hair, and the other sitting on the floor at her feet, wearing just a slip. You could just smell the cloud of cheap perfume. At the bottom of the book cover were the words, "Theirs was a kind of love they dared not show the world . . ."

She could take a joke. Doing so these past weeks, time and again, had won her the scientists' respect. And yet, she had to draw a line. Arkansas, her perfectionism, even her chain-smoking were all fair game, but this particular little bud of humor had to be nipped. Her best guess was Bader with his love of anything scurrilous. He undoubtedly found the pulp novel in some drugstore and thought it would be a jolly little joke.

She wrote "Very funny" in large letters on a sheet of white paper and placed it squarely on his desk. An hour later he came into her office flapping the paper and asking, "What?"

His blank expression made her doubt his guilt, and so she quickly tried to formulate another reason for having left the oversized note. Thankfully he had the attention span of a gnat. He wadded the paper and tossed it into her wastebasket and then asked her when she'd be done with the Camp Century site plans.

That night she decided that the best course of action would be to pretend the book had never arrived on her desk, to just play dumb. What choice did she have? Wave the book around in the lab and cry out, *Ha ha ha!* along with the boys? Hand out scientific tracts about homosexuality so they would better understand? Maybe Kinsey's female study? Nope. The best course of action was to swallow the tacky little book whole, to pretend the incident had never happened.

Still, all that week she watched the scientists for signs of guilt. They were none of them good actors. She'd see it. Instead, all she noticed was their increased kindness and respect for her work, at long last.

Late on Friday night, after getting home from drinks in Chicago with the guys, she read the book in one go. Then she tossed the paperback across the room, startling L'Forte. The book angered her: the wretched level of dependency the female lovers had upon one another, their shame, and the corrective ending; how this kind of trash served to define her to the rest of society. She needed to know who sent it to her. Phyllis would never have bought, or even touched, one of these books. Nor would Harry, unless, somehow, it was a follow-up to his statement that she needed to "play." But no, Harry saw the world through Freudian eyes and probably had never read a book by a woman in his life. If he'd determined to help her, he would have sent something about penis envy. She called him anyway.

"It's one in the morning, Lucy."

"Someone sent me a paperback book. One of those drugstore ones about girls."

"Well, that's nice." She heard Wesley muttering in the background.

"No, it's not nice. It's horrid. The writing alone—"

"Don't be self-hating, honey. Look, it's too late to talk now."

She wasn't self-hating. People who sent lurid lesbian tales anonymously through the mail were self-hating. "I need to know who sent this to me."

Harry yawned. "Clare?"

Why hadn't she thought of that? She was probably also guilty of telling Phyllis her whereabouts.

"She talks about you sometimes. I figured you were in touch."

"Do you have her telephone number?"

"Well, yes, I do, somewhere. But it's past one in the morning and I—"

"Please just get it for me, and then you can go back to sleep."

"For Christ's sake," she heard Wesley groan.

Harry clunked down the telephone. The bedsprings creaked as he got up, and she wondered why a man who made a good income as the self-proclaimed "shrink of inverts" didn't buy a better mattress. A minute later, he read the information to her from his address book. Lucybelle thanked him and hung up.

"Why did you send me that book?" she said when Clare answered the telephone.

"Who is this?" Clare asked eagerly. Unlike Harry, she was pleased, curious, about someone calling her in the middle of the night.

"And to my place of work. You well know that could get me fired. You also told Phyllis where I am. I need you to leave me alone." With a girl like her, only absolute candor would work.

"Oh! It's Lucy!" Still pleased. "Is it a secret?"

"Is what a secret?"

"Your place of work."

"No. But Clare, anyone with a modicum of discretion would know to not hand out that information to someone's ex."

"You should know I have no discretion, not a modicum or any other kind."

True, she *should* know that. Yet she'd allowed herself that interlude in the entryway; she'd told Clare where she was moving, even where she would be working. It could be argued that she deserved *Whisper Their Love*.

"However," Clare continued. "I haven't sent you any books. I haven't even written you a letter." There was a pause followed by an intake of breath. "But truth be told, I've thought about you. A lot."

"You didn't send me the . . . the book . . . by Valerie Taylor?"

"That new one? *Whisper Their Love?* The ending really ticked me off, although I guess you could argue that running off with a man is better than suicide or insanity, which is usually what they do to us in books." Clare paused, as if she expected Lucybelle to have a conversation about the book, as if they were sitting in a bar with drinks. "Yes, I told Phyllis where you'd gone. Like I said, I didn't know it was a secret, and if it was, you shouldn't have told me. But no, I didn't send you a book."

Lucybelle almost believed her. Clare was nothing if not vigorously candid.

"I'm sorry," Lucybelle said. "I shouldn't have involved you in my life the way I did my last night in New York."

"'Involved you in my life,'" Clare quoted. "Wow. Nice way to put it."

Lucybelle lit a cigarette, deeply regretting this phone call. "It's late."

"But you called me, didn't you? You're still 'involving me in your life.'"

"I thought you'd sent something that was an endangerment to me."

"I'm an endangerment to you. Whether I sent you anything or not. Just my status in the world, my commitment to being true to myself. That threatens everything, doesn't it?"

The anger building in Clare's voice was the last thing she needed. But she understood it. Clare was right and deserved a better apology. Lucybelle knew exactly why she'd kissed her that night. Clare was a marvel of genuineness. Lucybelle didn't want to be Beverly wadding up her sandwich paper, or Ruthie laughing hysterically, or Phyllis marrying a poofter, as if that somehow protected her. Clare's lack of fear was an aphrodisiac.

"I'm sorry," Lucybelle said again.

"They're having a baby, you know."

She didn't know.

"Everyone's been laughing about it. No one thought they'd ever, you know, carry through with the actual marriage act." Clare's laughter was like a bell, and it lightened something in Lucybelle's chest, despite the news.

Clare sighed and said, "I'd never do anything to hurt you."

61

"I know." She refrained from apologizing yet again.

"You're a sweet woman. Don't let 'em eat you alive, you hear?"

"No. I won't," Lucybelle said, chagrined that it came out in a whisper.

"If you ever make it back to New York, look me up, will you?"

"Good night. Thanks for talking."

"You're lonely," she said. "I hear it in your voice."

Lucybelle hung up. What else could she do? Clare would never say good-bye.

## Monday, April 29, 1957

By the end of the weekend, she'd decided on a course of action. Beverly and Ruthie's hostility angered her, and the anger emboldened her. Something had to be done if she was to have any peace at work. Even if they weren't the culprits, there was a good chance they'd know who was. She had to take the offensive, rip the Band-Aid off the wound and give it some air.

Lucybelle waited until midmorning when everyone would be immersed in their work. Beverly and Ruthie were alone in the foyer, the first pursing her lips at an order form, a sharpened pencil in her firm grip, and the latter typing with wicked speed, her fingers as nimble as a concert pianist. Lucybelle stood watching for a moment, listening to the sharp *tat* of each key striking the paper, impressing its neat ink letter. She almost hated to disturb them; a symbiosis of purpose seemed to hold the two women together—and everything else at bay.

Lucybelle dropped *Whisper Their Love*, face up, on Beverly's desk, and then stepped back to monitor the reaction.

Beverly stared, reddened, and then pushed back her office chair as if the book were a tarantula. "Where'd you get that trash?"

"I'm asking you. It came to me in the mail."

"Get it away from me."

"Look. I know about you. I read your file."

"You what?" The words were a soft hush of fire.

Ruthie wheezed.

Beverly looked at Ruthie, and then back at Lucybelle. Her expression was unreadable, but it wasn't quite hatred and it wasn't quite fear. It was like resolve hardened to amber. Beverly picked up the book. She tore off the cover and title page. She shredded these into bits of paper, and then she set to work on the rest of the pages.

Ruthie's wheezing intensified.

"Is she okay?" Lucybelle asked.

"No, she isn't," Beverly said as she proceeded with her destruction of the paperback.

Ruthie was seriously having trouble breathing, and Lucybelle went quickly to her side. She put a hand on her shoulder. "Can I help?"

The secretary was bent in two, coughing great desperate gasps, but she found enough energy to shrug away Lucybelle's hand.

Beverly scooped all the bits of paper into her wastepaper basket and tossed in a lit match. As flames leapt up the metal sides of the can, she snatched their coats off the coat rack and ushered Ruthie, who was fighting for breath, out the door.

Lucybelle stood watching the fire in the wastepaper basket die down to embers, wondering what had just happened. She picked up a file folder and tried to wave away the smoke.

Bader stepped into the foyer. "What the hell?"

"I dropped a cigarette in the wastepaper basket," she told him. "It was stupid."

"I'll say it was." He paused and then smiled. "You're lucky Beverly isn't here. She runs a tight ship. You'd be walking the gangplank."

Lucybelle nodded, feeling the full measure of dread in what she'd set in motion. A gangplank would be a relief. More likely the ladies would find a way to dangle her, indefinitely, over the high seas, with no hope of rescue.

"Where are they, anyway?" Bader asked.

Lucybelle didn't answer and he stomped back to his office.

Two hours later, she heard the women return and take their places at their desks as if nothing had happened. Lucybelle saw Beverly bring Ruthie a glass of water, and another time saw the secretary holding a damp washcloth on her own forehead. The voices coming from the foyer were softer than usual.

Neither woman spoke to her that entire week. If Lucybelle asked them to type something, or inquired after the whereabouts of one of the scientists, they acted as if she were invisible and inaudible. She did her own typing and searching. Bader repeated her explanation about tossing the cigarette in the wastepaper bin, and the scientists teased her mercilessly about trying to burn down the lab. The smell of smoke didn't leave the foyer for days.

## Friday, May 3, 1957

On Friday night Lucybelle skipped drinks with the scientists and instead walked to the Evanston address. She knocked on the door and Ruthie answered.

"I want to apologize. And make sure you're okay."

Beverly appeared behind Ruthie. Indignation flared across her face and she tried to shut the door. To Lucybelle's surprise, Ruthie put her foot in the way, blocking the move.

Lucybelle took quick advantage of the opening. "That was such an insensitive thing for me to do. I'm sorry."

"Come in," Ruthie said.

"No," Beverly said, and yet, unaccountably, she stepped aside.

Dorothy stood in their living room, in front of the couch, looking downright pleased by the unfolding spectacle. She must have recently arrived because the tray of egg rolls on the coffee table looked untouched. The bright red dipping sauce emitted a sweet, tangy aroma.

Lucybelle moved quickly into the room before they had a chance to change their minds and evict her. The coziness of the apartment surprised her; she'd unconsciously pictured them living at desks in their own home. Tan-and-orange plaid wool covered the chunky couch. A large rug, brown with golden flecks, warmed the floor. A walnut coffee table, with rounded corners, stood on copper legs. The leather armchair with a matching ottoman had to be Beverly's, and the huge collection of porcelain figurines, displayed in the breakfront, must be Ruthie's.

"I'm truly sorry for the mess I made on Monday."

"Well," Beverly and Ruthie said simultaneously.

"Someone sent me that book and I was so exasperated by . . . by *it*. I thought you might know who sent it."

"How could we possibly know anything at all about that book?" Beverly asked.

"You told Bader that you started the fire with a cigarette," Dorothy said.

"I guess you could say that I did start the fire, at least indirectly."

"Though not with your cigarette." Dorothy gleamed and nodded, urging the story forward.

"I have asthma," Ruthie said.

"Triggered by unnecessary emotional strain," Beverly added.

"I'm so sorry."

"One could go through life apologizing if one wasn't careful," Ruthie said, and Lucybelle didn't know if the remark was meant to be forgiving or a warning.

"That does seem to be my pattern of late," Lucybelle said, unwittingly picking up Ruthie's formal diction.

"You've apologized," Beverly said. "It's best if you leave now."

"Have a seat," Ruthie said, and Beverly didn't oppose her.

Dorothy plopped down on the plaid couch and fingered the fabric weave, her eyes shining, as if she'd lucked into witnessing a murder.

"I do take some responsibility," Ruthie said. "I should have had my inhaler with me."

"Show her!" Dorothy said. "It's small enough to fit in her purse. It's really something. She used to have to use this big glass bulb contraption. I swear, modern medicine!"

"No one wants to see Ruthie's inhaler."

"I do," Lucybelle said, making every effort.

Ruthie opened a side table drawer and withdrew a small device shaped like an L. "It was invented to dispense perfume. Then some man whose daughter had asthma thought to make it into something that could administer the right amount of medicine to the lungs."

"It's changed her life," Dorothy said.

"It *would* change my life, if I kept it with me. I've only had it a few months. I'm just not used to there being such an easy solution."

"Hardly easy," Beverly said.

In the long silence that followed, Lucybelle who still stood in the middle of the room knew she was supposed to graciously say her good-byes and leave. Instead she said, "Nice prints." She'd have expected painted bouquets of violets rather than the Van Gogh and Picasso.

"We get them from the library," Ruthie said. "We change them every few weeks."

"The library here in Evanston?"

65

"Chicago Public. Dorothy used to work there. She told us about the art collection."

Lucybelle could feel Beverly ticking away at her back, her hand probably still on the doorknob. She searched for a way to keep the polite conversation going. "That must have been a great job."

Dorothy rolled her eyes. "It was. But I got involved with someone who also worked at the library, and when we broke up, well, it just seemed like a good idea to leave."

"You left to find a job closer to your mother," Beverly corrected.

"That's the official story. It's a lot easier to get help up here, and now I'm a quick walk away if I need to rush home. But Bev, the timing was good, you can't deny that." She looked at Lucybelle and said, "I have a bad habit of getting involved with people at work."

"I don't believe Miss Bledsoe came to hear your life story," Beverly said.

"It's a pattern I have to break. I mean, you can't change jobs every time a relationship ends."

"Dorothy!"

"Relax, Bev. Why doesn't everyone just sit down." Ruthie hadn't giggled once here in her own home. She settled into the leather chair, and Lucybelle sat on the other side of the plaid couch from Dorothy. Beverly carried a hardback chair from the kitchen, clunking it down loudly and shifting her behind back and forth on the wooden seat, making it clear that the apartment could only accommodate three comfortably.

"You said you read my file."

Lucybelle almost smiled. It didn't take Beverly long to take back the offense.

"I did. So I guess we're all in the same boat."

"Which boat is that?" Beverly spoke with slow heat.

"Can we have drinks?" Dorothy asked.

Ruthie pushed herself out of the big leather chair. "Gin okay?" It was as if she wore a personality costume to work. Here at home she was much more relaxed, even genial.

"Perfect," Lucybelle said. "Thank you."

All three of the other women retreated to the kitchen to make the drinks, and Lucybelle let them have their little conference. When they returned, Dorothy carried the tray, the ice cubes tinkling pleasantly, as if this were any cocktail party. A bowl of pretzels and a bottle of tonic water sat on the tray next to the glasses of gin.

When everyone was seated again with drinks in their hands, Beverly said, "I have a job and I intend to keep it." She ran a hand through her hair, loosening the short auburn waves. She'd washed off the dark-red lipstick, foundation, and eyebrow penciling. Freed from the makeup, with her hair a bit mussed, she was a striking woman.

"Good plan," Lucybelle said, wishing desperately for a cigarette.

"Just tell her," Dorothy said. "The whole story."

"Yes." Ruthie spoke with her eyes closed, as if she were a soothsayer reading the situation. "One feels that it's okay."

Beverly huffed.

"Ladies, it *is* okay," Dorothy said. "She's friends with Djuna Barnes!"

"I didn't say friends. I only met her once."

"And you charmed her," Beverly added drily, as if Lucybelle charming anyone was hard to believe.

"I did a bit, yes. They say so."

"They?"

"Friends who were at the party."

"Lucky you," Dorothy said. "Living in the Village."

"Tell," Ruthie said again, looking at Beverly, her pixie features nearly fierce in the command. Funny, Lucybelle thought, how power dynamics in couples sometimes reversed themselves in public and private spheres. Here was Ruthie calling the shots from the leather chair with the ottoman.

"I'm gay too," Lucybelle said. "Just to be clear."

Dorothy clapped.

"That hardly calls for applause," Beverly said.

"What fun," Dorothy said. "Four out of four. That's really something!"

Beverly rolled her eyes. "Not exactly shocking."

"Actually, it is too shocking. All four women working at SIPRE?" Dorothy glanced quickly around the room, meeting eyes with each of the other women, as if trying to understand the significance.

Lucybelle couldn't help but think of Bader's words that day in Morningside Park. *You're smart as a whip. You have the exact skills we need.* She'd been wooed by his flattery. Had his praise just been a decoy? Had his real intent lay in the sentences that followed? *There really would be no sacrifice on your part. Just stay out of the bars. Don't get arrested.*

Four out of four, Lucybelle realized, were ideal subjects for blackmail. Or at the very least, they were all easily controlled.

"Don't be ridiculous," Beverly said. "We"—her voice hitched at the admission imbedded in that one word—"have always made up most of the female workforce. The other ladies are busy at home with kids."

"Just tell her the story, Bev," Ruthie said.

Everyone took sips. The gin tasted acrid. Lucybelle preferred British brands. A cigarette would go a long way toward mitigating the unpleasant taste, but that was clearly out of the question.

"Go on," Ruthie said, scooting deeper into her chair. Dorothy crossed her legs and threw an arm over the back of the couch, her hand grazing Lucybelle's shoulder.

"Very well," Beverly said. She looked at Lucybelle for a long moment, decided something, and then loosened. "It was a Friday and I wore my light-blue suit and dark-blue heels."

"Which you don't have anymore."

"She wants nothing associated with this event," Dorothy explained to Lucybelle.

"It was a very hot day and they took me into a room with no windows. I didn't want to take off my suit jacket because of the dampness under the arms of my white blouse. I felt that vulnerable. The two civil service investigators sat me down across from them. A big oak table separated us. They had stacks of file folders on the table."

"Piles and piles of evidence," Dorothy said.

"It was not evidence!" Ruthie said.

"Would you two like to tell the story?"

"It's your story."

"That's what I thought." Beverly raised her eyebrows and pursed her lips, but without the makeup the familiar expression was almost appealing.

"I don't see how a bit of elaboration on the side can hurt." Dorothy batted Lucybelle's shoulder gently. With her gap-toothed grin and protruding eyes, she looked as if she were about to burst.

"Just go on," Ruthie said.

"It was not evidence. That's the point. It was, for all I know, photographs of their own families and letters from their grandmothers. But they did stack thick file folders on the table. One started out by saying, 'You're an attractive girl, Miss Turnbull. Why would you wear such a manly suit?'

It *wasn't* a manly suit, anymore than any other woman's suit. It was a suit, yes, but not a manly one. Then the other said, 'Your voluntary appearance here today has been requested in order to afford you an opportunity to answer questions concerning information that has been received by the US Civil Service Commission.' He laid his hands on the stacks of files, again implying that they were chock full of incriminating information. Of course I knew immediately where this was going. I was not there 'voluntarily,' I might add. It was not an option for me to stand up and walk out of that room."

"Legally, she should have been able to have a lawyer present," Dorothy said.

"A lawyer wouldn't have changed anything," Ruthie defended.

Lucybelle realized they'd told this story many, many times, if only to one another.

"They started out with benign questions about my name and date of birth, things like that. Finally they got around to asking *the* question. They wanted me to comment." Beverly's demeanor softened. She held her folded hands in her lap and her mouth quivered as if she might cry. Perched on the edge of that hard upright chair, she looked defenseless, like a bird on an exposed tree limb.

"How'd they phrase the question?" Lucybelle asked.

Dorothy batted Lucybelle's shoulder again. "Aren't you a live one."

Ruthie wheezed, as if focusing too sharply on the devastating topic would bring on an asthma attack.

Lucybelle refrained from saying that words mattered, but she wanted to know, exactly, how they chose to frame the threat.

"Shall I go on?" Beverly looked at each of their faces. Dorothy bugged her eyes and Ruthie pulled a pretend zipper across her mouth. "Good. So I said, 'No comment.' They seemed to accept that, and I started to feel almost light. I thought I was going to get out of this, though why I thought that tactic would work is anyone's guess. They launched into asking about certain bars, whether I'd ever been, and continued pretending to have photos. Let me tell you right now, Miss Bledsoe, Ruthie and I do not frequent bars, nor have we ever. The women there . . ." She huffed her disapproval. "Nevertheless, on one or two occasions, we'd been coaxed by someone to attend what had been billed as a private event in certain establishments. I never saw the actual images on the photographs, but one of the men kept sliding shiny pictures out from one of the folders and flashing them quickly. The more I've thought about it, I'm quite sure they wouldn't have featured me. How could they have? I didn't patronize those places, and no one took pictures at the private parties we attended. But at the time . . . he scared me."

Beverly stopped talking and took a big gulp of her iced gin and tonic. A sheen of fear heightened the color in the pocks in her skin, and yet, underlying the fear, a raw and angry determination projected itself as beauty. Yes, beauty. She was like a mountain, daunting and a bit cold, but lovely nonetheless. Lucybelle felt her own loneliness slough away, all in one go.

Nobody made encouraging noises for Beverly to go on. They waited for the alpenglow to fade, for her to regain control on her own, and then she continued. "It was when they began asking about my friends . . . Do I know so-and-so? Had I had dinner with Miss R—? I see now that I answered incorrectly. Of course I should have denied any association with these women, but they were my friends, and in the heat of the moment, my response was to claim them, both for myself, as if I could bring them into the room with me for comfort, but also because I didn't want to deny them. It felt as if, were I to say, no, I don't know her, I'd be pushing her off a cliff. Of course, as it turned out—and I should have known this—the opposite was true."

"How could you have known, how could anyone have known, how to answer those men? They were monsters," Ruthie said.

"Stop blaming yourself," Dorothy said.

"Finally one of them—truly, I couldn't tell you what they looked like now; they were identical with their crew cuts and blunt fingers—asked me if I knew that all of these girls were known to be. Certified, he said."

"Certified," Lucybelle repeated. Like crazy.

"They meant homosexual," Dorothy clarified. The word took flight, circled over their heads, both free and menacing.

"Well, obviously," Beverly said, glad for an opportunity to be irked. "After that, they became obscene, describing acts and asking about my experience." Tears came into her eyes, and to counter them, she shifted forward in her chair toward Lucybelle and said, "So if you're a spook, go write your report."

"Who turned you out?"

"That's the hardest part of the story," Ruthie said.

"A former friend."

"A former *beau*," Dorothy said. "Who to this day has a well-paid, high-level job in the State Department."

"Besides firing Bev, they told her parents and her brother."

"If I ran into her on the street," Beverly said, "I might spit on her. I really might."

"Spit?" Dorothy called out. "I'd shoot her dead."

"You don't have a gun."

"If I did."

"Two other friends were also fired."

"Jane hung herself."

Beverly gave Ruthie a look that said every detail needn't be shared, but for Jane's sake, Lucybelle was glad to know. She felt a pang of love for the unknown girl. It was nearly erotic, a desire to touch her most private anguish, to ease it. Lucybelle craved the truth. Yes, Beverly did need to share every detail.

"They even called Ruthie's boss at the bank. Mr. McGregor was wonderful, though. He said to not worry, he'd stand behind Ruthie's fine work record."

"But Beverly would never get work again in Washington. Anyway, gossip about us would reach every corner of the city."

"Already had," Ruthie said.

"So we moved to Chicago with our savings, hoping to get any kind of jobs. At least here no one knew us."

"Well, my parents," Ruthie said.

"Yes. That's one of the reasons we chose Chicago. We knew that if we had to, we could live with them until we got our feet back on the ground. They've been kind."

"Thank god we didn't have to do that."

"I never dreamed I'd ever work for the government again."

"It's kind of a fluke that we are." Finally Ruthie giggled.

Maybe a fluke, Lucybelle thought. And maybe not.

"They were setting up this lab, and I saw the listings for an office manager and a secretary. Of course when we applied, we didn't tell them that we knew each other."

"I said to Beverly, 'What do we have to lose? They can't do anything more to us.'"

"Which wasn't exactly true. They could have destroyed Chicago for us. Then where would we have gone?"

"We both got the jobs."

"I figured they somehow hadn't done background checks."

"Now we know," Ruthie said quietly.

"You didn't know, before this?" Lucybelle asked.

"How could we have?" Beverly tightened up again.

"I thought you would have seen your files."

Beverly stared at Lucybelle with deadpan forbearance. Of course they wouldn't have snooped, as she had done; they couldn't afford one misstep.

"We've all been waiting for the other shoe to drop," Dorothy said.

"Well, it's dropped," Ruthie said.

"Miss Bledsoe—" Dorothy rested her hand on Lucybelle's shoulder.

"Please. Just Lucy."

"Lucy," Dorothy started out again. "You've—" She stopped herself and looked first at Ruthie and then at Beverly. Her open face seemed to turn inside out with wonderment. "You've freed them. Us! If they know . . . if they already know, then . . ."

"They know," Lucybelle said. "They definitely know."

Dorothy grinned. "And you two thought you were so clever."

"We will not be changing a single habit of our lives," Beverly said firmly.

"Since we were hired at the same time, it made sense that we'd get an apartment together," Ruthie said. "So that looked natural."

"Still, at any time," Beverly said.

"We're saving money. In case it happens again."

"They won't even take a vacation," Dorothy said to Lucybelle. "It's not like *I* can ever go anywhere. My mother is a full-time job. After paying Sally, the girl from across the street who watches her, I'm saving nothing. Zilch."

"Which is why you should be more careful. You of all people can't afford to lose your job."

"One doesn't let down her guard," Ruthie said. "One doesn't advertise anything."

"You're right. You're always right." Dorothy winked at Lucybelle.

"I'm serious," Beverly said. "Just because Miss Bledsoe here, or Lucy, or whoever, has provided some information that might indicate a bit more safety than we previously thought we had, the situation can deteriorate at any moment. Are you forgetting Martha?"

Dorothy turned to Lucybelle. "A friend who's still in Washington is going through this right now. We've been pretty upset about Martha."

"You don't even know her," Beverly said to Dorothy.

"But I know it's reminding you of the ordeal all over again."

"True," Ruthie said.

"She hired a lawyer, which means the whole thing is dragging out for months, and also that the investigation is spreading far and wide."

Lucybelle understood: Martha's decision to fight could bring probing eyes back around to the lives of her friends. No wonder they'd been so touchy these past months.

"There's always San Francisco!" Dorothy said. "If you had to move again."

"God forbid," Beverly said.

"I'm making another round," Dorothy said. "Everyone?"

Beverly scooted her chair up to the coffee table and picked up an egg roll. "These are cold." She dipped it in the sticky red sauce anyway and took a bite. "Help yourself," she said around the mouthful of fried crust and shredded cabbage.

"But wait." Ruthie spoke so quietly it was almost a whisper. "Who did send Lucy that book?"

## Friday, August 23, 1957

"No more setups," Lucybelle told her new friends. "I've chosen a life of the mind." She meant the latter comment to sound ironically comical but no one laughed.

"Well, la-dee-da," Beverly said.

Throughout their efforts to find her what Beverly called "an appropriate match," as if romance were just like hiring employees, Lucybelle hadn't told them that Bader had warned her against "acting on it." She knew that the question was moot; there would be no one upon whom she wished to act, at least from their pool of applicants. But she'd wanted to please her friends and maybe make some new ones.

"You're stubborn," Dorothy said.

"It's true."

"You're going to have to settle for something a bit more ordinary than a movie star," Ruthie said.

"Phyllis was a stage actress."

"Well, excuse *me*."

"You said glamorous, though," Dorothy said. "You said gorgeous."

"I thought so."

"La-dee-da."

"You can't expect to feel that way at the start," Ruthie said.

"I'm not willing to 'settle' for anything at all."

Dorothy's eyes gleamed, as if Lucybelle had said something daring. Maybe she had. She would hold out for what? Love? Beverly and Ruthie tightened their lips and straightened their spines, looking both defensive and disdainful. Lucybelle hadn't meant to suggest that *they'd* settled, but to say so would only dig herself in deeper. Still, she'd had enough of their matchmaking and had to make that clear.

"I'm serious," she said. "No more women. If you arrange something behind my back again, I'll walk out."

"That would be rude," Ruthie said.

"Yes, it would be. So let's avoid the situation altogether. Agreed?"

"If an opportunity comes along," Beverly said. "I'd hate to pass it up."

"*You* wouldn't be passing it up. You have Ruthie."

"You're so difficult."

"Thanks. From you, Bev, I'll take that as a compliment."

Beverly smiled.

"Why aren't you setting up Dorothy, anyway?"

"She has her mother."

"What's that got to do with it?"

"Think about it," Dorothy said. "I have to be home every night, except occasionally when I can get Sally to stay. Relationships are hard enough. Who wants to take on someone's mother on top of all the rest?"

"It's not like your mother would know. She has dementia."

The picture this created, of Dorothy and a girlfriend carrying on under the same roof as her uncomprehending mother, triggered a laughing fit.

"It's not funny!" Ruthie cried out, but the more they tried to stop, the harder they laughed.

"Oh, no!" Beverly rocked in uncharacteristic merriment. "This is wrong! Stop! *Stop!*"

They spewed mouthfuls of gin and cracker crumbs. No one laughed harder than Dorothy who had tears streaming down her face.

"In any case," Lucybelle said when they finally calmed, "I'm not looking for a relationship. Please respect that."

Each of the dates they'd set up for her had been disastrous. One woman flinched every time Lucybelle spoke, as if her words were knife jabs. Another, with whom she spent an afternoon at the Art Institute, stood before each painting scowling before offering criticism, always negative. When Lucybelle showed her *The Song of the Lark*, she said, "Ugh. Farmland. What's more boring than that?" In July, a friend of Beverly's, a literature professor from Vassar, visited for the weekend. That woman spoke primarily in lines of memorized poetry, impressive, but off-putting by the end of the weekend. When Lucybelle asked if she'd read *HOWL*, Geneviève recoiled as if Lucybelle had offered her a hallucinatory drug.

"No 'angelheaded hipsters staggering on tenement roofs illuminated' for you, huh?" Lucybelle asked, and the look on Geneviève's face dismissed her for good.

Lucybelle liked a little better the one who owned a red Mustang and drove too fast along Lake Shore Drive, but it turned out she could *only* drive, not talk. After a great deal of racing about in the Mustang, they finally stopped for dinner at a mediocre pub, and Babs shoved french fries around on her plate and made monosyllabic remarks. Lucybelle tried her best to ignite a conversation, but then gave up halfway through the meal and they ate in silence until the check arrived.

The last one, a woman named Leslie, she liked well enough to accept three dates, though she was aware that her loneliness was getting the best of her, because while Leslie was nice-looking and well spoken, Lucybelle had more fun with L'Forte. On the third date, while having drinks at the Drake Hotel, Leslie cocked her head shyly and asked whose apartment would be best.

"Best for what?"

"Us."

"Us?"

"I only have a studio. You mentioned that you have an extra room, so . . ."

"No. I'm sorry. No."

Leslie left the Drake Hotel in anger, as if by accepting three dates Lucybelle had agreed to an entire relationship.

But the months of dating had been useful. She needn't feel bad about adhering to Bader's rule because there were no temptations. The dates also proved that she wasn't afraid. No threat would stop her from doing as she pleased. The fact of the matter was, she'd agreed to be a widow for her own sake, not for Bader's. The clarity of the agreement appealed to her. No women. No messes. No heartbreak. She and L'Forte were doing just fine on their own.

On Friday nights Lucybelle often had to choose between having drinks with Beverly, Ruthie, and Dorothy in Evanston or taking the train into town with the fellows. She felt guilty for sometimes preferring the company of the scientists. They hewed to facts, searched with unbound curiosity for truths about whatever interested them, even when it was only ice. They were freewheeling, raucous, hell-bent on finding answers to questions, while the women did the opposite, used nearly all their energy to cover up the truth about their lives. But how unfair her judgments were when the scientists and their wives enjoyed the full support of society. No one called them perverted, twisted, inverted. No one threatened their jobs.

Everyday Lucybelle looked for a hairline fracture, a place in the social fabric of not just SIPRE, but Chicago, the whole country, where truth might collect like rain, freeze, and force open the gap. This was the story she wanted to tell, the novel she wanted to write, but first she had to find the chink.

Late that summer she bought a table and chair for her typewriter, and she began writing pages of story under the words "Chapter One." They weren't any good. What did she have to write about? Crows, rice fields, her love for a desperate actress. Cather had made stories from the prairie, from actresses and trains, dirt and sky. And light, mostly just light. She'd managed to sneak in subversions too, and yet they *were* snuck, tucked, hiding. Cather didn't go far enough, nowhere near far enough. Most nights Lucybelle tore up her pages.

## September 1957

The week Little Rock tried to integrate Central High School, Lucybelle bought a television set for her apartment. Everything, it seemed, drew her back to Arkansas.

The one girl hadn't gotten the message that she was supposed to meet the others so they could climb those stairs and walk in the front door together. She endured the jeers and projectiles of fruit all by herself. When the mob prevented her from getting near the high school entrance, she turned around and walked to the bus stop, where she sat and waited, alone. She wore a white blouse and a full skirt she'd made herself. A pair of sunglasses, her only shield, didn't hide the expression on her face. The girl's mouth was a bruise, her chin a balustrade holding up the entire country, her thin bare arms, hugging books to her chest, utterly vulnerable. She walked away from the tormentors, away from the Arkansas National Guard's guns, with her head held steady, a slim insistence in her stride.

Lucybelle knew how that Arkansas sun, its muddy light, felt on bare skin. How the eyes of those insensate boys and girls could scrape and tear.

The summer she was nine years old, a witless neighbor boy snuck into the yard and peeked into her sunshine pen. She heard him approach, even saw his eyeball in the crack between two boards, but she refused to gather her clothes to her body or call for help. Penned and naked, she lay on her back, her arms at her sides, her legs slightly spread, and looked back at his greasy pupil. A couple of years older than her, he was a scrawny boy, high-voiced and always looking for small acts of revenge. He'd found a situation in which he could dominate.

Already though she'd learned to toss her imagination far beyond the pen. She flew with the crows, way above the town, effortlessly riding sweet lilting drafts, not even bothering to look down on the little square houses and parched fields and stupid boys. The second time he came, she lifted a finger and pointed directly at his eyeball in the crack between the boards. He gasped, as if she'd put a hex on him, and she heard the thump of his bare feet running across the weedy grass.

Lucybelle's heart hurt with admiration for the young people attempting to attend Little Rock's Central High. Eventually the president ordered the Arkansas National Guard to protect, rather than target, the children. How strange to see the same men who'd threatened the students with their aimed guns now escorting them. Helicopters circled the sky over the school and tanks rolled down the surrounding streets. A few white kids stood inside the high school entrance and extended their hands, welcomed the new students. How slight a gesture, though, a handshake, next to the wet food hurtling toward their faces, along with the spit, the shoves, the ugly words. Worst of all, the ugly words.

This was America. This was Arkansas.

## Thursday, October 31, 1957

Lucybelle decided to go to the Halloween party as Djuna Barnes. At least Dorothy would appreciate the costume. She spent an entire Saturday haunting secondhand stores, shopping for her ensemble. She found a perfect black cape, a white scarf with black polka dots, and even a silver-headed ebony walking stick. The hat would be key, and she ended up buying that new. The black snap-brim fedora with a gray hatband was Djuna Barnes to a tee.

Now she just hoped her friends didn't chicken out. Dorothy had received the invitation and suggested they all go. Beverly, of course, said that the timing was poor, maybe another time. Ruthie threw caution to the wind and said they needed to have some fun. "Okay," Beverly said, caving in as she always did to Ruthie's wishes.

"Besides," Dorothy pointed out. "We'll be in disguise."

"Remember," Lucybelle said. "They already know. And they haven't fired you."

Beverly huffed.

The day of the party Lucybelle starched and ironed a white shirt so that the collar stood up stiffly. She pulled on her own black trousers and wrapped the polka dot scarf around her neck. She fastened the black cape at her throat. As the final touch, she applied lipstick so deeply red it was nearly black. She positioned the fedora on her head, slightly to the right and tipped forward over her right eyebrow. Her thick-lensed, cat-eye glasses looked ridiculous, and so, at the last second, she tossed them on top of the stack of books on her bedside table.

When Dorothy came to pick her up, she squealed with delight at the costume. Beverly and Ruthie, peering through the windshield of their Pontiac, were less enthusiastic. Lucybelle swished the black cape at their skeptical faces and then twirled with her walking stick aloft.

"Dracula?" Beverly asked as Lucybelle got into the backseat.

"She's Djuna Barnes!" Dorothy adjusted her oversized pirate hat. She wore a patch over one eye, a billowy red blouse, and a real sword in a sheath at her waist, which had made getting in the car rather difficult.

Beverly wore a clown suit, complete with a strap-on red-ball nose and a bright pink wig of curly hair. Ruthie was dressed as herself, in a simple green sweater and black skirt, driving the car like a chaperone.

"I couldn't think of anything," she said. "I was going to be a geologist, but Bev nixed that."

"I could just see us getting pulled over, and there would be Ruthie with her blue jeans and flannel shirt, pickaxe in hand. You count the number of things we could be arrested for."

"Why would we get pulled over?" Lucybelle asked.

The women in the car were silent, and for the millionth time she remembered that Beverly lived her life expecting to be pulled over, one way or another.

"For being a pickaxe murderer?" Dorothy finally suggested, and they all laughed.

Dorothy reached across the backseat and squeezed Lucybelle's hand. "You look great. But can you see?"

"No. Stay close, okay? Make sure I don't walk into walls."

"You won't be at a disadvantage without your glasses," Ruthie said, maneuvering the car into a parking space several blocks away from the party, in case anyone collected license plate numbers. "Everyone will be in costume. No one will know who they're talking to."

"You're not in costume."

Lucybelle wished Dorothy hadn't stated the obvious. Did Ruthie intend to wait in the car? Maybe she saw herself as their getaway driver. But she surprised Lucybelle by nodding sharply, bravely, and stepping briskly out of the Pontiac.

Lucybelle was excited about the party, and she took the lead walking to the front door. She rang the bell and as they waited, Beverly nervously adjusted her pink wig and Ruthie checked their surroundings.

A large woman with very short hair, blue jeans, a plaid flannel shirt, and a man's jacket opened the door. Dorothy had to grab Beverly's hand to keep her from retreating.

"What are you?" Lucybelle asked. Somehow she was pretty sure the woman wasn't a geologist.

"I'm a dyke. How do you like my costume?" the woman boomed and then laughed heartily.

Beverly said, "Ruthie."

Ruthie said, "I want to go in."

"I don't bite, ladies, but are y'all sure you're at the right party?"

"Yes," Dorothy said. "We're friends of Dorothy."

"Actually, she *is* Dorothy," Lucybelle said, "and *we're* the friends."

Beverly exhaled her exasperation. Lucybelle was botching the code for getting in the door. Lucybelle and the big greeter laughed at the irritated clown.

"Her real name," Ruthie said gesturing at the pirate, "is Dorothy."

"What are you dressed as?" the woman in the dyke costume asked. "A secretary?"

"Ha ha," Ruthie said. She glanced down the street where they'd parked the car.

The dyke bellowed her laugh again. "Welcome, ladies. Come in."

Lucybelle plunged in the door before her friends decided to not attend the party. The house was already packed with lavishly attired women, the festivities in full swing. Over the shouts of conversation and laughter, she heard the tinkle of ice cubes and the *pfft* of beer bottle caps being removed. She made her way through the bright blotches of color to the makeshift bar on the far side of the front room, answering the question, "Who are you?" five times on the way. She hadn't expected people to recognize her costume, but their blank expressions when she said the author's name was disappointing. She asked for a gin on the rocks and then realized she'd left her friends and couldn't see a thing. Surely she could find Dorothy's red blouse in the fuzzy tableau before her. There!

Dorothy's hand gripped the hilt of her sword as she talked to a sailor. "Lucy! Guess who I found!"

"Popeye?"

The woman in the sailor cap and white bell-bottomed pants smiled. "Who's this lovely lady?"

"Djuna Barnes!" Dorothy said.

"Really. I'm extremely pleased to make your acquaintance." The sailor held out her hand.

"You know Barnes?" Lucybelle asked.

"Her work, not the woman."

"Lucy has met her." Dorothy's cheeks were already rosy. The prominent gap between her two front teeth worked well with the pirate garb.

"Do tell."

"I used to live in the Village. She was at a party once."

"And even though she hardly talks with anyone, she talked with Lucy for *hours*."

"Maybe ten minutes."

"Lucy—?"

"Bledsoe." She shook the sailor's hand as the woman said, "Valerie Taylor."

Dorothy elbowed Lucybelle and then couldn't contain herself. "*Whisper Their Love*. I loved it. It's so nice to meet you in person, Miss Taylor."

"Please. Val."

Lucybelle felt the shock of opening that brown paper package all over again. That the book had an actual flesh-and-blood author jolted her to the core. Well, of course it did, but until now she'd imagined it coming from some generalized cloud of malevolence. She hadn't pictured a person—a woman, a gay girl herself—sitting down and penning the story.

Furthermore, Dorothy had read and "loved" the novel.

Valerie Taylor wore cat-eye glasses much like her own, but she'd had the good sense to keep hers on with her sailor costume. Lucybelle wished she could see her more clearly.

"It's a great book, Val," Dorothy was saying. "Thanks for writing it. Are you going to write a sequel? Tell you what, write a sequel and have Joyce leave John, don't you think?"

Valerie Taylor looked a bit fatigued by Dorothy's enthusiasm, but she was kind. "I'll give that some thought."

"Do," Dorothy said. "I hate to think of Joyce stuck with him for the rest of her life."

"What do you do?" Val asked Lucybelle, and so she began to explain about the ice research, but a slim blond woman beelined over to Val's side and gave her a juicy smack on the temple, right at the hairline. Dorothy elbowed Lucybelle again.

"Sweetie," the woman said to Val, "we need to get to our next party."

Val nodded as she lit a cigarette.

Lucybelle thought she might faint from the need for a smoke, another casualty of her rushing out the door without her purse. "May I bother you for one of those?"

The blond girlfriend slung a possessive arm around the author's waist as Val lit a cigarette for Lucybelle. Inhaling gratefully, she watched the couple make their way to the door.

"Wow!" Dorothy said. "That was exciting."

The woman's voice had been intelligently intriguing. Lucybelle wished they could have talked more.

"I'm going to get us more drinks," Dorothy said.

"No, thanks. Not for me."

"Really? Well, don't move. I'll be back."

Lucybelle weaved through the costumed women to the front door and was disappointed to find the dyke away from her post. She slipped outside and sat on the porch smoking. It was a cold and damp night, but clear. Lucybelle wished she could see the stars. When she squinted she thought maybe she could see smudges of light. She pictured her parents at the door of their house in Pocahontas, handing out homemade caramels to the children. Daddy would first request tricks and then guffaw at their crestfallen faces before giving over the candy. John Perry's children were probably haunting the streets of Portland, all but the baby, Lucy, who'd stay home with Helen.

"There you are." Dorothy the pirate stood on the step behind her. "We'd better stay inside."

"I know." Yet another unspoken rule: when at parties, give the neighbors as little to see as possible.

"You look great in that costume, by the way." Dorothy nudged her with a knee.

Lucybelle looked out at the blurry neighborhing homes. "Thanks, but—"

"But?"

Her fun had soured. Valerie Taylor was the only one who'd even heard of Djuna Barnes, and anyway, these women's relationships to their costumes were too complicated for real fun. Half of them needed total disguise to attend a party at all.

"Are you okay? You look sad. Are you thinking about Phyllis?"

Lucybelle waved her cigarette at the sky. "Farthest thing from my thoughts."

Dorothy allowed herself a big smile. "We should go back inside. That person watching the door told me we aren't supposed to be out here."

"I know."

"Beverly says I'm reckless, and I guess she's right. I have my mother. I can't afford to lose my job."

"People go to Paris," Lucybelle said softly. "People write books. Some people, like Ruthie, have families who accept them. Every street is not a dead end."

"I'm going to get you another gin. Come in with me."

"Okay. I'll be right there. I'm just going to finish this cigarette." She heard the door open and close again as Dorothy went back inside. She crushed out her cigarette, stood up, and wrapped the black cape more tightly around herself. A group of children came down the sidewalk, brown paper bags in their tight fists, shouting with excitement about their growing wealth of candy.

"Boo!" she said.

"Dracula!" shrieked the oldest one.

As they started up the walk to the front door, Lucybelle opened her cape and roared. That did the trick. They backed up and then ran all the way to the next house, looking over their shoulders.

Back inside, Lucybelle took a seat on the couch and watched the shimmering party shapes bounce and swoop. A few moments later, Dorothy handed her a glass of gin and sat on the arm of the couch. "Can you believe Valerie Taylor was here?"

"Who was the blonde?"

"I bet she has a lot of options, women-wise."

"I don't doubt it."

"So did you ever read *Whisper Their Love*? I mean before Bev burned it."

They both laughed and Lucybelle didn't answer. Instead she said, "I just finished Rachel Carson's *The Sea Around Us*." Now there was someone she'd love to meet: Carson, who wrote about the sea with the passion of a shark, swimming restlessly, mouth open, head swinging from side to side.

"I read that."

"You have very eclectic tastes."

"What choice do I have but to read everything, what with being stuck at home most nights?"

83

"You're not home now." The sentence popped out staccato. Dorothy's constant references to her homebound mother grated.

"No. That's true." Dorothy dutifully glanced out at the roomful of women, as if she were perusing the best route over difficult terrain. Then she sighed and shrugged. "She's family, you know."

"Yes, but you do take such good care of her, and you have a right to a life too." Lucybelle was glad for the opportunity to speak more sympathetically.

"I don't mean my mother, and I don't mean that kind of family."

"Who do you mean?"

"Rachel Carson."

"How would you know that?"

All Lucybelle could see of Dorothy's eyes was the flash of green as she breathlessly explained her source, a friend whose family had a house in Maine, and how nothing had ever been *said*, but via the power of observation of certain visitors and their walks on the beach, well, it was plain. "Quite plain," Dorothy emphasized.

The news almost hurt, like a sharp injection of truth. Lucybelle cared too much. She was already half in love with the author, just from reading her books. How she would love to be the one walking with her on Maine's shore. She imagined crouching before crusty orange starfish and gazing into shallow pools inhabited by green anemones waving their tentacles, waves crashing on the rocks, wetting their faces. She could just taste the rubbery seaweed brine. Most of all, most welcome of all, would be the conversation about things that mattered: books and the planet, stories and the sea.

It was discommoding, this interest in like souls, this feeling of *yes, mine, Rachel Carson*. It was as if she knew already, could read the depth and nature of Carson's affectional tendencies in the texts about the sea, but how could that be possible? It showed in her willingness to embrace complexity, an enormity of love, all bursting out from behind a shield of sorts, an invisible shield, but one felt even in her books.

"Everyone knows about Sappho," Dorothy rattled on, excited and maybe a little drunk, "and Gertrude Stein and Virginia Woolf, of course. That's all public knowledge. But I've heard that Eleanor Roosevelt is one of us! Imagine!"

Lucybelle liked Dorothy. Even without her glasses she could see the liveliness in her face as she talked. Who but a librarian read *Whisper Their*

*Love* alongside *The Sea Around Us*? She refrained from touching her friend's flushed cheek. The impulse surprised her. Maybe it was her blindness; if she couldn't see, she could touch. The full, red blouse was easy enough to see. Dorothy's multifarious reading habits complemented her lubricious figure.

"You don't believe me," Dorothy said.

"I don't *not* believe you. I just think people need to name themselves."

"You're right. Of course you're right."

"Have you read Allen Ginsberg?"

Dorothy shook her head hard. "Goodness, no."

"Ah, so you haven't read everything."

"Drugs and penises I can do without." Dorothy pulled her lips tightly around her teeth and it seemed as though her whole face sagged a bit, as if the very existence of that poem spoke of a world rocketing past her. "Come on," she said getting up from the arm of the couch. "We should circulate." She pulled Lucybelle to her feet, misjudging her slight weight, and Lucybelle came forward too hard, falling against the pirate. She was soft and yielding.

"I've been looking for the two of you." Ruthie's voice startled them both.

"Where's Beverly?" Dorothy asked, as if everyone needed to be accounted for.

"In the hall closet with the butch who answered the door," Lucybelle said.

To say the joke fell flat would be an understatement. Maybe she'd spent too much time with the SIPRE scientists. "Come on. It's funny, isn't it?"

"No," Ruthie said.

Dorothy pasted on a weak smile, but she put a supportive arm around Ruthie's shoulders.

Fine, she'd go look for the big bomber herself. Not that she could see a thing as she made her way across the room, but the woman in plaid flannel and blue jeans working as the front door bouncer would be hard to miss. As Lucybelle approached, she thought better of the plan. If her work friends saw her so much as converse with the flagrant dyke, she'd be shunned for at least a week.

Lucybelle swerved from her course toward the front door and made instead for the kitchen, where she found the telephone book, looked up Acme Transport, dialed the number, and gave the dispatcher, a nasal-voiced fellow this time, the address of a major intersection a few blocks away. Then she looked for the bright pink blob that would be Beverly's head, found her in the den, and told her she was going home.

"Are you okay?"

"Yes, I'm fine."

"Hon." It was the first time she'd ever used a term of endearment for Lucybelle; perhaps she'd made inroads into the office manager's labyrinthine trials of trust. Beverly leaned in and whispered, "I heard that author was here. The one who wrote that book. You must be upset. But she's already left. I think it's safe."

"It's not that. I shouldn't have gone out without my glasses. Don't worry, I asked the dispatcher to have the cabbie stop four blocks away. He won't know about the party."

"I'll walk you."

"A clown and Djuna Barnes walking down the street? Do you think that's safe?"

Beverly laughed. Lucybelle was happy to see her loosening up and enjoying herself. A drink sloshed in her hand, and Lucybelle reached down to level it for her. Then she tweaked Beverly's red-ball nose. "I'm fine. I really am. See you Monday morning. Please give my regrets to Ruthie and Dorothy."

Someone in the den cracked a good joke and under the cover of gales of laughter, Lucybelle slipped out, passed through the kitchen, and stepped back out into the night. It was well past the bedtimes of most children, and the streets had cleared of the little goblins and witches. She walked the four blocks as quickly as she could and then stopped on the corner to wait.

As cars whizzed through the busy intersection, she wondered how she would even be able to distinguish a taxicab from other vehicles. Black and white, she thought, with checkers. Or would it be yellow? She hadn't told the dispatcher to have the driver look for a woman in a long cape and fedora. She couldn't wait to get home, tear off this costume, and sink into a hot bath with a book. Meeting Valerie Taylor had unnerved her more than she wanted to admit. The intelligent amusement in the author's voice, a kind of happy irony, surprised her. It was curious that she'd written that silly book.

But more unnerving was that house full of women she might like to know, but couldn't even *see*, in large part because she'd been dumb enough to go out without her glasses, and also because they were all wearing disguises. That inflammatory rub between fear and desire: Beverly's touchstone word "safe" and Dorothy's lush presence.

Where was that taxicab?

A flash of lightning jagged through the sky to the east, probably over the lake, followed by a long growl of thunder. Any minute the clouds would dump their wet load. Should she run back to the party?

A shiny black-and-white cab, with no yellow or checkers, just stripes of dark and light, swerved up to the curb, its roof light illuminated. Lucybelle pulled open the backseat door and fell in with relief.

"Yes, ma'am?"

She gave the fellow her address and he turned in the seat to look at her, suppressing a grin at the sight of her flamboyant outfit. The black cherry lipstick had probably smeared across her cheeks and chin. "All the way up to Evanston? That's going to be a steep fare."

She recognized that voice. "That's okay."

"So who are you supposed to be? Costume-wise?"

"*Stella?*"

The driver snapped on the interior light. "Do I know you?"

"Michigan Avenue Bridge, about a year ago. You took my picture and gave me a copy of Allen Ginsberg's book."

"Hot diggity. So I did."

"I thought you'd given me a false telephone number. I called once. To give you your book back."

"I'm supposed to believe that?" Stella grinned now, suppressing nothing.

"I did. Your dispatcher answered."

"Why didn't you ask for me?"

"It didn't occur to me that you worked for the taxicab company."

"I own it. I don't usually drive anymore, but it's Halloween. We're busy."

"I could run in and get your book when we get to my apartment."

"Like I said, Evanston is a long way."

"So drop me at the train station." Lucybelle was surprised by the petulance in her own voice.

"Nah. I'll run you home. What with it being Halloween and that getup you're in, I don't suppose we'll find any trouble."

"Trouble?"

"Chicago is nothing but trouble these days." When Lucybelle didn't answer, Stella turned off the interior light and added, "For my people."

"Yes," Lucybelle said. "I know. I've been reading the paper."

"Yeah, well, reading the paper is a lovely place to be. I've been living the heat."

"I can't imagine."

"No," Stella said as she pulled out into the traffic. "You can't."

Lucybelle settled into the backseat, relieved to be going home and unaccountably pleased that Stella hadn't given her a fake telephone number after all.

Stella glanced repeatedly in the rearview mirror until she said, "Arkansas. I remember."

"Not Little Rock."

"And other parts of the state are any better?"

Lucybelle started to object, but of course the girl was right. "Probably worse."

"I have to take a little detour before we head up to Evanston. It's a longer run than I thought I'd be on."

"I said you can drop me at the train station."

"I won't charge you for the detour." Stella looked over her shoulder, as if she couldn't believe what she saw in her rearview mirror, and exhaled a little laugh. "Or are you in a hurry? Even with the stop, you'll get home faster with me."

Truth be told, Lucybelle could drive around all night in this plush car. The chrome trim gleamed and the leather seats smelled like quality. Stella drove expertly, taking the turns smoothly and coming to stops so gently Lucybelle didn't hitch forward even a bit. It was relaxing, lounging back there on the cushioned bench. "It's okay. Take your detour."

They rode in silence until Stella said, "South Side," and then a few minutes later, "Wentworth." When she pulled up in front of a plain boxy building with no signage, she turned in her seat and said, "Wait right here. Don't get out of the car." Stella disappeared inside the establishment, and a second later, a short, very fat, brown-skinned woman emerged, stood in front of the building's one door, crossed her arms, and stared at Lucybelle. She rolled down her window and said hi, but the round woman didn't answer. Fats Domino's "Blueberry Hill" wafted out of what must have been a club, followed by Sam Cooke's "You Send Me," interfused with flashes of lightning and claps of thunder.

Finally Stella bounded out the door, slapped the fat woman on the shoulder, and said, "Thanks, Tiny. You're a pal."

"What took you so long?" Tiny asked with exaggerated irritation. "You said ten seconds. That was more like ten minutes."

"Had to dance that last one. You know women. My luck to step in the door just when the mushy one comes on."

"Who's she?" Tiny pointed with her chin.

"A fare. What's with the questions?"

"You bring a fare, a pale one, to my club, and I'm gonna ask questions."

"I didn't bring her to your club. I'm parked in the street, which as a taxpayer, I own same as you."

Tiny bobbled her head, meaning maybe and maybe not, but smiled. "All right. Be safe. You coming back tonight?"

"Sure. See you in a while."

Stella climbed back in the driver's seat, turned the key in the ignition, and put the taxicab in gear. She pulled onto Wentworth. Lucybelle wished she could see her better.

"What'd you have to do in there?" It was none of her business, but she'd waited patiently and so maybe deserved to know.

Stella ignored the question. "So, Arkansas. Were you there in September?"

"No. But I watched the coverage on television."

"What'd you think?"

"It's heartrending. They're children." Then thinking she should be very clear, Lucybelle added, "They have a right to an equal education."

Stella nodded. "Yeah, I've said a lot of nasty things about Arkansans in the past couple of months. I would have been shocked just yesterday had someone told me I'd be having a pleasant conversation with a white girl from the state."

"We don't have to converse." Damned if she wasn't flirting with the taxicab driver.

"You're the one who started in with the questions."

"It's a bad habit of mine."

Stella smiled. "No, that's a good habit."

"Where are we now?"

"See? Good question. Another detour. Thought we'd spin along the lake. Don't worry. I'm not charging you extra. In fact, I'll give you a deal."

"I'm not worried. But I probably should be."

"Yeah. You probably should be." Stella glanced over her shoulder with another grin, and then threw her arm across the back of the seat and drove with one hand on the steering wheel. Lucybelle wanted to ask who she'd had to dance with on the Sam Cooke number.

"I didn't recognize you, with the, you know . . ." Stella circled the air in front of her face with her palm. "And don't you wear glasses?"

"Yes."

"Can you see without them?"

"No."

"You should have at least put them in your purse."

"That would have been a good idea, but I didn't bring a purse either."

After a full pause, Stella said, "Don't worry. I'll get you home safely."

"Thank you."

"I'll tell you what. However I feel about Arkansas, I do wish I'd been at Central High in September."

"Really? Why?"

"To bear witness."

"With your camera."

"Yeah." She looked in the rearview mirror, nodding. "Exactly."

Lucybelle wondered if Stella had developed the pictures of her on the bridge. She'd said it was too dark, that she hadn't captured her image, but maybe she'd just said that to put Lucybelle at ease.

"Just as well I wasn't there. The reporters got it worse than the kids. I can't afford to lose my camera."

"Are you also a reporter?"

Stella didn't answer for a long time. When she did, her voice had changed, become infused with resolve that she was overriding, as if she didn't want to reveal so much but couldn't stop herself. "I learned photography in the service. Not that they let me in the photography division. I was lucky to just get out of kitchen or laundry. I got motor transport because I already knew a lot about mechanics." She laughed. "To this day Mama argues with Dad about teaching me."

"Why?"

"She wanted me to go to college. I wanted that too. I thought I would after the war. But can you picture me in a girls' dorm?" She took the fast breath of a narrow escape. "Anyway, what good would a college education do me? I could teach maybe. Dad was determined I'd become a doctor. Not just a doctor, but a surgeon. He said the automobile mechanics would be good training in connecting minute parts." Her laughter tumbled a mix of humor, sagacity, and sadness. "*Maybe* if I'd done the eight to twelve years of extra schooling I could be making more money than I am now, but it's questionable. Nope, I hopped right in the service, got training in motor transport, and after the war, the GI Bill bought me my cars, and I set up Acme Transport. I got a fleet of three vehicles, and I'm always making improvements. Just this year I fitted them all out with the new Motorola radios, and I'm looking to buy a couple more cars, probably one next year and another the year after. Would I have more prestige as a surgeon? Sure, in some small circles, but I'd likely take a lot more flack too. This way I do what I please and dress how I'm comfortable. All in all, the service wasn't a bad deal, for me anyway.

"But I did want photography, which wasn't open to colored. What happened was this white fellow, from a real fancy family and everything, but good people, *fair*, he took me under his wing, taught me all about taking pictures." Stella reached across the front seat and lifted her camera. "I go nowhere without it."

When they reached Lake Shore Drive, Stella stepped on the gas and they soared along Lake Michigan. Storm clouds puffed over the lake and wind splashed waves a good five feet in the air. The rain held off.

"So what's your line of business?" Stella asked.

"I'm an editor."

"*Time? Life?*"

"Nothing that glamorous."

"Storm coming in. Good thing you're tucking in home," Stella said as the biggest wave yet frothed into the air. "Not to be nosy, but I picked you up on a busy street corner. You're in that . . . that costume. You left a party in a hurry, am I right? Why?"

Lucybelle laughed. "I wish I had a good story to tell you, but I don't."

"You're not saying. I get it. Still, not fair. I just spilled a lot of beans. Here's another question. An easier one. Who are you supposed to be?"

"Djuna Barnes."

"Really? Hot diggity! I tried to read that book, but man oh man, does she twist up the English language. So what'd you think of *HOWL*?"

"Stupendous. But the Arkansas part unnerved me."

"What Arkansas part?"

"'Who passed through universities with radiant eyes hallucinating Arkansas and Blake—light tragedy . . .'"

"Wow! You memorize the whole thing?"

"No. Of course not."

"Do you suppose that part is about you?"

"I don't know. I did study Blake at Columbia."

"It is! It's about you!"

Lucybelle laughed, relishing Stella's eagerness to connect her to Ginsberg's poem. "Our time at Columbia overlapped only briefly. He left the program. I heard he went traveling."

Stella exhaled a long, reverential breath. "I'm going to San Francisco one day."

"I think about Paris."

"That too. That too." Stella's laugh rolled out, perfectly synchronized with another thunderclap. She stomped down harder on the accelerator and they shot through the night. The first splats of rain hit the windshield.

"So it's All Hallow's Eve," Stella said. "Do you know the history?"

"Tell me." Talk to me all night.

"There're a lot of interpretations." All she could make of Stella's face in the rearview mirror was mobile roundness. "I should probably do some fact-checking in the library before running my mouth."

"Run your mouth."

The smile, she could see that. "Okay, so it's the one day of the year honoring demons and lost souls, the people society despises, which is the same thing as saying the people society fears. This is the day we get to gather, be free, spook everyone. This is *our* day. Well, my day, anyway."

"Mine too."

"Yeah. I thought so."

Lucybelle thought at first that it was an unusual flash of lightning, a red one, but she turned to see the lit and twirling cherry.

"Damn." Stella hit the brakes, but she'd probably taken it up to seventy miles an hour by then and there was no disguising the fact that she'd been speeding. When she got the taxicab pulled to the side of the road, she dropped her forehead onto the steering wheel and muttered, "Damn, damn, damn," while the police officer called in her license plate number from his squad car.

When he approached the driver's side of the taxicab, she reached into her back pocket and withdrew her wallet, and the cop, undoubtedly seeing the color of her skin, pulled his gun. Stella rolled down her window and shouted, "I'm getting out my license." The cop did not put away his gun. He aimed it at the hood of the car while he gave Stella a good looking over and then squatted down so he could examine her passenger.

"Whoa," he said, as if there were a dead body in the backseat. "Whadda we have here?"

"Lady wants to go to Evanston. I'm taking her."

"Evanston? What are you doing on Lake Shore Drive?"

"Taking her to Evanston."

"Don't get smart. License."

Lucybelle couldn't see what Stella handed over, but she saw him shuffling through what must have been a roll of cash. "Dunno," he said after pushing it into his back pocket. Stella withdrew more bills from her wallet and flapped them out the window. It was her own threat: take the money or risk someone seeing the bribe. The cop snatched the cash.

"Move aside," he said, and Stella leaned toward the passenger side of the front seat. He put his head in the window so he could level his eyes at Lucybelle. "You look crazy enough," he said. "So I guess you know what you're doing. But next time why don't you call a white taxicab company?" He waited for her to make some kind of response. When she didn't, he said, "I get it. You're one of the troublemakers." He shook his head slowly. "Riding about town with a colored boy. You have no idea what you're getting yourself into. Where're you from, New York?"

Finally he pulled his head out of the window and walked slowly back to his squad car. Stella waited, but he didn't go anywhere, so she started the engine and pulled out. He followed them closely.

"I'm sorry," Lucybelle said. "Look, I know that went a lot worse than it might have because I was in the car."

"Don't talk."

Driving well under the speed limit, they left the city limits of Chicago, and still the cop rode Stella's bumper, so close that if she braked quickly, he'd ram into her.

"For the love of god, stop turning around and looking at him. He'll decide you're a kidnapped heiress and pull me over again."

"Stella, I can pay you back for that. I'm sorry."

93

"Just keep quiet."

Lucybelle was hurt by Stella's harsh reprimand, but she shut up. The cop finally made a squealing U-turn and headed off in the opposite direction. When they finally pulled in front of 814 Michigan Avenue in Evanston, Lucybelle reached into her pants' pocket and took out all of the cash she had, which wouldn't be nearly enough, and held it over the top of the front seat. "Take this and I'll run upstairs and get the rest."

Stella didn't turn around, didn't look at her in the rearview mirror, just waved her hand at the handful of money. "Keep it and get out."

"Take it. I owe you a lot more."

"Would you please get out of my cab?"

By now the rain slanted down, and it drenched Lucybelle as she ran down the walkway to her entrance. She went directly to her bedside table and put on her glasses, and then hurried to the window overlooking the street. Stella was gone.


## Monday–Friday, November 4–8, 1957

"Luceee! Get in here!" Bader no longer bothered stopping by her desk when he wanted her. He just shouted.

"Yes, sir." She saluted, but he didn't laugh. He didn't even smile.

"Sit down."

Sometimes, when facing a deadline, his depth of concentration wiped out his sense of humor. But she'd never seen this expression before: he looked murderously focused.

"You've been here over a year," he said. "We haven't done any kind of evaluation. I'd say it's time. What do you think?"

"Of what?"

"Your performance. I said, sit down." He leaned across the table and lit her cigarette. "We're not measuring the length of the Amazon here. We're not calculating the amount of ore in a mountain. We're not wondering how many dinosaurs walked on this continent a few years ago. Who cares how many inches the glaciers have advanced or retreated in the past decade, for fuck sake? We're about to look at the history of the planet. The *entire* history. Forget Napoleon and Jesus Christ. They happened yesterday. When we reach bedrock, we'll be able to give a picture of earth's climate going back *tens of thousands* of years. It's epic. It's mankind's biggest, most important story ever."

Bader stood and paced to his door and back. "God, these walls make me feel crazy. I can't breathe in a box. Can we talk outside? No. There's no time. I'll just finish up fast.

"It's been a crazy year. By all accounts, the International Geophysical Year is a smashing success. We have fourteen countries on board—from both sides of the Iron Curtain—with 302 stations in the Arctic and forty-eight in Antarctica."

Lucybelle loved when he talked like this, how he seemed to draw passion from the very soles of his feet, the way he nearly vibrated with purpose. She nodded her agreement. What he'd accomplished this year, what *they'd* accomplished, was deeply satisfying.

"We still have a lot to work out. The pilot drilling has been problematic. The ice cores have been disappointing."

"The '57 core is fantastic," she interrupted.

"A lot better than the '56, to be sure, but still, we've only got down to a thousand feet. I want bedrock. The hitch right now is the technology. We keep breaking the drills."

"Yes, I know, but—"

"We expected that. We knew we'd have to figure it out as we went along. I have to convince the Army Corps and the National Science Foundation that we can reach bedrock, and will, and soon, and that the results will be spectacular. I already have Hansen working on a new kind of drill. A thermal drill. Along with a souped-up electric transformer. We'll melt our way to bedrock. We're innovating the hell out of geology. They have to know, as I know, as you better well know, that the results we get are going to change our view of the planet.

"That's your job. Your words must convince them. It's up to you to make sure our successes shine through so brightly they'll be blinded into writing the biggest checks. They have to understand, and in this case, that means seeing how history illuminates the future. Your job. Do it. And do it brilliantly."

"The future of the planet in my hands," Lucybelle said. "But no pressure."

It was the kind of comment that usually drew at least a smile from Bader, but he nodded, as if it were in fact completely true. She sat back and tried to relax. His intensity this morning wasn't about her perform-ance; it was about his nervous anticipation of the new thermal drill and the fickleness of their funders. He often used her for thinking out loud, stating the already known facts, so he could sort them, make a strategy for his next moves.

"Your June report to the National Academy of Sciences carried the day," he said.

"Thank you."

"But good writing isn't enough. The point is, we're all going to have to make sacrifices. Work long hours. Focus on our target like a goddamn Russian missile. We need to get this done." Finally his wolfish smile broke rank with his lecture. "Then, sugar, I don't care if you want to dance naked with Marilyn Monroe. Capiche?"

What did *that* mean?

"I'm leaving for Byrd Station on Friday. I need a complete report on the '57 ice core before I leave."

"But Russell isn't even half-finished. He told me—"

"All the data. Organized, analyzed, charted, written up, on my desk. Thursday night—okay, fine, Friday morning by three o'clock should be okay."

Lucybelle worked sixteen-hour days the rest of the week. Two of the nights she slept under her desk. Half the time she spent in the cold lab with Russell, wearing her plum wool coat, taking down his data as he coaxed it from the ice, interpreting its meaning herself and then making corrections after the scientists read her words. All the scientists worked the same long hours, helping collect the raw data, but none of them could write, and un-fortunately, she'd finally convinced them all to admit it.

She finished three hours early. On Thursday night, a little after mid-night, she took a cab to Bader's apartment in north Chicago. Exhilarated and relieved, she pounded on his door.

"Come in." Bader waved an arm at the interior of his apartment. A dark-haired woman slept on the couch in nothing but her panties and bra. "Can you give her a ride when you leave? I gotta be out of here in a couple of hours."

"No."

"No? I'm your boss, sugar."

"I don't have a car. I took a cab."

"Of course I'll pay. Here, I'll write down her mother's address." He scribbled on a corner of one of the reports she'd just handed him and tore off the scrap. "Have the driver drop her there and then ride on home yourself." He reached for the wallet in his jean's back pocket and pulled out a hundred dollar bill. "This will cover it, plus a big tip for a job well done."

"You aren't going to look over the report?"

"I don't need to. You're flawless."

The urge to cry pressed so hard on her eyeballs that they burned. The lack of sleep, the long hours of concentrated writing, nearly freezing to death in the cold labs, and now this, a floozy (one who lived with her mother) asleep on his couch, and her assignment of babysitting duties. She herself was supposed to "not act on" her "inclinations," while he indulged every appetite.

"Gin?" he asked. "You look a wreck."

Lucybelle pushed the girl's bare feet off the couch and they thudded to the floor. There was nowhere else to sit. Bader roared his laugh, and the girl sat up, squinting and rubbing her milk white arms. "Wha—? Who's this? Henri? Who is this?"

Lucybelle stared at the girl, who made no effort to cover herself. Her face led with its nose, long and humped on the bridge. Below, her small mouth and dainty chin retreated into her neck. Above, sooty eyes held their own against the large creaseless forehead. Cleopatra might have looked like this; she was lovely.

"She's taking you home," Bader told the woman as he handed Lucybelle her drink. "Put your clothes on."

"I'm tired. I'll stay here and go in the morning."

"You'll be happier at your mother's. Come on, Adele, put your clothes on."

"I don't know where they are," Adele pouted.

As before, the apartment was strewn with clothes and their man-musk odor saturated the air. Bader glanced around. "I need to do laundry. Are there any places open at this hour? Lucy, could you find out?"

She swallowed down the gin in two gulps and said, "If she wants a ride. I'm leaving now."

"I can't exactly go naked," Adele said.

As Bader pawed through the piles, presumably searching for her dress, Lucybelle walked back to see the jaguar.

"What happened to your cat?"

"I gave him to a friend for his birthday."

"Lucky fellow." Lucybelle returned to the front room to find the woman pulling on a pair of Bader's jeans. He knelt and rolled up the bottoms.

"We can't find her dress," he said. He grabbed a short electric cord. "Cinch them with these. My belt will be too big."

Lucybelle picked up a T-shirt between her thumb and forefinger and tossed it at Adele's chest.

"Thanks. Who are you? Henri, who is she?"

"She's my right hand," he said. "Now come on, put that shirt on."

In one stride, he was at Lucybelle's side. He kissed her cheek. "Thank you, sugar. See you in a couple of months. Behave yourself."

"Right." She couldn't help the affection she felt for this man. His voraciousness swallowed up even her anger. "Be safe."

"You want to go sometime?" He paused and pinned her with his intense gaze, as if it were possible, as if he might need to take an editor with him to Antarctica.

"To Byrd Camp," she said with slow deliberation.

"The sea ice is this breathtaking bottomless blue. Once you look into it, you're ruined for life. You never want to be anywhere else."

"Well, thanks," Adele said, running a hand through her hair. "Love you too."

"In a couple of months," Bader went on, ignoring the woman and also the fact that he had a flight to catch, "when the sea ice starts breaking up, whole pods of killer whales leap and play in the cracks. I can breathe there. And the sky—"

Lucybelle opened the front door and walked out. This time she had remembered to ask the taxicab driver to wait. Bader hustled Adele out the door behind her and put her in the cab, kissing her tenderly before shutting the door.

Adele slept all the way to her mother's house, where Lucybelle helped her in the door and then rode up to Evanston, where she fell into bed fully dressed.

## Friday, November 8, 1957

She awoke at noon the next day and didn't even bother to call in to the lab. When she retrieved L'Forte from the Worthingtons across the hall, the poor fellow whined his disapproval at having so little time with her the past few days. She took him out to the patch of grass next to the sidewalk and then brought him back inside for breakfast. As she ate her own bowl of cornflakes, he pawed her shins for more attention, holding his sweet long ears back in anticipation of her hand on his head. She reached down and stroked the short fur on his bony skull. Did Phyllis miss L'Forte at all?

Despite all the sleep, she had a headache. She couldn't stop thinking about Bader, that woman in his apartment, his full-bore go at life, his mineral honesty. What had he meant with that bit about Marilyn Monroe?

She could have run all her errands in Evanston, but she craved a bigger, denser, more complex picture. She showered and put the copy of *HOWL* in her purse, along with change from Bader's hundred-dollar bill. She felt guilty leaving L'Forte yet again, but promised him a long evening together in the wingback chair.

Her headache vanished as she stepped out of the train station in Chicago and looked up at the vertical city with its angled pieces of sky. She laughed out loud. Sure thing: Marilyn Monroe! First she went to the bookstore and bought another copy of Rachel Carson's *The Sea Around Us.* Then, seeing a drugstore a block down the street, she stopped in for some toothpaste. As she walked past the rack of paperbacks, she could practically hear the clatter at her back, the mischief and shenanigans in those cheap stories. She found the toothpaste and then decided to grab a bottle of aspirin too. She realized that she was stalling. If Bader wanted to read a trashy book, he'd read it in public on the train. She snatched a box of sanitary napkins, to use as a decoy, and then walked purposely to the paperback racks and perused the offerings. Valerie Taylor's book was right there, front and center, and she plucked it off the wire rack.

The druggist rang up her purchases, averting his eyes from both the sanitary napkins and her paperback, completing the transaction as quickly as he could. She rolled the top of the brown paper sack tightly, put the parcel under her arm, and walked out of the drugstore with her chin up.

By the time she got to the Michigan Avenue Bridge it was nearly dusk, just as it had been the first time she stood in the middle of its expanse. But everything was different now. She'd made friends at work and won the respect of the geologists. Bader was a bucket of icy water, tossed repeatedly in her face, and for that she was grateful. Last year at this time, in this exact spot, she'd thought of jumping, the oblivion of a river bottom a strong lure. Today, strangely exhilarated after the hardest workweek of her life, she felt embraced by the pale blue glaciers capping the earth and reached for Bader's epic future.

From a telephone booth she called Acme Transport. Would it be the nasal-voiced fellow from Halloween night or the melodiously voiced woman from New Year's Eve? Ah, good, the latter.

"I'd like to speak with Stella, please."

"May I ask who's calling?"

"Lucybelle."

"And who might Lucybelle be?"

"I owe her some money. I was short the night she took me home."

"Aren't you the honest one."

Lucybelle hesitated and then matched the attitude with her own. "I do pay my debts, yes."

"Just watch what kinds of debts you accrue, sister."

"Excuse me?" Did Stella know how rude her dispatcher was? "Look, if you could just tell me how I can get in touch with Stella."

"Give me your number. I'll have her call you."

That evening Lucybelle sat down at her typewriter. She wrote about the Halloween party and her ride with Stella. She kept these pages, reading them over and making corrections with a pencil. Then she folded them in half and looked through *Shakespeare: The Complete Works* for a place to steep them in poetry, wisdom, and maybe even a bit of humor. There was Phyllis's letter, bobbing on the waters of Venice. She shifted a couple hunks of pages forward and found a good spot in *Hamlet*. To be, or not to be, that *was* the question. She put the book back on the shelf before she ruined the evening by rereading Phyllis.

She'd promised L'Forte a night in the armchair. She settled in with her new copy of *Whisper Their Love* and patted her lap. He jumped up.

Lucybelle cringed, as before, at the dean's desperation, but this time found the jest in the writing, a subversive digging at society's mores. She read the ending with a fresh interpretation as well. Yes, Joyce appears to accept that she must marry John and live a "normal" life. But he's drawn with such ridiculous pomposity, and he offers an entirely unrealistic carte blanche amnesty from what he views as her moral missteps. The girl is still a teenager; her life has barely begun. Taylor makes it clear that John is not her destiny. That last scene, where he buys her dinner, the joke seems to be that she's going for the large steak he buys her, not him. The closing dialogue too tells a different story. Joyce whispers, "I never thought it would end like this," and John replies, "Stupid, this isn't the end. This is only the beginning."

"Ha!" Lucybelle cried out loud, startling L'Forte. Valerie Taylor was a sly one. Indeed, this would never be the end. And who was the stupid one?

Now she was sorry she hadn't recognized the author's feat before meeting her. Taylor had managed to write a lesbian protagonist who didn't kill herself or go crazy. Better, she'd winked at her lesbian readers behind the backs of heterosexual readers, behind the back, no doubt, of even her publisher.

Lucybelle still had no idea who'd sent her the book, but meeting the author, and now understanding the playful subtext, she felt better. She experimented with putting the book on her bookshelf, right next to her row of Cather novels, but thought better of the placement. Instead she tucked it in back of the thick Shakespeare and then smiled at the juxtaposition. Actually, she decided, the bard himself, with his goofy sense of humor, would quite appreciate her shelving choice.

## Thursday, November 14, 1957

The week careened forward. She submitted Bader's report to four agencies, all in different formats, and cleaned up a number of letters he'd piled on her desk and asked her to correct and send. Lucybelle found the letter in her inbox late in the day on Thursday.

When she opened the envelope, the picture fell into her lap. The child looked to be a few months younger than her niece, but baby Lucy had a sturdy and frank demeanor, while this baby was Shirley Temple all over, eyes already sparking with an actor's deception, hair as curly as a lamb's.

*My dear Lucy Heart*, Phyllis wrote.

> *Here's my precious Georgia. She says Ma and Da already, and Fred swears she says Theater. I know you won't believe me! But she does. Every day the girl who watches her says Ma and Da are at*

101

*the theater, and so it's not really that surprising because of course she longs for us. But don't you think it's good for my daughter to know that Ma is doing what she loves, what she needs to do? Of course you of all people hear the guilt in my voice, even in this brief letter. But isn't Love what counts, and oh, I love her so much. She's changed my Life in ways I can't count. Please come visit. I'll teach her to say Lucy, and then you'll never be able to resist us again. Us. Now I'm using her as a lure. But it is Us. And you should come.*

*The production is going so well and I love the cast. We have such fun parties, you'd be in Heaven. I'm sorry, Lucy, I know I was impossible our last year. Maybe our last three years. Maybe the entire span of our Friendship. But I'm so much better now. I needed this.*

This, Lucybelle supposed, meant Fred. It was shocking to the point of appalling how much approval—in so many categories, including society, family, on the street, maybe even in the theater—could result from association with one negligible man.

*I ran into Harry on Bank Street the other day, a block from our apartment.*

Her use of the word "our" sent spikes up Lucybelle's spine.

*He said he'd talked to you a couple of times. Why won't you call me? Or send me your number and I'll call you, on my nickel.*

*Truly, my Sweet One, you should be here in New York now. This new crowd, my friends from the production, are ever so much more engaging than any others we ever found in the Village. Come Home.*

Home. That punched her in the solar plexus.

*At every single party, with every cup of coffee, I hear your sharp wit slicing up the conversation. Your Reviews, we used to call them. Remember how hard we laughed? Why can't we have that still? Fred—this will make you mad, no doubt, but I'm going to say it anyway—is hardly ever around. His job is wildly demanding. You*

*don't know Mielziner. He's brilliant but requires so much of Fred. It
exhausts the poor man. The upshot, however, is quite a bit of Freedom
for me and sweet Georgia.*

*I offer the above only as an Enticement for you to visit. You won't
have to see much of the Dreaded Husband.*

*Say yes. Buy a plane ticket. And a theater ticket!*

*Yours always,*
*Phyllis*


Theater ticket? Lucybelle looked at the picture of Georgia for a long
time.

That night she sat in her wingback chair, lifted the telephone's receiver,
and held it in both hands. Twice she put it back on the hook. Then, at last,
she picked it back up and dialed her own former number. Phyllis answered.

"She's beautiful."

After a dramatic intake of breath, Phyllis gushed, "Lucy! Oh, Lucy!
Oh!"

"Georgia is a lovely name too."

"I wish you could see her. She's perfect, all pink and glowing. She looks
like Fred. Exactly. Only miniature and female."

Lucybelle held up the picture and realized that what Phyllis said was
true. She forced herself to ask, "And how is Fred?"

"He's well. He's building sets for Jo Mielziner, which is such a relief
because with Georgia we have bills coming out our ears."

"Good for him then."

"I don't want to talk about Fred." She said his name as you might say
the word "hamburger." Phyllis caught herself, gasped a little laugh, but
then added, "And neither do you."

"She does have his features, but on her they come together in a much
more pleasing way."

"God, I miss you. As long as she doesn't get his personality, we'll be all
right."

"Phyllis!"

"You do know what I mean."

"You married the man."

"I did. And look what I got." On cue, a baby's cry rasped into Lucybelle's ear, as if Phyllis had put the telephone to Georgia's tiny mouth. "I
wish you could see her. You'd understand."

103

"You're happy then."

"It's so good to be working again."

"You mentioned a production and cast but didn't say what."

"It's just a small part, but a part just the same. *Look Homeward, Angel*, opening in two weeks on Thanksgiving Day at the Barrymore. Fred's working with Jo on the set."

"That's wonderful news."

"Oh, it is!"

"So Fred watches Georgia when you're on stage?"

"Well, no, but . . ." Phyllis's voice hitched.

Lucybelle refrained from asking if Fred had given up men.

"So, are you seeing anyone?" Phyllis asked shyly.

Lucybelle closed her eyes. She hadn't been touched, beyond handshakes or accidental jostling, in months. She could distract herself and make Phyllis laugh with stories of the women her office friends had tried to set her up with, but Phyllis would just feel sorry for her. She could make a story out of sweet, artless Dorothy, but she felt protective of her new friend. Probably Phyllis would be quite understanding of Bader's proviso, but she wouldn't give Phyllis the satisfaction of knowing her hands were tied.

"I went to a really fun Halloween party a couple of weeks ago."

"You didn't answer my question."

"Did you send me a book?"

"A book?"

"Yeah, called *Whisper* something something." She knew the title, of course, but having met Valerie Taylor, she didn't want to hear Phyllis's shrieks of condescending laughter.

"No. Why? Oh damn. Georgia just threw up. I love you! Please call me again! Wait! What's your number so I can call you? Oh, gotta go, she's puking. Call me!"


## Saturday, March 15, 1958

On a cold Saturday night in the middle of March, Lucybelle pulled on her brown wool slacks, a white blouse, and the cream cabled cardigan her mother had knitted. She put the cash in her purse, tucked the Allen Ginsberg and Rachel Carson books under her arm, kissed L'Forte's forehead, and walked to the train station. The cold air stabbed right through her plum wool coat. Once in Chicago she hailed a taxi.

"2711 South Wentworth, please."

"That's colored, miss." The driver stared straight ahead and waited for her to give a different address. When she didn't, he asked, "Where you trying to go?"

"The address is 2711 South Wentworth."

His wrist rested on the top of the steering wheel, the fingers dangling over the backside. He let his eyelids drop and dulled his entire face.

"Shall I find another cab?"

"It's your neck."

"Exactly."

"See what I mean?" he asked when they got to Wentworth and started trolling for the 2711 address. Despite the cold night, there were lots of people on the street, which was, she supposed, what he meant: people, dark-skinned people, on the street.

"There it is. I'll get out here."

"You want, I'll wait for you."

Lucybelle remembered hearing "You Send Me" wafting out the club door. The round bouncer staring at her. Stella might not even be there tonight. "No, thank you."

"Your neck."

Lucybelle paid him, without a tip, and slammed the door extra hard to make sure he understood she was finished with him. Then, before she lost her nerve, she pulled open the door to Tiny and Ruby's Hot Spot.

The patrons were two- and three-deep at the bar, shouting their drink orders and laughing at jokes. A dozen couples danced in the middle of the club, some of the women in full-skirted dresses with fitted tops, silky fabrics printed with splashy abstractions or colorful flowers. A few wore men's pants and suit jackets, polished shoes and shiny ties. On the far side of the room a small stage held a live band, fronted by Tiny, that short basketball of a woman, playing the hell out of a trumpet.

Lucybelle felt a profound and immediate happiness in being there, swallowed up by the laughter and music, even as she regretted not dressing more appropriately for a Saturday night on the town. There were a few other white women in the club, but everyone stared at her anyway, standing just inside the door in her wool slacks and plum coat, clutching a purse and two books, looking like someone's aunt. Even Tiny spotted her from the stage, and when she finished that tune she set the trumpet on its stand and held out her hand for someone, anyone, to help her off the stage. She rolled right toward Lucybelle.

"Help you?" she asked.

"I'm looking for Stella."

Tiny cupped her ear, signaling that she couldn't hear, and then stepped around Lucybelle and opened the door to the street. When they were outside, Tiny said, "We're full tonight."

Lucybelle could tell that Tiny thought she'd stumbled into the wrong club, or worse, that she was some kind of undercover snitch. You couldn't really look more square than she did. "I'm looking for Stella. She owns Acme Transport."

Tiny narrowed her eyes and lied, "Don't know any Stella. Good night."

"We, I mean you and I, actually met a few months ago. On Halloween."

Tiny reared back and looked at her hard. "Arkansas."

That stung. She'd been a story for Stella. She pictured Tiny and Stella, and maybe the sultry-voiced dispatcher at Acme Transport, sitting around laughing at the farm girl out alone on Halloween night, dressed in a cape and fedora.

"My name is Lucybelle."

"Hoo wee. What are you doing here? I thought you were a fare."

"Well, yes. That's right. And I shorted Stella a bit. I want to pay her."

"A *bit*? That cop stripped her wallet. And she'd just been to the bank that day."

Despite the temperature having dropped into the twenties, Lucybelle felt a hot flush of chagrin. She *had* been a story. And the cause of Stella's grief with the racist cop.

"You say you're here to pay her?"

Lucybelle nodded.

"Wait here."

Lucybelle wanted to go back inside, but she did as she was told. The sidewalk was cold, dim, lonely.

Not thirty seconds later, Stella stepped briskly out the door, as if Lucybelle's appearance were an emergency. She looked pained, glanced at the cars passing on Wentworth, nodded at a couple on the sidewalk. She took

Lucybelle's elbow, guiding her around to the shadowed side of the building. "What are you doing here?"

"I owe you some money."

Stella reared back. "You came all this way to pay a six-month-old fare?"

"Well, I thought maybe I'd have a drink—"

"I don't expect a fare to pay when you're subjected to what you were subjected to."

"It was my fault."

"It wasn't your fault. The color of my skin caused that particular fuss. Which is to say it was the fault of the cop's attitude."

"Fair is fair. Here. Just take the money." Lucybelle pulled the wad of cash from her purse. "And here's your book too. Plus, another one I thought you might like."

"Hey! Don't be pulling all that money out right here on the street. I can't take it, anyway." She ignored the books.

"Why can't you take the money?"

Stella chuffed. "What happened that night is what I call the bulldagger tip. It happens. Part of business. Nothing that I worry about."

"He called you a boy."

"Sure he did. But he knew exactly what I am. He won't stop me again, in any case."

"How's that?"

"So it's a thousand questions again."

"I thought you liked questions."

"Look, I'm going to have Rusty run you home."

"Who's Rusty?"

"One of my drivers."

"I thought I might have a drink."

Another chuff, and then, "Suit yourself." The words were short, but Stella's face softened into what looked like an involuntary quizzicality. She didn't leave.

"I'll buy you one," Lucybelle said. "Since you won't take my fare money."

Stella smiled at the ground.

Lucybelle grinned too. This club was a relief. So was a woman who read poetry and studied photography, who owned her own company and dressed as she pleased. Why had she tolerated Phyllis's complicated artifice all those years?

"Sorry," Stella said, lifting her head, the smile gone. "I'm busy. But let me know when you're ready to go." With that Stella turned and went back inside the club.

Lucybelle stood shivering, wondering. Was it the color barrier? She ought to hail a cab and just leave, but she'd come all this way, and she really would like a drink. She pushed open the door and made her way to the bar.

A butch girl with bad acne, so young she still had baby fat, slid off the end barstool and gestured at it.

"I'll stand," Lucybelle said.

"No you won't. Come on, sugar, have a seat."

Sugar. Ha. That's what Bader called her.

"Ruby!" the girl shouted for the bartender. Beneath the veneer of bravado, the kid seemed anxious, maybe a little scared.

Lucybelle sat and the tall bartender strolled down and asked what she'd like to drink.

"Gin. Rocks. Thank you."

"Pour her something from the top shelf," the girl told Ruby. "Don't give her that gut rot you pour for the rest of us."

"That's not necessary," Lucybelle said.

"Oh, yeah it is." She was adorable with her adolescent skin and smile, her reach into adulthood on this cold Saturday night.

"Thank you. But you look too young to be buying women drinks."

The kid grinned. "I'm twenty-one."

"Sure you are."

Tiny was back on stage, swinging a sweet ballad with her horn, and the floor was packed with slow dancers. The sight of all those embracing women knotted Lucybelle's throat to her heart. Tiny's trumpet hollered, crescendoing and then backing down, while the guy on piano shimmied into the opening and the woman on bass kept time with a soothing thrum.

"Ruby's the drummer," her self-appointed hostess said. "But she don't like to let go of her bar. Not when it's this crowded."

The drink arrived at the same time Stella stepped up with another kid, who didn't look much older than Lucybelle's new friend. "This is Rusty. She'll run you home when you're ready." Rusty was a scrappy character, so skinny she looked hungry, dressed like a boy from another era, including a cap and suspenders. Her elbows and knees jabbed at her shirt and pants. Her full lips, and the freckles dotting her light-brown face, compromised the tough-girl act. Her burnished hair, pulled straight up from the nape of her neck and back from her temples, was tied in a knot that showed under the cap. Lucybelle imagined the hair styled entirely differently for when she attended church on Sunday with the family. Rusty shifted her weight from one foot to the other, nodding her head in judgment, though she didn't even look at Lucybelle as Stella introduced them.

"Why can't she sit a spell?" the kid at the bar asked. "Why're you sending her off? We're just getting to know one another."

Lucybelle took a sip of her drink.

Babyface pressed her case. "You know Ruby don't like nobody being snooty in her bar. Everyone gets the welcome mat, same as everyone else."

"Yeah, sure," Stella said. "She can stay as long as she likes. Just find Rusty when you're ready." Clearly she was trying to get rid of her but managed to make it sound like she was being chivalrous. Lucybelle felt a hot embarrassment about the two books in her lap, one a return and the other a gift, evidence of a misconstrued intimacy.

Yet Lucybelle remained stubbornly at the bar, sipping her gin, while Rusty stood waiting at the door, scowling at her, as if Lucybelle were ruining her evening by not leaving. When she finished her drink, she thanked the underage girl, slid off the barstool, and left the club.

Rusty stepped out right behind her. "Car's in back."

"I can call a cab."

"What do you think it is that I drive?"

Lucybelle looked at the kid in her suspenders and shirtsleeves, no jacket or coat, as if to underscore how quick she wanted to make this interruption to her evening. She figured that she might as well give Stella's taxicab company business, rather than call that one with the racist driver, so she nodded her acquiescence and followed Rusty around to the parking lot behind the club. Rusty opened the back door of a black-and-white Acme Transport car and stared off into the distance as Lucybelle climbed inside.

"I have the address," Rusty said. She drove under the speed limit and it took them a full forty minutes to get to the apartment in Evanston. When Lucybelle asked the amount of the fare, Rusty said, "It's covered already."

"What?"

"I said the fare is paid."

Lucybelle dropped a five-dollar tip in the front seat and got out.

Rusty got out too. "She said I was supposed to see you to the door."

"That's all right. This is my building."

"Suit yourself," Rusty said, sounding like Stella. She jumped back in the cab, and Lucybelle heard the door lock clunk down.

That night she dreamed she was wading through the flooded rice fields at home in Arkansas, slogging thigh-deep in muddy water, the thirsty roots soaking it up, the seeds of grain fattening. She awoke feeling plumped with a painful but nourishing anticipation.

## Sunday, March 16, 1958

The doorbell sounded at a quarter to nine. Still in her pajamas, Lucybelle padded to the window and looked out. An Acme Transport taxicab was parked across the street.

She scrubbed her face, brushed her teeth, and pulled on last night's trousers, blouse, and sweater. By the time she yanked open her front door, the stoop was empty. She ran down the stairwell and then along the glistening, ice-covered cement path between her building and the neighboring one. Just as she reached the Michigan Avenue sidewalk, her feet flew out from beneath her. She landed so hard on her hip she thought she might have broken it. Her eyes squeezed shut in pain.

"Hey," Stella said softly. "Hey. You okay?"

Something warm and wet touched her face. She opened her eyes to find the Worthingtons' basset hound snuffling its way down her body, happily detecting L'Forte.

"Winston!" Mrs. Worthington called. "Come!" Then, "My dear girl, are you all right? Anything broken?"

The three of them, Stella and the Worthingtons, huddled around her.

"You can go, boy," Mr. Worthington said to Stella.

"That's my cab," Stella said. "She called me."

Her brain was a soup of pain, but Lucybelle appreciated the quick-thinking lie.

"Clearly she's not going anywhere now. Run along."

"Yes, I am," Lucybelle managed to croak. "I'm going somewhere. Please stay." She tried to clear her head in spite of the throbbing in her hip. "Please stay," she said again. She forced herself to look up at the elderly white couple and said, "Thank you, Mr. and Mrs. Worthington, but I'm fine."

"Oh, no you're not, dear. Come upstairs. We'll make you a nice cup of tea." She shooed Stella with a flapping hand.

"Stella," Lucybelle said. "Stay. Please."

The Worthingtons glanced at one another. Mr. Worthington grabbed Winston's collar, as if the hound needed to be protected from the crazy white lady on the ground and the Negro girl-boy cab driver, and they continued on down the street. Lucybelle had never been so glad about anyone's departure.

"Can you get up?" Stella asked.

"It's questionable."

"That was a pretty fall."

Lucybelle rolled over onto her hands and knees, and from that position pushed slowly to her feet. She brushed the grits of rock and ice off her pants and then took a couple of experimental steps. "Nothing's broken, I don't think."

"You tore your trousers." Stella gestured at her hip where the wool had ripped a good three inches, revealing a sliver of her white panties and the top of her thigh.

"Charming," Lucybelle said. Her hair, she knew, was a mess of curls on top and flattened in the back where she'd slept on it. "I have to take L'Forte out. Do you want to walk with us?"

"Who's L'Forte?"

"My dog. Just a minute, okay? I'll get him and be right back." She began limping up the walkway and then turned. "Will you wait? Please?"

Stella nodded.

Upstairs Lucybelle tried to brush her hair, but the dry cold air sent her curls in all directions. She pulled on a hat her mother had knit to go with the plum coat, but it was the wrong shade of purple and clashed. When she took it off again, her hair was even more witchy, so she tugged the hat back on, called L'Forte, and then made her way back down the stairs and out to the street.

Stella leaned against a tree trunk, hands sunk in the pockets of her creased trousers, which hung to the perfect length over polished black shoes, her black wool overcoat opened at the front. She'd put on a pair of sunglasses, and bursts of sunshine glinted off each of the green lenses. Lucybelle thought she ought to be surprised to see Stella, but she wasn't. She owed her money, after all, and Stella's refusing to take it last night somehow compounded the debt.

L'Forte stopped to lift his short back leg on a tree and then headed east at a clip.

"He's going to the lake."

"I only have a few minutes. I got church soon."

"It's just two blocks."

"A hot dog on legs."

"Are you making fun of my dog?"

"Wouldn't dream of it. Hey, let me get my camera. Hold on."

L'Forte turned and watched Stella jog across the ice-free street to her cab. He sat down and drew back his brown ears, as if he were worried about her departure, and then wagged his tail when she returned. He barked twice, cheerfully, before leading the way to the lake.

"I can't figure him out," Lucybelle said. "He seems to like you."

"That's so difficult to understand?"

"He has such strong opinions, is all. For example, he'll only go to the lake on sunny days. He can't abide gloomy ones."

"Sounds like he has good sense, me and sunshine."

L'Forte pranced around the frozen puddles and climbed up on a rock to look at the lake. A hard, cold silver light sparkled the water. The ice floes popped and tinkled as a breeze jostled them against one another. Lucybelle still wasn't used to that expanse of water, a lake so big it might as well have been called a sea. It daunted her, like a border, but also enticed her.

"He looks like he's considering a voyage," Stella said, snapping a picture of L'Forte. She tossed a stick and the dachshund shot out after it. For the next few minutes he ran, fetched, and dropped for his new best friend. Stella laughed every time he leapt up in the air to catch the stick, his plug of a body with the short stubby limbs flying. She took a series of pictures of him in action, giving Lucybelle directions about how to toss the stick so she could get the best light on the little dog. Catching on to the more sophisticated game of photography, L'Forte scrambled onto one of the shore rocks and then, holding the stick in his mouth like an Olympic relay runner, turned and looked at Stella, as if to say, photograph me *now*. Stella did.

While they played, Lucybelle fervently wished she hadn't taken that spill, wasn't limping along in torn trousers and bed-wrecked hair, wearing mismatched clothing. She took off her glasses and held them up to the light. They were smudged as well.

"Cigarette?" Stella knocked a Chesterfield out of the pack she drew from her coat's inside pocket.

"God, yes."

Stella loosed her full smile, the one that caved deep dimples on either side of her mouth. She cupped her hands around the lighter's little flame and lit Lucybelle's cigarette. She wore a class ring, platinum with a green stone. Lucybelle wanted to put the pad of her index finger on the stone. It looked like it would be icy and clarifying to the touch.

"My brand too," Lucybelle said inhaling gratefully.

"Sometimes I roll my own," Stella said.

"I'm sure you do."

Stella cocked her head and twisted her mouth to the side.

"Why are you here?"

Stella sat on a bench and waited for Lucybelle to sit as well. They smoked in silence for a minute. "I'm sorry about last night. I guess I was a jerk."

"You guess?"

"I was a jerk."

"I embarrassed you."

"No. It wasn't that. I'm pretty hard to embarrass. It's just that . . . I felt responsible. For you. And also to the club. To Tiny and Ruby. I mean, look, I don't know you. You come in the club like that, and if there's trouble, well, I feel responsible. Because you were my fare."

Lucybelle laughed. "Me, trouble?" Then she remembered she'd asked the same question on Halloween night.

Stella kicked out her legs, and then drew them back in, revealing an appealing uneasiness. "You never did tell me what you were doing alone on a street corner on Halloween."

"You must have thought I was a lunatic. Or think."

"I just thought—think—there's a story."

"Not much of one. I went to a party with some friends from work. It was fun putting that costume together, but once I was there, at the party, I felt impatient with all the disguises. Of course it was stupid of me. I mean, it was Halloween. People were just having fun. But I thought, what am I doing at a party with a pirate and a clown? Besides, no one knew Djuna Barnes."

Stella nodded as she listened.

"I like what you said about Halloween being the night when we can be ourselves. Maybe I just wanted to be myself."

"Yeah," Stella said, taking off her sunglasses. "I'm not good at disguises."

"I can see that. But—" Lucybelle didn't know if she was allowed a personal question. Stella cocked her head, bunched her mouth to the side. "What about when you were in the service? You must have had to—"

Stella chuckled. "Nah. It was fine. I even showed up for my recruitment interview in my suit trousers and polished wingtips. My hair might have been a tad longer than it is now, and yeah, okay, I did style it a bit for that afternoon, gave it a faint whiff of girlishness. But look at me. A girl's hairdo won't take me far.

"So my recruiter asks, 'Have you ever had a crush on a girl?' She practically winked at me. 'What?!' I said. 'Heavens, no. My goodness gracious!' Sitting there in my wingtips and trousers, two feet of air between my knees. She was white too, so you know, I threw in words they like, 'gracious' and such." Stella paused, snagging on the word "they." "Nah, it wasn't a problem. They were dying for smart girls, people who could actually *do* stuff. I can fix anything." She grinned and repeated, "Anything."

It was nearly noon by the time they got back to Lucybelle's building on Michigan Avenue. Surely Stella had missed church. They stopped at the place Lucybelle had taken her fall.

"How's that hip of yours?"

"Hurts like hell."

"Aspirin and ice."

"Thanks, doc. I have something for you. Wait here a moment?"

"Sure. I'll be in my car."

Lucybelle remembered how Rusty had locked herself in the moment she'd gotten out of the cab. Maybe Stella wouldn't feel safe just standing around her neighborhood. "Do you want to come up?"

She shook her head no.

Lucybelle tried to hurry, but her bruised hip made walking difficult. As she returned to the street, Stella rolled down the driver's window. Lucybelle ignored that and climbed in the front passenger seat. She handed Stella *HOWL*, as well as the copy of *The Sea Around Us* that she had bought in November. "Do you know Rachel Carson?"

Stella shook her head. She flipped through the pages of the book, her mouth softly ajar, and then left it lying on the tops of her thighs. "Thank you. But you keep the Ginsberg."

"Thank you."

Stella nodded.

"Also, I need to pay you for my ride on Halloween and the police bribe, and last night's fare, as well." By now it was pretty clear that Stella hadn't come for the money, but it was also clear that Lucybelle wanted no festering misunderstandings, of any kind, between them.

Stella chuffed. "I thought I told you that's just part of doing business. Fifty bucks for the color of my skin and another fifty for being a dyke. It's not so bad, really. I'm pretty lucky."

"Lucky?"

"You really want to know?"

"I really want to know."

"I got a little sweetheart deal on the side. I drive a guy around for free, whenever he needs me. He gives me some protection, not a lot, but some. He never asks for cash payments for the protection. He's a gentleman. Just wants the free rides and a whole lotta discretion. He can count on me to get him anywhere and no one's the wiser. For most of his business, he doesn't want a Negro company carting him around, you see? But it's a nice cover when he needs it. Works for both of us."

Lucybelle understood that "a guy" meant a mobster, but she didn't see how it worked in Stella's favor. "Seems like you had to fork over a lot of cash that night."

"Yeah, that kid cop who pulled me over is new on the force. These relationships take time, and I have to roll with the process. My guy's already had a word with him, and okay, here's the part I guess you should know: an envelope with all that bribe money arrived in the mail shortly after the incident. I got it all back.

"You're staring at me. I don't do anything illegal, Arkansas. I just—"

"Don't call me that."

"Arkansas?"

"Tiny called me that too. You've been making fun of me."

Stella looked at her hands, twisted her mouth to the side. "I'm sorry. I guess I have been a little."

"I'm just a joke among your friends."

"I don't think you've reached that level of importance among my friends. We take jokes seriously."

"Who's the woman with the sultry voice?"

"You do ask a lot of questions."

"The one who sometimes answers your company telephone."

"That's Wanda. My dispatcher. So you really did call?"

Lucybelle wouldn't be a fink by mentioning the woman's rudeness on the telephone a few months ago. She just nodded, wishing she hadn't used the word "sometimes," which implied she'd called more than once.

"I better go," Stella said and put her hand on the keys dangling from the ignition.

"Thank you for walking L'Forte with me."

"Thank you for the book. I'll read it tonight."

"You will? Tonight?"

"Sure. Why not?" Stella dropped her hand from the keys and smiled. "But you do still owe me."

Hadn't she just told her, for the umpteenth time, to forget about the Halloween fare?

"I put my telephone number inside the book I gave you." She fanned the first pages of *The Sea Around Us* and then dug a pen out of the pouch on the inside of the car door.

As Lucybelle wrote her telephone number on the title page, her hand shook as if she were signing a confession.

"So that was kind of gutsy, you coming to Tiny and Ruby's club last night."

"I'm sorry it was awkward for you."

"Nah. It wasn't awkward."

"Now you're lying. I can't abide lies."

Just like that, an understanding sprung up between them. Stella's cheeks and chin slackened, her mouth opened slightly and her hazel eyes caramelized. She nodded, looked away, and started the engine of the car. Lucybelle reached for the door handle just as Stella spoke again, "Okay then. Yeah, it was awkward."

"Thank you for that. You better get to church."

"I missed church."

Lucybelle laughed at the additional truth-telling, opened the door, and limped across the street in her purple homemade hat and plum overcoat, torn brown wool pants, and tie oxfords. She felt ridiculous, and yet, also, unaccountably, ridiculously beautiful.

## Monday, March 24, 1958

The next book arrived that week. She knew right away, before opening the brown paper package tied up with twine, that it would be the successor to the one sent nearly a year ago. It was addressed in the same blocky lettering. The sender had all but cut and pasted letters from magazines, the writing so obviously someone's attempt to disguise his own. Presumably that meant the sender thought she'd recognize his handwriting. She tore off the wrapping and found Willa Cather's *Lucy Gayheart*.

Lucybelle was floored. This literary missive was quite an improvement over *Whisper Their Love*. In fact, it was one of Lucybelle's favorite novels. She loved that character's buoyancy, resilience, luminosity. But of course that Lucy drowned. Still, as a twelve-year-old girl reading the novel for the first time, Lucybelle had thought the ending was pitch perfect. What other ending could be as true?

The title read a little differently now in 1958 than it had read in 1935 when Cather published the novel. Lucybelle supposed that, given the book was delivered in the same furtive manner as *Whisper Their Love*, it also was intended as a threat.

She flipped through the pages, looking for a note, but there wasn't one, so she put the book under her desk and took it home that night. She reread it in one go, staying up way too late, and cried at the end when Lucy Gayheart fell through the ice, got her skates tangled in the submerged branches, and slowly died. Not so buoyant, after all.

The story struck Lucybelle as even more poignant than it had when she read it as a girl. This was a love story about a young woman for herself. Lucy Gayheart wanted so much more than a simple marriage and safety. But her lively presence in the world couldn't be accommodated. Her vision for life, a primary partnership between herself and music, just wasn't possible. Lucybelle was glad, as she had been the first time she read the story, that she drowned rather than succumbed. Dramatic maybe, but true. At least it was true.

## Tuesday, April 15, 1958

A full month after their Sunday morning walk, Stella called and asked her out to lunch for the following day. Lucybelle suggested the soda fountain at Lyman's drugstore on the corner of Fourth and Linden in Wilmette.

In the morning she washed her hair and tried to comb it into submission. The air here was either too dry or too wet; she never could do anything reasonable with her blond curls. She might as well have been feral, fresh from the woodlands, the way it swept off her head in random swirls. Clothes presented another problem. It was a beautiful day, cool but clear, and so she thought she might even be able to wear her summer dress, the polka dot one, with a sweater. But the sight of herself in all those dots made her feel like she was at the circus, and so she stripped off the dress and left it wadded on her bed. The tweed skirt and white blouse made her look like a librarian, especially with her thick glasses, and so she settled on a lavender short-sleeved blouse, a dark blue straight skirt, her black heels because they were all she had other than the tie oxfords or Keds, and the cream cardigan her mother had knit. The lavender was pretty, anyway.

It was plain stupid how nervous she felt all morning. It had taken Stella a month to ask her out, if this was even a date, so her heightened anticipation was unwarranted, at least unmatched. Still, she had no appetite, couldn't imagine choking down a hamburger in Stella's presence. Maybe she'd just have a soda, but that would reveal her nervousness.

Stella stood in front of Lyman's drugstore, her taxicab parked at the curb. She smiled at Lucybelle coming down the sidewalk, which made Lucybelle's knees give a little, and she swerved. She looked drunk at noon.

"How about hot dogs for lunch?" Stella asked.

"Sure. They have tunafish, hamburgers, whatever you want."

"I was thinking of Comiskey Park. It's opening day. The White Sox are playing the Detroit Tigers."

"I love baseball. But I only have an hour for lunch."

"The game starts at two thirty. Maybe you could get a stomachache."

"I love baseball," she said again, unable to cap the wellspring of pleasure.

118

"Let's go then." Stella stepped to her gleaming cab and opened the front passenger door.

"I should tell them I'm not coming back this afternoon."

"I'll swing you by."

"It's just a few blocks away. 1217 Washington Avenue."

"Yes, ma'am," Stella said, pretending to be just her driver.

Lucybelle ran up the stairs to the SIPRE office. Beverly and Ruthie were already at lunch. She checked the lunchroom, but they weren't there. She even looked in the library, just in case Dorothy hadn't yet left. Somehow telling someone in person felt more honorable than leaving a note, but she had no choice, so she wrote, "I won't be coming back after lunch today" on a piece of paper and left it on Beverly's desk. It was quite possible that friendship would trump office management, and Beverly wouldn't even mention her absence to Bader. It was even more likely that he wouldn't notice.

As she got back into the taxicab, Stella reached into the backseat and fetched a folder, which she laid in Lucybelle's lap. Inside she found two large photographs of L'Forte. In the first, he was running full speed, all four paws off the ground, his ears flying, toward an also airborne stick. The picture captured his joy. In the second, he stood on a rock by the shore of the lake, stick in his mouth, long nose tilted toward the sky, the most regally proud dachshund ever.

"L'Forte 'Christopher Columbus' Bledsoe," Stella said.

"Perfect. They are hilariously, endearingly perfect portraits of the little beast. You captured his spirit exactly."

Stella pulled away from the curb, pleased by Lucybelle's delight in the photographs. Maybe it was the pictures of L'Forte, the example of his abandon, but Lucybelle's nervousness fell away. She couldn't stop talking as they drove south to the ballpark. She told Stella about leaving the note on the office manager's desk, and then described Beverly and Ruthie, making Stella laugh and herself feel guilty for making fun of the couple. She also told Stella about receiving *Lucy Gayheart* in the mail three weeks ago.

"Strange. You have no idea who sent it?"

"There's this girl in New York." Lucybelle paused, trying to decide how to describe her relationship to Clare. "She collects everything that's ever printed about gay girls. She carries this big maroon velvet satchel around, like a walking queer library." Lucybelle had never before used that word out loud. Some "on" button seemed to have gotten pushed and un-edited words flew from her mouth. "But I don't really think it's her. I mean, she's genuine to a fault. There's nothing furtive about her."

"That's funny," Stella said. "So you and this girl were an item?"

"No." At least she could keep that little incident bottled up.

"So if not her, then who?"

"I don't know. But it's the second one. Almost a year ago someone sent me a book called—"

"Called?"

"I hate the title. It's like a crooked finger luring readers to view the freaks. *Whisper Their Love.*"

Stella shouted her laugh and suddenly it wasn't at all freakish, just funny.

"Whisper their love," Stella stage-whispered.

"Have you read it?"

"Nah. Someone sent that to you anonymously as well?"

"Yeah."

"I guess you have an admirer."

"An admirer? I think of the books more as threats."

"Who'd want to threaten *you*?" Stella's glance lingered. It was such a simple question, but the "you" in Stella's mouth swelled with complexity. You who's sitting next to me in my cab in your lavender blouse and unruly hair and thick, cat-eye glasses, talking too openly. You, being so fully, so quickly, you.

"I met the author," Lucybelle said. "Valerie Taylor. She was at the Halloween party. I think she's a smart woman. But I don't want . . . I don't know . . . to be that kind of writer."

"You're a writer?"

"I want to write a novel." Words spilling out.

"Why not a writer like Valerie Taylor?"

"The book is pretty trashy."

"So you want to write about genteel people?"

"No." She wanted to talk with Stella about Willa Cather and Carson McCullers. She wanted to write luminous stories about real people. No code, no disguises.

"So what was wrong with *Whisper Their Love*?"

"I suppose Taylor had to marry the girl off to a boy in the end. But . . . I don't know. Does that *have* to be the end?"

"Did she at least have girls in the interim?" Stella grinned, making those dimples.

Lucybelle laughed. "Yes, she did."

"Hot diggity. I'd like to read those parts."

Lucybelle wanted to tell Stella more about the end, how maybe Taylor intended to leave a door open for the protagonist, a secret door visible only to her lesbian readers. But they'd reached the parking lot for Comiskey Park, where Stella saluted the attendant as if she knew him, and steered her Acme Transport cab to a parking spot.

"You two together?" the ticket taker asked, scraping his eyes across both women.

"Yes, sir," Stella answered and kept walking.

"Why did you answer him?" Lucybelle asked when they were a few paces away. "He doesn't have a right to ask us questions. Why did you call him sir?"

"Because we *are* together." She took Lucybelle's elbow and guided her to their seats. "I'll be right back. What would you like for lunch?"

"A hot dog, lots of mustard, and a Coke. And a bag of peanuts, please."

Stella stood looking at Lucybelle. "I like you," she said before turning to go fetch lunch.

Lucybelle glanced around at their neighbors on the bleachers. Likely most of them thought Stella was a man. Fine. Their color difference might be challenge enough for public consumption. She felt another surge of pleasure. She did love a baseball game: hot dogs and spring weather, a crowd cheering a team, the crack of a well-hit ball, the clouds of dust as players slid onto bases, losing herself in a story that mattered not at all. She wanted the White Sox to win. Of course she did. But who really cared?

Apparently Stella did. "We gotta win this one," she said emphatically as she handed the box of food to Lucybelle and got situated on the bleacher next to her. "First game sets the tone. This year we're gonna blow through the Yankees."

Lucybelle broke open a few peanut shells and dropped the peanuts into her Coke.

"You're something else, girl."

"It's good."

"A southern thing."

"It is."

"How's the mustard level?"

"Perfect. Do you always take game days off of work?"

"I shouldn't."

"But you did today."

"Yeah. It's not my time so much as the car. I had to give a driver the afternoon off." She hesitated and then looked straight ahead as she said, "But I wasn't going to take you to the game on the train."

"I love riding in your cab."

"It's a bit chilly. Here." Stella took off her jacket and fitted it around Lucybelle's shoulders.

After finishing lunch, Stella rose to her feet each time there was hope for a White Sox play, shouting her encouragement, but they lost three to four. The two women walked with the dejected crowd out to the parking lot, Stella talking the whole time about the doggone Yankees and how the Sox had better improve if they ever expected to win a pennant.

When they reached the taxicab, she said, "Let's just let the crowds leave. I can't risk someone denting my fender. You in a hurry to get anywhere?"

"No." She couldn't stop looking at Stella. Why didn't she feel shy? She'd never felt this at ease in her life. No, it wasn't at ease. It was a kind of energy, an expanding zest.

She sympathized with Valerie Taylor. How did a writer find words to describe this feeling? The floral and volcanic metaphors were laughable. Tingling, pulsing, throbbing all boorish. And yet, she did want words, accurate ones, true ones.

Stella rested her back against the car door interior and her arm across the top of the seat. "I've never seen the ocean. Have you?"

"Yes."

"So, it's like Miss Carson describes?"

"You read the book?"

"Twice. Once in a big gulp. Then sentence by sentence so I could really see."

"You liked it."

"I loved it. Is that what the ocean is like?"

"I love swimming in the waves, but I don't have the kind of eyes Rachel Carson has."

"Let's go."

"Okay." Lucybelle pivoted so that she was facing forward again, disappointed that Stella was already through talking about *The Sea Around Us.*

"I meant to the sea."

"Oh!" It was all she could do to stay on her side of the car seat. "You and me?"

"Yeah."

"How would we get there?"

"What? You don't like my car?" Stella gestured at the dashboard and then the roomy backseat.

"I love your car."

"How many days would it take us?"

"We could do it in two. If we drove through the night."

Stella turned and looked out the window, as if the sea were just there, a bit beyond the edges of the parking lot.

"Really? You read the book twice?"

"We're gonna go some day. We'll just start driving east, okay? Take whatever roads are in front of us. Small roads, so we can see stuff. We'll stop whenever we want. I'll take pictures and you'll write. We'll take two weeks, not two days. We'll have time." The way she said the word "time" made Lucybelle picture a very large mountain, layers and layers of time stacked high, grand, beautiful.

The parking lot had emptied, and Stella drove straight across the painted space lines. She saluted the attendant again and drove out without paying. A few minutes later, as she pulled in front of Lucybelle's apartment building, she said, "You asked me a question when we were entering the ballpark. Why I called that boy 'sir.'"

She wanted to tell Stella that she didn't have to explain anything. She wanted, even more, to hear everything.

"I don't look for trouble. If one three-letter word can keep it at bay, I'll use it. Respect never hurt anyone, even if it's a one-way street. I learned that in the service."

"What else did you learn in the service?"

"Lots."

"Thank you." Lucybelle touched Stella's hand and climbed out of the cab, the folder with L'Forte's photographs tightly tucked under her arm. When she got upstairs to her apartment, she looked out the window as

Stella pulled away from the curb and drove down Evanston's Michigan Avenue.

## Friday, April 25, 1958

"It's obviously Phyllis," Beverly said leaning forward to take the last egg roll. She slid it around in the red dipping sauce and took a big bite. "She's hurting, the little coward."

"You said she drinks, am I correct?" Ruthie said. "It fits. Get a little tight. Send an ex dirty books."

"*Lucy Gayheart* is not a dirty book."

"Lucy *Gay*-heart. Please." Beverly rolled her eyes.

"It's not," Dorothy said. "Willa Cather is a famous author."

"La-dee-da."

"I actually think Phyllis is happy. Finally. She said in her last letter that she's quit drinking. Because of the baby." It hurt that their own relationship hadn't inspired sobriety, but still, Phyllis had so much to give the world and now she was back in the theater and off the sauce. Baby Georgia deserved a fully present mother.

"Happy, my foot. This is exactly the sort of thing people do. Their fear twists up their insides and they go a little . . ." Beverly twirled a finger around the air beside her ear. "Seriously. You need to cut ties. I don't think you should be allowing her to write to you. You just never know."

"I'm in full agreement," Ruthie said. "She needs a connection to her true self and she's using you to get it. The books are links for her. Like lifelines. Only you can't be that for her. It's dangerous."

"Where was it mailed from?" Beverly asked.

"I didn't think to look at the canceled postal stamp."

"It's Phyllis," Ruthie said.

"I don't know," Lucybelle said. "Phyllis is a little nuts, you're right about that, but I don't think she's organized enough for this kind of a prank. Anyway, she *is* happy. She adores her baby. And her play is doing great on Broadway."

"Huh," Beverly said. "La-dee-da."

"Happy is as happy does," Ruthie advised. "I don't care what her story is, you don't turn on your friends."

"She didn't exactly turn on me."

"No. She left you for a man."

"Okay, enough, Bev." Dorothy patted Lucybelle's hand.

"It's okay. It takes a lot to offend me."

"That's what we like about you," Beverly said. "You're a straight shooter. A person knows where he stands with you."

"She," Dorothy said.

"I was using the universal. 'He' is correct in that instance."

Dorothy sighed and looked to Lucybelle for editorial support.

"Speaking of grammar," Beverly said. "We had an idea." She paused so long both Lucybelle and Dorothy were forced to say, "What?"

"We think," Beverly smiled at Ruthie, "that Geneviève would be perfect for Dorothy. I don't know why we didn't think of this in the first place."

"Yes," Ruthie agreed. "Bookish. Attractive. Gainfully employed."

"Bookish!" Dorothy shrieked.

"And so are you."

"I like to read. That's different from bookish."

"The Vassar professor?" Lucybelle asked, appalled at the way this crowd talked about available women as if they were circling through on a conveyer belt, waiting to be plucked off.

"She's quite safe," Beverly said. "As a professor at a fine liberal arts college, well, she's not going to be stopping in at the Bagatelle."

"You've been to the Bagatelle?" Lucybelle asked.

"Absolutely not."

"It's not that bad."

"You haven't been there either," Dorothy said to Lucybelle, making fun of Beverly, and they all smiled.

"The best part, though," Beverly continued, "is that she lives in Poughkeepsie."

"So you'd never have to see her," Lucybelle said.

"That's not what I'm saying."

"She's saying," Ruthie clarified, "that Geneviève has a very full life of her own, that a long-distance relationship might suit both of your needs. Nice weekends here and there. I like her very much."

Dorothy gave a theatrical shake of her head followed by an even more dramatic shudder. Lucybelle approved of the reaction. Dorothy was delightfully lively. She deserved someone much more interesting than that Vassar professor.

"Why don't we invite her down for a weekend?" Beverly clapped her hands.

"You forget," Dorothy said. "You already did that. For Lucy."

"And it didn't work," Ruthie said. "Lucy's loss, your gain."

"Stop." Dorothy held up her hands. "Enough. I'm making more drinks. Strong ones. Everyone?"

Lucybelle sometimes felt claustrophobic in Beverly and Ruthie's apartment but she'd never noticed until tonight that there wasn't a single window in their front room. She heard Dorothy drop the metal ice tray in the kitchen. Ice cubes clunked and slithered across the linoleum floor. Dorothy smiled at her as she stooped in the doorway to pick them up. The other two sat smugly sharing the leather seating, Ruthie in the chair itself and Beverly next to her on the ottoman. They were so obviously happy here in their nest of homemade comforters and revolving prints by famous painters. The place was strangely reminiscent of Lucybelle's girlhood home, the way it held its inhabitants, and also confined them.

"I'm awfully tired," she said after quickly finishing the new drink. "I should probably go walk L'Forte."

"You don't look tired," Beverly said. "You look all lit up. You have ever since you went out sick last week. Are you sure you don't have a fever?"

"Of course not." She stood and reached for her coat.

"I should go too," Dorothy said. "I'll give you a ride home."

"I need the air. I'm fine walking."

But Dorothy pulled on her own coat anyway, and when they reached the street she stepped alongside Lucybelle. "I'll walk with you and then come back for my car."

"Sure. That'd be nice."

"So. Last week. Tuesday afternoon. Were you really sick?"

When Lucybelle didn't answer, Dorothy said, "I saw that girl pick you up in her cab. It seemed like you knew her. I mean, the way you got in the front seat. And how you sat and chatted for a while."

"I can't believe you were spying on me. Where were you watching from?"

"You were on the sidewalk in downtown Wilmette at lunchtime. It would have been hard to miss. You need to be careful, that's all. I don't know who she was, but yowzer. I don't think she's a good idea."

"I didn't ask for advice."

"Don't get tetchy." Dorothy spoke softly, almost sympathetically. "How's your mother?"

"You're changing the subject. Look, I didn't say anything to Beverly or Ruthie. I absolutely covered for you. But I did see what I saw."

"You saw me get into a taxicab."

"I know what it's like to be lonely. I'm just going to say it. We have so much in common. We both love to read. We both love to laugh. We both drink Booth's dry gin! I really like you. I think you like me."

They'd reached her building and Dorothy kept going, heading up the walk that led to the stairway that ended at her front door, as if she could physically walk right into the center of Lucybelle's life.

Shocked into submission, Lucybelle started to follow her but then stopped and called out, "Wait. Dorothy." A full twenty yards separated them and she had to shout, "I do like you."

The prospect of neighbors overhearing brought Dorothy back to her side. "Just give us a chance. I mean, we can just try it." She reached for Lucybelle's hand and held it too tightly.

The moment was unbearable. Dorothy's face, with that sweet gap-toothed smile and the dancing eyes, could break a woman's heart. She was right too. They had so much in common. A weird logic fitted them together. Lucybelle thought: this is what I could have, here, now. She watched herself almost acquiesce, as if her id rose out of her body, floated above, and gawped down at her libido rolling into the wrong woman's arms. That fast. And then where would she be? How would she ever free herself? She squeezed Dorothy's hand, and oh, that was the wrong thing to do.

Dorothy whispered, "Let's go upstairs."

Lucybelle felt wretched, but she had to tell her friend the truth. "I care about you so much. As a friend."

Dorothy twitched as if she'd been touched with an electric probe.

"I'm sorry. I just . . . I'm not at liberty." Then, unable to bear hurting her friend, she made her next mistake. "I made a promise to Bader. I have a high security clearance."

"That's what I mean." Dorothy spoke in an excited whisper. "We have access to the same classified information. There'd be no risk for anyone."

"You forget your vow to never again get involved with someone at work."

"I know, but that's what I'm saying, this is different."

"I'm so happy to have you as my friend. I don't want to ruin that."

"It's because of my mother, isn't it? Please just be honest."

"Dorothy, your mother isn't the impediment you make her out to be. In fact, just the opposite. Your loving care for her says so much about the wonderful, kind person you are. It doesn't have to get in the way of your life."

"So then why not?"

"I need you as my friend."

"Of course." Dorothy finally released her hand. "I understand."

She set off down the street, into the dark, alone, her gait weighted with emotion, as if she were trying to move quickly while carrying a piano on her shoulders. Lucybelle almost called out to her.

## Friday, June 13, 1958

How could she have felt all that expansive happiness by herself? Maybe she'd insulted Stella by asking her about calling the white kid sir. Maybe Stella thought she could never understand what it meant to be in her skin. As the days, and then weeks, went by, she looked for her everywhere: out her living room window on Sunday mornings; curbside in front of Lyman's drugstore; walking across the Michigan Avenue Bridge on her way to Friday night drinks with the fellows. She almost called Acme Transport a dozen times but managed to restrain herself. Clearly she'd been dropped, if there'd ever been anything substantial enough between them in the first place to warrant the word dropped. Dorothy had been right: she had no business running after a woman like Stella. The difference in the colors of their skins was an issue, of course it was: they inhabited different worlds, ones that didn't intersect, at least not gracefully; but more, Stella wore men's clothing, owned her own company, and danced slow tunes with women in public. Lucybelle had been a moment's distraction for her.

On a warm June evening two months after opening day of the White Sox season, Lucybelle rode the crowded train into Chicago to join the scientists for drinks. It was Friday the 13th and had indeed been a rough day. Nothing disastrous had happened, but she felt foiled at every turn. A key on her typewriter had snapped off. She not only ran out of cigarettes, but Lyman's had been out too. Ruthie had an asthma attack brought on, according to Beverly, by some potted plants Peter Hauser's wife, Emily, put in the foyer. While Ruthie gasped for breath, Bader threw a temper tantrum because he wanted her to take dictation right then. By five o'clock Lucybelle needed the raucous but impersonal company of the scientists, and she looked forward to an ice-cold martini. She stood pressed to one of the silver posts, reading the *New Yorker*, as the train rocked along its tracks.

"You're Djuna Barnes, aren't you?"

Startled, she dropped the magazine. Her behind slammed into the man in back of her as she bent to pick it up.

"I've been staring at you," the voice continued, and Lucybelle placed it as coming from a woman seated on the bench to her right. "I just couldn't figure it out. Usually I'm very good with faces. But of course you'd had the whole costume on when we met." The woman smiled and held out a hand. "Val Taylor."

"Yes, I remember." Again, that jarring dissonance of there being a real person, a normal-looking person, behind that flashing siren of a book. Lucybelle remembered to say, "How are you?"

"Excellent. Very well, thank you." She had the most forthright voice. "Where're you headed?"

"Into town for drinks with people I work with."

"Sounds dull. Come with me. I'm going to a party to raise money for Lorraine Hansberry, a Chicago playwright. Should be a good time."

"Oh, thank you, but—" Oh, why not. "I'd love to."

They got off the train in Hyde Park and walked a few blocks, Val talking nonstop about a group of Cuban rebels, led by the Castro brothers and Che Guevara, who were staging a revolution against Batista's government from some mountains on the tiny island. About ten years older than Lucybelle, Val projected a larger-than-life attitude, a saucy dismissal of the everyday, as if she could only be bothered by excellent food and big ideas. Her skin was the pasty color of uncooked dough, and her hair, hacked off at a medium length, looked as though she'd done it herself in front of the bathroom mirror. She wore a short-sleeved white blouse with red stitching on the top edges of two breast pockets and an ill-fitting gathered brown skirt, worn askew. The zipper and clasp sat on Val's hip, and Lucybelle kept wanting to move it to the back for her. She wore glasses, cat-eyes much like Lucybelle's, only Val's were bedecked with ornamental curlicues.

Party guests—men and women, Negro and white—crowded the wrap-around porch. Val shouted greetings and pushed through to the front door. For once Lucybelle was pleased with her own appearance. Last Saturday she'd bought a new summer dress to replace the outdated polka dot one. The polished cotton fabric was covered with green and violet hydrangea blossoms, the fitted top snugged against her breasts and ribcage and the full flowery skirt announced summer. Friday the 13th be damned. She was at a theater party in Chicago, wearing a pretty new dress. She planned on having a good time.

Val went directly to the table spread with potato salad, dinner rolls, collard greens, and a giant platter of fried chicken. Realizing she was famished, Lucybelle followed. She dropped fifty cents in the coffee can sitting on the inside corner of the table and fixed herself a plate. Other guests filling their plates gave her warm smiles and asked how she was doing. She was doing wonderfully, now that she was at this welcoming party. Someone pointed out the drinks table, and Lucybelle dropped a dime into that coffee can and fetched herself a frosty bottle of beer from the ice-filled metal bucket.

"Aren't you looking fine." A slight, brown-skinned man in a shiny blue suit looked her up and down.

"Thank you." It was curious how some men could compliment you and it seemed to mean exactly what they said and nothing more, while others could say a sentence like, "Aren't you looking fine" and mean to reduce you somehow. She liked this fellow right away. He told her that he too had moved to Chicago from New York, having been unable to break into theater there. Someone told him the color barrier wasn't as bad here, although he wasn't finding that to be the case.

"Have you met Lorraine Hansberry? She's right over there." The fellow nodded toward a knot of people gathered around a pretty young woman with a wide, warm smile. "I'm trying to get up my nerve to speak with her."

"Why not just walk up and say hi?"

"I heard she's looking for producers. The last person she needs to meet right now is some aspiring actor."

"What if her play makes it big? And you passed up this chance."

"I like the way you think," the fey man said and gave a sweet little shrug. He stared wistfully at the playwright and took a deep breath.

"Come on. We'll go together."

"Oh, no. I can't. I don't know her."

"I don't know her either. But what if this moment is the one that changes your life? What if she said, 'Look at that face. He's exactly who I need to play the lead.'"

The man groaned. "In my dreams, sister."

"What's your name?"

"Joe Mack."

"Okay, Joe Mack. I have an idea. Trust me?"

His expressive face cycled through a series of obvious thoughts: why should he trust; she did look trustworthy; and really, what did he have to lose?

"Exactly. Neither one of us has a thing to lose." She set down her plate and bottle of beer and took his hand. He was actually trembling. Oh, Joe Mack, she thought, I like you. She loathed interrupting people, but now she couldn't let him down. All this confidence because of what, a new dress? They stood on the periphery of the group surrounding Lorraine Hansberry. She didn't see how anything other than extreme rudeness would get them inside. She needed a strategy.

"Maybe later," Joe Mack whispered.

"I'm a reviewer with the *Nation*," Lucybelle said in as friendly but firm a voice as she could muster. It was not a complete lie. "May I have a word with Miss Hansberry?"

The crowd parted, Lucybelle yanked Joe Mack forward, and there they were, in front of their target audience.

"It's a pleasure to meet you, Miss Hansberry. I want to congratulate you on your play and also introduce you to my friend, one of the best actors I've had the pleasure of seeing on the stage, Mr. Joe Mack."

Joe was indeed a good actor. His fear appeared to have evaporated and now not a muscle twitched in his face as he stepped forward and shook her hand. "*Raisin in the Sun* is a play I want to be in. *Must* be in. I can't tell you enough, Miss Hansberry . . ."

Lucybelle breathed deeply, happily, pleased to be wearing a pretty dress and helping a pretty man. Maybe she could write a review for the *Nation* once the play got produced. She'd write her old advisor, Joseph Wood Krutch, tomorrow. The world felt capacious and joyful right then. She looked out over the room full of people—writers and actors of all colors celebrating Miss Hansberry—and that's when she saw, teething on a chicken bone and laughing at someone's joke, Stella.

As rude as a hiccup, she turned and walked away from Joe Mack and Lorraine Hansberry. A second later she stood before Stella.

"Hey, there!" Stella said with too much joviality.

Rusty stood on one side of Stella, but she didn't know the woman on the other side. Since no one introduced her, she said, "I'm Lucy."

"Arkansas," Rusty said.

"Oh, so *this* is Arkansas." A good head taller and several shades lighter than Stella, the woman was gorgeous, her long hair spilling over bare shoulders, her wide mouth rubescent with lipstick, one eyelid drooping sexily, and long sleek eyebrows. Her golden form-fitting gown made Lucybelle's dress feel like a schoolgirl's. She put a hand on Stella's shoulder and said, "Darling, get me another plate of that chicken. Might as well throw on a spoonful of potato salad too. I like how she puts sweet pickles in hers."

Lucybelle recognized the dispatcher's low, sensual voice.

Stella allowed her eyes to meet Lucybelle's, ever so briefly, before she took the tall woman's plate and headed for the food table.

"I'm Wanda," she said. "That's a pretty dress."

"Thank you."

"Tell you what, don't let these jokers get to you." She nodded at Rusty. "I'm from Arkansas too. That's why they like to carry on about the state."

"Which part?"

"Jonesboro."

"I'm from just up the road, Pocahontas."

"You don't say. It's a small world, ain't it?"

"Yes, ma'am."

"Where's that plate of food? I swear, Stella can't walk a straight line. She's got to take a detour every single journey she sets out on, even if it's ten yards to the food table. It's a wonder she ever got the business off the ground, back when she was driving."

"So you're the dispatcher for Acme Transport?" She knew she should keep her mouth shut, walk away, let go. But she couldn't resist her need for absolute confirmation.

Rusty made a hostile coughing sound.

Wanda cocked one of those beautiful eyebrows and said, "Dispatcher, bookkeeper, secretary. I even drive fares from time to time, someone out sick."

Lucybelle understood that Stella wouldn't come back with Wanda's plate of food as long as she was standing there. "I came with a friend. I guess I'll go see how she's doing."

"Yeah, good," Rusty said.

"Nice to meet you," Wanda said, dragging the words like a body through a swamp. "Don't let no one disparage Arkansas to your face, you hear? Lots of famous people have come out of the state. Scott Joplin. Florence Beatrice Price."

"Johnny Cash," Rusty said, "might be more her speed."

"Come on now, what's wrong with you, Rusty? Besides, I like me a little Johnny Cash now and then. That new one?" She sang the first couple of lines. "'Keep a close watch on this heart of mine, I keep my eyes wide open all the time.' Yeah, I like Johnny Cash just fine." She winked at Lucybelle and her eyelid stuck shut for a moment.

Lucybelle managed to say pleased to meet you and walk away. She squeezed past the food table, where Stella was not making a plate for Wanda, and checked the kitchen and even a bedroom in the back of the house, where when she tried to open the door, someone slammed it back shut from inside. A puff of marijuana smoke wafted out.

A fireball of hurt and anger burned in Lucybelle's stomach. She was afraid of what she might say to any stranger who tried to speak to her, so when she saw a door leading to the backyard, she took it. Air. Just some air. She landed on a screened-in porch where a group hotly debated the merits of a play currently off Broadway. She opened the screen door and stepped into the warm night sky. A host of mosquitoes jumped on her bare arms but she didn't care. Let them have me. She saw the end of a lit cigarette in the furthest recesses of the yard and headed for it. She smelled the sweet lilac blossoms, their scent mingling with the tobacco smoke, before she recognized the figure taking shelter next to the bush.

"Let me have one of those."

Stella knocked a Chesterfield out of her pack and lit it from her own. She handed the cigarette to Lucybelle.

"Your dispatcher is beautiful."

Stella nodded.

"Maybe I misunderstood something."

Stella inhaled the smoke, furrowed her brow.

"You promised not to lie to me."

"I didn't—"

"Don't."

"Okay. I'm sorry. I made a mistake."

"You mean taking me to the baseball game."

"You know, I don't really deserve this." Stella stubbed out her cigarette in the grass and then ground her heel into the butt. "Yeah, we went to a baseball game. I don't recall asking you to marry me."

"I'm not a fool," Lucybelle said, "and I don't want you making me out to be one."

Stella lit another cigarette. At least she didn't walk away. In fact, despite her hard words, she looked miserable.

"I thought we were going to drive to the seashore."

"That was just talk."

"Of course. I knew that then too. But it was a certain kind of talk." She absolutely wasn't going to cry. She thought of how Dorothy had gripped her hand too hard, how unpleasant that had felt. She didn't want to do that to anyone. She ought to turn, right now, and walk back into the house. Instead she stood there in her hydrangea dress, drenched in lilac fragrance, wanting this woman to kiss her. It was crazy to have that thought. "I knew we weren't really going to drive to the coast, but I believed in the feeling between us. I knew when you didn't call that I'd been wrong. But that afternoon, and for a while afterward, I believed."

"Lucybelle. Please."

"There's only one thing I have, one thing I can insist on in my life. The truth. That's all. And it's a bitch to find. Anywhere." Now the tears did come, damn it. "You better go get that plate of food for your dispatcher."

She'd left no wiggle room for Stella and she was glad. She didn't even move out of the way, forcing Stella to step around her on her way back into the house.

Lucybelle stayed out in the backyard, the mosquitoes eating her alive, and composed herself. She'd left the party on Halloween; she wasn't going to leave this one. If only because they were honoring Lorraine Hansberry, who'd written a play some people said was brilliant. If only because Valerie Taylor had invited her. She'd go back inside, get another cold beer, and find Joe Mack.

"What happened to you, girl? She took my telephone number!"

"I'm glad, Joe."

"You took off like you'd seen a ghost."

"I had."

"Old flame?"

"New flame. Already extinguished."

"Oh, honey. Parties can be land mines. Let's get more food. Simone just brought out another platter of chicken. You're as skinny as I am. Put some fat on you, girl, and whoever's troubling you will be sorry he— she?—whatever, don't matter to me, they'll be sorry they let you go. Real sorry."

They put a couple more fifty-cent pieces in the can and filled their plates, Lucybelle being sure she kept her back to Stella's crowd, and then she suggested they take their food out to the screened-in porch. She allowed herself to be drawn into the lively conversation and had a lovely time. Yes, she did. Stella, whose last name she didn't even know, be damned. She'd been a fool to allow her romantic imagination so much leeway. When Val found her an hour later to say she was leaving, Lucybelle kissed Joe Mack on the cheek and said good-bye.

"Lucybelle Bledsoe," he said. "I won't forget your name. And when *Raisin in the Sun* opens on Broadway, come backstage to my dressing room, you hear?"

"That won't happen," Val said as they weaved through the party guests on their way to the front door. "Broadway isn't ready for Lorraine's play. I wish it was, but no way."

Lucybelle wished Val would keep her voice down.

As they stepped off the front porch, someone tapped Lucybelle on the shoulder. She turned to find Rusty's freckled face inches from her own.

"Fifteen years," Rusty said. "Stella and Wanda."

"What's that got to do with me?"

"My question exactly."

Val was barreling down the walkway toward the street. Lucybelle turned to follow but Rusty put a hand on her shoulder, gripping too hard. "I don't think you understand."

"This isn't your business."

"Oh no? My mother and father, my brothers and sisters, none of them speak to me. I was put on the street when I was fourteen years old. You know who picked me up? Trained me? Gave me work? Stella and Wanda are my family." Rusty's copper eyes rang with alarm.

"Your family is safe," Lucybelle said. "I came to the party with someone and I'm leaving with her now, if you'll let me go." Lucybelle nodded toward Valerie Taylor standing on the sidewalk, hands on hips, scowling back at the porch.

"Go then," Rusty said, sinking her hands in her front pockets, just a scared kid.

The warm, buggy walk back to the train station, with Val talking loudly the entire way, was dreadful. So was the jarring train ride all the way back up to Evanston. It had been a doozy of a Friday the 13th, after all.


## Thursday, June 19, 1958

Lucybelle stopped under the golden dragon topped by the lighted blue ball in front of the Drake Hotel. Friday night's revelation put her in need of some serious reinforcement, a boost of any kind, and one from her boss—she was thinking a pay raise—would be most welcome. Why else would he invite her to dinner at the swank hotel? Bader had said to meet him in the Coq d'Or bar, so she went inside and ordered a dry martini.

The place was too dark and woody, the waiter too formal, as if he meant to intimidate rather than comfort the patrons. Of course Bader was late. She'd almost finished her martini by the time he strode in the bar and yanked out the chair across the table from her. He looked startlingly handsome, if a bit disheveled, in his evening attire. He wore black slacks, too short, a white shirt that had been maybe ironed but definitely not starched, and an unconventionally knotted tie. He looked like a man who couldn't be contained by clothes, and she liked that about him.

"Bottoms up," he said. "I'm hungry. Let's go to the dining room."

The maître d' of the Camellia House pulled a moue at the sight of Bader, but with a show of great indulgence, he said, "Come with me." They stepped into the coatroom, not at all out of sight, as if this was more a punishment of humiliation than a correction, but of course Bader was far outside any possibility of humiliation. The maître d' used his hand to brush off, one might say crudely "iron," Bader's suit jacket, and then he unknotted Bader's tie and quickly redid it, patting him on the chest when he finished. As he was being groomed, Bader made funny faces over the man's shoulder. Lucybelle smiled at her boss.

Bader ordered for both of them, including another martini for Lucybelle. Then he leaned across the table and said, "Look. We've talked about this."

"Yes, we have. I told you I can order for myself."

"Not that. Drop it, Lucy. The sole is excellent. You want it. But yes, I *am* referring to the same conversation, the day we discussed terms at the diner in Harlem."

So here it came. She quickly assessed her chances of gaining anything by taking the offensive. She could toss out the accusation that he'd hired her for this very moment, so he could extract something from her by means of extortion. She hesitated. The charge would make her seem paranoid. The drinks arrived and Lucybelle took two generous swallows of her martini.

"I personally couldn't care less," he said. "You know that. But the fact of the matter is, you have more information about SIPRE's doings than anyone else in the lab, including the scientists. They're focused on the ice, on chemistry and physics and drilling. Everyone knows a little bit, but I've trusted you, and that means pretty much every piece of paper leaving SIPRE is seen by you." His accent was thicker this evening, and she'd learned that this was a sign of emotional discomfort, a rare condition for Bader. Normally he loved the outer fringes of both ideas and feelings.

"What are you trying to say?"

"I'm not *trying* to say anything. Drink your drink. You don't have to be an editor tonight. What I *am* saying is that Camp Century is almost there. We'll be manning it next year. You know I'm not that keen on the military stuff, to put it lightly." He grimaced and pushed back from the table, having finished his shrimp cocktail. His right knee bashed the edge of the table and all the beverages sloshed out of the glasses. "'City Under the Ice,'" he quoted in a mock grand voice. "I could be much more enthusiastic if I didn't think it was a great big waste of the taxpayers' money. Don't you dare quote me on that, ever. In any case, it's going to be fucking fantastic, if you look at it from the point of view of the most elaborate Boy Scout camp ever built."

"What's your point?"

"You even know the exact location of Camp Century."

Of course she did: about 140 miles from the Thule Air Force base in Greenland. She'd edited the site maps. Camp Century, an entire city under the ice sheet, would house two hundred men. Besides dormitories, there were shops, theaters, clubs, a hospital, a library, a nuclear power plant.

"Sometimes," Bader said looking nervously thoughtful, "I feel like I've made a pact with the devil."

"Don't be dramatic," she said to make him laugh, and he did, briefly.

Then he leaned halfway across the white tablecloth and tried to speak softly, but his whisper was a hoarse rumble. "Our sponsors don't care enough about the ice cores. They can't fathom the importance of the knowledge we stand to gain. They're too blinded by their fear of the Russians. Which is why we're really in Greenland. Moscow is right there, just over the hump of ice."

She'd heard the scientists' conjectures about Camp Century being a missile launching site, but frankly, she thought the idea was just a bit too absurd, even for the government. How could you contain a thing like that? You couldn't. It was more likely that Bader was fanning the flames of that rumor to scare her into submission. Submission to what, though?

"You know this for a fact?" she asked.

"I don't know anything."

"Would you get to your point?" She found that she was shaking.

He nodded and held eye contact. "I believe in knowledge. Science is mankind's only hope. I need to keep the government not just interested in the ice cores but committed to them. I like to think of our work as a distraction. Maybe we don't need to launch any missiles if we have instead earth's history, and future, in our sites. Are you following me?"

"Yes."

"I need flawless performance coming from every single team member at SIPRE."

"Is there a problem with my work?"

"Our bosses aren't going to tolerate a single slip. Or more to the point, even the perception of a slip. The threat of a slip."

"What are you getting at?"

"It doesn't look good. You gotta play the game. You gotta try harder."

"Have there been errors in my work? Have you gotten complaints?"

The waiter put a plate of sole wrapped around crab, garnished with a half dozen bright green beans, in front of each of them. He backed away from their table, bowing. Bader dug in as if he'd forgotten they were in the middle of a conversation. He polished off the sole in about thirty seconds.

Lucybelle looked around the dining room and tried to gather her wits. The black, white, and sapphire color scheme didn't help. It was both too rich and too harsh at the same time. She kept feeling as if she were about to slip off her chair, the polished cotton of her dress not adhering to the blue-striped silk upholstery. The blue camellias on the china, together with the hydrangeas covering her body, made her wish for garden shears. It was much too floral. The dining room's opulence was meant to soothe, but it only made her edgy. "Would you be so kind as to tell me what you're talking about?"

"I think you know. It wouldn't be helpful for me to spell it out."

She pushed her plate toward him. "Go ahead. I've lost my appetite."

"Don't be that way. You're a ballsy girl. You can buck this. You just have to be more savvy."

"So what do you think you have on me?"

"Don't smirk at me. You're too smart to pretend that you don't understand what's at stake."

"I know all about Beverly and the State Department."

He waved away the admission. "That was just silly. State Department nonsense."

Silly? Nonsense? Families had been severed. Homes had been lost. Beverly's friend Jane hung herself.

"Sure," he said. "You could lose your job. But jobs are the least of it."

"So what's the most of it?"

"What's at stake," he said, "are the ice cores."

He finished off his wine, mopped a piece of bread across the plate's pale blue camellias, wiped his mouth, and exchanged his plate for Lucybelle's. "You really don't want your fish? I've had better. It's a bit swampy. Maybe it's the crab. The sauce too is so-so. It's almost coagulated. The best fish I've ever had was in Chile. You sit on the edge of a fjord, at little tables on perfectly swept cement slabs, covered with beautiful Moroccan rugs, and you watch the guy with a homemade fishing pole and line, just a few yards away, haul in your dinner. Patagonian hake. He walks it up the beach and hands it to your waiter. It all takes about half an hour, from fjord to plate. By the way, Chilean wine is also excellent."

"What *about* the ice cores?" Lucybelle asked.

"The best part about Camp Century is that our labs will be right there, on site, and we'll have state-of-the-art everything. I'm not willing to let anything compromise our progress. It's been too damn slow as it is. If some silly socializing choice affects my ability to keep going, my ability to keep our sponsors' eyes trained on knowledge rather than war, well, that's unforgiveable."

Lucybelle laughed out loud. "My attendance at a party could alter the future of mankind."

Bader grinned. But after the waiter cleared away the dinner plates, he leaned forward and said, "Seriously. It's fascinating, isn't it? Your attendance at a party *could* alter the future of mankind. The future of the planet, even."

"Don't be ridiculous."

"It's insanely ridiculous. I'll grant you that. And yet, I have my life-work to protect. So tell me. Where've you been?"

"You know where I've been. I'm in the lab more hours than is humanly acceptable."

"Where've you been?"

"Did you purposely hire us, all of us: me, Beverly, Ruthie"—she didn't have evidence that anyone knew about Dorothy, so she left her name off the list—"so you could blackmail us if necessary?"

Bader's wineglass stopped halfway to his mouth and he looked truly stunned. Then he burst out with a loud guffaw. "Good idea. I think I'll keep that in mind for future hiring. But actually, sugar, the argument usually goes the other direction. We can't trust homos because they can be pressured so easily by the enemy. Anyway, you three are women, for god's sake. No one . . ."

There was some satisfaction in seeing him stall himself out.

"Cares?" Lucybelle offered. "Now you're contradicting yourself. What women do doesn't matter, so my socializing choices, as you call them, shouldn't matter. To you or anyone else."

Bader sighed dramatically. "Right. Of course. They shouldn't. But look. There's a big difference between you and the girls in the foyer. They're not privy to classified material. I really don't care what they do and where they go. They're expendable. You're not. I hired you because of your reputation for excellent scientific editorial work. Period."

Lucybelle hated the tears that came into her eyes, but she prized having Bader's respect. "So then why are you threatening me now?"

"I'm not threatening you. They are. In any case, I can't have it. I just don't have time."

"They?"

"Come on. Surely you know how this works. I got a letter. Never heard of the guy who signed it, but he's official, that much is clear."

A letter.

She felt transported back to her sunshine pen, lying naked, the crude wooden structure maybe protecting her and maybe caging her, overhead the pale sky, hot with circling crows. Where is the place where shame morphs into anger?

A letter meant an informant.

"Don't give me that hot look of yours," Bader said. "You're in no position to get huffy."

"No one can blackmail me if I'm not afraid of exposure."

Bader sat back in his chair with a slow smile of surprise. "True enough. They can't." He waited a few beats, watching her closely, letting her think about what she was saying. Because, after all, he had his own interests to protect. Quietly, he said, "No, you don't care about any of that . . . exposure."

Lucybelle pictured her mother's thin-lipped expression of distaste; her daddy's overhanging eyebrows and gleam of pride; the little blue house on the shady street, the interior draped with homemade quilts and the exterior dwarfed by the giant oak tree; the front steps of the First Methodist Church of Pocahontas, where big ladies with big hats clasped their hands on her cheeks; the face of her best childhood friend, whom she hadn't seen in two decades, a girl whose character she suddenly realized was echoed by Dorothy's.

She looked down at the blank white tablecloth. She had no way forward.

"I thought so," Bader said. "You don't want to do that."

Lucybelle straightened her posture, leveled her gaze at Bader, and tried to calm the scrabbling.

To his credit, Bader looked uncomfortable. Yet he persevered. "I know you care about our work too."

"I work myself to the bone for you. I thought you'd invited me to dinner to offer me a raise."

He nodded slowly and she saw the affection in his eyes. He'd invited her to dinner at the Camellia House in the Drake Hotel because he wanted to compensate for his unsavory message. He knew he had no right.

"I'll cut you a deal," he said.

"I can't wait to hear this."

"You're right. You deserve a fat raise. In exchange for—"

"How about in exchange for the work I do. Isn't that why I'm paid?"

"No more deviant parties." His eyes lit with an imagined view of that party.

"Who ratted me out? I want a name."

"I told you. I got a letter. Never heard of the fellow. FBI, though. You should feel honored."

"What I feel is paranoid."

"Well, you should. That's appropriate. You need to keep your hands clean. Eyes on the prize."

Lucybelle laughed even though it wasn't funny, not even a little bit. She couldn't believe she was having this conversation.

"Bottom line: I need you. And I don't need any goons breathing down my neck about you." He sighed and signaled the waiter, from whom he ordered coffee for both of them, a slice of chocolate cake, and a French custard. "Look. I wasn't going to go into detail. But I didn't expect this, shall we say, resistance from you." He held up a restraining hand. "Hear me out. I like your easily triggered indignation. You have a sense of fairness you don't find all that often in Americans. It reaches far in my view. I'd do anything for you. I would. Short of spoiling—"

"Your ice cores."

"Exactly. So I'm going to lay it out even more clearly. You were at a party for some Negro playwright, a woman named Lorraine Hansberry. You apparently arrived with an author who goes by Valerie Taylor. Am I right so far?"

"This was all in the letter from the spook?"

"Taylor is a member of the American Socialist Party. In Europe, no one would give a rip. You know it's a bit different here. They take great offense when citizens who have access to highly classified information socialize with commies."

"You said she's a socialist."

"Believe me, they don't differentiate. Adding insult to injury, your date—"

"She wasn't my date."

"Really? I heard differently. Taylor is also a member of some new organization out in Los Angeles called Daughters of Belugas, or something like that."

"Belugas are whales, Henri."

"So then what is the name of the organization?"

"I haven't a clue," she said looking him right in the eye.

"Good girl."

"You know, you're one to talk." She took a sip of her black coffee. "You with that floozy Adele in your apartment last month."

The expression on his face surprised her. Since when did Bader ever take offense? She was pleased to have scored a point. He stirred four sugars into his coffee, added cream, but didn't pick up the cup. "That floozy," he said, "is my wife."

"What?"

"Adele."

"You're married?"

He nodded slowly.

She could have asked all kinds of questions, like how come he never talked about her, and did she really stay with her mother when he was in Greenland or the Antarctic, but none of it was her business, any more than her intimate life was his. She decided to end the evening on the proper playing field. "So. How much of a raise do I get?"

"We're in agreement then? We see eye to eye? I can count on you?" He rarely allowed vulnerability to show. She knew how much he cared about the ice work and she'd seen just now that he loved his wife. Even Henri Bader could be hurt.

"Yes," she said. "You can count on me."

"I'll increase you by twenty percent." He pulled out his wallet and counted out the dinner cash.

"Thirty percent."

"That's a lot."

She didn't get up from the table as he did. The truth was, renewing this agreement with Henri Bader felt good. She had not and would not "act on" her feelings, as he'd put it in the Harlem diner. Fine. The options presented so far hadn't been exactly irresistible. All those dates set up by her lab friends had felt like job interviews at best. Stella had Wanda, which explained why she hadn't called her after the baseball game. Then there was Dorothy, who Lucybelle needed too much as a friend. Finally, most recently, there'd been the socialist sapphist Valerie Taylor, for whom she didn't feel an iota of attraction.

"Are we agreed?" she asked.

"I'll find the money. Thirty percent."

As usual, Bader didn't even say good-bye. He left her alone at the dining room table, looking every bit the part of a jilted lover. The other women in the room gave her sympathetic half-smiles as she rose from her seat, with the help of the now solicitous waiter, and walked out of the dining room.

Dinner had lasted just over an hour. She'd had too much to drink, and not enough to eat, but that wasn't why her hands shook. Lucybelle Bledsoe, farm girl from Pocahontas, Arkansas, with an FBI file? She didn't know whether she was about to disassemble due to hilarity or terror. She wanted another martini. She looked in the Coq d'Or, but the cave-like atmosphere was intimidating, a movie-set den of spies, so she walked the hallways of the hotel's ground floor until she found a placed called the Cape Cod Room. It was perfect: small and cozy, a red check motif throughout, and a giant crab mounted on the wall.

As she took a seat at the worn wooden bar, a man slid down from the end to sit on the stool next to her. "May I join you?"

What did it matter? The rules were utterly twisted. She was pretty sure, however, that talking to strange men in public places was approved behavior. He made a big show of lighting her cigarette, extinguishing the match with a big flourish.

"What'll you have?"

"Dry martini, please, up with an olive."

"Two," he told the bartender holding up two fingers. He looked like a salesman with his mussed hair and ill-fitting suit, sad eyes and sadder mouth, downturned at the corners as if he were perennially on the verge of tears. "I like it here," he said. "I'm in Chicago a lot, and this is my favorite haunt. The food is good and even when the place is empty, you got company." He wiped a hand across the wooden bar top into which hundreds of people had carved their initials. "Famous people too. Look." He leaned across Lucybelle, falling too much against her breasts, and tapped a place on the left end of the bar. "These were carved in 1954. J. D. and M. M. Those initials mean anything to you?"

"Yeah," she said. "Joe DiMaggio and Marilyn Monroe."

"Bingo. Right here, same as you and me."

*Then, sugar, I don't care if you want to dance naked with Marilyn Monroe. Capiche?*

"Sure, if you say so. You can call me Marilyn and I'll call you Joe."

This unduly pleased the fellow, as if it were the first yes he'd heard in months. "You're on, Marilyn!" He downed his drink, motioned for another, and then threw himself into a river of words. The monologist began with a description of his unhappy marriage, moved on to the woes of being financially responsible for his institutionalized mentally retarded sister, the week's string of unsuccessful sales calls, the fleabag hotels where he sleeps, and the elegant ones where he drinks.

Normally Lucybelle wouldn't suffer a fool like this for a second, but tonight she sipped her drink and took refuge in the boredom of his soliloquy, wanting the dull patter to muffle her disturbing thoughts. They broke free anyway, her thoughts, flew overhead like a flock of anxious birds, darting here and there, checking the ceiling and corners for danger. Was anyone in the restaurant watching her? This drunk man talking to her, was he a mole? How she'd hated the insidious way paranoia oozed into every crevice of her friends' lives, and now the cold sweat was on her own skin.

"You seem like a nice lady," the man said. "I wouldn't want to insult you. But maybe. I mean, if you wanted. My hotel is a few blocks away, but . . ."

Lucybelle slid off the barstool and put a hand on his shoulder. His face brightened and it reminded her of Dorothy. She removed her hand. How does one say, yes, I understand loneliness, and yet you aren't the one to relieve mine?

"You haven't insulted me. Thank you for the drink. Good night."


## Friday, June 27, 1958

Lucybelle was running so late she considered just taking L'Forte into work with her. She could walk him in Wilmette. Besides, it was promising to be a hot day and she hated leaving the poor little fellow cooped up. This weekend they could take long walks by the lake.

She gathered the dachshund under her arm, still unsure whether she was going to carry him with her to the train station or take him back upstairs after he did his business, and hurried down the stairwell and out to the

145

street. The chrome fender of the taxicab glinted in the already hot sun. Stella stood against a tree in the shade, hands in her pockets. She waited for Lucybelle's eyes to find her before pushing off from the tree trunk and approaching.

"What are you doing here?" She set down L'Forte and he ran to Stella, jumping up on her thighs as if they were long lost friends.

"I came to apologize." She scratched the short fur on the top of L'Forte's bony head. "He's forgiven me, anyway."

"I have to get to work."

"Why not take the day off? The Sox are playing the Washington Senators. It's going to be a good game."

"You think this is funny?"

"Nothing funny about baseball."

Lucybelle willed her feet to walk away, but they didn't move.

"I'm sorry. I should have called. I should have explained. I was confused. Whatever happened between us just happened. Then I didn't know what to do. I'm sorry. I'm truly sorry. I guess I figured staying away would be the best thing."

At least Lucybelle hadn't imagined that something had happened between them. "So then why are you here now?"

"I don't see why we can't be friends."

"I can think of several reasons. Wanda being one."

Having greeted Stella and also relieved himself, L'Forte trotted down the sidewalk in the direction of the lake and then turned to look over his shoulder, as if to say, come on, what are you waiting for?

"I can have a friend," Stella said.

"I liked Wanda."

"Good. That's good."

"She's from Arkansas too."

Stella laughed. "So. Ozark solidarity?"

"Maybe."

"I'm only asking you to come to the baseball game with me this afternoon. Please."

Lucybelle did love baseball: the sun passing overhead, its yellow glare and pockets of blue shade; the sharp tang of mustard; the audible wave of cheering fans, yelling in unison for a bunch of men running around on a field, playing a game, just a game. It was almost as good as theater.

"I'll pick you up at noon."

She wanted to say, don't pick me up in front of SIPRE, but she didn't. She wouldn't. She knew Bader considered baseball a cultural excess, a waste of human energy and money. In his view a game that didn't advance an idea, or at least satisfy a bodily need, was useless. But she'd only promised to not have a homosexual entanglement; she hadn't promised to have no friends. Stella was not a member of the socialist party, as Valerie Taylor apparently was. Stella was a veteran who'd served her country. Even better, romantic involvement with Stella was out of the question. And baseball, no matter how Bader felt about it, was the number one American pastime. Even Joe McCarthy couldn't complain about her attendance at a baseball game.

This kind of thinking was how people ended up in the loony bin. Was she seriously considering whether she was allowed to go to a baseball game?

Stella's eyes never left her face. Lucybelle nodded her yes.

Right before lunch she walked into the foyer and told Beverly, "I'm leaving for the afternoon."

"Oh no, you're feeling ill again. I want you to see a doctor. You've been looking piqued all week. Here. I'm going to call mine now. He's excellent. I'll tell his girl you need in this afternoon."

"Please no. I just need an afternoon off."

"I don't like this. It's a long time until Monday. You look awful."

Lucybelle laughed. "Well now you're getting downright insulting."

The office manager didn't look any too chipper herself. She had a smudge of pinkish pancake makeup on the Peter Pan collar of her beige blouse. Her eyebrows were asymmetrical, as if she'd been in a hurry drawing them in this morning.

Ruthie coughed. She too looked ragged, her pageboy limp and her gray eyes flat.

"She had a spell this morning," Beverly said. "We barely got to work on time. Which, I noticed, you did not." The office manager held her two hands aloft and immobile over her desk, her lips pursed, and waited for an explanation.

"I'm so sorry," Lucybelle said, meaning about Ruthie's asthma attack, but Beverly dropped her hands and unpursed her lips, making a show of forgiving her tardiness.

"I'm concerned about you," Beverly persisted.

147

"I appreciate that. No doctor today, however. I'll see you on Monday."

"Ruthie and I will stop by tonight to see how you are."

"That's sweet of you, but it's not necessary. Have a good weekend."

Lucybelle walked out of the foyer, down the stairs, into the sunlight, and climbed into the front seat of the waiting taxicab.

At the ballpark, Stella appeared to be far more interested in the game than in her company. This time there were no prolonged looks or draped jackets. Stella entered a nearly prayerful state as it looked like Billy Pierce was going to pitch a perfect game.

"Take that to the Yankees!" Stella shouted at the top of the ninth, her voice joining all the other cheering fans. Everyone was ecstatic about Pierce's performance and Lucybelle was having even more fun than she'd had at the opening day game, if that were possible. Did she really look piqued? She'd never felt more hale.

Then, with two outs in the ninth, pinch hitter Ed Fitzgerald hit Pierce's first pitch down the third baseline, the ball landing just inches inside for a double.

"Foul!" Stella shouted. "That was out!"

"It was clearly inside the line," Lucybelle said. The entire audience of Sox fans groaned in unison.

There was no consoling Stella at the end of the game. "We still won three to zero," Lucybelle said. "Come on. We won."

"Damn!" She banged the base of her palm on the steering wheel as they waited in a line of cars to exit the parking lot. No lingering until the lot emptied this time. "So close. *So* close. I can't believe he gave away that pitch."

"He didn't give it away, he—"

"He did. He gave it away." Lucybelle watched Stella as she segued from Pierce's letdown of his fans to a tirade against the Yankees, rattling off season statistics and probabilities for upcoming games. Watching her rave about her beloved White Sox—including manager Al Lopez and the players with Dickensian names like Nellie Fox and Early Wynn—was almost as good as watching her take pictures of L'Forte. Her voice rose and fell, her hands flew about the steering wheel, her scowl as endearing—yes, that was the word, and it was okay to say it silently to herself; no one could police her mind—as her smile.

Stella finally quieted as she pulled up on Evanston's Michigan Avenue.

She parked the car, turned off the engine, and then reached into the back-seat for her camera.

"I want to photograph you." As if that sentence followed baseball statistics as easily as a cart followed a horse. "What do you say?"

"Why on earth." It was an exclamation, not a question.

"I just do."

"Well, no." She wanted to say, *I'm not beautiful enough*, as if that were the reason for the no.

"I like the way you are in your body. You have this fierce presence, even though you're so skinny and pale. You're like a cirrus cloud. Wispy. White. Floaty. High. Bringing in weather. Undeniable."

She felt x-rayed, seen all the way through.

"What do you say? It doesn't get dark until after nine o'clock. I bet you have plenty of light in your apartment."

Lucybelle shook her head.

"It's just practice. I don't mean to scare you. It's just that, well, when a subject compels me, it's difficult to turn away. There's nothing more expressive than the human body."

"No."

"You don't think so?"

"I mean, no, you may not photograph me."

Stella smiled, and Lucybelle knew that even answering the question was opening the door far too widely. "Are you going to walk L'Forte now?"

"I thought I would."

"Mind if I come along?"

She was not able to say no again. Stella got out of the car, with her camera, and followed Lucybelle up the stairs to her apartment.

"Ice tea?"

"That would be nice." L'Forte ran to greet Stella. "I'll take him out while you fix the tea."

That hadn't been what they'd agreed on, and anyway, she had a pitcher all made up in the refrigerator, but Stella was out the door with L'Forte and Lucybelle didn't stop her. Instead, she opened her window and watched while L'Forte lifted a leg on the nearest tree trunk. Stella smiled up at her. Then she ran down the block with the dog, both of them frolicsome and happy, as if they belonged to one another. When they returned, a light film of sweat covered Stella's face, and she took the glass of ice tea.

"Anywhere is fine," Lucybelle said gesturing at her rather bare living room.

Stella sat on the couch. "I wanted to give him a little run too. Poor guy. Shut up inside all day." L'Forte jumped up on the couch and settled next to Stella.

Lucybelle remained standing in the doorway to her kitchen. The line "very poor judgment" tapped through her brain like the ticker tape of a telegram.

"What's in that other room?"

"My desk. And typewriter."

"Where you're writing your novel."

"Where I might one day."

"Tell me about it. Who will your characters be?"

Phyllis had never asked. No one had. She should say she didn't know. But she did know, even though the words were still missing. They existed, those words. She knew they did. But they needed to be gathered and combined.

"May I look at your books?"

"Of course."

Stella bypassed the shelves in the living room. She walked right into the desk and typewriter room. She found the picture of Willa Cather, held it up, and smiled, and then the picture of Elizabeth Eckford in her dark glasses and white blouse, trying to enter Little Rock Central High, the jeering white girl at her back. She held this one up too, but her smile faded. Stella placed both pictures back on top of the typewriter and continued on to the bookshelf. Head cocked to the side, she called out the exact right three authors: Cather, McCullers, Shakespeare.

"Have you read Baldwin?" she asked.

Lucybelle nodded. "They're in the front room."

"He's brilliant."

"He has more eloquence and courage in his pinkie than any other living writer has in his whole body."

"True." Then Stella clapped her hands in a businesslike let's-get-to-work way. "The light in this room is softer. It's perfect. A little dusty. Warm-smelling."

Lucybelle leaned against the doorframe, arms tightly crossed.

"I'm not propositioning you. I'm not asking for anything improper. I'm asking as one artist to another."

"I'm not an artist."

"You're a writer."

"I want—"

"You are."

*I'm not even beautiful,* is what she wanted, again, to say.

"You want honest," Stella said. "I've never photographed a white woman. I don't know that I've ever even seen a white woman without her clothes. Except in pictures. I'm telling you this so you'll understand. I mean to make art." Stella looked out the window. "Just art."

Without clothes? Lucybelle looked for the word *no* and didn't find it.

"It's just practice."

It was time for Stella to leave.

"You're wondering why you. There's a reason. I'm not sure you'll believe me."

Another opportunity for *no* and *please leave now.*

"I trust you," Stella said, raising her hands, palms up, as if she were at a loss, as if she had no idea why this would be true.

Yet it was exactly how Lucybelle felt. She trusted Stella. The words made her want to undress.

"I just want to take your picture."

When Lucybelle still didn't speak, Stella said, "I'm going into your bedroom. I'm going to get the bedsheet, okay? You can use it as a drape, until we're ready."

"I'll go. Wait here." Lucybelle went into her bedroom and took off her glasses first, and then her dress, slip, and shoes. She took the top bedsheet off of her bed and wrapped herself Roman-toga style. She couldn't move. She couldn't leave the room.

Then she did. Stella was sitting on the chair at her desk, twisting the rings on her camera. She looked up and smiled when Lucybelle walked in barefoot with the sheet tight around her torso.

"I've been studying the light in here. At first I thought, right here on the floor, in this late afternoon yellow light, but now I'm thinking half in and half out."

"Which half where?"

They both laughed.

Stella took several steps back, cocked her head at the wooden floor, and used her toe to trace the line where the windowsill cut off the pool of light. "I'm not sure. We can try different things. Start with your legs in the light, up to the tops of your thighs. The rest of you will be somewhat obscured by the shade. Except with your pale skin . . . maybe . . . well, we'll see. Will you do that? I hate to ask you to lie on the floor. Do you have a broom? Let me sweep first."

"Don't look."

Stella turned her back. Lucybelle dropped the sheet and lay on the floor. She scooted until her legs were in the sun, her pubis and torso and arms and head in the shade. She rolled onto her side and brought her top leg forward, for modesty's sake. "Okay," she said.

Stella stared flatly, as if she were looking at a field of corn. "Can I fix your hair?"

"What's wrong with it?"

"Nothing. Nothing at all. I just want to maybe loosen it up a little. Okay?"

"My hair is always a little too loose."

"I know. I want to exaggerate that." With crisp, businesslike movements, Stella approached, squatted, and used her fingers to fluff Lucybelle's hair out from her face and head. "Good. You comfortable?"

She considered the question. Yes would be too strong. And yet she wasn't anywhere near as uncomfortable as she ought to be.

Stella took the first picture. She took two more from the same angle and then lowered her camera and scowled. "You're too bifurcated. The contrast in light is too much. Will you lie right on the line between the two, but with most of you in the sun? Say, just part of one leg and one arm in the shade."

Lucybelle found she couldn't move. She couldn't lift her covering leg up and over. She couldn't flip onto her back. Stella approached with both caution and impatience, took hold of her ankle, and gently pulled it over, turning her onto her back. "Now bend the other knee. Yes. Good. Scoot your head into the sun. Okay, and your upper body too. No, too much. There. Perfect."

She felt beautiful. A kind of beautiful she'd never known existed.

"Such ferocity under that pale, vulnerable skin," Stella said.

It was as if she were being seen for the first time in her life. She closed her eyes to keep the intensity of feeling at bay. The hot sun mellowed her muscles and she couldn't stop herself from relaxing into the pose.

"Yeah," Stella said.

Her daddy hadn't meant to shame her in the sunshine pen. The wooden planks of the pen were like the exoskeleton of an insect, a shell to protect the soft inner self. He'd meant to strengthen her, as if she could draw energy directly from the sun like a plant. Nor had the circling crows been sent to mock her; they'd come to show her how a body could soar.

It had been a start, isolating her with the sun, the top of her pen an aperture to sky and flight. But this. A photographer's eyes on her skin changed everything into light and beauty.

"All right, good. Can you roll onto your stomach now? Yeah, and fold your arms under your left cheek. Eyes open, please. Good. Tell me about your work. What's SIPRE?"

"It's part of the Army Corps of Engineers." Lucybelle was glad for a factual field, a place to ground herself. "Snow, Ice and Permafrost Research Establishment."

"What does the Army want to know about snow and ice?"

Lucybelle knew that Stella asked the question to distract her, so that she could get better pictures, but she didn't care. She wanted to tell Stella everything. "They look at ice as a kind of rock, though it's not. They want to find out how it can function as a building material. You know, landing strips and bomb shelters in the polar regions. So we're looking at questions like, how hard *is* ice?"

"Bated breath. Tell me."

Lucybelle laughed. "That's the stuff the Army cares about, but what the rest of us care about is far more intriguing. My boss, Henri Bader, is inventing ways to drill into the ice and pull out whole cores. It's like traveling back into deep-time. The ice cores, if and when we can pull them up whole and still frozen, will give us a picture of ancient climates."

Stella lowered her camera. "Wow. It must be exciting to be a part of that."

"It is." Being naked gave her the sense of being in another world, one where she had no responsibilities whatsoever. She felt lulled by the warm sun-yellow room, dust particles floating lazily about her head, her views of everything fuzzy and blurred without her glasses, the satisfying sound of the camera's aperture opening and shutting. *Click, hum, click.*

Stella knelt by her feet and picked one up, fingertips pressing the thin bones leading to her toes, and thumb on the arch of her sole. She pulled the foot, with the leg following, outward. "Just a bit," she said. "There." *Click, hum, click.*

"Have you ever been to the Arctic?" Stella asked.

"No. But I want to go. We're building this whole city under the ice in Greenland. It's phenomenal. I'd like to see it."

"What do you mean, city under the ice?"

Lucybelle couldn't believe she'd just revealed that. What's more, she wanted, more than anything, to impress Stella by describing Camp Century with its barbershop and nuclear reactor, its tunnels of ice, the way it was completely concealed from aerial view by the Arctic ice cap, how it hid an entire brigade outfitted to respond to a Russian attack. What she really wanted, she realized lying there naked and now afraid, utterly unprotected, was to unburden the secret of Project Iceworm, the possibility of the United States launching its own attack from Greenland, and worst of all, Bader's view that it was their job to prevent that. Suddenly she felt crushed by the responsibility.

"A place for the scientists to live," she extemporized, "while they pull the ice cores."

"Amazing," Stella said. "I'd like to see the aurora borealis."

"Me too."

"Actually, I want to go everywhere," Stella said.

"We'll start with the coast." Oh, she shouldn't have said that either!

Lucybelle was glad Stella didn't answer. *Click, hum, click.* She knew Stella loved Wanda. That much had been clear, even if Rusty hadn't outlined their history for her.

"Tell me about Rusty." There, better footing.

"Rusty's just a kid."

"She said you helped her out."

"I hired her. If that's helping her out, okay."

She was being modest. The emotion in Rusty's voice, as she gripped Lucybelle's shoulder on the front porch at the Lorraine Hansberry party, told a much larger story. Lucybelle forced herself to picture Wanda: her long hair, drooping eyelid, red lips, regal bearing. Rusty said fifteen years.

Lucybelle reached for the sheet and covered herself. "You better go now."

Stella slung the camera strap over her shoulder and nodded. "Okay. Thank you." She paused and said her name. "Lucybelle."

"You can just call me Lucy. Most people do."

"I like Lucybelle."

She stood and with the sheet wrapped around her body, from the neck

154

down to her ankles, walked to the front door and opened it a crack. "Thank you for the baseball game."

"I take it you'd like me to leave *now*." Stella only half smiled.

Lucybelle didn't trust her voice. She nodded.

Stella walked past Lucybelle and out the door without so much as a good-bye. A minute later, though, a soft clunking drew her attention to the window. Dirt clods burst against the glass, dispersing as smaller particles. She knelt, so that only her shoulders and head could be viewed, and pushed open the sash. Stella stood below, arm cocked back about to pitch another dirt clod. She lowered her arm and smiled her big unabashed smile. "Thank you," she called up. "I'll see you later."

No, Lucybelle thought, no you won't.

Tears! They came all at once, and hard, as if she'd lost a sweetheart of many years. She slumped to the floor, out of sight, and cried from a much deeper place than she'd ever cried for anyone. The sorrow she'd felt after Phyllis had been for herself, for the hollow prospect of loneliness, but this sadness was for that crazy smile and those able hands, cradling the camera and depressing the shutter release. For eyes that truly saw.

How much time had she actually spent with Stella? Two baseball games, a long and troubled cab ride, ten even more troubled minutes in someone's backyard while Stella's lover waited inside for a plate of chicken and potato salad. And this past hour, here in her apartment, Lucybelle as naked as the day she was born, letting the woman photograph her. All of her.

That evening Beverly and Ruthie did stop by with some chicken soup. Lucybelle had no choice but to pretend a sore throat so that they would leave quickly.

## July–September 1958

The month of July passed with one hot, sticky day after another. When she joined the women for drinks on Friday nights, they talked about the crisis of Ruthie's niece's wedding. Though her parents had been kind and protective of their daughter when Beverly had been fired, they weren't ready to have the pair at an extended family event. They insisted she come alone or find a male date. Beverly was all for the ploy, Dorothy thought Ruthie should find a gay fellow and have fun with the situation, and Ruthie burst into tears every time the topic came up.

Lucybelle kept quiet, tried to listen to their endless machinations, but couldn't stop thinking of Stella's hoarse voice shouting at the White Sox players, the feel of the wooden floor on her bare skin, the soothing sound of the camera shutter opening and closing. The freedom in full exposure.

At the end of the month, Dorothy's mother took a bad fall while Dorothy was at work, which called into question caretaker Sally's competence. After much discussion it was decided that she was still the best choice. She lived right across the street and anyway getting someone else would be next to impossible, especially now with the broken hip. All the women agreed that accidents happened and that this was the first time something bad had happened on Sally's watch.

To support their friend, Lucybelle suggested a Friday night in the hospital, so they brought a couple of flasks of whiskey into Dorothy's mother's room and had their cocktails bedside, eventually falling into terribly inappropriate and noisy laughter. The nurse came trotting down the hall and into the room, looking quite attractive in her little white hat and shoes, and they convinced her to take a few swigs of whiskey. Dorothy's mother, who understood very little in her dementia, declared that her daughter had the best friends in the entire world. They all drank to friendship, and Dorothy held a flask to her mother's lips, right in front of the nurse, for a swallow. It was one of their funnest evenings.

Lucybelle passed other Friday nights with the scientists, where ribald jokes were told and too much alcohol was consumed. Peter Hauser admitted to being kicked out of the house by Emily and sleeping on the roof of the SIPRE lab for four nights. He said the stars were magnificent. Bader told stories about Antarctica: the Russian scientist who'd shot dead a colleague over a game of chess; the time they became snowbound on a field trip and survived on penguin stew; the contest between Oscar, an American, and Philip, a Brit, over which "race" was the heartiest, culminating in a jump into the polar sea, accessible between great crusts of ice, coarse ropes tied around their chests and held by their fellow countrymen. Both lived, though barely.

Early on the second Sunday morning in August, Lucybelle finished her coffee, put on her Keds, a pair of madras shorts, and a light-yellow, sleeveless blouse. L'Forte scampered down the stairwell ahead of her, excited about the promised long lakeside walk. Instead he and Lucybelle found Stella sitting on the curb, across the street, and not in her church clothes.

156

Lucybelle held out a hand, and Stella shook it formally, without a smile, the need to touch so great that any ruse would do.

"Why are you sitting on the curb?"

"It's early. I knew you'd be bringing L'Forte out."

"Why aren't you going to church?"

"Wanda went to visit her folks."

"In Jonesboro."

"Yeah."

A breeze blew off the lake. Their bare arms brushed, repeatedly, as they walked. Neither spoke much and when they did it was about anything other than what they were thinking and feeling. Lucybelle said she'd gotten a letter from her mother and that it was all about her brother and his children. Stella said she'd made a down payment on two new cars for Acme Transport. Lucybelle said that she'd written a short story and sent it off, foolishly, to the *New Yorker*. Stella said that Lorraine Hansberry had found a producer for her play and that *A Raisin in the Sun* was going to premier on Broadway some time in the spring.

"Take me to New York to see it," Lucybelle said, turning at last from inconsequential matters.

"Okay."

Their words were shells, rough and gnarly on the outside, the pearly insides glimpsed but unreachable. Saying them felt good anyway, even if they held no attainable substance.

"What did you do with the pictures?"

"I developed them."

"Where? Couldn't you get arrested?"

Stella laughed. "I have my own darkroom. I do my own developing."

She ought to ask Stella to hand them over, or to destroy them, but she couldn't bring herself to do so. The existence of those pictures projected her into that place of light and beauty, and she couldn't bear to wreck it. "Well, we did almost get arrested together on Halloween."

"True. Did you find that exciting?"

Lucybelle smiled picturing herself in the Djuna Barnes getup, sitting in the backseat of Stella's cab.

"Can I come up?"

Lucybelle didn't answer, nor did she stop Stella from following her up the stairwell. The Worthingtons came out of their apartment just as

Lucybelle was keying hers open. L'Forte growled and then lunged at their basset hound, a dog that looked just like him but lighter in color and bigger in size. L'Forte had never exhibited aggressive behavior toward other dogs, and certainly not toward people, and Lucybelle could only imagine that he felt she needed extra protection just then.

She tried to apologize to the Worthingtons but they were busy collaring the hound, looking outraged by the attack and downright undone by the sight of a butch Negro girl practically on their doorstep. Lucybelle hurled a smile at the elderly couple and pulled both L'Forte and Stella inside. She threw the deadbolt and latched the chain lock.

As she turned, pressing her back against the inside of the front door, Stella cupped her chin and looked at her. Saw her. Moved her hand down her neck, along her clavicle. Their lips didn't touch on the first kiss, a sliver of air separated their mouths. Their hands too fell against their own sides, as if anything more would be too potent, impossible to bear.

The tenderness stretched out time, making it transparent. In the beginning there was pure longing.

Then, probably much sooner than it seemed, the tenderness snapped, split open, and they crashed against the door and fell to the wooden planking, grief already profound between them, snarled in with the love. It couldn't be any different if it was to be true and Lucybelle wanted, more than she wanted anything else in life, true. They must have touched every part of one another, inside and out, and they probably talked, said words, maybe made oaths. That first time became sacred in their legend of themselves, and sometimes they tried to remember the chronology of touch and feeling, but the story changed every time they told it.

Lucybelle didn't even try to talk herself out of the affair. She knew she'd fail. She wanted this: making love with Stella, talking for hours afterward, then making love some more. She was going to have it. She just was.

Stella came when Wanda was at work or at church or just at home. She drove one of the cabs, meaning she kept it off the street and from earning income, if that was the best way to get to Lucybelle. Sometimes she took the train. They walked L'Forte, they made love, they talked, and they ate dinners in the park, lying on a blanket, using their fingers to pry pickles out of jars and to peel sliced roast beef off the deli pile. They made each other sandwiches and drinks, handed over the creations and concoctions with raw affection.

People sometimes stared. Maybe they saw that the two women were more than casual companions. Maybe they were curious about Stella's boyishness. Maybe they disapproved of interracial friendship. Lucybelle and Stella laughed so hard their sides hurt at the looks the Worthingtons gave them. They didn't care what people saw or thought they saw. Love is a painkiller and nothing, physical or psychic, could touch them.

Thankfully Wanda hated baseball, so they got to go to all the games, where they shouted for the White Sox and for themselves. Lucybelle loved how Stella loved baseball. They managed, but just, to not get arrested. They kept their hands, but not their eyes, off of one another in public, and twice they had to move seats at the ballpark before other White Sox fans reported the vibrant aura surrounding the two women.

Lucybelle was the happiest she'd ever been in her life.

She hadn't forgotten her agreement with Bader, or his warning in June. In fact, in her lust-warped judgment, she viewed the agreement and warning as justifications for having the affair. Stella was not free to be in an open relationship either. They both needed the secrecy, and that shared hiding created a stasis of its own, bound them as tightly as their desire. One evening, as they lay in Lucybelle's bed at dusk, she made the mistake of telling Stella about her arrangement with Bader.

She'd only seen Stella angry two other times, the first with the cop on Lake Shore Drive and the second when she'd shown up at Tiny and Ruby's club, but neither of those times compared to this one. Stella flung her feet to the floor and sat up.

"*What?*" she asked as if Lucybelle had said she'd committed herself to an insane asylum.

Hearing her own words through Stella's ears shamed her. It had made sense, before she said it out loud, but now she couldn't unscramble even her own understanding of the commitment she'd made to Bader.

"Why would you *do* that?"

Lucybelle pulled the sheet up to her chin. "My relationship with Phyllis was over. I needed to get out of New York. It seemed like an opportunity, one that took care of a lot of things at once. Anyway, I can always leave my job. It's not forever."

"Everything I know about you goes against this thing you've told me."

She hated Stella knowing. Yet she didn't wish she'd kept silent.

"And if he finds out that you are in fact 'acting on it'?"

She shook her head. Out loud it did sound absurd.

"Answer me," Stella said roughly. "I really want to know."

"You're hiding as much as I am."

"I'm not hiding my character, my soul. The whole world knows who I am. They just have to look at me. I'm my own boss."

"No, you don't have to lie on the street or at work. Only to your life companion."

"The point is," Stella continued, undaunted by Lucybelle saying what they'd never said aloud, "you would never actually be with me, would you? Open and free?"

"You're the one who's not free. It's not a fair question."

"Answer it anyway."

*I would,* Lucybelle thought. But the question hurt too much to answer because Stella did have Wanda at home. Instead she threw out, "Would you take me to Tiny and Ruby's?"

At last she'd damped Stella's indignation. "What do you mean, would I *now*? Or would I *if*?"

"Either."

"You don't belong there." Stella paused. "Not because of color. You're a sophisticated lady. You read the *New Yorker*."

"That's ridiculous. And you're not sophisticated?"

"Bulldyke and sophistication will never go together."

"Don't use that word."

"See? Your fear of that word makes my point. That's why you're not going to Tiny and Ruby's."

"I'm not going to Tiny and Ruby's because of your girlfriend."

"She knows about you."

"What do you mean?"

"She knows I have a friend."

That hurt more than anything else Stella had said. "Just a friend."

Stella lay back down beside Lucybelle. They'd already said too much. She pushed her face into the crook of Lucybelle's neck, but maybe that felt too vulnerable, too like home, because she quickly rose up to kiss her collarbone and breasts, grasping at the silky eroticism that bound them. If nothing else, they had that.

They didn't fight again. The balance was too delicate. But their lovemaking shifted slightly, became edged with hopelessness, as if each time was going to be the last.

Baseball season ended and it began to rain. They went to the movies when they could, read short stories aloud to one another, and still walked L'Forte. A couple of other regular dog-walkers smiled and said hello, while still others made wide swaths around their path, scowled, caught on, or just disapproved of what they saw on the face of it. Stella and Lucybelle didn't care.

One time they held hands while walking along the lake. Their joined palms felt like a fuse in an outlet, as if their touch was the source of everything that mattered, as if by doing this, holding hands in public, they'd be able to make better photographs and write better stories. Make better love. The power of those few minutes of not hiding felt like it could fuel an entire country.

## Tuesday, November 18, 1958

Daddy died of a quick heart attack in the courtroom. He was seventy years old but Lucybelle hadn't yet considered the possibility of his death. She told her mother that she loved her, hung up the telephone, and wanted to call Stella.

The only number she had was for Acme Transport. Wanda was the dispatcher. Lucybelle had never been to their house.

Even before she felt the full impact of her grief at losing Daddy, she was hit by the realization that not only did she have no viable way for contacting Stella, her lover wasn't available to her. At all. In any real way. These past three months had been an illusion of closeness.

The double whammy near about killed her that night. She drank too much. She smashed some dishes. L'Forte ended up peeing in a corner of her study.

In the morning she called Dorothy and asked if she'd keep L'Forte, then took a taxicab to the airport and booked a flight to Little Rock. The airplane bumped down on the tarmac, the wings wagging side to side, and the brakes screeched to a slow stop. Her brother, John Perry, having flown in from Portland, met her flight and they drove together to Pocahontas.

They found the house full of women, Mother on the couch holding tightly to her Bible, casseroles and cakes covering the dining room table. The smell of the lard-rich food made Lucybelle nauseous. She went directly to the little yellow cube that was her girlhood bedroom, closed the door, and sat on the small single mattress. Her arms and legs felt as brittle as sticks. Her face ached. Home without Daddy was impossible. If no one before Stella had truly seen her, at least Daddy had glimpsed her. He'd struggled to fit her into his picture of the world, the small-town Christian life he believed in with all his might. He'd viewed her intelligence as an anchor she'd have to forever drag, could not conceive that it might be her ship out, but he'd seen it. He had loved her.

Lucybelle was shattered.

She wanted a cigarette with a level of desperation that felt life-threatening. She had to smoke or she would die. The only feeling stronger was her shame: neither her brother nor her mother knew that she smoked. What a stupid thing to hide. But it felt like the nadir of her self, indicative of her lack of discipline, her vulnerability, her unworthiness.

John Perry had married a smart and beautiful woman, Helen, and they had four wholesome children. They took hikes after church on Sundays and talked politics at the family dinner table. She, by contrast, was involved with a woman who was cheating on her lover of fifteen years, a woman whom she couldn't call even when her daddy died. She smoked cigarettes and didn't even own a dinner table. She'd lost eight pounds since she began seeing Stella.

By the end of the week, she felt so diminished she seriously considered staying in Pocahontas. Someone had to care for her mother. John Perry had his family in Oregon. If Dorothy could do it, she could too. For that matter, there might be an available hog farmer. What would it be like to not have to fend for herself? To live in a place where people trusted her?

But then she remembered that Daddy was dead. This could never be home again.

## Tuesday, November 25, 1958

Stella had the nerve to be irritated. "Where've you been? I came by on Sunday, three different times, and knocked and knocked." Then Stella smiled. "I was afraid the Worthingtons were going to call the police."

"Daddy died."

"What?"

"Daddy died. I had to go to Pocahontas."

"Oh. I'm so sorry."

"It's eleven o'clock at night."

"I know. I had a fare in the neighborhood, so—" She caught herself too late.

"So it was convenient. For you."

"I'm sorry about your daddy. Is there anything I can do?"

"Do? How about be here for me. When I actually need you. Not in the middle of the night before a work day."

"Baby, I know. I'm so sorry. I—"

"I'm supposed to sit in my apartment and wait for you to show up." Stella shook her head.

"You don't do that, show up, as much as you used to either. I've noticed, in case you think I haven't."

"I'm sorry. It's been crazy busy. I've had two drivers quit."

Lucybelle went to the window and looked for the sliver of moon. She'd seen on the news that Pioneer 3 would be launching soon and attempting a lunar flyby. She couldn't see the moon from her window. The sky was black. "My daddy died."

"I'm sorry. I don't know what to say." She held her camera in her right hand, hanging by her side, her fingers gripping extra hard.

"You're afraid," Lucybelle said.

"What are you talking about?"

"You're afraid of the intensity of my grief."

"Look, I got a lot going on too."

She wanted to break more dishes. "You can't put a camera between yourself and death."

Stella cocked her head, chuffed. "I'll keep that in mind."

"When your turn comes."

"You're acting crazy."

"I'm not acting crazy. My father just died."

"I would have come over sooner if I'd known."

"Exactly. If you'd known. You can't know anything about me or my life unless you knock on my door. When *you* feel like knocking on my door."

"Look, it's probably the wrong time to mention this. But Tiny and Ruby had to close the club. It's been a really hard time for everyone. It just seems like things are falling apart."

Lucybelle was tempted to comment on the comparison between one's father dying and the closing of a bar, but she knew that Tiny and Ruby closing the club was a significant loss in its own right. "I'm sorry about the club."

Stella looked relieved at Lucybelle's understanding. "Let's lie down for a few minutes."

"No."

It was the first time she'd ever said no to making love and Stella looked startled.

"It's almost midnight. I have to be at work at nine. And I'm sad. I don't want sex."

"Okay. Fine."

"Will you come by on Thanksgiving? Just for a couple of hours?"

"I thought you were doing Thanksgiving with your work friends."

"I'd rather see you."

"You know I can't."

"Why?"

"Come on, Lucybelle. Don't do this now. Everything's too . . . too sad already."

"*Why?*" She didn't feel desperate so much as she felt resolute. She needed to know exactly what they had.

"You want me to say it?"

"Yes."

"Okay. We have people coming over for Thanksgiving. Wanda's cooking."

"I'm tired of this."

"You're exhausted. Let's talk later, okay?"

"Let's talk now. Put down your camera."

"No."

"No?"

"Why are you giving me orders?"

"I want to talk."

"So I'll talk holding my camera."

"It's like your blanket. It's a shield you hold between you and the world."

"That's deep. Real insightful."

"Don't you dare be sarcastic with me."

"And don't you talk to me about being disingenuous. You're the one who made a deal with your boss, with the United States government no less, to never have a lover. Talk about a shield."

"I love my work."

"Baloney. You're hiding."

"No, I'm not."

Stella thumped her chest with her palm. "This is what living honestly looks like."

"You're so hypocritical. All high and mighty about being out in the world when you're cheating on your girlfriend."

"Wanda has nothing to do with us."

"No? Then take me to the opening of *Raisin in the Sun*." She'd thought about this. Wanda hated to travel. There was no reason she and Stella couldn't go. They could have so much fun in New York.

"What are you talking about?"

"Your favorite stalling sentence: 'What are you talking about?' You know what I'm talking about. I want to be with you. I want to be with you for the important things. I love you."

Stella set her camera down on the coffee table. "No. Don't cry. I love you madly. You know that. What we have is . . . is . . . I know what it is. You know what it is. It's rare and priceless and beautiful. I love you so much. Please don't cry."

"I do know that. And I try to tell myself that our lovemaking is all that matters, that the depth of happiness we have is something few people ever get to experience in their lives. But I know this too: you also love Wanda. I'm jealous of her. Wild crazy jealous. And yet I love you for loving her. I can't help it. I love your devotion to whatever it is you're devoted to—Wanda, baseball, your camera. I love all of you. But I also want all of you."

Stella tried to approach but Lucybelle held out an obstructing arm. "I can't do this."

"I'm not the only one who keeps us apart. I'm not the one pretending to be a widow."

"No, you're the one pretending to be unmarried."

"There's no such thing as married for us."

"So that means Wanda doesn't mind you sleeping with another woman? Because you're not married? Nice try."

165

"I guess I do think of you and me as somehow outside of time. Like we have our own universe."

"My bed."

"You know perfectly well that our universe is much bigger than your bed. Our life in that bed is so important, so beautiful, *because* of our big universe together."

Lucybelle wanted to hold that close. She knew it was true. But it was still nothing if it existed in isolation. "Our universe is a fairytale if we can't have friends, spend holidays together. If I can't call you when my daddy dies."

"It's not a fairytale. I love you. You know that."

She did. She also knew that Stella would not leave Wanda and that she would never ask her to leave Wanda. They had a house, a business, a family of friends. Lucybelle was on the outside of all that. With every passing week, she felt colder and colder out here in their private galaxy, like Pioneer 3 attempting a lunar flyby.

"I love you too," she said. "Now leave, and please, if you love me as much as you say, don't come back. Ever. Let me get on with my life."

"No. This works."

"Works for who? Not me."

When Stella opened her mouth to speak again, Lucybelle shook her head. She knew she looked fierce with the grief from her daddy's death etched on her face. If Stella was going to honor their promise to tell the truth, always, she'd walk out that door now.

She did.

## Sunday, December 21, 1958

Four days before Christmas, at two o'clock on a Sunday morning, Lucybelle awoke to a rhythmic thumping, as if someone were using a blunt object to bash in her front door. She crept out of bed, eased the window curtain open half an inch, and saw, parked across the street, an Acme Transport taxicab. She made out the shape of Rusty's cap on the head of the person in the driver's seat. The front door pounding continued, the sound surely echoing up and down the stairwell. The Worthingtons would be calling the police, if they hadn't already.

As Lucybelle pulled open the front door, she jumped out of the way, which was a good idea because Wanda's baseball bat was in the forward arc of its violent swing. The momentum pulled her into the room, and the bat clunked onto the floor. Lucybelle quickly shut the door. Wanda raised the bat again, her eyes wild with fury.

Then she scoffed so hard it was like retching. "You're nothing. Look at you. A flimsy piece of shit nothing. I tap you with this bat and you'd die. One thing I know: I'm not going to prison for the zero of you."

Lucybelle could offer no words that would be equal to the situation, so she had the good sense to remain silent.

"I could destroy you. I could find out where you work. I could call your mama. I could leave notes under the doors of all your neighbors."

Wanda wore a pair of black satin slacks, a red mohair sweater, and matching red heels. Her earrings were sparkly green Christmas ornaments. A large black purse was slung over her shoulder. She let herself down on Lucybelle's couch and laid the baseball bat across her thighs.

"You mute?"

"I don't know what to say."

"That's okay, baby. You don't have to say a thing. These say it all." She yanked a couple of eight-by-ten photographs from her bag. They were creased every which way, as if she'd crumpled them in her fists and then flattened them back out again. "Stupid me. I almost tore them to bits. What use would they be to me then?"

Wanda may as well have slammed the baseball bat into Lucybelle's gut. She buckled, would have fallen to the floor if some survival instinct hadn't kicked in hard and fast. She somehow knew that standing up to Wanda was going to work a lot better than groveling.

"I'll take those," she said and began making her way toward Wanda, moving slowly as one might approach a wild animal.

"Nah. I'm gonna keep 'em. Arkansas might be interested. You said Pocahontas, right? Nice little town. Bet your mama and papa go to a nice little church—I'm gonna guess a First Methodist kinda joint—just teeming with upstanding white folk who'd love to have a look at the prodigal daughter."

"Not prodigal."

"Why do you even talk? How do you think words can do a thing for you now?"

She had a point.

Wanda stuffed the pictures back into her bag.

"Please. Just let me have them. Please. I won't ever interfere again. I—"

"Interfere? Is that the word you people use for fucking other people's girlfriends? That's rich."

"Just let me have the photographs. You have my word that I'll stay out of your way for the rest of my life."

"Your word. Do you know how much value your word has with me?" She pounded the end of the bat on the floorboards. "I want an answer to that question."

"I'm sure none."

"Exactly. Besides, what good would my giving you these photos do? I'm sure there're more where they came from. Stella always shoots and prints a lot, and I know I could find them. Let me ask you this: Who in her right mind would let someone take pictures of her buck naked? You crazy, right?"

Lucybelle nodded.

"Aw. Poor baby. Poor repentant baby."

"Look. It's over, completely over, between Stella and me."

"Between Stella and you? Over? You truly believe there ever *was* anything? Delusional, crazy bitch."

"I'm sorry." The ridiculously inadequate words reminded her of the times Stella had said them.

"Not as sorry as you're going to be." Wanda stood and held the baseball bat by its top knob, letting the shaft swing like a pendulum.

Lucybelle had the absurd urge to offer Wanda a drink.

"I'm actually a very nice person," Wanda said, her face easing into something akin, maybe, to mercy. "I don't hurt people. Until provoked. Until they do something to deserve it. You are smack in the bull's-eye of that category. But I'm going to walk out of your apartment now. I have a Christmas party to get back to. This is your one warning. There won't be another one." She chucked the baseball bat across the room and it landed in front of Lucybelle's television set. "That's your souvenir. In case you forget. And these"—she patted her big handbag—"are my guarantee."

Wanda let herself out and Lucybelle went to the window to watch her climb into the front seat of the cab. Rusty started the engine and carefully pulled into the street.

168

# Friday, July 31, 1959

On the last Friday in July 1959, a bevy of military types descended on the SIPRE lab to celebrate the occupation of Camp Century. A crew of men had successfully flown to Greenland and begun living in the city under the ice cap. Their post was more lavishly outfitted than some towns in America. They had a recreation hall and theater; a library and hobby shops; and a dispensary, operating room, and a ten-bed infirmary. They had a laundry facility, a post office, scientific labs, and a cold storage warehouse. A nuclear power plant provided their energy and was backed up by a diesel-electric power plant. They could get their hair cut in the barbershop and pray in the chapel. Sixteen escape hatches allowed them to pop up from the city and onto the surface of Greenland's ice cap, should they choose to do so.

How Camp Century would stop the Russians from staging an attack via the Arctic was less clearly detailed, but perhaps the Army would figure that out now that they were situated under the ice. In any case, the Army was quite pleased with its accomplishment. Men in uniform swarmed through the Wilmette lab offices, popped open bottles of champagne, shook hands with the scientists, grinned at the support staff, inspected the cold labs, and then began an endless ceremony of speeches. Attendance was mandatory.

Lucybelle sat with Beverly, Ruthie, Dorothy, and the scientists' wives, who'd been invited but knew they were supposed to appear simultaneously proud and confused. The project was still top secret. The laudatory language was vague and general, as in "a job well done" and "exemplary service," leaving many in the room in the dark as to why exactly they were drinking champagne.

The SIPRE wives were accustomed to being held outside the content of their husbands' work lives and they didn't let the lack of information stop them from availing themselves of the bubbly and adding to the festive atmosphere. It was a party and they did their part. They wore shiny, flouncy dresses, had had their hair done, and several had brought cheese balls and Chex party mix.

Lucybelle tried to appear attentive as the hard voices sailed overhead, but she'd drifted into a decidedly carnal reverie by the time she felt Dorothy's elbow in her side. "Go," Dorothy whispered. "They want you up front."

Everyone was looking at her.

Again Dorothy whispered, "Go!" and gave her another shove. She rose from her chair and walked through the silence to the front of the room to stand with the men in uniforms, multicolored bars pinned to their jackets, brass buttons up their chests. She looked into the grates of white teeth, what passed as smiles for these men, and hoped they meant her well. Wasn't that what smiles meant? And yet her recent thoughts were ever so much more vivid than anything happening here in this room. It was irrational, downright crazy, but she felt as if everyone could see those thoughts. With all eyes on her, she was about to be publicly renounced. For loving someone of the wrong gender and wrong race. Why not throw in adultery. Lasciviousness. As the decorated officer began talking, she couldn't listen because she wanted a cigarette so badly. Bader caught her eye and flashed his best canine grin. Then he winked. She heard the words "outstanding service" and took the framed certificate. The applause beat at her ears. As she worked her way, as quickly as possible, out of the limelight and back to the women's section, Bader intercepted her. He took her arm, leaned in, and said, "Try to smile, sugar." She whispered, "Go to hell," which he enjoyed immensely. Everyone had dressed up for the occasion but Bader, who seemed to have purposely dressed down. He wore blue jeans and his red plaid, short-sleeved shirt, partially untucked.

As soon as she could slip away, Lucybelle took refuge in her office. She lit a cigarette and flipped through the day's mail. At the bottom of the stack was another book wrapped in twine and brown paper, the address painstakingly written in that same blocky printing. She said "For god's sake" out loud and this time checked the canceled postal mark before tearing off the paper. Chicago!

Even creepier was the timing: why had it arrived on the very day they were not only celebrating the occupation of Camp Century but giving her an award? It did seem as though someone were trying to intimidate her, remind her of her classified status and all that was at stake.

*Odd Girl Out* had been published two years earlier, she saw on the copyright page, by a woman named Ann Bannon. Again the cover was designed to suggest lewdness, the blond girl hovering desperately over the brunette, her hands attending to the shoulders of the desired one.

"Here you are," Dorothy said, entering her office without knocking. "Why aren't you at the party?"

"Just taking a break. Look. Another book."

"Give it to me." Dorothy snatched the book and stuffed it into Lucybelle's purse. "Ugh."

"Ugh? Have you read it?"

"Maybe, but—"

"Maybe?" Lucybelle laughed and pulled the book back out of her purse.

"All the brass is right outside your door. The last thing you need is for them to find you with this."

"You said you liked the Valerie Taylor one."

"It's trash," Dorothy said, but she sounded as if she were saying words she thought she was supposed to say, not ones she believed. "Look at the cover."

"It's just a book."

"One that implicates you."

"It's just a book."

Dorothy sighed, her fingers tapping the desktop as if she were searching for difficult words, but finally just said, "Come on. They gave you an award. You need to be out there. Bader needs you out there. You're his best advocate. He certainly doesn't do himself any good."

Lucybelle smiled. "You'd think he could put on a suit and tie. I know he has one."

"He loves being difficult."

"That's the truth." She touched her friend's forearm as she passed back out into the foyer to join the party.

Lucybelle read the book that night. Like *Whisper Their Love*, Bannon pulled a major switcheroo for the conclusion. The desperate girl, Laura, jilted by Beth for a man, suddenly develops a measure of self-respect as she's leaving on the train. She not only stops begging for love, she declares herself openly queer and prepares for a life of loving women with dignity. From a literary point of view, Laura's sudden self-respect is an unearned character inconsistency. As a subversive message to lesbian readers, it was kind of a neat trick. Laura didn't get the girl, but she was going to get some girl, soon, at the end of her train ride.

The sender had to be Bader. He'd been extra itchy lately. His frustration with the Army's other interests taking precedence over the ice cores made him more and more obstreperous in his demands for attention and additional funding. The scuttlebutt was that the Army was trying to get rid of him. Surely he was aware of the rumors, if not outright negotiating to save his position. She knew he'd commit murder if it advanced his ice cores. And yet, he could not shut his mouth. All week he'd been unable to contain a litany of jokes about the Russians. Lucybelle told him to curb himself, reminded him that his ice cores hung in the balance. That did shut him up, at least temporarily. It also left him without an outlet for his perverse sense of humor and unwieldy intensity. Who else would send these books? It had to be him.

## Tuesday, September 22, 1959

The White Sox had a spectacular year, and on September 22 they were playing the Cleveland Indians, in Cleveland, to decide the American League pennant. Chicago was wildly excited and WGN was televising the matchup for the hometown fans.

It promised to be a hot night. Lucybelle was glad she'd gotten a haircut on Saturday. She put on a sleeveless white blouse and her sky-blue pedal pushers. She looked good and wished she were looking good *for* someone. Stella and Wanda had gotten a new RCA last year, and she bet they'd invited friends over to watch the game. Wanda didn't even like baseball.

She needed a distraction. She looked out the window at her neighbors who were gathering with their coolers of beer on the slab of concrete that separated her building from the one next door. A television set, its electric cord plugged into a long extension that ran into a window on the ground level, sat blaring on a card table. A man with a crew cut fiddled with the antennae, looking for the best reception.

She knew better, but called Dorothy anyway.

"Come watch the game with me."

"You know I don't give a hoot about baseball." A big smile filled her voice.

"Everyone within a hundred miles of Chicago is watching the game. You'd be culturally remiss not to participate."

Dorothy laughed. "Let me see if Sally will look in on Mother. I'll call you back."

A half hour later, Dorothy arrived with a six-pack of cold beer. They put the beer in the refrigerator, next to the pitcher of gin and tonics that

Lucybelle had mixed, and carried kitchen chairs downstairs to join her neighbors on the patio.

After her first gin and tonic, Dorothy started whispering humorous comments about Lucybelle's neighbors, making fun of the way Mr. Worthington bobbed his head and Mrs. Worthington's chignon pulled her face tight. The guy with the crew cut who manned the television set, endlessly adjusting the antennae and dials as if he could tune the Sox into playing their best game, threw his hands into the air after every significant play and made a strange whooping sound, which got them both laughing uncontrollably every time he did it. About the masculine teenaged girl who watched the game with her parents, Dorothy whispered—her voice becoming louder with a second gin and tonic—that she was "on her way to invert hell."

"That's enough," Lucybelle said. The girl was young and her unwitting boyishness reminded her of Stella.

"Everyone is laser-beamed on the game," Dorothy said. "They aren't listening to me."

"I'll refill our glasses."

"Oh, good! These are delicious. Beverly never allows more than two drinks."

"Two and a half," Lucybelle said, "if there's something to celebrate."

"Like a new chair."

"Or the conquest of an ant infestation."

It felt so good to laugh.

Dorothy's commentary about the gathered neighbors became more pronounced with more alcohol, and eventually it was noticed by a redheaded fellow with one polio-withered leg and a sunny smile. He lifted his wooden chair by the back rails and set it down close to Dorothy's. He said he liked the wild way she laughed, and Lucybelle realized that she too liked the wild way Dorothy laughed. He nodded at a pair of young lovers, holding hands and murmuring to one another, and then took Dorothy's hand, meaning to imitate them as a joke.

"Oh, you!" Dorothy said, slapping him away, but flirtatiously. He introduced himself and Dorothy said, "I'm getting Roger a gin and tonic." She turned and winked at him from the bottom of the stairwell.

When she returned, she handed him the frosty glass and scooted her chair away from his. "What are you afraid of?" Roger asked, and Dorothy answered, "You!"

173

The false flirting annoyed Lucybelle, especially since by moving her chair away from Roger, Dorothy got herself right up against Lucybelle. It was too hot to sit thigh to thigh like this, but when she saw Mrs. Worthington note the leg contact, she chose not to move. She was tired of the hostile stares from that old couple. Anyway, maybe she kind of enjoyed the way Dorothy poked her with an elbow every time someone said or did something funny. They were both getting bombed and the White Sox were winning. Stella could go to hell.

She held the rail as she went upstairs to make another pitcher of gin and tonics. She closed her apartment door and leaned her spine against the wood, just as she had done the first time with Stella. A chorus coming from radios and televisions all over the neighborhood entered through the open window and crowded the room. The sounds of baseball had been the music of their eroticism, and now the sweat on her own skin reminded her of Stella's touch. The way her mouth moved. The way Lucybelle had discovered her own soul, parts of herself she hadn't even known existed until she had Stella inside her. The way they found that making love and telling the truth were the same thing. Were they reckless or honest? How could anyone possibly know the difference?

"You're drunk," she told herself. She went to the kitchen and gulped right from the pitcher, finishing off the watery gin and tonics. She mixed a fresh pitcher and carried it back downstairs, where she refilled Dorothy and Roger's glasses. Roger appeared puffed up, confident that something would happen between himself and Dorothy.

When he got up for the seventh inning stretch to go smoke with some of the men on the far side of the concrete slab, Dorothy said, "Phew. I was getting tired of him."

"It'd be difficult for him to know that by the way you're flirting."

Dorothy's whole face wiggled, as if her ongoing attempts at containment were failing and her joie de vivre was about to burst out of her features. "Did you know that your Arkansas comes out when you're drunk? You sound real southern."

Phyllis had called it her hillbilly accent.

"Me, drunk? Look who's talking."

"Thank god," Dorothy said. "For this scene, I need to be."

Lucybelle lowered her voice. "What: baseball or my neighbors?"

"Both."

She smiled. It was hard to be miffed at Dorothy.

"I'm just joking. Hey, can I tell you something?"

"About what?"

"What do you mean, about what? Are there any out-of-bounds topics?"

"That depends."

"Seriously, you and I know a few things that pretty much no one else in the world knows. Well, Bader and a few high-ups, notwithstanding."

"Notwithstanding," Lucybelle said, trying to stay jocular, but she felt disappointed. *Those* secrets. She was tired of them. A swarm of flies buzzed around the collection of empty beer bottles. The air stunk, hot and fermented.

"I mean, don't you think it's magnificent?" Dorothy said. "A whole city under the ice and no one knows it's there?"

Lucybelle glanced around. All her neighbors were a few sheets to the wind. Mr. Worthington was pouring beer into a bowl for the basset hound that lay panting on the pavement. The butch teenager and her parents gnawed intently on cold pieces of chicken. The young lovers, sitting a few feet behind the Worthingtons, were making out. Roger still posed with the men across the way, watching Dorothy as he smoked.

"Don't worry. No one's listening." Dorothy nudged her with a knee. "I like secrets. They're kind of sexy, don't you think?"

"I should go check on L'Forte."

"Admit that it's fun sharing classified information."

"Actually, those secrets make our lives rather radioactive." In April Congress had funded a new lab and it was being built in New Hampshire. SIPRE would merge with the Cold Regions Resources and Engineering Laboratory, known as CRREL and pronounced like the tiny shrimp, krill. Even if she wanted to leave her job, stay here in Chicago, or maybe return to New York, could she? They'd want to bury her, at least metaphorically, where she could not, would not, leak. It was as if she herself were being swallowed by the ice in Greenland.

"Oh, pooh. Don't be so serious!" Dorothy slurped up an ice cube and sucked on it, her eyes dancing, enjoying the merging of gin, classified information, flirtation.

"The ice cores are terrific, and we're so close—"

"The ice cores!" Dorothy waved a dismissive hand through the air. "Who cares?"

The sweat chilled on Lucybelle's skin, despite the heat. She cared. She cared a lot. She loved the patience and exactitude of scientific inquiry, the way tiny bits of data collected, over years, to tell huge stories, solve giant problems. But human beings weren't patient. They weren't exact. Most were motivated by fear. Project Iceworm—if it even existed, who knew, it was outside her purview, but people talked—would base newly designed Icemen ICBM missiles in a network of tunnels dug into the Greenland ice cap. The United States would be ready for the Russians, maybe make the first strike. Ice cores? Hauser said he heard one official actually say that a few popsicles would contribute nothing toward thwarting the communist threat.

If Bader lost this fight, if the missiles won out over the ice cores, then Lucybelle could be an accessory to what might amount to World War Three. She had edited the plans for Camp Century. The thought made her sick.

She could walk away. She could quit. They'd find a way to guarantee her silence, if she did. But that's not why she stayed. She stayed because she was betting with Bader: she wanted to move toward knowledge, the hope of an enlightened future. They, and the other scientists at the lab, might be the only people who saw the glimmer of that hope, but if no one tried for it, how would we ever get there?

"I don't want to talk about this," she said to Dorothy.

"Me neither!" Then Dorothy lowered her voice with exaggerated caution. "Actually, I want to tell you a different secret. You can't tell anyone. Only Beverly and Ruthie know. You'd know too if you ever came on Friday nights anymore. You're so busy all the time. I keep wondering what you're doing that's so important."

The Worthingtons were lavishly praising the basset hound for lapping the beer, their voices loud and their attention wholly absorbed by the dog, and yet Dorothy finally spoke in a real whisper, her personal life apparently a much greater secret than national security. "I've started seeing Geneviève."

"Dorothy, that's . . ." Lucybelle got stuck on what word to use. She felt suddenly giddy, thanks to the combination of relief and gin and tonics, and it was all she could do to not laugh.

"Wonderful." Dorothy filled in the appropriate word.

"Yes!"

"I know you already discarded her."

"I didn't discard her. We never started dating."

Dorothy shrugged. "Beverly and Ruthie think it's a good situation for me."

She made it sound as if she'd become a governess for a widower's children.

"I'm glad for you."

"She has a very nice house."

"Good."

"She travels to Europe most summers. Later . . . when I don't have so many responsibilities at home . . ."

Why doesn't she just say it? When her mother dies.

"I'll be able to accompany her. Assuming I can get the time off."

"Of course you'll be able to get the time off."

"She doesn't laugh much."

"There's no need to make lists of her possessions or personality traits. Just enjoy yourself."

"Once she relaxes she's a lot of fun."

Lucybelle squeezed Dorothy's hand. "This is great news. I'm happy for you."

"It's hard not telling her things, though. Like about Camp Century. Do you know what I mean? Don't you feel tempted sometimes?"

"No," Lucybelle said. "Not really."

"She asks about my work, and I have to tell her I can't talk."

Lucybelle suspected Dorothy liked saying she couldn't talk. "There's plenty you can say. You're a librarian for a research lab that studies the properties of ice."

"The sex is better than you'd think."

"Especially when you whisper state secrets to her."

Dorothy batted her arm. "I do not! You're making fun." She leaned in and said, "Whoops. I think I said the word 'sex' too loud. Look at Butch Junior's parents."

"These are my neighbors," Lucybelle said softly. "I have to live with them."

"Sorry! I'll be quieter. Anyway, she's all buttoned up, but that just means when she unbuttons, there's more to release."

"That might be more than I need to know."

"Oh, I know you're not a prude."

Lucybelle laughed. "You're the one who panics at the sight of saucy book covers."

Dorothy hooted so loudly everyone on the patio turned to look.

The guy with the crew cut put a finger to his lips. "Shh. The game is starting up again." He cranked the television set's volume.

Roger limped back and moved his chair closer to Dorothy. "Hello again, ladies."

"You'd be surprised," Dorothy whispered to Lucybelle. "All that ancient poetry stirs up the old girl."

"Do you read it to her in bed?"

Another hoot, followed by another shush. "I would. But it doesn't take that much. She spends all week reading it, so she's primed by the time I get to her on the weekend."

"How long have you been seeing her? I can't believe you haven't told me."

"She's really worried about exposure," Dorothy whispered. "Losing her position at Vassar. I swore I wouldn't talk to anyone but Beverly and Ruthie, so already I've gone against my word. I can't hold it in, though."

"I understand."

"You do?" Her voice was gaining volume.

"Sure."

"Are you seeing someone?"

"How about you?" Roger leaned forward to ask Dorothy.

"I can't believe you're eavesdropping on our conversation!" Dorothy said with mock exasperation. She winked at him again.

All of Lucybelle's gathered neighbors groaned in loud unison and she felt laid bare, naked. The breath in her throat thickened, choked, as the entire city seemed to discharge a cacophony of shouting. Protests rang out from the open windows of nearby apartments and streets.

The game. It was just the game.

Roger filled them in. Until now the White Sox had held their four to two lead, but they were poised to lose everything. "Indians just loaded the bases. Only one out. Lopez put in relief pitcher Staley. Vic Power at bat. It's all over for the White Sox."

Television broadcaster Jack Brickhouse sounded as though he were announcing the death of a president, his words strangled as he reported on the about-to-be-dashed hopes of White Sox fans. *"A crowd of over 54,000 people absolutely rooted to their seats, riveted to the edges of their seats at Cleveland. WGN Television."*

"No!" Lucybelle suddenly, vehemently, wanted this win. It would make Stella's whole year.

"Gee whiz," Dorothy said. "It's just a game."

*"Here we go!"* Brickhouse announced. *"Power has one for four, an infield single. There's a groundball . . . Aparicio has it, steps on second, throws to first! The ballgame's over! The White Sox are the champions of 1959! The forty-year wait has now ended! The White Sox have won it! The White Sox have won it! A double play by Luis! He grabbed the ball, he stepped on second, he fired to first, and pandemonium reigns in Chicago I know! Start those sirens! Blow those whistles!"*

Roger reached into the nearest cooler and grabbed a beer. He shook it hard before peeling off the metal cap. The beer sprayed into the air, dousing Lucybelle and Dorothy. Everyone laughed and grabbed their own beers, shook and sprayed. The entire population of greater Chicago erupted in celebratory pandemonium. Car horns blared. People banged metal spoons on pans. Firecrackers exploded. Human voices roared beastlike across the cityscape. It was a long and joyous few minutes of pure jubilation.

Roger picked up Dorothy and began twirling, her legs, skirt, and hair flying. Only someone reading her lips would be able to know she was crying, "Put me down!" His bad leg gave way and he fell, both of them crashing to the cement, his hands grabbing onto Dorothy's bottom even as blood burst from the cut on her cheek.

Lucybelle went for her friend but was stopped by a new sound rising up through the noise. A siren, starting low and escalating to a scream, followed by another and then another, tore through the hot night like the climax to everything.

"The air-raid sirens," Lucybelle said, transfixed by the intensity and pitch of the sound. It matched how she felt exactly.

Roger was trying to help Dorothy up, but she kicked him away with both feet. The lovers who'd been kissing pulled apart but their mouths remained open. The boyish teenager and her parents ran to their apartment. Roger kept grabbing for Dorothy's kicking feet, laughing.

"Khrushchev has done it!" Mrs. Worthington shrieked. Her husband hefted the basset hound as if the Russians were going to pluck up the dogs first.

179

"The basement!" shouted the crew cut guy. "Let's go! Everyone!" He trotted back and forth on the patio, pushing people toward the stairwell that led to the building's basement. "Let's go! Let's go! Everyone *now!*"

Lucybelle put a hand on Roger's skinny chest and pushed him away from Dorothy, and then helped her friend get up.

"What's going on?" Dorothy asked, panicky.

The racket of revelry that had been intensifying across the city morphed into sounds of panic. People screamed, doors slammed. Radios hissed out nothing but static.

"World War Three!" Roger crooned, beginning to twirl again, all by himself. Maybe he hadn't even noticed Dorothy's smashed-up face.

"I think it's just Daley's way of celebrating the White Sox win," Lucybelle said. "Let's go upstairs."

"What if they're right, though?" Blood streamed down Dorothy's cheek and onto the front of her blouse. "Khrushchev threatened. He did."

"I'm not going into that hot dark basement with these people. I'm just not."

"It's the end of everything!" Roger sang out, laughing drunkenly, until the crew cut guy collared him and dragged him toward the basement door.

Lucybelle took Dorothy's arm and pulled her up the stairwell before they had to fight anyone about not going into the basement. She locked the door behind them.

First she found her sweet dachshund under the bed, shaking so hard his jowls wobbled. She scooted on her stomach until she could pull him out, and then petted and nuzzled him for a minute before handing him over to Dorothy. "Hold him and sit on the couch."

Next she wetted a washcloth with warm water and cleaned up Dorothy's face. She pulled a blouse from her closet, took L'Forte, and told Dorothy to change. They both laughed at the tight fit and straining buttons. Dorothy tossed the blouse aside and sat with blood dripping onto her D-cup Maidenform as Lucybelle retrieved her bathrobe. This barely fitted around Dorothy's generous figure, but they secured the terrycloth wrap with a belt. The effort got them laughing even harder, and they sat side by side, each doubled over her own lap, gasping with hilarity. This caused more blood to spurt from the cut on Dorothy's face and Lucybelle wrapped two ice cubes in a kitchen towel. "Put this on your cheek."

"Do you think I'll have a scar?"

"It's not that deep."

Lucybelle mixed two more sloppy gin and tonics, measuring nothing, pouring and clinking.

"The air-raid sirens," Dorothy said.

"Were for the White Sox. It's just baseball."

"Still," Dorothy said. "It's perfect chaos."

Perfect chaos appealed to her right then. She handed Dorothy the new drink and took a good swallow of her own.

"Oh, Lucy, what if it *were* the end of everything?"

"It's not."

"Kiss me," Dorothy said. "Just in case."

So she did.

## Thursday, October 8, 1959

On the day of the sixth game in the World Series, being played in Chicago's own Comiskey Park, Lucybelle had the entire lab to herself. Even those who didn't have tickets to the game stayed home to watch it on television. Lucybelle hadn't wanted to watch the game alone, so she sat at her desk and tried to edit a paper on isotopes, choosing as difficult a project as she could find in her work pile, reasoning that it would be the best distraction. She was deep into those abstractions when the sound of flesh on wood startled her.

The knocking reminded her of Wanda's holiday visit, nine months ago. Stella had sent a letter of explanation, as if knowing how Wanda had found the photographs—while digging in Stella's bag for some cash during a party at Tiny and Ruby's—helped in any way, and also of apology. Sorry: the most inadequate word in the English language.

The knocking persisted, like in the Edgar Allan Poe story, but it was not coming from beneath her floorboards, and she wasn't going insane. She'd been spending too much time alone. It was just someone at her door. But who? Earlier in the day she'd checked all the other offices, even the cold storage labs upstairs, and there had been no one.

The door opened a crack. "Are you in here?"

"Dorothy! You scared the daylights out of me." She hadn't looked in the library. "Have you been here all day?"

"Yes. I didn't know you were here. I figured you'd be watching the game."

"I wanted to use the quiet day to catch up."

"Me too. Drink? It's after six."

"I should go home and walk L'Forte."

"You've been avoiding me."

"No, I haven't."

"We should talk about it."

"I'm really happy about you and Geneviève."

"She's in Poughkeepsie." Dorothy paused, leaving the meaning of that statement unclear. "All I want to say is that I had a blast with you that night. It was really fun." Dorothy threw herself into the easy chair Lucybelle had put in the corner of her office for comfortable reading. "Don't worry about it. It was just a little collision of too many gin and tonics, the air-raid siren, the White Sox win. They all kind of combusted."

"Yes." That was exactly what it had been. Lucybelle smiled, glad for Dorothy's understanding about the kiss. Kisses. If it'd been just one quick kiss, they wouldn't even be talking about it, but it had gone on rather long. She's pretty sure their hands had gotten involved. Never mind. Let the incident plummet into the abyss of that hot, drunken, and yes, okay, even kind of fun night.

"Did you really have a husband who was killed in the war?"

The question stunned her. She'd nearly forgotten her fictitious husband.

"That's what I heard," Dorothy said. "I just wondered. You've never mentioned him."

"How do you know about that?"

"Were you in love with him?"

"No." The answer worked for both of Dorothy's questions.

"It must have been awful losing him. Even if you weren't really in love." When Lucybelle didn't respond, Dorothy carried on. "I've never married. I know a lot of us girls do, you know, give it a try. Funny, though, because I can't picture you that way."

"The move to Hanover will be wonderful for you," Lucybelle said to change the subject. "You'll be so much closer to Geneviève."

Dorothy took a short breath. "Accent grave over the third e."

Lucybelle laughed. She knew exactly what Dorothy was referring to. Anytime someone asked her name, the Vassar scholar said, "Geneviève, four *e*'s, accent grave over the third one."

"I don't mean to make fun of her," Dorothy said, waving her hand in the air as if to erase the comment. "It's just my insecurity. She's so . . . fine-tuned . . . particular. I'm afraid I'm too unbuttoned for her."

"Opposites attract." Such hooey, but she wanted to smooth this conversation along.

"I hope so. I think I love her, all four *e*'s, even the one with an accent grave."

Lucybelle laughed again.

"The thing is, I'm going to have to move my mother too, and I don't even know if that's possible." Hail tapped at the one office windowpane. They both looked out at the hard balls of ice slanting down from the sky. "Good thing the weather held off for the game," Dorothy said, and then, "I think Geneviève likes that I have my mother in tow. She talks about her more than I do. It's a good cover."

"That's lovely to have a girl who cares about your mother."

"That's not what I'm saying."

Lucybelle knew what she was saying.

"I think she wants there to be obstacles between us."

"No one's perfect." Yet another banal comment. Dorothy stared at her with those clear, green eyes, waiting for her to say something more meaningful. The best she could muster was, "You know what I mean. There're problems with every relationship."

Dorothy sat up straighter without taking her eyes off of Lucybelle. She appeared to be considering her words carefully. "The move will be good for you too."

Lucybelle dreaded the idea of relocating to New Hampshire.

"You know," Dorothy said. "To get away from that girl." She scooted to the edge of her chair, excited to have broached the subject. "The colored girl."

"Her name is Stella."

"Her name is Trouble."

Lucybelle found her purse under the desk. She stood and reached for her coat on the hook.

"Oh, don't look so thunderstruck. I've seen you with her. You haven't exactly been discreet. The only reason I bring it up is because I'm worried about you."

She hadn't seen Stella in months, but it wasn't any of Dorothy's business.

"You have a classified position with the Army Corps of Engineers. You can't afford to play around with people like her."

"People like her?"

"She might be a perfectly nice girl. But look at her. She doesn't play by the rules. You need to."

"I need to get home."

"Come on." Dorothy waved her hand toward the office door. "Drinks."

"Thanks, but no."

"Now you're mad," Dorothy said as they stepped out into the light drizzle that had replaced the hail. "Don't be. Look, the move to Hanover is an easy solution to your difficulty. In a few months, you'll be out of her reach."

"I don't have a difficulty."

"I'm just trying to help. Get in." She motioned toward her car at the curb. "I'll run you home."

"It's out of your way. I like taking the train." Lucybelle knew that walking through the cold rain to the station, refusing a ride, was tantamount to admitting guilt. To what, though?

"You *are* mad. Come on. Life is too short."

Lucybelle made herself smile and say, "Of course I'm not mad. I appreciate your concern. I really do. But everything is fine." Then she made herself get in Dorothy's car, accept the ride home. Thankfully her friend didn't use the opportunity to insist on the drink.

That night she turned on the radio and learned that the Los Angeles Dodgers had won the game, nine to three, taking the World Series.

"Well," Lucybelle said to L'Forte. "There you go. That's that."

## Thursday, July 14, 1960

In the middle of July, Lucybelle received a letter from her brother, John Perry, describing a backpacking trip his family had taken in Oregon's Mount Jefferson Wilderness. One morning, as the group of friends, with all their children, was getting ready to start the day's hike, someone noticed that three-and-a-half-year-old Lucy was missing. The women stayed in camp with the little ones, and the older children joined the men in the search. The child was found in a nearby ice cave, deep in the melted out cavern, sitting on some wet stones, smiling.

"Smiling," John Perry wrote. "Apparently happy to be alone. To be encased in ice. Fearless. Maybe just witless."

The picture of Lucy Jane's brave and maybe witless smile cheered her. She laughed out loud at the juxtaposition: a little girl sitting on wet stones in the translucent light of an ice cave, smiling; the army of men under the glacier at Camp Century, grinding away at their endeavors.

Lucybelle went out that weekend and finally bought her car, a brand new Chevrolet Bel Air two-door sedan, the model Stella had recommended for her. The light-blue paint was like summer itself, the elegant chrome trim announced clarity of purpose, and the arched tail fins said see you later. She drove fast, L'Forte riding shotgun, up and down the western shore of the lake, enjoying the relief of speed and air.

## Sunday, August 14, 1960

A few days before her birthday, Lucybelle packed a swimsuit and L'Forte's dish, and they drove north along the lake, looking for new beaches. While she swam, he ran back and forth on the edge of the water, ears flying, eyebrows knit, barking for her to come out. She called for him to join her, but he'd have none of it. On Saturday night, Lucybelle found a diner, where she ate a dinner of steak, baked potato, and cherry pie, saving generous portions for L'Forte, which she fed him in their Holiday Inn room. They drove home on Sunday.

As she carried her bag, the wet swimsuit soaking through the canvas, toward the stairwell leading to her front door, a voice called out, "Finally! Where have you been? On some romantic escapade, no doubt."

The musical laugh echoed down the stony shaft of the stairwell.

L'Forte barked at the familiar voice.

The sight of Phyllis and little Georgia sitting with their backs against her front door rendered Lucybelle speechless.

"We've been here since midday yesterday. Don't worry. I made friends with the people across the hall. Their basset hound almost bit Georgia, but I made nice. The lady gave us some snacks and didn't call the cops about us sleeping on your doorstep, though she threatened. I told her that I'm your sister. It looks a bit seedy, sorry, but not as seedy as it could look. If I'd told them the truth, that is." She deployed more of that musical laughter.

185

Lucybelle had all but forgotten the way it cascaded in tone from high to low. L'Forte kept barking.

She hadn't seen Phyllis since she'd walked out of their 12th Street apartment four years ago. Lucybelle stood halfway up the stairwell, the wet canvas of her bag soaking into her blouse and shorts, dumbstruck.

"Sweetie," Phyllis said to the little girl. "Meet your Aunt Lucy. It's her birthday in two days. Tell her happy birthday."

Lucybelle finished the climb and unlocked her door. Phyllis dragged Georgia inside by the hand. "We're broke and I've left Fred. There, that's out." She didn't stop in the front room but kept walking through the apartment, popping her head in the kitchen, Lucybelle's bedroom, and the typewriter room. "Look, you have a spare room."

"That's where I work."

"I thought you had a job in a lab."

"I'm working on my novel."

"That's wonderful!" Phyllis let out a long breath as if much had been decided. "Can we have cocktails?"

She looked bad. Maybe it was just her unwashed hair and the wear of travel—they must have come by train—but she looked weary beyond her years, and the travel couldn't account for the weight gain.

"I thought you quit drinking."

"Sure, for as long as I was nursing Georgia. Okay, maybe I laid off for a while longer than that, but I haven't gotten any more parts since *Angel*, and so . . . why bother?"

"Georgia needs her mother."

"Georgia needs her mother to be relaxed."

Lucybelle took off her glasses, as if she could blur this new development into something more acceptable. Actually, it was her response to the development that was problematic, and she could see that even now, in these very first moments. She rubbed the bridge of her nose, wanting to feel outrage and clarity. She searched for a strong sense of resolve, but instead felt a simple slump of happiness at seeing her old friend, at the lovely comfort of predictability, at the possibility of an episode that didn't require restraint and discipline.

"We won't stay long," Phyllis said. "We just need a place to roost for a few days. Until I gather my wits. Anyway, you obviously have another place to roost yourself."

"I just went away for a little weekend. By myself."

"Right. By yourself. I don't believe that for a second. Do you, Georgia? Look, I'm a fat mother now, soon to be a divorcée. You can tell me all there is to tell. I take my titillation where I can get it these days."

Lucybelle filled the silver shaker with ice and added a healthy splash of vermouth. She shook hard, making a sloshy ice-cube music, and then poured off all the liquid so that the ice cubes were just coated in the vermouth. She knew exactly how Phyllis liked her martinis, with miniature ice floes on the top, and so she shook the gin for an extra long time before pouring it into two martini glasses. She speared an olive each on two toothpicks and dropped them in the glasses. She poured some orange juice for Georgia and split an orange slice to fit over the edge of the tumbler. The poor child fell asleep before taking even a sip, her legs curled tight and her head in her mother's lap on the couch. Lucybelle took the wingback chair.

She told Phyllis the entire story of Stella Robinson, including the Michigan Avenue Bridge, the nude photographs, the baseball games, even, with a bit of prodding, the soul-shattering sex. Phyllis loved all the details, begged for more, and Lucybelle loved telling them. The confession was cathartic.

Phyllis told her the slim story of Fred Higgins. Not surprisingly, he spent most nights out with boyfriends, and once Georgia had been born, he couldn't bear to sleep at home. She'd been a colicky baby and her crying, he said, was more than he could take. He was an artist and needed to keep what he called the "plane of his psyche" as free from interference as possible. Phyllis embellished the details for Lucybelle's entertainment, and she hadn't laughed so hard in months.

"Those pictures, sweetie," Phyllis said. "You need to get them back."

Lucybelle shook her head. "It doesn't matter."

"There's that fatalistic part of you. It's sexy. No, it is. But I won't let you succumb to it. Listen to me. No, Lucy, *look* at me. Wanda might never use them, but do you really want that axe hanging over your head? No, you don't. And what if she *does* use them?"

Phyllis wouldn't understand the real reason she hadn't demanded that Stella hand over all the photographs, plus the negatives. For Phyllis, everything was illusory. Perceptions and feelings were created, manufactured for effect. All of life, if you were honest about it, Phyllis contended, was theater. Lucybelle had once loved this about her, as if the cynicism, her

187

insistence that nothing authentic existed, were a deeper understanding of human nature.

But she was wrong. The pictures were a raw and naked revelation of Lucybelle. They literally captured her. More, they held Stella's view of her as beautiful. Asking for them back would be like rescinding that afternoon, their short time together, everything. She wouldn't do it.

"Don't underestimate Wanda," Phyllis said knocking back the last of her third martini. "Anything could retrigger her ire. Those photographs could show up on your boss's desk. Don't smile. You think this is funny?"

"I like to think of them showing up in someone's attic a hundred years from now. I picture some girl finding them and wondering about their story."

"Stop it," Phyllis said. She did look old. Worry lines creased the skin between her eyebrows. "Stop that dreamy stuff. You need to watch out for yourself."

Lucybelle nodded at the child asleep in Phyllis's lap. "*You* giving *me* advice."

Phyllis sighed, petted her daughter's curls, and said, "I still love you, you know."

"Baloney. Now *you* stop it."

"No. I won't stop it. I'm not trying any funny stuff. Nothing like that. Fat old me? I'm quite happy with celibacy, seriously. I'm just saying that I admire you so much, the way you've always stayed above the fray."

"Celibate? Give me a break. You seemed to enjoy hearing the details of my sex life."

"Exactly. *Hearing* the details. I love a good story. But I've got Georgia now, and it's all I can do to keep my own loose ends tied up. But you know what? When you and I were together, those were the very best years. We helped each other, didn't we? It was like a real partnership. I miss you."

"I have to go to work tomorrow. I'll get sheets and pillows for you and Georgia. You can sleep in the typewriter room if you want, but there's only the floor. The couch might be comfier."

Lucybelle crawled into her own bed and then lay awake for hours, not worrying about her new houseguests, as she should have been doing, but instead about the photographs. Her choice—to ask for the prints and negatives back or not—was existentially impossible. She either erased herself, burned the evidence, let fear rot her from the inside out; or she risked exposure of her most precious possession, her fully eroticized authenticity, the documentation of her love. Which, if exposed, could erase her anyway.

## Friday, November 11, 1960

"It's like having a wife," Lucybelle said. "She picks up my dry cleaning, makes dinner, even cleans the bathroom, which I have to say, I'd have never expected from Phyllis."

Beverly exaggerated her scowl, making sure Lucybelle didn't miss it.

"When will we have the opportunity to meet her?" Ruthie asked.

"Are you sleeping with her?" Dorothy asked.

"That is none of our business." Beverly practically spit the words. She and Ruthie both looked at the golden-flecked brown carpet as they waited for the answer.

"Of course not. You've asked me that about five times. You know I'm not."

"You can be cryptic at times."

"What are you referring to?" she asked, drilling her gaze into Dorothy's. Dorothy laughed and blew her a kiss.

Ruthie coughed, always the barometer of tension, and Beverly got up to get her a glass of water.

"It's just temporary. Until the alimony and child support checks start coming."

"Don't hold your breath," Dorothy said. "I bet Fred is in Paris by now."

"As if you know Fred," Ruthie said. "You always have opinions about people and situations with which you have absolutely no familiarity."

"Lucy has told us plenty."

"I thought you said Lucy was cryptic."

"Thank you," Lucybelle said, "for pointing out Dorothy's contradictions. Look, Phyllis can be a pain in the neck, but I do have a spare room, and it's temporary." She didn't mention how Phyllis had bought and set up a crib, hung all her dresses in Lucybelle's closet, and made friends with the neighbors, including the Worthingtons, who still thought she was her sister. "And the child is fun."

"Fun," Beverly said. "Which part, the noise or the mess?"

Ruthie arched her eyebrows in agreement rather than scolding Beverly for rudeness.

Lucybelle didn't tell them how she liked coming home to the smell of roasting chicken, a companion for cocktails, and most of all, good hard laughs about everyone from the Worthingtons to these women in the room right now. With Phyllis, she could speak her uncensored mind and it felt ever so good.

Ruthie made a show of girding her loins and said, "I think you should invite her for Thanksgiving."

Beverly shot Ruthie a sharp look.

"Yes!" Dorothy clapped her hands.

"But Geneviève is going to be here," Beverly said, as if the woman herself were a classified document.

"Exactly," Ruthie said. "It'll be a party."

The word party in Ruthie's mouth sounded nearly scandalous.

"The child too?" Beverly feigned—was she feigning?—a look of horror.

"For god's sake, Bev, what are you suggesting? That Phyllis leave the child home alone?"

"There won't be anyone for her to play with."

"We'll take turns," Dorothy said, clearly thrilled at the idea of meeting the actress who'd left Lucybelle for a fey man and then appeared, fat and worn for wear, four years later on her doorstep.

"I don't know," Lucybelle said.

"Yes, you do," Beverly countered, acquiescing as she always did to Ruthie's ideas. "You'll come, all three of you."

And though the idea had been hers, Ruthie now began wheezing in earnest. Beverly couldn't find the inhaler, which brought everyone to their feet, searching, until it was safely planted in Ruthie's mouth.

Dorothy, Lucybelle noticed, suppressed a grin through the whole episode.


## Thanksgiving Day 1960

Dorothy gasped at the sight of Phyllis and then tried to pretend she was choking on a cracker.

"Well, la-dee-da," Beverly said, semiquietly, pretending to be speaking only to Ruthie.

"What an interesting shade of . . . purple." Ruthie spoke the color as if it were morally questionable.

"Lucy told me I was overdressing," Phyllis said, running her hands down the hips of her formfitting knit dress. She kicked out a foot to show her deep purple matching heels. "I was nervous."

"We don't bite!" Dorothy called from the couch. "Come on in."

"I'm sorry we're late," Lucybelle said. Not only had Phyllis spent all morning trying on outfits—ignoring Lucybelle's pleas to just wear a sweater and slacks like everyone else would be doing—she'd decided to touch up her hair. The truth was, she looked stunning, her black hair soft and glossy, the gray of her eyes velvety, and her cheek color high. She'd reached deeply into her bag of theatrical tricks and transformed herself from old, disappointed, and fat to elegant, fateful, and voluptuous. She'd decked out Georgia, as well, in a white dress covered with little pink roses, puffed short sleeves, and white lace trim.

"Would you like a drink?" Ruthie asked.

"Would I!"

Dorothy pulled Georgia by the hand over to the breakfront to show her Ruthie's collection of porcelain figurines. The three-year-old squealed with delight.

"No touching," Beverly said. "Those are Hummels."

Georgia reached up and smudged the glass with already sticky fingertips. Dorothy bent and whispered something to the child, and the two of them laughed together. "Let's tell stories," she said and sat Georgia on her lap on the couch.

"You're a natural," Phyllis said sitting next to Dorothy. She took a generous sip from her cocktail and said, "Mm, good."

"Where's Geneviève?" Lucybelle asked.

"Late, as always," Beverly said.

"I'm glad we weren't the only ones." Phyllis gave Lucybelle an I-told-you-so look.

"Why didn't she come with you?" Lucybelle asked Dorothy.

"She's staying at the motor lodge. It just makes more sense."

Even Beverly rolled her eyes.

Lucybelle couldn't hold her tongue. "You're a few hundred miles from Poughkeepsie."

"She likes privacy. Besides, she has work to do this weekend. She thought she'd be able to get more done if she stayed at the motor lodge."

"She's a delightful woman," Ruthie said to Phyllis. "You're going to love her. So erudite. So cultured."

"I should think so," Phyllis said, "with those four *e*'s, and the third one with an accent grave."

"Phyllis," Lucybelle said.

"I agree entirely," Dorothy said with a brave smile. "Geneviève has a responsibility to live up to all four *e*'s, and especially to the one with an accent grave."

Ruthie coughed.

"Tell us about Broadway," Dorothy said. "Have you met Rita Hayworth? How about Marilyn Monroe?"

"I'm quite sure they're both in Hollywood, not New York." Beverly used her most caustic tone.

A soft but assertive knock brought both Ruthie and Beverly to their feet. The minute Geneviève walked in the door, Lucybelle knew the matchup was going to be rousing. She and Phyllis even looked a bit alike, though on opposite ends of the glamour scale. Geneviève wore not a speck of makeup, a tweed skirt, and a tan blouse. She looked a bit like a raven with her black hair, narrow face, eyes bright and omnivorous. Lucybelle tried not to think of what Dorothy had told her about the professor's sexual appetite.

"I'm so sorry I'm late. I got to working this morning and lost all sense of time. 'The mind is its own place, and in itself / can make a Heav'n of Hell, a Hell of Heav'n.' Milton."

"We've taught her to give us plebeians the sources," Dorothy said. "Milton. The poet."

"Ah!" Phyllis openly assessed the new arrival.

"You're here now," Beverly said, more interested in the schedule than literary references. "Drink?"

"I'd love another," Phyllis said.

"Did the morning's work go well?" Dorothy asked.

"'Things fall apart; the centre cannot hold.' Yeats."

"My center holds just fine, thank you," Phyllis said.

Lucybelle watched Phyllis working out what role she might play this afternoon and didn't know whether to be relieved that Phyllis was finding a way to amuse herself or worried about the character she would decide to embody.

"So you're the actress," Geneviève said. Even her posture was slanted forward like a raven, and her hands were like delicate claws, the fingers crooked and spread as she spoke. She appeared ready to peck.

"And you're the professor who . . ." Phyllis wore her naughtiest smile, oh she was playing this to the hilt, and if she said, "has a healthy libido," Lucybelle would put her on the street tonight. " . . . speaks in verse."

Rude, but not as bad as it could have been.

"The turkey came out two hours ago," Beverly announced. "It's probably stone cold."

"My goodness," Phyllis said, and Lucybelle knew she was annoyed that there wouldn't be a proper cocktail hour.

"The child!" Ruthie wheezed.

Everyone turned to see Georgia on her tiptoes trying to reach the knobs that opened the glass doors of the breakfront.

"Georgia!" Phyllis cried. "Come away from there."

"I want the little shepherdess," she said, still reaching.

"It's my fault." Dorothy scooped up the little girl. "I showed her the figurines and kindled her interest."

"Why don't we all remove to the dining room," Ruthie said.

Phyllis leaned toward Lucybelle and whispered, "Remove?"

Beverly poured small portions of wine into everyone's glasses while Ruthie carried in the platters of brussels sprouts, sweet potatoes, and the turkey. Beverly carved.

"I want a drumstick!" Georgia said.

"That's a bit much for a little girl, isn't it?" Beverly said.

"Give the child a drumstick, for crying out loud," Dorothy said. "Here honey. There's lots of marshmallow on the sweet potatoes. You'll love 'em. I do."

Georgia smiled adoringly at Dorothy. She then used her fingers to separate the marshmallow from the potatoes and ate the white stuff with her fingers. If Phyllis noticed, she didn't reprimand the child. Nor did she say a word when Georgia used the giant turkey drumstick as an actual drumstick, pounding the table with it and singing out, "*A-rump-a-dump-dump.*" Everyone stared except for Phyllis, who reached for the wine bottle and refilled her glass. Dorothy wrested the meat from Georgia's pudgy grasp.

A horrendous silence, the most protracted one Lucybelle had ever endured in a social setting, ensued. The quiet was broken by the sound of

Phyllis swallowing a healthy drink of wine. Lucybelle wished with all of her heart that she hadn't succumbed to this invitation. The afternoon was well on its way to disaster.

"So," Phyllis broke the awful spell. "The wine is lovely. Thank you so much for including me and Georgia."

Beverly took a deep breath but didn't speak. Ruthie murmured, "But of course."

Lucybelle saw the little hitch of insult cross Phyllis's face, that moment when she decided she owed these boorish people nothing. "Poetry," Phyllis said with an aggressive smile directed at Geneviève. "I'm a Walt Whitman kind of girl, myself. All that grassy sensual stuff. e.e. cummings is nice too. Simple and straightforward. You don't get a headache trying to figure out his meaning."

Phyllis looked around the table. "Did everyone else see that? I think our poetess shuddered at my taste."

Geneviève looked genuinely abashed. She set down her fork with a brussels sprout speared on the end. "I guess I did shudder a bit. I didn't mean to offend. I'm sorry."

Phyllis answered with a delighted laugh. "Not at all. I love your honesty. Thank you. So you like the really old poets. Lucy and I love Shakespeare ourselves. Don't we, hon? 'All the world's a stage, and all the men and women merely players: they have their exits and their entrances; and one man in his time plays many parts, his acts being seven ages.' He nailed that one, didn't he? Please pass the wine."

"Well, la-dee-da."

"Not just the old ones," Geneviève said. "I'm quite fond of Elizabeth Bishop and Edna St. Vincent Millay."

"Ah!"

"They're family, you know," Dorothy said, eyes shining.

"They're *poets*," Geneviève said.

"How about 'a rose is a rose is a rose'?" Phyllis brandished her wineglass in mock professorship.

"I loathe Gertrude Stein." Geneviève's narrow face and long nose looked fierce with her dislike. The intensity was rather appealing.

"Ha!" Phyllis cried out, smiling quite sincerely at Geneviève. She raised her wineglass. "I shan't mention her name again. To Milton, Yeats, Shakespeare, Bishop, and Millay!"

With that Phyllis launched a refined and subtle flirtation with Geneviève, using impeccable timing with eye contact and body language to reel in her target. Geneviève appeared to understand the game instantly, in all its complexity, and resisted with equal skill, but also obvious enjoyment. The two of them orbited one another in mock derision, working and sweetening the tension. The flirtation was so surprising, and carried out with such reserve, that it seemed harmless, while still providing a much-needed structure to the afternoon. For a couple of hours, everyone had fun.

Then, perhaps feeling threatened, Dorothy asked Phyllis a question to which they all already knew the answer. "So are you involved with anyone?"

"That's none of our business," Beverly said.

"I have no secrets. My marriage has ended. I'm just trying to make ends meet and take care of my little girl."

Ruthie nodded approvingly.

That might have been that, but Geneviève threw out some more Yeats. "'Too long a sacrifice / Can make a stone of the heart.'"

"Yeah, well," Phyllis said. "'Human kind / Cannot bear very much reality.'"

That got the biggest smile Lucybelle had ever seen on Geneviève's face. The professor had long since deduced that Phyllis wasn't as unschooled as she pretended, but that she could quote Eliot won her big points. Geneviève's radiant delight reminded Lucybelle of her secondhand knowledge of the professor's sex drive.

"And yet," Geneviève shot back, "'Earth's the right place for love.'"

Phyllis laughed and clapped her hands. "I give up. You win. Who?"

"Just Frost."

"*Just* Frost," Lucybelle said, rolling her eyes.

"Let me ask you a question." Phyllis reached a hand across the table to gently tap Geneviève's wrist. "Why all the poetry? I mean, in place of just talking?"

"'Life in itself / Is nothing, / An empty cup, a flight of uncarpeted stairs. / It is not enough that yearly, down this hill / April / Comes like an idiot, babbling and strewing flowers.'" She turned to Dorothy and said, "Millay."

"Babbling," Phyllis said. "You've got a point."

The scream sounded a second before the crash. Then the ragged tinkle of breaking glass, followed by splitting wood. All five women ran into the living room, where the breakfront had fallen forward and broken across the chair placed in front of it. Georgia lay on the floor, next to the chair, covered in shards of glass, now screaming in earnest. The chair had kept the piece of furniture from falling directly onto her. Most of the porcelain figurines were spilled across the floor.

"Darling!" Phyllis crouched next to Georgia and began picking the glass out of her curls, off her dress and tights, keening, "Oh my god oh my god oh my god."

"She's fine. Just scared." Lucybelle lifted Georgia to her feet and helped check her for cuts.

"She must have pulled the chair over on her own," Dorothy said. "To get to the figurines. I'm so sorry. It's my fault."

Ruthie clasped a hand at her throat, rasping for air.

"It most certainly is *not* your fault. This is the most undisciplined child I've ever met." Beverly's mouth pruned tight and a hot red flushed up her chest and neck, highlighting the pocks on her face.

"For Christ's sake," Phyllis nearly shouted. "I can't believe you don't have that thing secured to the wall."

Ruthie dropped into the big leather chair, hunched over, coughing.

"Where's her inhaler?" Lucybelle asked.

Ruthie gasped, her throat making high choking sounds, as if she couldn't get any oxygen at all.

"Too late," Beverly said. She yanked their coats out of the closet, threaded Ruthie's arms into hers, and moved her out the door.

Georgia's chubby legs were wrapped around her mother's waist, her face pressed into her neck, and she was still sobbing. Phyllis sat on the couch and soothed her daughter while the others righted the smashed breakfront and picked up the figurines.

"Only a few are broken," Dorothy said.

"The breakfront, though."

"We'll pay for it all," Lucybelle said.

"Why don't the three of you go on home. Geneviève and I'll wait for them to get back from the hospital."

"I don't want to leave you . . ."

"Please," Dorothy said, and Lucybelle nodded. The sooner she cleared Phyllis and Georgia out of there, the better. She retrieved their coats, handed Phyllis hers, and gave her a little shove toward the door.

But Phyllis circled back into the room and kissed Geneviève on the cheek. "'Hell is empty and all the devils are here.'" She winked at Dorothy and said, "Shakespeare."

Dorothy said, "Would you just leave?"

Phyllis drew herself up, as if she were about to deliver a soliloquy, lifted her chin, tilted her head, and like magic, made herself gorgeous. "It was so nice to meet you at last. Good night."

"It's five in the afternoon," Dorothy said.

Lucybelle lifted Georgia and pushed Phyllis out the door.

"That went well," Phyllis said climbing into the front seat of the Bel Air and settling Georgia in her lap. "I like the professor. Vassar, you say?"

## Friday, March 17, 1961

When Lucybelle got home from work, she found two green leprechaun hats, each with a black hatband, on the floor of the front room. One of the hats was smashed in, as if someone had stomped on it. The doors to both her typewriter room and her bedroom were closed. She quietly opened the typewriter room door and found Georgia sound asleep in her crib. She shut the door again and stood in the living room, listening.

She heard hissing whispers. The sound of a belt buckle clanging to the floor. Legs sliding into the fabric of trousers. The bedcovers getting yanked and smoothed.

Phyllis emerged first. "You're home early." Then, as if the bedroom door were a stage curtain, she threw it open and said, "This is Tom."

A man stepped forward still buttoning his shirt, his suit jacket tucked under his arm. "Good day," he said.

"Out." Lucybelle jerked her head toward the front door.

"Who's the bitch?" the man asked.

"Tom!" Phyllis said. "How dare you speak to my sister like that." Though she hadn't attempted any steps, she stumbled anyway and fell against the doorjamb.

"Where's your purse?" Lucybelle asked. "Do you have your purse?"

"How dare you imply that I'm a thief," the man said.

"My purse . . ." Phyllis gestured at the couch and Lucybelle quickly located her wallet within.

Then she said, "Get out of my apartment."

"It's her apartment too. She invited me. You can't make me leave."

"Actually," Phyllis slurred. She slumped to the floor and purposely banged her head against the doorjamb. "It's hers. Not mine."

"Suit yourselves. I'm done here."

Lucybelle locked the door behind Tom and then turned on Phyllis. She felt such disgust that she couldn't even speak directly to her. She went to the kitchen and drank two big glasses of water, as if she could wash the scene from her system, and then went back into the living room. "I'm taking Georgia to the movies. You'll clean yourself up. Change my sheets. When you're sober, we'll talk about where you're going."

## Friday, May 26, 1961

"Luceee! You've got some 'splainin' to do."

She took her time moseying into Bader's office. "The Ricky Ricardo thing is old. I thought you'd dropped it."

"Have a drink with me."

"I can't." She'd promised to have drinks with the girls tonight. They'd all been civil with one another but had avoided socializing since Thanksgiving. Lucybelle was glad for the opportunity to make friendly amends. Still, when Ruthie poked her head in her office this morning and said, "I don't think I need to say it, but *sans* Phyllis, okay?" it had angered her. As if Beverly and Ruthie's rigid lifestyle or Dorothy's poetry-spewing companion and bedridden mother were all that more palatable than her shipwrecked ex with child. God knew what they'd say if she told them about the Tom episode. Obviously she needed to find a solution to the problem, but she couldn't exactly put a woman with a young child on the street.

"Yes, you can," Bader said. "It's an order."

"I'll try. Where're you meeting?" The truth was, she'd love a jolly night out with the scientists.

"Here. Now." Bader pulled a bottle of whiskey and two tumblers from his bottom drawer, poured a couple of fingers into each. He pushed hers across the desk. She didn't like whiskey and liked even less what the early afternoon drink portended.

"Look," he said. "I'm not going to New Hampshire." Bader feigned a shudder, as if the mere mention of the rural state gave him anxiety tremors.

She nodded. She'd heard. The new management was even less interested in Bader's ice cores than the previous one. He'd become increasingly outspoken about his impatience with the military uses of his work, the disproportionate piece of the pie that went to preparing for the Russians. He loved joking about Daley's air-raid sirens after the White Sox pennant win, how so many Chicagoans thought the Russians had attacked. He made fun of these fears, right in the faces of the top brass, and the result was that his passion about climate research was losing, rather than gaining, ground in his employer's imagination. "There's a difference," she'd heard the new director say, right out loud, standing in the foyer, in front of Beverly and Ruthie's desks, "between science and obsession. If a scientist crosses the line from dispassionate observer to advocating ideologue, then he is no longer a scientist."

Lucybelle was relieved that he'd brought up the topic of his departure. She scooted to the edge of her chair, took a swig of the whiskey, and said, "I've been meaning to talk to you."

He held up a hand to quiet her. "I've convinced them to keep me on contract."

This was news.

"Despite their inability to recognize the importance of our work, they've poured far too much money into it to let it go now. So I'll be up to Hanover now and then. But I simply can't live in the boondocks."

That he wasn't actually leaving the work, the ice cores, wavered her own decision. But she braced herself against her resolve. "I fully understand. Neither can I."

"To the contrary. I think you can. You were raised in the boondocks."

"Exactly. I'm not going back."

He started as he caught her meaning. He stood up, planted his hands on the desk, and leaned toward her, anger darkening his eyes. "I need you to stay with the lab. I need you to go to Hanover."

"I've made my decision. I'm sorry."

He sat again and ran his fingers through his goatee. He kept his eyes on her as he calmed himself, calculated. "I think it'd be the best move for you. I have some motivators too. Some deal sweeteners."

"Why do you care? You're not going." She'd given this so much thought. Moving to Chicago, or at least a short train ride from Chicago, was one thing. Rural New England was quite another. Without Bader, without the fuel of his passion for the ice cores, there was nothing holding her to this job. His leaving had made her decision to leave a lot easier.

"That's why I need you to go. Some consistency. Someone I can count on. Management is going haywire. It changes every five minutes. I can't talk to those guys. My ice cores . . ." He closed his eyes, and if she didn't know him so well, she'd think he was praying.

She reached for her boldest voice and said, "I want to have a life."

He waved a hand through the air: a life, how trifling. As if she were a petulant child asking for a cookie. "I need you in Hanover. I need you to keep an eye on the ice cores, and on everything else. These fools will use Camp Century to launch a missile at Russia, if you let them."

"I'm a science editor. I can hardly prevent that."

Bader threw back his drink and poured another, topping off Lucybelle's too. "Yes, you can prevent that. You know I hate handing out compliments. I expect ace work every single moment you're in my department. But the fact of the matter is, you're the best editor I've ever worked with. You actually manage to convince those fools of things they don't even know they're being convinced of. You, your reports and funding proposals, make them value what we're doing. I cannot afford to lose that. I just can't. We're this close"—he held up his thumb and forefinger, leaving a space of one centimeter between them—"from getting the technology we need to reach bedrock. Saving us from whatever the Russians want to do tomorrow is nothing compared to the information we'll get about this planet, saving *all* of us.

"I'm a terrible advocate for my own goals. I know that. I just piss everyone off. But you're quiet and steady and brilliant. Words, Lucy, your words: that's what is going to convince them to keep their eyes on the prize. The real prize."

He might be a bona fide megalomaniac. His work, her words, saving the planet, mankind. She opened her mouth to say as much, but he interrupted.

"You don't know men, sugar. They love pushing buttons. They love explosions. But what if we could distract them with the story the ice cores tell? What if we convinced them that the knowledge we'll gain from our work is more important to our survival than any weapons can ever be?"

"The ice cores," Lucybelle said, "will tell us the history of the planet's climate. They won't stop the Russians or our government from launching anything."

Bader shook his head. "Nice. A very succinct statement of how everyone else views me: hyperbolic, outsized ego, crazy. But not you, sugar. You can pretend you don't understand, but you do. I see it in your eyes, in the way you're holding your mouth this very moment, tight as if you don't want my medicine. But you do want my medicine. You know it's the truth. You're fighting me because it's a monster responsibility, what we're doing, convincing the world of its importance. *Vital*"—he pounded the desktop with his fist—"importance. Who the hell wants to move to Hanover? I understand. You think I don't, but I do. Of course I do. All I'm asking is that you give it a year or two. Until we get the cores."

"If it's so vital, why aren't you going?"

"I would. Actually, I would. Despite my loathing of small-town America. But the truth of the matter is, I've not been 'invited.' On contract is the only way they'll allow me to continue my work. God knows I'd endure even Hanover, if I had to, if it would help me get to bedrock. Don't you see? This is why I need you there."

For all his bravado, he drooped for a moment, done in by his own exuberance. He sat with his rumpled shirt and uncombed thick, black hair, staring at her, waiting for her to acquiesce. His chin may have even briefly trembled.

But of course while Lucybelle was softening, while she considered his rare flash of vulnerability, he used the pause to reload.

He straightened his spine and asked, "Have you heard of a woman named Rachel Carson?"

"Of course."

"She's working on an extraordinary new book about the ways that man is poisoning the planet. The planet *today*. Our work is like the control study for hers. The ice cores will be the first ever pure evidence of what exactly the atmosphere was like, a hundred, two hundred, a thousand years ago. I need you to interpret this evidence. I need you to be on the team with me and Rachel Carson."

She laughed at his reach. "Rachel Carson is not on your team."

"*Our* team." He knew Lucybelle well enough to know that Carson's name, her brilliance and passion, would be a powerful magnet.

She took a swallow of the whiskey. It burned going down her throat. She'd seen photographs of Rachel Carson. The writer was as slim and as plain as she was. But dogged. Those serious sad eyes on the future, that patient persistence. The only difference between Carson and Bader was their contrasting prim and indecorous demeanors.

Bader saw his opening and smiled. "Do you care about the ice cores?"

She practically felt the hemp of the net falling loosely over her head and shoulders.

"Do you?"

"You know I do." She looked at her watch, as if the schedule of one day could save her.

"We've got all afternoon," he said. "Relax."

"I hate men who tell me to relax."

"You hate *when* men tell you to relax. You don't hate the men who do it, because I just did and you rather like me." He smiled again.

"I've got work to do." She stood up. No one could force her to keep a job, to move anywhere at all. She had a right to—

"Were you really dating a communist sapphist?"

"Now you're threatening me?"

"Answer the question."

"I thought you said socialist."

"Answer the question."

"You forget. I'm a grief-struck widow."

"Admit it: going to New Hampshire could solve a few of your problems."

"I don't have any secrets."

He raised his eyebrows. "I didn't say 'secrets.' I said 'problems.'"

"Are you finished?"

"Here's the deal. You move to Hanover, we up your pay grade. I've already gotten this approved. You get two assistants. And—" He held up a finger and grinned. "Here's the part you're going to like. You're to learn Russian, on paid time."

"Russian! In preparation for my transfer to Siberia?"

The wolf smile. "If you're good, we'll keep you stateside. I've already engaged a tutor. His name is Boris."

"His name is not Boris."

"It is."

They both laughed.

"It's an easy language. You'll pick it right up."

"Why?"

"Because I won't be up there and they need someone to read the studies the Russians are publishing. I've convinced them that you're the perfect choice. Anyway, it'll clear your record."

"I don't have a record."

"Really? You forget the letters."

"Letters, plural?"

He nodded.

"From the goon."

"Yes. Him." He continued on as cheerfully as if they were discussing breakfast cereal. "If you're learning Russian, you'll look like a spy. For us, not them."

"I'm sorry. But I'm staying in Chicago."

"You're forcing me to play hardball."

"Why can't you understand the word no?"

"I'll just say two names. Stella Robinson. Phyllis Dove."

Her brain cells did the jitterbug. He was going for a psychological lobotomy.

Bader leaned back in his chair and shrugged. "I think I can help you."

"You're trying to blackmail me."

"I wouldn't call it blackmail. Maybe adding a bit of incentive to the deal, but seriously, this is as much for you as it is for me. You don't need that drunken actress in your apartment. As for the taxicab driver, she's already got a girlfriend."

"Who *are* the goons feeding you this garbage?"

"Garbage? That's what you call your life?"

"Go to hell."

He shook his head. "Lashing out at me is pointless. You're the one who's made a mess of your life. Take the job. At least until you have a clear idea about your next move."

"You mean at least until we reach bedrock."

"Exactly. I like how you track."


## Saturday, May 27, 1961

Lucybelle skipped drinks with the girls and went straight home after her little tête-à-tête with Bader. Phyllis and Georgia were out, and if this were like other Friday nights, they'd be gone for hours, if not a couple of days. Lucybelle sat down at her typewriter and began writing.

She wrote against the goons, to keep their tentacles from reaching inside her, to ward off the killer paranoia. They thought they knew her story. She wrote against *Whisper Their Love* and *Odd Girl Out* too. Those books didn't describe her world. She wanted to write a story that did.

The stupid informant didn't seem to even know that she hadn't seen Stella in well over a year. Ironically, his outdated intelligence brought back the heartache. Lucybelle missed Stella. She missed having a companion who wasn't afraid, who explored her own mind and aesthetic, who understood the complexity of lust.

By four thirty in the morning, Lucybelle had written what might be the first chapter of her novel. L'Forte sat on his short haunches, next to her feet, crying. She hadn't taken him out all night. She stood up, stiff and exhausted, but deeply satisfied.

She and her dog walked in the dark to the lake. A cool breeze blew off the water. She stood on the shore, watching the dim morning light begin to polish the surface of the lake, and smiled thinking of Bader's hard sell. A life of the mind meant writing her novel. It meant seeing the ice cores through, all the way down to bedrock. Those translucent columns would be like lenses, ones that looked deep into our history, and just as Bader had said, help humanity see its future.

A thin bright line formed on the water's horizon, a crack to something brilliant and lovely. It looked as though, if only she had a boat, she could sail right through it, arrive in that place of new light.

Part Three

**Hanover, New Hampshire, 1961–66**

## July–September 1961

There were black crows everywhere, but not the dusty ones like back home. These were sleeker, glossier, fatter. Perhaps they had more to eat in this verdant landscape. They slitted their eyes at her wherever she went, as if to say, we know you. You can leave the farm, dabble in New York and Chicago, but we will always be watching you, claiming you.

Lucybelle tried to let the roar of quiet support rather than unhinge her. After all, Willa Cather had kept a writing haven in New Hampshire, an attic in a hotel to which she retreated whenever she needed to get work done, and this consonance inspired Lucybelle. Every day she came home from work and wrote. She wrote all weekend too. She wrote with an intense focus, zipping page after page out from the top of her typewriter. She'd had no idea it would feel like this, the profound relief in telling a true story. Each page felt like tossing a stone of ballast from her soul. She became lighter and lighter. It didn't even matter what happened with the fat stack of paper or whether the sentences and paragraphs were any good. They weren't, they most decidedly were not any good at all; they were clumsy, unwieldy, purple, and tepid, all at once. Yet this growing pile of paper illuminated everything.

Lucybelle had come to Hanover with the front guard, a handful of employees sent to be the liaison between the old lab and the new one, which was far from completed. There was a great deal of hostility toward the new residents in town, based on rumors that the new lab would be a military target, or that it would accidentally blow up, leveling everything in sight, or that they were making atomic bombs rather than studying ice. The displaced scientists and staff did their best to dispel the rumors, but everyone from the bagger at the grocery store to the clerk at the dry cleaners treated them with brisk animus. This friction was unpleasant, but she braced against it and used the products of loneliness—time and clarity—to write her novel.

In September, she and L'Forte drove back to Chicago to help Dorothy make the move. With Mrs. Shipwright in a makeshift bed in the backseat and L'Forte settled on his blanket on the floor beneath her, they drove the thousand miles straight through, taking turns at the wheel, stopping only to walk L'Forte and to change Mrs. Shipwright's diaper and give her spoonfuls of the baby food Dorothy brought for easy nutrition. The two women in the front seat ate roast beef sandwiches and apples and drank thermoses of coffee. When they were both awake, Dorothy read pages from Lucybelle's novel out loud. Lucybelle cringed and shouted, "No!" at all the bad sentences, but Dorothy insisted that it was a beautiful piece of writing and a gripping story.

Lucybelle knew it was neither beautiful nor gripping. She knew it would require many more drafts to make it a passable novel. But the experience of someone reading the story, coupled with Dorothy's kind enthusiasm, was alarmingly gratifying. She could see perfectly well that her fondness for Dorothy increased in direct proportion to her friend's compliments, and yet she couldn't help letting herself bask in them. The pleasure in having her novel appreciated gave her a nearly erotic charge, and there they were, encased in the steel of her blue Bel Air, driving the highways of America, a demented woman in the backseat, and an aging dachshund on the floor. They laughed a lot and even sang songs Daddy used to have the family sing on road trips, like "Red River Valley" and "If You're Happy and You Know It."

"I'm very happy," Dorothy said somewhere in upstate New York.

"I know you are," Lucybelle said. "Geneviève is a treasure."

Dorothy laughed and Lucybelle knew why: she never used words like "treasure" and using it only suggested a falseness to her statement. Lucybelle added, as if a patch were needed, "You love her."

"I do," Dorothy said carefully. "I actually do. She's so . . . what's the word? Concentrated. Intense. In good ways. It scares me a little. I wish she'd loosen up. But I do love her."

"She might loosen up with time. And you'll be so much closer now."

"But that isn't what I was talking about when I said I was very happy. Right now."

Lucybelle knew it wasn't what she'd been talking about. She too was very happy. Right now. She loved the smell and feel of the hot tarred pavement under the rubber of her spinning tires, the autumn air blowing in the car windows, her novel in the seat between them, helping her friend do something she thought impossible, move her mother, while her friend in turn helped her to do something *she* thought impossible, write a novel.

By the time they arrived in Hanover early in the morning, their eyeballs felt like sandpaper and their stomachs like cement mixers. Mrs. Shipwright was limp and breathing shallowly as they carried her into the furnished apartment Lucybelle had found for Dorothy. They laid her on the bed, stood and looked at her for a long moment, and then walked back out to the street.

Dorothy kissed her cheek. "What would I do without you?"

"We made it."

Dorothy nodded and didn't look away.

Lucybelle laughed, though no one had said anything funny. "Poor L'Forte. I'm getting him home to his proper bed."

"Thank you," Dorothy said, loading up the words too much.

"It was so much fun," Lucybelle answered, trying to unpack the load.

At home Lucybelle put a fresh sheet of paper into her typewriter. Hearing parts of her novel out loud gave her ideas. She didn't want to lose them. She wrote until suppertime, and then after a meal of canned mushroom soup, she allowed L'Forte under the covers with her. They both slept hard for nearly twelve hours.

The ringing telephone woke her at six o'clock the next morning. Mrs. Shipwright hadn't lived through the night.

## Friday, October 20, 1961

"It was not your fault." Beverly nearly growled at Dorothy.

Lucybelle felt as if it was her own fault. She'd convinced Dorothy that Mrs. Shipwright could make the trip.

"Honey." Ruthie spoke much more softly than Beverly had. "Listen to me. She was close to death. Did we hasten it by a day or two? Perhaps."

"Or months," Dorothy said, the tears rising yet again.

"Her life was hell," Beverly said. "She didn't know where she was or even who you were half the time. She lay in bed all day, with bed sores and who knows what other pains."

"Honey," Ruthie said again. "I know you're grieving. Time will heal. But do please hear me out on this. You were a devoted daughter. You cared for your mother until the end. Also—" Ruthie held up a hand and put on her strict voice. "You have a simply wonderful companion. Moving here, so you can be closer to her, was absolutely the right thing to do. You have your entire life ahead of you. Now Geneviève is a mere 250 miles away. I couldn't dream of a better situation for you."

Dorothy blew her nose.

"Ruthie is right."

"What I don't understand is why I can't just move to Poughkeepsie. I'm sure I could get a job in the college library."

Beverly and Ruthie exchanged a look.

"What?" Dorothy asked. "We wouldn't need to live together. I'm not suggesting we make an announcement. It just would be a heck of a lot easier than a four-hour drive. Why not?"

"Geneviève has a very good job. As do you."

Lucybelle sighed and kept her mouth shut. She wondered when she could go home and get back to work on her novel. Beverly and Ruthie's Hanover apartment was oddly similar to their Evanston one. Maybe it was just that they'd moved the tan-and-orange plaid couch, the golden-flecked brown rug, the copper-legged walnut coffee table, the leather armchair and ottoman, and of course the repaired breakfront. They'd somehow managed to arrange the furniture in the exact same configuration too. At least this apartment had nice, big windows. Lucybelle looked out at the brilliant yellow foliage, the tree trunks creamy white, the sky a hard blue. She stood and walked to the window, where she could feel the bracing cold seeping through the glass. Maybe she could claim a headache.

"Geneviève is quite late." Beverly looked at her watch.

"She's always late."

"Like I said, it's a four-hour drive."

The telephone rang and Ruthie went to the kitchen to answer it. "Where are you? Are you all right? Yes, of course. Hold on. I'll get her. See you soon."

They all listened as Dorothy answered the telephone, her voice full of enthusiasm. They kept listening even though Dorothy, just out of sight around the corner of the kitchen, didn't speak again. Beverly made a face at Ruthie and then at Lucybelle, meaning to ask, what in the world could Geneviève be saying? Dorothy hung up without saying good-bye.

She swayed back into the front room, putting a hand on the breakfront to steady herself. Her green eyes had gone murky.

"What's happened?" Beverly barked.

"She's not coming."

"Is she okay? Did she take ill?" Ruthie asked.

"She's fine. She thought this would be a good time to tell me, while I'm with friends."

210

Lucybelle helped Dorothy to the couch.

"Tell you what?" Ruthie had to ask.

"Let me have the goddamn telephone." It was the first time Lucybelle had ever heard Beverly use profanity.

"Don't," Dorothy said.

"I've known that bitch since she was a coed. How dare she."

"Is there someone else?" Ruthie asked. "How could she—"

"No. There's no one else. Unless you count the chorus of dead poets she lives with. And her esteemed Vassar colleagues who surely have worse secrets than a female lover."

"Surely." Ruthie's voice brimmed with ire.

"What exactly did she say?" Beverly asked.

"You really want to know?"

"You don't have to say," Lucybelle said, dreading the answer.

"She quoted some poem about dark woods and promises she has to keep and all the miles she has to go before she sleeps."

"She didn't."

"She did."

"What miles does she have to go?" Ruthie asked. "What exactly does she have to do that's so important?"

"Promises to whom?" Beverly asked. "Herself? And is she calling a relationship, calling Dorothy, 'sleep'?"

"If she is, it's a compliment," Lucybelle said. "The woman can't allow herself even the pleasure of sleep. She's plodding endlessly in pursuit of—"

"Of *what*?" Dorothy wailed.

"Oh, honey," Ruthie said. "She doesn't even know."

"At least she didn't toss out that 'loved and lost' one, about it being better," Beverly said.

"I did everything she wanted," Dorothy cried. "I tried to speak more quietly. I tried to chew with my mouth shut. I avoided eye contact with her in public places."

"You're much better off without her," Beverly said. "Trust me. I've known her for years, and she's only gotten worse."

"She uses poetry as a fortress," Lucybelle said.

"We'll never speak to her again," Ruthie said with a hard nod at Beverly.

"Mother is gone," Dorothy whispered. "Geneviève is gone. I have nothing. *Nothing.*"

"Now you're being a bit dramatic," Beverly said.

"You have us," Ruthie said, the words sounding too stringent.

Dorothy waved her hand through the air as if to say, spare me the platitudes. Then she straightened her back and looked up at the corner of the room. "I moved my mother for her. And it killed her."

She spoke as if possessed, and it gave Lucybelle a shiver.

"You moved to be with us," Beverly said. "None of us could bear this backwater without you."

"The move did not kill your mother," Ruthie said. "You know that."

"It did. I moved for Geneviève and it killed Mother." She looked furiously alone.

Lucybelle put her arms around Dorothy, who began to sob.

"This calls for strong drinks," Ruthie said as she hustled to the kitchen.

## Friday–Wednesday, December 22–27, 1961

They'd had enough driving for the year, but Lucybelle wanted to bring L'Forte, so she and Dorothy took the train. They didn't bother with a sleeping car, agreeing that it would be fun to watch the views change. As they chugged south, the grazing cows and trim, white clapboard houses of New England were replaced by the bone-skinny dogs and plank-and-hammer dwellings of Appalachia. Crossing the Mississippi and rolling into the fertile farmland of her origins brought on both relief—home!—and apprehension, as if the dreaded hog farmer sat at his kitchen table, rifle across his knees, waiting for her.

Gus Fritchie, who'd taken over running the farm for Mother after Daddy died, picked them up at the train station in Memphis, drove them to Pocahontas, and gave Dorothy a tour before taking them home. They sat squeezed together in the front seat of his ancient pickup truck, bumping down the dirt roads that crisscrossed the rice and soybean fields. He reported on last year's yield and next year's expected one, assuring Lucybelle that he'd sent all the necessary information to John Perry in Portland, that she needn't worry one whit about any of this. A bit of frost clung to the dirt clods and the sky was a dull blue. Black crows pecked at the winter ground, finding edible bits, scattering and taking flight as the truck barreled through their gatherings. In town Gus Fritchie stopped first at the cemetery so Lucybelle could pay her respects to Daddy's grave, and then he circled the quiet town square, the courthouse at its center, talking nonstop about what a good man Judge Bledsoe had been. Lucybelle was emotionally exhausted by the time he finally dropped them off at the house.

A pile of washed greens filled the kitchen sink and a still steaming lemon chess pie sat on the sideboard. The chickens were squawking something fierce, and Lucybelle opened the door to the backyard to find Mother in their midst, feathers flying and wings flapping, all the birds shrieking, their beaks open and their little leathery tongues panting in and out. Mother pounced on one, caught its neck in her fist, and hefted the bird in the air above her head. Standing with her sturdy legs braced apart, she swung the chicken hard, once, twice, until she heard the sharp crack of its neck breaking. Lucybelle winced and Dorothy gasped. The other chickens huddled against the back fence, as far from Mother as they could get.

"Lucybelle," Mother said, clopping back toward them in her chunky heeled shoes, thick support hose, and housedress covered by an apron, the dead chicken hanging from her hand. "And this must be Dorothy."

Dorothy showed her mettle that afternoon by willingly taking on the task of plucking the chicken. The operation had always turned Lucybelle's stomach and did so even more now that she hadn't had to see it done in years. As a child, her presumed sickliness gave her an excuse, but now, according to her mother, "anyone who can make her own way in New York and Chicago can certainly prepare a chicken for the table." She sat at Dorothy's side and pretended to help while Dorothy did all the work.

Dorothy also knew how to mix and bake fluffy biscuits and even say grace at the table. During the meal she asked about Mother's handiwork, and after the lemon chess pie, admired all the quilts, afghans, sweaters, hats, dolls, and doll clothes that Mother had made for the upcoming church bazaar, commenting in detail on the stitching and fabric choices, and admiring especially the economy in using rags and scraps to such "professional" effect. Mother mentioned that every year she made over half the merchandise for the church bazaar and that the proceeds went to local needy families. Dorothy said, "You're doing God's work, Mrs. Bledsoe." Lucybelle rolled her eyes, but Mother was well pleased.

After church that Sunday, Dorothy complimented Mrs. Fritchie's hat and praised the minister's sermon. At the bazaar, she spent over fifty dollars at Mother's table, so much that Mother actually protested. "Surely you've already bought and sent your Christmas gifts."

"This is for next year. Where could I ever find such perfect gifts, and so well-made, all the while contributing to charity?"

"Well, yes," Mother agreed.

Lucybelle had never learned how to sew or knit or even cook, but her deficiencies didn't feel like failures this Christmas. Dorothy took up the slack.

On the morning they were leaving, as Gus Fritchie loaded their suitcases into his truck and Dorothy stepped into the bathroom, Mother called Lucybelle into the kitchen. She shut the door. Her voice curdled with the effort, and yet she said, "I like Dorothy."

"Oh."

"I don't know what your father would say."

"Oh. It's not—"

"It's none of my business. You're a grown woman. I've said what I have to say. Come home again soon."

It was as if Dorothy had single-handedly delivered Mother to her. She'd always known Mother loved her. She'd also known she admired her good grades in school, the number of books she read as a child, but she had felt cared for at a distance, respected as a foreigner might be respected. Dorothy was like a translator, someone who could speak both languages. Lucybelle wanted to thank her friend, but it was difficult to even name that for which she was grateful. Anyway, Dorothy was so busy thanking Lucybelle for bringing her home for the holidays, for saving her from a lonely Christmas.

"The best part is still ahead," Lucybelle told her on the train. They were on their way to New York for the second part of their holiday. The metal wheels screeched along the rails, the windows steamed up with their conversation, and it felt grand to have escaped Arkansas once again.

"I can't wait to meet your friends."

"I'm so glad you're feeling better."

Dorothy didn't speak for a long time. Then she said, "The saddest part is I don't think I ever actually loved her. I was glad to have found someone. I told myself I loved her. I wanted to love her. It was more like"—Dorothy laughed—"like Beverly said, a good situation."

"Apparently not that good."

"Apparently not. You never really loved Stella either, did you?"

"Actually I did."

"She had a whole life without you. So does Geneviève, without me. We were both delusional."

"I suppose you're right."

"I *am* right," Dorothy said. "There's no such thing as a healthy relationship for us."

"That can't be true. What about Beverly and Ruthie? They love each other."

Dorothy made a face. "Spare me. There's no room for slippage there. They feel so, I don't know, tight."

"Ball and chain."

"Exactly. No, it just isn't possible. If you can't live openly, the relationship gets poisoned. You're right to live a life of the mind. To write your novel. That's the way to handle who we are. Find a way to sublimate the feelings."

"I didn't know you were being analyzed," Lucybelle teased.

"Ha. I would go for it if I thought I could afford the treatment."

"You sound like you hate being a lesbian."

Dorothy shuddered. "I hate that word."

It did sound rather slimy, like a species of slug.

"I'm napping," Lucybelle said. "I bet the boys will want to go out tonight."

"Out? Where?"

"You'll love everyone. You'll fit right in, just like you did in Pocahontas."

"From Pocahontas to Greenwich Village. That's one stretch."

Lucybelle snorted.

"You're a brave woman, Lucybelle Bledsoe."

"Only my mother gets to call me that."

"Your mother and me."


## New Year's Eve 1961

Wesley sat in his armchair, his satin face mask strapped across his eyes, and thick, padded headphones over his ears, listening to his Renaissance music.

Harry pulled one of the rounded headphones away from Wesley's ear and shouted, "Get up. You're coming to dinner."

Wesley didn't respond.

Harry pushed the face mask up onto his boyfriend's forehead. "I scored New Year's Eve reservations at Lutèce. I've laid out your tux."

Wesley squinted at the light. "No."

Harry hadn't mentioned the agoraphobia when Lucybelle called to say that she and Dorothy were coming to New York and he begged them to stay at their place. Wesley had always been a bit antisocial, but in the past six days he hadn't left the house once. Surely his condition was aggravated by the two women moving into his study during their visit. He'd moved his operation, the chair and stereo and entire record collection, to the front room, and so while he wasn't willing to go out, it was impossible to enjoy staying in, since he took up so much space, both physical and psychic, in the small apartment. L'Forte's presence made everything worse. If he so much as scratched a paw on the carpet, Wesley nearly gagged, as if the dog were vermin. Yesterday, on their third morning in the apartment, Lucybelle had taken Harry aside and told him they would move to a hotel. She hated causing more stress for the couple. He adamantly refused and she realized that their visit was a badly needed respite for him.

Wesley's illness had taken a big bite out of Harry's trademark affability. During their meals out, he talked incessantly about the symptoms and his efforts to relieve them, discussing Wesley as if he were one of his patients rather than his boyfriend. Lucybelle was sorry to see Harry, a man who'd always had unfailing good cheer, brought down by Wesley's diminishing world and increasing phobias.

After they finished their coffee and dessert at Lutèce, Harry hailed a cab and they rode down to the Village. So far they'd seen two Broadway shows and been to the Metropolitan Museum, the Museum of Modern Art, and the Natural History Museum. They'd gone to the top of the Empire State Building and to the viewing deck of the stock exchange. Harry was an excellent tour guide, and Dorothy nearly vibrated with the thrill of New York. She was entirely charmed by their big, sophisticated host, and even, Lucybelle suspected, enjoyed the drama in the men's home.

"The Page Three," Harry announced, holding open the club door for the women. He and Lucybelle grinned at each other. Oh, she had missed the city.

The place was packed for the holiday, but a group was just getting up from a table and Harry grabbed the backs of two emptied chairs. "Sit. I'll get drinks."

"I don't know," Dorothy said as her eyes adjusted to the darkened club. She didn't sit. "Should we be here?"

"Why not?"

"What kind of place is this?"

They'd had cocktails and wine with dinner, and Lucybelle felt warm and loose. She enjoyed watching Dorothy's big appetite handle *this* meal. She said, "Welcome to your life."

"Not mine."

"Oh, come on. What are you saying?"

"We both have jobs with the government. I don't think we should."

Harry set two martinis down on the small table. "Dorothy, my love, sit. I'll just go fetch mine, and another chair, and be right back."

"It makes me uncomfortable," Dorothy said as he left again. "Those two women over there—if they both even are women—are kissing."

"Lucky them." Lucybelle lifted her martini. "To kissing."

Dorothy had that bursting appearance again, as if she just couldn't contain herself, and Lucybelle laughed out loud. "And to 1962, may it bring us happiness."

"To happiness," Dorothy acceded and took a gulp of her martini. "Holy cow, do you know that woman? She's walking this way, looking at you like you're her long lost . . . something."

Clare wore a black beret, a black turtleneck sweater, a purple velvet vest, and tight black pants. She'd replaced her burgundy velvet satchel with an even bigger lavender brocade one. Lucybelle stood and embraced her, surprised at how pleased she was to see her. She smelled faintly like pine needles.

Clare thrust a hand at Dorothy's chest. "So happy to meet your lover."

Lucybelle expected an emphatic correction from Dorothy, but after another large gulp of her martini, she just smiled her beautiful, gap-toothed smile.

"You're a lucky woman," Clare added, her tone suggesting intimate knowledge of just how lucky. "She owes me, you know. She once stole a photograph from me."

"It's a picture of Willa Cather," Lucybelle told Dorothy. "She gave it to me."

"Not exactly. When you refused to return it—went so far as to lie about losing it—I let you have it."

217

Dorothy's alarmed look blinked back on.

"How are Helen and Serena?"

"Never see them anymore. Married. Boring."

"Charles?"

"She's right over there." Clare nodded at the bar. "I'll go get her. I know she'd love to say hi. Oh, here she comes."

Harry had Charles, who was decked out in a red satin dress, hosiery, and a red pillbox hat with a black lace veil, on his arm.

"Oh my goodness," Dorothy whispered.

"I'll find chairs," Clare said, but she didn't move away from the table.

"Oh, my darling Lucy." Charles gave her a big smack right on the lips, leaving a smudge of cherry lipstick. "I'm so happy to see you. The place has gone entirely downhill since you left. No one holds a candle to your style."

"My style?" Lucybelle laughed. "It's nonexistent."

"That's what you think. You're the real deal, honey. That's the whole point of you. *I* need all of *this*." Charles flourished a hand through the air, from the top of his head down to his feet. "But you've got those self-styled blond curls, no-nonsense frock, and smart-girl glasses. All you need is a pencil behind your ear. It all just makes you so unique and—"

"Stop while you're ahead," Harry said.

Lucybelle laughed again and told Charles, "You certainly look beautiful tonight."

"Thank you! If I can't have fun on New Year's Eve, when can I?"

"Agreed!" Dorothy tossed out bravely.

She was trying, Lucybelle had to hand her that.

"I'd stay and talk," Charles stage-whispered, "but I have a date." He gestured toward the bar and winked. "Happy New Year, girls!"

"Wow," Lucybelle said as he sashayed back to the man at the bar. "I guess he's left Alabama far behind."

"We've all changed," Harry said and sighed.

"How long have you two been together?" Clare asked.

"Actually," Dorothy said. "We're both single."

"Oh!" Clare said happily.

Lucybelle wished Dorothy had let the misperception stand.

"I'm going to leave you girls," Harry said, draining his cocktail and standing up. He didn't like to leave Wesley alone for long. Clare quickly took his seat.

218

"We better go too," Dorothy said.

"I like your smile," Clare told her.

"Gosh, I wish more guys did!"

"Dorothy!"

She stomped on Lucybelle's foot under the table.

Clare assumed a smug look, like she now knew everything there was to know about both Lucybelle and Dorothy. She swung her lavender brocade satchel into her lap and began digging through it, as if looking for the right recruiting pamphlet.

"We should go," Dorothy said again.

"It's almost midnight. Celebrate with me." Clare touched Lucybelle's hand, reminding her of the dark entryway.

"Go ahead." Dorothy stood and pushed in her chair. "I'll catch a cab."

"I'm coming." Lucybelle got to her feet as well. "It was great to see you, Clare."

She slipped her arm through Dorothy's, and they pushed through the crowd at the Page Three as Chubby Checker's "Let's Twist Again" segued into The Drifters' "Please Stay." Dorothy hurried out the door, and Lucybelle, practically getting dragged, turned, trying to see Clare, but the crush of people blocked her view.

When they hit the cold air on the street, Lucybelle said, "Let's walk back."

"You could have stayed," Dorothy said.

"'I'll catch a cab,'" Lucybelle quoted her. "Give me a break."

"You looked like you wanted to stay!"

"I'm with you."

Dorothy laughed, pleased.

As they headed down 7th Avenue, people began honking car horns and shouting greetings to the New Year. Dorothy kissed Lucybelle's cheek.

"In public!"

"It's allowed at midnight on New Year's Eve." Dorothy kissed her again, this time on the corner of her mouth.

"Five minutes ago you were claiming to want guys to like your smile."

Dorothy shrugged, grinned. "Not with you."

More than a little drunk, Lucybelle felt as if she'd toppled into a river of warm water. She would just let the flow carry her. They stumbled, holding onto each other and laughing at everything, all the way back to

Harry and Wesley's apartment. As they let themselves in to the dark rooms and tiptoed to Wesley's study, the effort to keep quiet only got them laughing harder. Wesley shouted for them to quiet down, and they threw themselves on the bed, buried their faces in the pillows, and laughed themselves out.

Lucybelle took L'Forte for a quick walk and then returned him to the kitchen. As she changed into pajamas, Dorothy, who was already in bed, asked, "So did you have a thing with that beatnik girl?"

Lucybelle got into bed. "She's just a friend. It feels funny seeing her again, after all these years. And Charles in a dress. And Harry so depressed. Everyone has changed. I wonder if I have."

Dorothy rolled onto her side, facing Lucybelle. "Are you kidding? You've changed more than any of them. In good ways, though. They're all just doing some different version of what they've always done."

"How do you know what they've always done?"

"It's sort of obvious."

L'Forte, shut in the kitchen, barked.

"You took him out," Dorothy said. "What does he want?"

"To sleep with me."

"Well, he wouldn't be the only one."

The dark entryway, the warm river, a new year; she let herself fall into it all. Dorothy clicked off the bedside lamp and kissed her on the mouth. They were loud and rambunctious, Dorothy's voluptuousness swallowing her litheness. She'd never been so purely lustful as she was that night, the beginning of 1962.

## Monday, January 1, 1962

For most of the train ride back up to New Hampshire, Dorothy slept or pretended to sleep. Then, in one swift turnabout, she faced Lucybelle.

"I'm sorry," she said. "You know how I feel about you."

She didn't, not exactly.

"But I can't do this."

"Wait," Lucybelle said, but for what she didn't know. She searched her friend's face, trying to figure out how to respond. She hadn't felt this happy in months, maybe even in a couple of years. Seeing her mother, that nearly tender moment of acceptance in the kitchen, spending an evening with her tribe—yes, her tribe—and then last night, whatever it was (did they have to define it?), all of that burned through some obstructive mass inside her. She was free. She'd almost finished the first draft of her novel. She knew who she was. And oh, expressing it as she and Dorothy had last night, that felt sacred to her. She wasn't in love with Dorothy, and that was almost the best part.

Dorothy was talking but Lucybelle wasn't listening. She was thinking of some lines from Willa Cather's *Lucy Gayheart*: "Something flashed into her mind, so clear that it must have come from the breathless quiet. What if—what if Life itself were the sweetheart?"

The train slithered through a birch forest, along an icy stream, and the movement and beauty satisfied so deeply. She reached for Dorothy's hand.

"No." Dorothy yanked her hand away. "Are you even listening?"

"I wasn't really. Honestly, look out the window! I just feel happy."

"I feel ashamed." Dorothy looked to the back of the train car, as if searching for an exit. Then she turned her entire body away, hunching toward the aisle.

"You're still recovering from Geneviève," she said, but Dorothy didn't, wouldn't, answer.

Lucybelle refused to let her friend's fear and shame wreck her joy. The trees and sky, the peace settled deep in her belly, the excitement in her thoughts. These were hers and she would not give them up.

They didn't speak again until the train rolled into Hanover where they said brief good-byes and took cabs to their separate apartments.

## Thursday, January 4, 1962

The basement floor of the new lab, which housed the machine shop and refrigeration equipment, was finally finished, and the scientists, most of whom had been commuting from Chicago and elsewhere, were moving in this week. The Cold Regions Research and Engineering Laboratory would at last begin functioning as the state-of-the-art research facility that had been so long in the dreaming and then building.

Early on Thursday morning, as Lucybelle drove down Lyme Road approaching the compound, she saw thick, black smoke billowing high into the sky. She drove in the gate anyway, parked, and ran to the small cluster of people standing a hundred yards from the small blaze that was causing so much smoke.

Dorothy turned to her with a look of fascinated terror. "Arson," she whispered, her breath a cloud of warm air billowing into the cold morning. They watched as the flames consumed a wall of the front building and then as a propane tank exploded. The brand new coldrooms went up in the blaze, hot fire against the icy blue sky. Fire trucks, their sirens screaming, raced down Lyme Road and turned onto the laboratory's grounds.

## Sunday, January 7, 1962

Lucybelle knew they had to talk, and so on Sunday morning she went without first calling to Dorothy's apartment. Dorothy was just stepping out of her new white Rambler, wearing her beige wool coat and nylons and high heels.

"Where have you been so dressed up this early on a Sunday?" Lucybelle asked.

"Church."

"You don't go to church."

"I do now."

This development threw Lucybelle off track for a moment. "Can we talk?"

"There's no need. I understand."

"What do you understand?"

"That you were . . . intoxicated."

"You were too."

"It was vulgar."

"What?"

"I was quite surprised, truth be known." She executed a tight, little head shake, as if freeing herself from a disgusting memory.

Lucybelle reached for the handle of her car door. She didn't need to hear any more of this.

"Wait," Dorothy said. "I'm sorry. I don't mean that. Not exactly. I just think . . . what I said before, women like us . . ."

"I'd hoped you would see it differently after New York."

"Why in the world would you think that? Your friends Harry and Wesley have a sick relationship, quite literally, wouldn't you say? And that beatnik girl? She has nothing in her life but a queer bar. Where else can she go? That fellow in the dress? I don't want any of that. I want to be normal."

Lucybelle felt herself teetering on the brink of perception. She saw beauty in Clare and Charles, and while Harry and Wesley were having troubles, the former had shown them a tremendous time in New York and the latter, poor fellow, at least he loved music. And yet, the sour words coming from Dorothy's mouth, they made her question how she saw anything at all.

"I'm sorry," Dorothy said again. "Maybe it's just because I've been burned too many times. But I need to make a sharp turn in my life."

If right then, Lucybelle could have said, *I love you*, Dorothy might have come around. Lucybelle did love her. Maybe could have even fallen *in* love with her. But it was too clear that the love would have to be proved, time and time and time again, and the shame overcome, also endlessly, and she didn't have it in her to do that. She wanted Life itself, the sweetheart, the truth, and yes, the lust.

"By the way," Lucybelle said, opening her car door. "That wasn't arson on Thursday. The workman who lights the fires under the kettles of tar accidentally started it. He's given a full report. It was an accident. Once the propane tank went up, the fire was out of control."

"Maybe," Dorothy said. "But maybe not. The way this town feels about us, who knows what happened."

"Everyone knows what happened. I just told you: the man who started the fire has given all the details. Why would you want it to be something sinister?"

Dorothy raised her eyebrows as if there were dozens of unanswered questions.

"If it was arson, they would have done a much better job of it. In the end, there wasn't even that much damage."

Why were they arguing about fire? Lucybelle sighed and tried to think of something kind to say. Dorothy looked so defeated, so thickly sad, and she couldn't join herself to that feeling, she just couldn't. She got in her car and drove away. When she looked in the rearview mirror, she saw Dorothy standing in the street, unmoving, arms at her sides, her pale face watching Lucybelle leave.

## Wednesday, September 19, 1962

For the past year, Lucybelle had been meeting Boris once a week for her Russian language lessons. He was a delightful and talkative fellow who much preferred practicing his own English to teaching Lucybelle Russian. But if she asked him questions about his home village in southeastern Russia, about his grandmother's cooking and the characters with whom he grew up, he forgot himself and talked at length, in Russian, and that was how she learned. He became exasperated every time she interrupted him to ask what a word meant or how to pronounce another, but by supplementing their conversations with texts she found at the Dartmouth library, and studying on her own, she was doing well enough by now to read a bit of Turgenev. It was a revelation to experience an author in his native language, how drastically different it was to reading him in translation, and the experience made her hungry to read other Russian novelists in their own tongue. Though to a lesser extent than gossiping about his childhood, Boris also enjoyed reading out loud, and that was what they were doing, taking turns with *Crime and Punishment*, when Dorothy came into Lucybelle's office without knocking.

"Oh!" Dorothy feigned surprise. "I didn't know you were in here. I was just going to drop something off."

"You've met Boris." Technically, Lucybelle wasn't supposed to talk about her Russian lessons, and so she hadn't, but her teacher did come to the lab every Wednesday afternoon, so it wasn't exactly a well-protected secret.

"I have not."

"This is Dorothy, our librarian."

Dorothy nodded tersely while Boris gathered up his overcoat and brief-case and copy of *Crime and Punishment*, kissed Lucybelle on the cheek, said, "До свидания, моя любовь," or "Good-bye, my love," and made his exit. Dorothy shut the door behind him.

"If I were a spy," Lucybelle said, "I wouldn't be meeting my contact in the lab."

"Don't be ridiculous."

"It's the look on your face." It didn't matter what Lucybelle did these days—from lighting a cigarette to using a swear word—Dorothy managed to convey her disapproval. Lucybelle lit a cigarette now, inhaled deeply, and blew the smoke into the room.

Dorothy said, "Sometimes I just don't know what's going on with you."

"Okay, I admit it, I've been sneaking off to Moscow regularly to reveal all. When I can't make the flight, I talk to Boris."

"You think I'm stupid. You've always thought I was stupid. Now you just make fun of me to my face."

"I don't think you're stupid. That's what angers me. You're so not stupid."

A tremor jiggled across Dorothy's face as she absorbed this backhanded compliment. Then, "So what *are* you doing with that man?"

"Learning Russian. It's part of my job. I need to read the Russian studies so we can know what they know."

The expression on Dorothy's face intensified as her imagination kicked in. The faster Dorothy ran from herself, the larger her phantoms loomed. How she would love it if Lucybelle *were* a spy. For either side.

"You said you were dropping something off," Lucybelle said.

"Yes. I thought these might interest you." Dorothy placed some photographs on Lucybelle's desk and then stepped back to watch her reaction.

The photographic shades of dove- to steel-gray sent a current of fear zipping through Lucybelle, all the way down to her toes. The response was brief and crisp, but so distracting that once she recovered, even after she saw what the pictures were not, it took her a long time to see what they were.

The photographs had been clipped from three different newspapers. Two showed members of an organization called the Student Nonviolent Coordinating Committee, who last summer, in conjunction with the NAACP, had gone to a town called McComb, Mississippi, for a month-long voter registration drive. The third depicted James Meredith, the young Negro man who was attempting to enroll at Ole Miss. The photographs were all credited to Stella Robinson.

Lucybelle went through the pictures again, looking at each one in careful detail, the faces beautiful in their resolve and pain. They were extraordinary pictures, each one a full story. And published. Stella had published her photographic journalism.

"You're smiling. I thought you'd be disturbed."

"I'm . . . I'm so happy for her."

"You must be kidding. I know you're not that naïve. That girl is trouble." Dorothy gestured at the clippings.

"Trouble?"

"I admire Martin Luther King. Pastor Lane says they're on the right track. But that girl is just an opportunist."

"She's put her life at risk to take these pictures. How exactly does that make her an opportunist?"

"Using prejudice to get ahead in her so-called career."

"You can't be serious."

"I'm not against them. It's just how they're going about it that's wrong. She's capitalizing on that."

"Who's 'them'? Who's 'they'?"

"The Negroes."

"How would you suggest 'going about it'?"

"Within the law."

"Taking pictures is well within the law. Anyway, James Meredith has the courts on his side. I'd call that within the law."

"They're stirring up violence."

"The racists who oppose them are doing the violence."

"Pastor Lane says that patience would be a better course of action."

"Patience." Lucybelle was surprised to hear herself nearly spit the word. "Where did you get these pictures, anyway?"

"It's part of my job," she said, using the exact words Lucybelle had used for learning Russian. "I read all the papers so I can clip relevant stories. I ran across these. But I'm sorry I showed you. I thought it'd help. You know, with your feelings."

"My feelings?"

"Getting over her."

"I haven't seen Stella in four years."

Dorothy looked surprised, but then said, "And counting."

Lucybelle controlled her anger because what she really wanted was to be alone with the pictures. "Thank you for showing them to me. They do help me with my feelings. I'm so proud of her."

"Proud?" Dorothy looked truly baffled.

"Why do you even care about my feelings for her? You have Mary."

"Mary? What in the world are you talking about?"

"You know exactly what I'm talking about."

A fresh smile played at the corners of Dorothy's mouth, and Lucybelle realized she'd just given the impression that she was jealous.

"Mary and I are just friends," Dorothy said in a pious, maybe even triumphant, tone of voice. "I think you know that."

"What I know is that people lie all the time about relationships."

"How dare you."

"I've got work to do. If you don't mind."

"How dare you suggest what you've just suggested."

Lucybelle shrugged, refusing to back down. She was so sick of the lies. Each one seemed to generate ten more. They rotted people from the inside out. She had no idea if Dorothy and Mary were having sex, but the look on Dorothy's face the couple of times she'd talked about her new friend told her that they were, nonetheless, lovers.

"In fact," Dorothy said, squaring her shoulders, "Mary and I have a double date this weekend with a couple of fellows from church."

"Have a good time," Lucybelle said and picked up her pencil. For nine months now, that drunken New Year's Eve sex had sat between them like an undigested meal. Since then Dorothy had refused to talk with her about anything but the most superficial of topics, and only at work. It hurt. Losing a friend. But also seeing Dorothy lose herself. That night in Wesley's study, Dorothy had allowed herself a bit of wild joy. A few hours later, she'd begun her campaign against that same joy.

Dorothy still stood in front of Lucybelle's desk, her lips pressed together, her arms folded tightly across her rounded figure, waiting for something that, even if it were offered, she wouldn't accept.

"Thanks for the pictures," Lucybelle said. "They delight me."

## Monday, October 29, 1962

"Well, isn't this the best international joke in a few decades!" Bader said banging the door to her office open.

"Henri! When did you get in town?"

"Here we've been spending millions of dollars to stop the Russians from invading via the Arctic, and like any rational people, they're coming instead through the tropics. We should have been studying sand, not ice."

"Shut the door, if you're going to talk like that."

He waved a hand over his head, dismissing the lab, the crisis in Cuba, maybe the entire United States government, and laughed. "They've essentially already fired me."

"Well, they haven't fired me." She got up and shut her office door. "How are you? It's good to see you."

"Furthermore," Bader continued, "we could have been drinking rum all this time, wrestling sharks, getting tans. All this polar business has been a big waste."

"What about your ice cores?"

"Sure, yeah, from my point of view, thank god the government was so badly duped and blinded. So, okay, here's the update." He treated her to a long and detailed accounting of the most recent technology and attempts at fetching the ice cores and transporting them to New Hampshire, all of which she already knew since she'd edited every single report. She sat back and looked at her mentor, the man who'd hired her, the man who'd threatened her. She smiled thinking that all you had to do was add the prefix "tor" to the word "mentor" to get a pretty accurate picture of her crazy relationship with this tall, disheveled, handsome man sporting a black goatee.

"But back to the Russians," he said after he'd satisfied his obsessive need to talk about the ice cores. "Think about it. Seriously. If they can drink rum under a palm tree, wearing their swimming trunks, why would they come any further? Let them have Cuba, for god's sake. The Ruskies and the Cubans, now there's the strangest marriage I've ever seen. Kennedy is actually worried? Give me a break."

"How's Adele?"

"Fine. Good. And you? Staying out of trouble?"

"I'm afraid so."

"Good girl. Hauser tells me you're already reading the Russian papers. I knew you were a quick study, but that's kind of impressive."

"What else is there to do up here?"

A scowl scrunched Bader's brow. "You're young. You should be having fun."

This man's contradictions hardly even irked her anymore. Him telling her that she should be having fun, that was a good one. Anyway, she wasn't young. Not anymore.

He looked around at her walls, searching for a clock. "What time is it? I have a meeting with the lieutenant. Or is he a corporal? I don't know the difference."

"You better get it right. They definitely know the difference. He's a colonel."

Bader saluted and stomped out of her office.

"Henri!" she called after him, and then went to the door to watch him stride down the hall away from her, the last of a species. Where else could you find that starch honesty and abiding passion?

"Henri," she said in a quieter voice. "Come back."

## Friday, August 16, 1963

The morning of her fortieth birthday, Lucybelle looked at herself in the mirror and didn't like what she saw. Her blond hair had muddied over the years; she could hardly even call it blond anymore; and now there were threads of gray. She supposed crow's feet on either side of her eyes were better than a frown line splitting her brow, but when did she start looking so tired? On some mornings, this one included, she looked as though she had two black eyes. Her nose looked swollen.

Single, fluent in Russian, a completed draft of her novel, nothing more than a stack of paper under her bed, that was her life. She missed her father.

She went to the west-facing window of her new studio apartment and shoved open the sash, startling a murder of crows perched in the giant oak tree. They cawed and flapped, taking flight into the early summer morning. It was her birthday. She'd try to make the most of it.

Lucybelle showered and put on her new robin's-egg-blue, sleeveless dress with the full skirt. The static electricity in the air made her hair even more frizzy than usual, but she didn't bother with any pins. Let it fly, gray streaks and all. She also decided against lipstick. The morning was cool, but sunny and clear, and she'd go into the day as natural as the light.

She felt much better by the time she got into her car. She did love her new place, one big room above a garage on a short dead-end street on the outskirts of the small town of Lebanon, New Hampshire. The houses on Placid Square Street all faced a round open field, where the handful of residents parked their cars. Not half a mile away, on the main highway, was Lander's Restaurant, where the scientists met every Friday evening for drinks. She almost always joined them. The staff at the lab had grown so much since she'd started in 1956, and now with the new facility, the ranks had swelled even more. Social alliances had shifted as well. Lucybelle enjoyed the Hausers and the Woos, as well as her assistant, Doug, and his wife. If Beverly and Ruthie still hosted Friday night cocktails, she hadn't been invited in a long while. But tonight they were getting together to celebrate Lucybelle's fortieth. Even Dorothy had agreed to come, although Lucybelle may have sabotaged that fragile agreement.

Yesterday at lunch she'd spotted Dorothy sitting with Beverly and Ruthie in the lab cafeteria, and so she'd joined them. As she set down her tray, she suggested that Dorothy bring Mary to the birthday party. Dorothy burst into tears and ran out of the cafeteria, leaving her uneaten lunch on the table.

"That wasn't necessary," Ruthie said to Lucybelle. "Why do you goad her?"

"I wasn't goading her. I was trying to be cordial."

"You were not," Beverly said but smiled.

"Okay," Lucybelle admitted. "Maybe not. I know she wouldn't dream of bringing the Virgin Mary to one of our den of sin parties, but why the tears?"

"I feel sorry for her," Ruthie said.

"Why?" Beverly used her best caustic tone, which Lucybelle had come to appreciate. She remembered how years ago Peter Hauser had told her that Beverly was "a real martinet." Code, she now realized, for dyke.

"We're lucky," Ruthie said. "She's not."

"I don't quite buy that," Lucybelle said. "I'm single too, you know. I've not exactly had an exemplary history of romance, and yet I haven't felt the need to denounce my lesbianism."

"Keep your voice down," Beverly said.

"I'm pleased she's decided to join us for your birthday celebration," Ruthie said. "Don't say anything more to scare her off."

"Sorry."

Lucybelle did look forward to the evening, for old time's sake, and she was glad that Dorothy was coming. She missed her sense of humor, her full-throated go at life, even if the *go* happened now to be at her church. Perhaps the outburst of tears was a good sign. Maybe her tolerance for disguise and fakery was crumbling.

Dorothy showed up a full forty-five minutes late for the party. They'd already polished off a bottle of champagne and exchanged news about their families. They were just moving on to lab gossip.

"I have exciting news!" Dorothy sang out the moment Ruthie opened the door. She was breathless and disheveled. She turned to Lucybelle and said, "Happy birthday. I don't mean to trump your holiday."

"Please. Help me forget. What's your good news?"

"Mary is engaged to be married! We're thrilled!"

Lucybelle, Beverly, and Ruthie stood motionless, staring at this bit of theater, completely at a loss for how to respond.

Dorothy began sobbing and dropped, right there in the doorway, to the floor and pounded the rug with her fists. "I hate you! I hate you! I hate you!" she wailed. It was not at all apparent to whom she was speaking. Herself? Mary? The women in the room? At least this cleared up the mystery about yesterday's cafeteria conniption. Ruthie helped her up and ushered her to the couch. Beverly shut and locked the door, then opened and poured more champagne, handing Dorothy a flute.

"I know what you all think," Dorothy said, sitting up straight, looking suddenly righteous, as if someone else, someone distasteful, had had the outburst.

"It doesn't matter what we think," Ruthie said.

"It's not that," Dorothy persevered.

Lucybelle felt a mix of anger, compassion, and impatience. Her arms ached for an authentic embrace.

"Of course I loved her. But we were quite happy being platonic friends. We had a happy—a very happy—agreement that way."

"Each to her own," Lucybelle said.

Ruthie scowled at Lucybelle and she shrugged back at her.

"You're speaking in the past tense," Beverly observed. "She didn't die. She's getting married."

"We were not together," Dorothy said, looking at Lucybelle. "Not in that way."

"Fine."

"But that doesn't mean my heart isn't broken. Again."

A bowl of mixed nuts, another one of Ritz crackers, and a plate of pale American cheese slices sat on the coffee table. Lucybelle made herself a cheese and cracker sandwich. The crumbs dusted the front of her blue dress as she bit into it.

Beverly looked as though she were trying with all her might to refrain from making an inflammatory comment, and Ruthie was concentrating on keeping Beverly from doing so. Lucybelle made another American cheese and Ritz sandwich.

"I'm sorry," Dorothy said. "I didn't mean to ruin your big day."

"Actually, I don't feel very celebratory about the beginning of my fifth decade, so I welcome the distraction." Callous again, she supposed, and so she added, "I don't mean I welcome your disappointment, just—" Thankfully Dorothy interrupted her because she had no idea how to finish that sentence.

"I'm not disappointed," Dorothy said, her emphasis managing to convey that no words could express the depth of her devastation. "I'm delighted for her. It's just that it leaves me rather in the lurch."

Ruthie patted Dorothy's hand.

"Get the cake," Beverly said, hurrying things along.

They sang "Happy Birthday" as Ruthie carried the round chocolate layer cake, adorned with four lit candles, from the kitchen. The singing triggered another crying fit by Dorothy. Lucybelle went to the window to look out as the other two tried to calm her, but then Ruthie started gasping for air. Once Beverly set her up on the leather chair with her inhaler, Lucybelle said that she was going home. She didn't offer an explanation.

"I ruin everything," she heard Dorothy say as she let herself out.

Lucybelle practically ran to her car. She was sorry to leave like that, to abandon the mess of Dorothy for Beverly and Ruthie to handle, especially with Ruthie coping with an asthma attack. But it was her fortieth birthday and she still had a horizon in her view.

## Monday, August 19, 1963

As Lucybelle turned left onto the long driveway leading to CRREL, she noticed a cream-colored Thunderbird convertible parked along Lyme Road, a short distance away from the entrance. Looking in her rearview mirror, she saw a short-haired, brown-skinned woman sitting on the hood of the Thunderbird, hands braced on the tops of her thighs, a pair of green-lensed sunglasses on her face.

Lucybelle braked, put the car in reverse, and backed down the driveway until she reached the highway. She parked a good twenty yards away from the Thunderbird, tried to calm her breathing, and then stepped out of the car.

"Happy birthday." Stella slid off the hood and walked toward Lucybelle, holding out a book.

She glanced at the cover and said, "I've already read it."

"I figured as much. Here, though. It's still your birthday present."

Lucybelle took the copy of Rachel Carson's *Silent Spring* and looked at the title page, knowing there'd be an inscription. Stella had written, "Always write in books. With love, Stella."

Lucybelle backed up a few steps so she could lean against her Chevy. It needed a wash, and the highway grit rubbed into the cotton of her dress.

Stella smiled. "Still all no-nonsense, aren't you?"

Lucybelle nodded and then felt foolish for having done so.

"You look beautiful. The blues of your dress, car, and sky are all exactly the same."

"Why are you here?" Lucybelle looked over her shoulder at the buildings of CRREL, a large complex with a hundred employees and dozens of windows.

"I'm here to say happy birthday. Forty is a big one."

"The Sox are playing the Yankees today. In Chicago."

Stella laughed. "Yep. I'm missing the game."

She wasn't here to say happy birthday. "How's Wanda?"

"She's fine."

"Rusty?"

"Rusty is Rusty. Can't do anything with her. Takes herself right up to the edge of trouble, time and again. Sometimes I wish she'd just mess up big time and let them put her away."

"You don't mean that."

"Of course I don't mean that. But she's not a kid anymore. I expected more of a learning curve than I've seen. I'm tired of bailing her out of tight spots."

"She depends on you and Wanda."

"She needs to learn to depend on herself."

"Acme Transport?"

"We're doing great. I have six cars now and good drivers. Solid protection from a few well-placed friends, which these days is even more necessary than it was back when you and I were stopped. Remember that Halloween?"

"I need you to tell me why you're here."

She nodded. "I forgot how you like to get right to the point."

"I haven't seen you in five years. So if this is getting right to the point, I'd hate to see your idea of a delay."

"I miss you."

"Stella."

"We were raided a month ago. They searched every room in the house, including my darkroom. They took the company books. They even tore through our clothes. Lots of us in the movement are getting this. It's intimidation, plain and simple. They hope to find drugs, anything they can stick you with, but all they found at our house was a lot of dirty dishes and more photographs than they'll ever want to look through."

The jolt of fear was so intensely visceral, Lucybelle thought she might vomit.

"They didn't find the ones of you. I had them well hidden."

It was as if she herself, not just photos of herself, had lain naked, well hidden, perhaps in an attic, while the men searched. She croaked, "You still have them?"

"Of course I still have them. I can't bear to destroy them."

Lucybelle struggled to reassemble herself. "I'm sorry for all the trouble I caused you and Wanda."

Stella grinned, her dimples caving. "I'm not sorry. Don't give me that strict-girl look. I'm just telling you the truth. That's what you asked for, isn't it?"

"You still haven't told me why you're here."

"I came to bring you the negatives and the pictures. I didn't want to put you at risk by mailing them. And they're not safe at my house anymore. We'll be raided again."

"You drove all this way to give them to me?"

Stella nodded.

"You could have just burned them."

"Yes. I could have." Stella opened the door to her Thunderbird, reached under the driver's seat, and withdrew a manila envelope. She handed it to Lucybelle. "But I didn't and I won't. Go ahead, if you see fit."

"What about the two that Wanda has?" Lucybelle still had the baseball bat. She kept it under her bed, alongside the novel manuscript.

Stella shrugged, looked off across the field on the other side of the highway.

"Where does she think you are now?"

"She knows where I am."

"Visiting me in New Hampshire?"

"Nah. I'm on my way back to Alabama to shoot another action."

"Yeah, and Hanover is right on the way."

"That's what I thought."

Lucybelle glanced over at the complex of buildings again. The sun glinted off the upper-story windows. "I should get in to work."

"Okay. I'd ask you to lunch, but . . ."

"Be careful in Alabama, will you?"

Stella chuffed and tapped the book in Lucybelle's hands. "Rachel Carson doesn't back down. She doesn't stop telling the truth. Despite Monsanto and the American Cyanamid Company attacking her every chance they get."

"Please be careful." They shot Medgar Evers in his own driveway. In the back.

"I know what I'm doing."

"I know you do."

"'If you're not ready to die for it, put the word freedom out of your vocabulary.' That's Malcolm X."

A long silence opened up between them. Lucybelle spoke the only words that would bridge it. "I love you."

Stella nodded.

"Please be safe."

"Look. Lucybelle. Honestly, I'm the one who should be cautioning you. Promising to not have girlfriends. Keeping classified secrets. Bound and gagged. It's going to corrupt your soul, sooner or later."

"I'm okay."

"They'll sell you down river the second it suits them."

"I'm getting out. Soon."

Stella studied her for a second, swallowing as if to rid her mouth of something distasteful. "There's something else."

Lucybelle waited.

"It was over a year ago. A woman came to the door. Asked a bunch of questions, including had I heard of a place called Camp Century."

Dread weighted Lucybelle's legs.

"No," Stella said. "Don't worry. She got nothing. I said I'd never been to camp. So she goes, 'Oh, I think you know what I'm talking about.' I said, 'I hate camping' and gave her my best dumb Negro look."

"Did she have a badge or anything?"

"Of course not. Just some low-level agent hoping for a find that would lead to a promotion. But what I'm trying to tell you . . . remember when you told me you couldn't abide lies?" She waited for Lucybelle to nod. "That's the safest place to be. Right there. They can't touch you if you're living the truth."

"I know." She hadn't meant it to come out in a whisper.

"I love you too." Stella touched her cheek.

"Do you have your camera?"

"Of course."

"Let me take your picture."

Stella got the camera out of her car and handed it to Lucybelle. She looked into the viewfinder, seeing only black, until Stella said, "You have to take off the lens cap." Stella guided her fingers to the focus ring, and as Lucybelle turned it, eyelashes came into focus. She took a few steps back and framed Stella, who looked right into the center of the lens, unsmiling, her eyes seductively perceptive. "Take your time," she said.

When Lucybelle lowered the camera, Stella took it from her hands. She advanced the rest of the film, opened the back, and dropped out the roll. She put the film—light and shape, even emotion, fixed in a translucent spool of tape—in Lucybelle's hand and closed her fingers around it. Stella climbed back in the Thunderbird and drove down Lyme Road toward Hanover.

That night Lucybelle lay in bed with her new copy of *Silent Spring*. The lovely writing, the woman's lyrical view of the planet and its life forms, and her tender defense of her positions sustained Lucybelle through the long, sleepless night.

## Sunday, September 15, 1963

Early on a Sunday morning in the middle of September, four men planted a box of dynamite, fitted out with a time-delay mechanism for its detonation, under the steps of the 16th Street Baptist Church in Birmingham, Alabama. A little after ten o'clock that morning, a group of twenty-six children walked into the church basement to prepare to hear a sermon titled "The Love That Forgives." The bomb went off, killing four little girls: Addie Mae Collins, Denise McNair, Carole Robertson, and Cynthia Wesley.

236

In her anger and grief, Lucybelle pulled her novel out from under her bed and began a rewrite, a search for deeper truth, for greater revelation. Stella once had called her photography bearing witness. It was throwing light onto lives, or more accurately, capturing the light already existing in lives. She hoped that words and stories could do that too.

## Friday, November 22, 1963

The festivities to celebrate the opening of the new lab had been postponed so many times that the colonel considered forgoing the whole formality. A few folks, including Lucybelle, already had been working there for two years. The date kept sliding for various reasons, including the tar-pot fire, followed by half the staff disappearing for their annual research trips to Greenland, Alaska, and Antarctica. The community in Hanover was slowly getting used to having the lab in its midst. Why remind them of their fears with fanfare?

However, the funders in Washington, who didn't have to live with the people in Hanover, insisted on a three-day gala event, and so on Thursday, November 21, when all the field researchers had returned to New England, General Britton cut the ceremonial ribbon and said, "This will open the door to the many friends of CRREL visiting today and throughout the open-house period. But more than that—it will signal, symbolically, the opening of the doors to new horizons in scientific and engineering achievements." On Friday the lab would be open for public tours. The grand finale, a big party, was planned for Saturday.

Lucybelle arrived in the late morning on Friday, as did Amanda Woo and Emily Hauser, to help set up. Beverly and Ruthie were already there, moving chairs about the cafeteria, flapping tablecloths onto tables, scrubbing stains off the walls.

"Music!" Emily cried and went off in search of a radio. She returned carrying the big one from the colonel's office and plugged it in. The voice of Elvis crooning "Love Me Tender" filled the cafeteria and Emily feigned a swoon.

"I'll find the classical station." Ruthie reached for the dials.

"I just tuned it," Emily said. "We need rock and roll for party prep."

"You can't be serious."

"As a heart attack."

"Elvis?"

"Heartthrob. Don't tell Peter."

Emily Hauser wore her ironic smile throughout the exchange and Beverly shot leave-it-be looks at Ruthie. It was a tough call, who in this situation had higher rank: the wife of a scientist or an actual employee of CRREL, even if she was a just a secretary.

"I'm surprised the new geologist isn't here." Ruthie retreated by impugning another. Vera Prescott was the first-ever woman scientist hired at SIPRE or CRREL, but apparently in Ruthie's opinion, femaleness trumped job title.

"She's just a geographer," Beverly said.

"She's got a PhD in both," Lucybelle said.

"Well, la-dee-da."

Ruthie did her nervous titter, quietly tumbling it into a cough.

"I don't care if she's the Countess of Hanover," Beverly said. "Helping out today would be a good way for her to get to know the other ladies."

"She's a scientist," Emily said. "She doesn't need to help with party setup."

"Well, la-dee-da."

"She keeps herself separate," Ruthie rallied. "Lucy is head of publications. She's here."

"She shouldn't be," Emily said. "For that matter, neither should either of you two."

"It's my job. I'm office manager." Beverly spoke with icy precision, claiming both resentment and authority.

"She's only been here a month," Lucybelle said. "She's probably shy."

"I invited her to help out today."

"Asking her if she'd like to help set up for a party is hardly a welcoming gesture."

Lucybelle was willing to cut Vera Prescott a lot of slack. She remembered how difficult it had been to break in socially with these women and nearly impossible to win the respect of the men. As a scientist, Vera was supposed to be their equal. It might take her years to be accepted, especially since, true enough, she didn't have an accommodating personality.

Twice Lucybelle had invited Vera to Friday night drinks with the scientists, both times writing down the address for Lander's Restaurant.

When on the following Monday mornings Lucybelle asked why she hadn't come, meaning to make it very clear how welcome she would be, Vera said that she was looking for a place to live and that the search took all of her time. Meanwhile, she'd had to make a long trip to Washington soon after starting the job. But even when she was in town, Lucybelle rarely saw her in the lab. She stayed holed up in the scientists' wing, not even emerging for lunch.

That too was understandable. What's worse than standing with a tray of food in a cafeteria full of people who all know one another, looking for a place to alight? On Vera's second day at CRREL, Lucybelle stopped by her office, introduced herself, and asked if she'd like to go to lunch together. The telephone rang as Lucybelle was making her invitation and Vera had lifted a finger, the wait-a-second gesture, and Lucybelle had done just that, waited there in the doorway while Vera entered into a lengthy conversation as if she weren't standing there at all. She finally left and Vera didn't mention the lunch invitation, or even smile, when they passed in a hallway later that afternoon.

The rebuff was so complete that Lucybelle didn't know why she tried another time. The woman was no-nonsense with her mink-brown hair and steely gray eyes. She wore her intelligence like armor, putting her brains on the outside, to ward off anyone who didn't want to engage on that level. It was almost fun to see what it would take to get her attention. She'd heard that Vera had been the only woman in her PhD program at MIT, and she wanted to hear the stories. They'd be doozies, she knew that. Vera undoubtedly survived by being perfect. Peter Hauser had said "her work couldn't be faulted," which meant that she was flawless. Keeping that up for a lifetime would take a toll. It also made Lucybelle curious.

The second time she asked Vera to lunch, she didn't even look up from the work on her desk. She continued making notes as she said, "Too busy, but thanks."

Lucybelle couldn't imagine her baking cookies or arranging flowers for a lab party, nor did she blame her.

And yet, a little after noon, just as the radio station began broadcasting the Kingsmen doing "Louie Louie" and Emily demonstrated the twist, who should come into the cafeteria carrying an uncovered plate but Vera Prescott. She smiled staunchly, looking as though she were making her best effort, and barked out, "I made Toll House cookies."

"Oh." Beverly took the plate, managing to convey with that one word some kind of disapproval.

"Sorry. I didn't have any waxed paper to cover the plate."

"I see that."

"We have plenty of desserts," Ruthie said.

"My favorite," Lucybelle said, rescuing the uncovered plate of cookies from Beverly's hands before she cited germs and dumped them in the bin.

Vera turned and left the cafeteria. Lucybelle thought she'd gone for good and was about to rebuke Beverly and Ruthie for their rudeness when she returned with a clutch of birch branches, the leaves a deep golden. "Color for the table. But perhaps you don't need them."

"Tree branches?" Beverly said.

"They're beautiful," Lucybelle said. "I'll find a container."

"How stupid of me to forget a container."

"We don't have anything that big," Ruthie said.

"Sure we do." Lucybelle took the branches and went off to hunt down a vase, but of course Ruthie was right and she couldn't find any large enough, so she took a tall bucket from one of the labs and glued black construction paper around the cylinder. She found shears for cutting the woody stalks to the right length and then arranged them as artfully as she could. The entire operation took her nearly an hour. She felt a little foolish for fussing so extensively over Vera Prescott's birch branches, but she was tired of Beverly and Ruthie's negativity, and she liked the new scientist. The energy and ambiguity in that rub between her PhD from MIT and the simple expectations of her femaleness must have affected every step she took, every word she spoke, maybe even the way she breathed.

Lucybelle carried the makeshift foliage arrangement into the cafeteria, calling out, "Ta da!" The size of the bucket and the branches themselves prevented her from seeing the women in the room until she set them down on one of the tables. That's when she saw that both Ruthie and Beverly were sitting on the floor, as if they'd collapsed, faces in their hands. Ruthie was sobbing. Amanda sat on one of the folding chairs, her mouth open, gasping. Emily sat next to her, holding her hand, tears streaming down her face. The only woman standing was Vera, arms at her sides, her chin held up, her eyes closed, as if she were wishing away something vile and terrible.

Lucybelle's first thought was that the new scientist had felled the other women with some scathing remark. That was ridiculous, of course, and

240

soon she heard the urgency in the voice of the radio announcer. The man was gulping air and choking out his words, and she felt the enormity of horror, the size of the disaster, before being able to make out details.

"The president has been shot," Vera told her. "He's dead."

## Wednesday, April 15, 1964

Vera walked past Lucybelle's secretary, Vivian, and her assistant, Doug, in the front part of the editorial offices. Vivian called to her back, "What can we do for you, Dr. Prescott?" but Vera ignored her.

Lucybelle looked up to see Vera standing in her doorway. "Hello?" Flirting with this woman was as easy as being ever so slightly less than businesslike.

"'We still haven't become mature enough to think of ourselves as only a tiny part of a vast and incredible universe.'"

Lucybelle couldn't help thinking of Geneviève, and yet quoting Rachel Carson seemed vital and relevant, rather than just pompous. Lucybelle had heard Carson say those very words on the recent CBS program.

"She died yesterday," Vera said. "Breast cancer."

"Oh." Lucybelle rose from her desk, feeling the immediate vacuum of grief.

"I thought you might be a fan too."

"I am, ever so much."

"She's been sick for a long while."

"Do you know her?"

"Yes. Not well. We have friends in common. I admire her hugely." Vera nodded again, just once and decisively, and departed abruptly, leaving the doorway empty.

Lucybelle didn't know which moved her the most: Rachel Carson's death or that Vera had come to her with the news.

She tossed some papers into her briefcase, told Vivian she was leaving for the day, and also stopped at Beverly's desk. "I'm working from home this afternoon."

"The colonel wants the Greenland statistics today."

"He'll get them tomorrow."

"That's not a decision for you to make."

"Bev. Please."

241

"Of course. I'll figure something out to put him off. Are you okay?"

"I'll be in tomorrow, I promise."

At home Lucybelle threw open her two windows and listened to the noisy spring day. At least three different songbirds were trilling their tunes. The faint fragrance of new green tinged the silky air. She took Carson's book in her hands and held it against her heart. The words in the book were anything but silent, and yet they predicted a silence she felt in the very cells of her own body.

She'd lost Phyllis to alcohol, Daddy to a heart attack, Stella to the rules of love, Dorothy to shame. The little girls in Birmingham and President Kennedy had been slain. Now Rachel Carson was dead. It was too much to bear.

## Saturday, June 13, 1964

"Hey, sugar." Bader's deep voice transcended telephone lines. It was as if a roar filled her apartment.

"So you're still alive."

"And kicking."

"I thought they fired you."

"It depends on who you think 'they' are."

"No riddles today. I'm tired."

"I'm sort of still on contract."

Meaning, he wouldn't go away, that he'd work for free on the ice cores, if that's what it took. "Why are you calling me at home?"

"What's the gossip?"

"The lab is a mess."

"So I hear. Lucky you, though. All you have to do is unscramble their incoherent sentences and drink with the boys on Friday nights."

"That's one way to look at it."

"But you care, so it's more complicated than that."

He wanted something. What?

"You're dedicated," he went on. "You can't just do your job and let go."

"You're one to talk." She missed Bader's intensity and focus, the way it had organized the entire lab. "Management bungles so much."

"As long as the military tries to manage science, you'll have a snarl of bullshit."

"There's an interesting metaphor."

"That's why I need you, sugar. To untangle my metaphors."

"Why are you calling?"

"What if I just wanted to find out how my favorite editor is faring?"

"Come on, Henri."

"All business. That's my girl. Okay, listen. Have you met the new scientist, Vera Prescott?"

"She's not around a lot."

"She's just back from Greenland. They got a lot of excellent images. She needs help writing up the data, though. I think she has two outstanding papers in her from the trip."

"Excuse me for having to say this, but you're not my boss anymore."

"I know. But she was my last stroke of genius at CRREL and I do care about my legacy."

"She's in the Photo Interpretation Research Division. She has nothing to do with the ice cores."

"Nevertheless, I convinced the powers that be to hire her. She's beyond capable, beyond exceptional, in her field. With one glaring deficit, and that's where you come in. She can't write."

"None of the scientists can."

"But she's female."

"Ah." Lucybelle got it, even if Bader didn't fully understand his own point. To the scientists, writing was a bit like housekeeping. Their brilliant ideas just needed tidying. A woman scientist should have these skills naturally.

"I want you to work with Prescott on the Greenland papers."

"And how does Prescott feel about this?"

"I haven't spoken with her yet. I wanted to get you on board first. Understand that this will have to be side work. Have her pay you."

Lucybelle laughed. "I've seen enough of the woman to know that she doesn't want my help. Anyway, I have plenty of legitimate work."

"This is legitimate work. It's your job to clean up the scientists' papers."

"So why can't she go through the same channels as all the others?"

"I can't believe that you, sugar, have to ask that question."

These moments of surprising insight were one of the reasons she liked Bader. "And you care why?"

"I told you. I hired her. Her success is my success."

"That's claiming a bit much, isn't it?"

"She has terrible writer's block. She can't even write a first draft. They'll boot her when they find out."

"I'm not a psychiatrist. I'm an editor."

"This conversation is going on way too long. Just do it." Bader hung up.

## Friday, July 3, 1964

"Would you like a drink?"

Lucybelle had already picked up her purse and jacket, made it to the door, and grasped the knob. She turned and stupidly asked, "A drink?"

Vera might have smiled, it was hard to tell. Dusk was a couple of hours away—outside the window to her right, above the couch, a late golden light slanted through the leaves of the trees—but the woody interior of the cabin prematurely gathered darkness. Lucybelle dropped her things on the couch and stepped back across the cabin, going to the window over the kitchen table to look at the pond. Yes, she wanted to stay. And yes, that was a smile.

"A cocktail," Vera clarified. "You do drink." It wasn't even a question.

"I'd love a drink."

"I have a friend in California who sends me lemons. You can't get lemons here like these. They're so flavorful you can eat them like oranges."

That seemed about right, this woman eating lemons as one would eat any other fruit.

"I make a mean Tom Collins."

While Vera began work at the kitchen counter, Lucybelle looked around at the remarkable contents of the cabin. When she first arrived, they'd gone directly to the piles of paper on the kitchen table and set to work, and she hadn't felt welcome to so much as glance at anything else in the cabin. The place had two doors to the outside, the front one leading to the road and woods and the back one leading right out to Post Pond. A third closed door presumably led to Vera's bedroom.

Vera put a cup of sugar in a cup of water and set this on a stovetop burner. She squeezed three lemons and poured the juice into two tall glasses. She added a healthy portion of gin to each glass, and when the simple syrup came to a boil, she put the pan in the freezer.

"While we wait for that to cool—I don't want to spoil the gin by heating it—I'll show you my collections."

They started with the biggest feathers. "I paddled down a river in Alaska two summers ago. Magnificent trip. We were guided the whole way by bald eagles. They were everywhere. Them and the grizzlies." Vera definitely smiled now, and Lucybelle wondered about a woman who reserved her smiles for grizzly bears.

She had stones from a cove in Nova Scotia and coral from an atoll in the Pacific. There were crystals from the Wind River Range in Wyoming and a seal's jaw, with a full set of teeth, from the Oregon Coast. A lovely piece of dried moss from the French Pyrenees and a shepherd's staff from the Peruvian Andes. Glossy seed pods, in a dozen shapes and sizes, from Mexico. Lucybelle felt as if she were being shown very special objects, and yet Vera was as terse as usual. With the exception of the bald eagle feathers, each keepsake got a phrase, none so much as a full sentence.

Lucybelle tried questions. Which river in Alaska? How far did she hike in the Wind River Range? Was the rest of the seal skeleton with its jaw? With whom did she go to the Andes?

Vera ignored most of the questions, but twice said, "Later."

The word opened like a door onto a long hallway, and Lucybelle's curiosity about what lay at its end was intense. Still, she felt an unusual patience, a pleasurable patience. She took Vera at her word. Later.

Vera measured two tablespoons of the cooled simple syrup into each glass, added club soda, and then ice cubes. They carried their glasses, the ice chiming, outside to the back lawn where she had two Adirondack chairs facing the pond. The drink was delicious, like the lemonade from Lucybelle's childhood, only with gin.

"Where are you from?" Lucybelle asked. She decided to conduct an interview. Perhaps a straightforward and aggressive approach would garner some information.

"A town in southern Illinois so small that I've already forgotten its name."

"Farm?"

"Yes. How did you know?"

"At home we'd have said you're unvarnished."

Vera looked almost hurt, but Lucybelle let it stand.

"So you too?"

"Yes. Northeastern Arkansas."

"Oh my. That's worse."

"Come on now. A small piece of Missouri separates us."

"True."

How could one simple word of agreement feel so good? "This Tom Collins is the best thing I've ever tasted."

"Surely you exaggerate."

"Nope."

"Then you're pretty easy to please."

"Wrong again. I'm difficult to please, in every category, and I have a particularly fussy palate."

"I'm a mean cook. I'll make you dinner sometime. You won't be fussy."

The whole world dilated. The leaves glowed in the late afternoon sunlight. The sparkles on the pond seemed to burst. The breeze was a soft fabric. This opening, this pleasure, wasn't quite welcome, as if she herself were in danger of coming asunder.

"Bader says you're brilliant," Vera said.

"He said that?"

"He said that you understand glaciology better than some of the glaciologists."

"That's my job. To communicate their work." She was drinking her Tom Collins too fast.

"I'm glad he appreciates you, but he's an annoying man."

"I like Bader."

"Do you?"

"Obnoxious as all get-out, sure, but people like him are necessary. They burrow tunnels and cut trails. And yes, definitely destroy things in their paths. But they get places they need to get to, and then others follow. His vision is unparalleled in the field."

"Well. The two of you have a mutual fan club."

"He speaks very highly of you too."

"Hm." Vera sipped her drink. "Well, I appreciate him asking you to work with me. I feel rather humiliated by my poor verbal skills."

"You're a geologist and geographer. Why should you be able to write?"

"As he pointed out, you seem to be able to handle both."

"Hardly the actual science. Just the muck of making it intelligible in the English language."

"He told me you've never married."

"He said that?" And how did the conversation swerve here?

"Yes."

"Why would he offer that information?"

"That's what I wondered."

What about her dead husband? Was Bader somehow testing her? And if so, why?

"He's a meddler," Vera said.

Now what did she mean by that?

"In any case," Vera continued. "I'm widowed."

Lucybelle laughed.

"What's funny?"

"I'm so sorry. That was rude of me to laugh. I . . . I can't explain what's funny."

"Well, it was many years ago. You needn't apologize."

"You really were widowed?"

"Why would I make something like that up?"

"It's just—"

"What?"

"Bader . . ."

"I'll make a couple more drinks, and after that you can tell me what's funny about my widow status."

She hadn't said "my husband's death" or even "my being a widow." It was a "status."

Vera put a second Tom Collins on the arm of Lucybelle's Adirondack chair. "What do you usually drink?"

"Martinis. But these are much better." She added, "Less dangerous."

"Dangerous." Vera had a way of asking questions without the upturned inflection in her voice at the end. It was unnerving, as if she were discovering you rather than asking you.

"Martinis tend to make people spill secrets," Lucybelle said.

"We could wait for martinis or you could just spill now."

"Back in 1956, when Bader hired me, he made me agree to a story about my past. I'm supposed to say that I'd been married and that my husband was killed in the war."

Vera gave her an indecipherable look. The gray eyes became nails. The high cheekbones plateaus. Only the mouth stayed soft, offered the possibility of forgiveness for such folly.

"You wanted the job," Vera finally said, but flatly, as if she were suppressing judgment.

"Yes, I wanted the job, but actually, that was the least of it. I also wanted to be an emotionally devastated widow who wouldn't consider another relationship." Lucybelle smiled out at the pond, wondering why this frightening woman didn't frighten her. "At the time, the story felt like protection."

"Someone broke your heart."

"I needed to get out of New York."

Vera nodded.

"So now you see why I laughed. But you really are a widow."

"William and I married very young. He died of tuberculosis two years later. But that isn't the relationship that put me in your camp."

"My camp?"

"Deciding against future involvements."

Lucybelle felt caught in yet another lie. She hadn't quite "decided" that, and she hadn't exactly done that. But she was too eager to hear Vera's story to correct the misconception right now.

"Foolish me," Vera said, softening even more. "I fell for another sensitive type like William. We were together for ten years."

Lucybelle wanted quite desperately to ask what a sensitive type was. Just the phrase tossed her back into her sunshine pen, naked, lacking.

"So you divorced?"

"Oh no. Nothing that satisfying."

They watched the last bits of sunlight leave the lake. Dark, flapping wings flew low over the water, the sound of air being displaced loud in the tension of silence.

"For god's sake," Lucybelle finally said. "Do you need another drink to tell me the story?"

"No. I just needed to know that you wanted to hear it."

This admission stunned Lucybelle. Her voice caught when she said, "Every detail."

"Susan was—is—terrified of life. She wouldn't even travel with me. God forbid what someone would think if they saw two women traveling together."

Susan! "Women travel together all the time."

"Of course. Fear dictated her every move. Over time, a dissonance built up inside her, a great clanging of her emotional needs. In private, she

248

became more and more clingy. In public, more and more jolly. But a brave kind of jolly, as if she were enduring some secret and deadly illness."

"You loved her?"

"I told you: ten years."

"And you're not the kind of woman who'd stay with someone for ten years if you didn't love her."

"Thank you." After another long pause, she said, "But your question is a fair one. What could possibly keep me in such a relationship? The early years were wonderful. Susan was smart and kind and even fun, if she felt safe."

"Safe. Sometimes I think I never want to hear that word again."

"Agreed. Who is safe, anyway? We could die of cancer next month."

"A tree could fall on us in five minutes." Lucybelle meant to be funny. But Vera said, "Oh no. All my trees are quite healthy."

"Your pond is beautiful. I thought you were just putting me off when you said you were spending all your time looking for a place to live."

"Well." Vera paused a long while and then said, "It's not exactly my pond. I have Trout Brook to thank for delivering the water caught in the form of snow by Smarts Mountain. Not to mention the recession of the last glaciers twelve thousand years ago."

"I hadn't meant to imply that you dug and filled the pond."

"I realize that. But I don't even think that I own a part of it. I'm squatting here."

"You have a cabin."

"Yes. Agreed. But I'm only dwelling here. Fleeting, temporary."

"'We still haven't become mature enough to think of ourselves as only a tiny part of a vast and incredible universe.'"

"Ah. You understand."

They sat in silence for several moments, and then Vera said, "About your other statement: I *was* putting you off."

"Thank you for that clarification."

"Do you hear the pileated woodpecker?"

She did hear a distant tatting, in the woods behind the house.

"Rachel Carson so loved the song of the veeries. I have them here."

"I don't believe I know what a veery sounds like. Or looks like."

Vera bolted from her chair and into the house, returning a moment later with *Birds of North America* and a flashlight. She showed Lucybelle pictures of veeries, male and female, adult and juvenile. "I have black bear too. There's a beech tree not far away with claw marks where the bears have climbed for the beech nuts."

"So you left Susan."

"No. She left me. For a lawyer."

"I guess he was a lot safer."

"She. And yes."

"She?"

"They keep separate apartments and only spend a night or two a week together. They both date men. From what I can tell, any men they can find, although lately they seem to have come up with an arrangement with a couple of fellows who want a cover as well. I haven't met them, but the lawyer praises them for being very masculine."

Night had arrived, but the stars weren't quite out and the moon was new. Vera sat a couple of feet away, but Lucybelle saw only her shape swell and sag as she heaved a big sigh. "You wonder why I stayed so long, why I waited for her to leave me. The confusing thing about Susan is that she gets it all. She's ashamed of her fear. She knows better. She's wonderfully perceptive." Vera's voice quavered a moment before she regained control. "Don't mind me. I'm not upset about her and me. I'm well over the relationship. I'm upset about *her*. She'd be capable of so much if she'd let herself. But her innate terror throws her into the arms of people like the lawyer."

"I'm sorry."

"I detest her." Vera caught herself and added, "Not Susan. The lawyer. I suppose that's wrong of me to harbor such intense . . . dislike."

"If you detest her, I'm sure she's quite detestable."

Vera laughed! "Well, she is. She works for IBM. They're developing computers, and she's perfect for the job. Not a single uncalculated word comes from her mouth. She makes a pile of money. I feel as if she keeps Susan imprisoned. That's actually not fair, though. Susan chooses the situation. So let them have their little purgatory."

"Strong language."

"Yes. Deserved." Vera sighed, as if letting go of something. "They probably don't have sex for fear of hidden surveillance cameras in the apartments. Whatever is between them, they're intent on keeping it secret. They're rigorous in their subterfuge. The lawyer is terrified I'll somehow blow their cover. I swear, I could probably blackmail her for a tidy monthly sum, if I wanted."

"That's so sad."

"Agreed."

"It's not all that uncommon."

"No, it's not. But I say, never again. No more sensitive types. No more secretive types."

A swath of the black sky shuddered across the yard, right above their chairs. Lucybelle gave a little cry of alarm, feeling as if she were revealing all her weaknesses in one outburst.

"It's just the crows. They're alighting in the bitternut hickory." Vera got up and waved her hands at the birds, calling out, "Shoo! Shoo!"

"You don't need to shoo them on my account. They just startled me."

"They harass the littler birds. I prefer that they have their conference elsewhere."

Vera didn't sit back down in the Adirondack chair. She stood with her fists on her hips, looking out at the dark pond, and Lucybelle knew without having to be told that this conference too was over. She left quickly, not wanting to be shooed like the crows.

## Sunday, July 12, 1964

The following Sunday, Lucybelle arrived at the appointed time, not a minute before or after, and knocked gently on the cabin's front door. When there was no answer, she knocked harder. Vera clearly had said eight o'clock. It seemed early for a Sunday, but Lucybelle agreed because she didn't want to sound like a slouch. Last week they'd met on Friday afternoon, which the colonel had given everyone off because of the holiday the next day. Lucybelle had suggested Saturday this week, hoping for more cocktails following their work, but Vera said she was busy.

Apparently, she was busy today too. Lucybelle got back in her car and started the engine, revving it just in case Vera was home and hadn't heard her knocking. She sat in the idling car for another couple of minutes and then shut off the engine. She imagined Vera inside the cozy two-room cabin with a friend, perhaps in the back room, the one Lucybelle hadn't seen, having forgotten their work appointment. But no, that was silly, Vera had made it quite clear with both her words and by inhabiting this backwoods cabin miles from the lab that, above all else, she wanted her reclusive independence.

Well. Good for her. Lucybelle got out of the car and slammed the door. She walked around the cabin to the back side, and there, emerging from the pond, water dripping off her like diamonds in the early morning air, was Vera. She wore a black bathing suit, no frills, and her hair was flattened against her head. She moved with a bold grace, backdropped by the shimmering surface of the pond. As she strode toward her cabin and Lucybelle, bare feet in the green grass, she said, "Is it eight o'clock already?"

"Quarter past."

"I spent all day yesterday—and night, I might add—working on the rewrite. It's on the kitchen table. You can get started. Help yourself to coffee."

She'd barely gotten seated when Vera joined her, toweled hair left all wonky, wearing a pair of blue jeans and an oversized T-shirt. Lucybelle felt prim in her cotton skirt and blouse.

"Do you like to swim?" Vera asked.

"Yes."

"Good."

"So should I spend a few minutes reading what you've done?"

"I didn't get any further than the first page."

"But you said—"

"Yes, all day and all night. I know."

"I could have come later in the week."

"That would have only prolonged my misery."

Lucybelle flipped through the pages they'd marked up last week. Bader had said there were two papers in this pile, and Vera had agreed. They'd teased apart the differences and made two outlines. Half the pages would be images.

"Let's do the photograph captions today," Lucybelle said. "Maybe that'll help me understand what all this is about."

"Help *you*?" Vera said. "Don't spare my feelings."

Four hours later, they'd written half of the captions and Lucybelle was starving, and she said so. As Vera made lunch, Lucybelle inspected the feathers, stones, and bones. She studied the books on the shelves—mostly natural history, not a single novel—and picked up the one on the coffee table, a technical treatise on flying. She looked up to see Vera drying her hands on a dishtowel and watching her.

"Want to go up some time?"

"You have a pilot's license?"

"Yep. We'll fly over the White Mountains."

She imagined Vera in a little leather cap like Amelia Earhart's, at the controls of a two-seater, herself flying shotgun. Below, the cold mountain peaks, and above, the endless blue sky. The fantasy left her with a vertiginous apprehension.

After eating their sandwiches, Vera suggested a "short walk" and lent Lucybelle a pair of sneakers which, being a size and a half too big, felt like clown shoes. Nevertheless, they hiked for over two hours, often pushing through dense underbrush, all the while Vera pointing out the species of trees, a schist cliff, a bobcat den in a fractured ledge, and the tree where the bear scratched. By the time they returned to the cabin, Lucybelle's legs were bleeding with a dozen scrapes and cuts, her feet were blistered, and her cotton skirt was torn.

"Next time wear jeans," Vera said handing her a box of Band-Aids.

With anyone else, Lucybelle would have just taken the pile of paper home and unscrambled the data and verbiage on her own. She knew she was capable of that. But she left it all right there on Vera's kitchen table and they planned to meet again the following weekend. The fact of the matter was, she enjoyed the look of helplessness on this capable woman's face as they wrote together.

Soon they both excused Vera from the process altogether, except to be available to answer questions, and Lucybelle buckled down at the table facing the pond and wrote the two papers, over the course of seven weekends.

## Saturday, August 29, 1964

As long as they met at Vera's cabin, and a manuscript sat between them on the kitchen table, Vera could pretend they had a strictly professional relationship, even if they did have drinks and take hikes. So when in late August, after the papers had been finished and submitted, one each to *Science* and *Nature*, and Lucybelle invited Vera over for dinner, she balked.

"What for?" she asked.

"Dinner," Lucybelle repeated.

"Dinner?"

"I'm not much of a cook. In fact, I can't cook at all, but I'd like to have you over to my place."

Vera stared without responding.

Lucybelle was well aware that she should be hurt rather than amused. The problem was, she liked Vera's walls. She enjoyed leaning against her resistance. In fact, she'd become quite infatuated with the walls, covered them in climbing roses, flew airplanes over them, took naps in their shade. She said, "Tell you what. Bring a briefcase and something you're working on. We'll lay it out on the coffee table."

"Very funny." Despite her sarcasm, a rare defenselessness—this one more deep-seated than the bad writer one—seized Vera's face. She turned away quickly but showed up for the dinner.

"You've met L'Forte." Lucybelle flourished a hand in the direction of her dog sitting upright, to the degree a dachshund can sit upright, in the wingback chair.

Early on she'd asked if she might bring him out to the pond, and Vera had said fine, if he didn't mind staying in the car. She said he'd be distracting to their work and also that he'd scare off her precious critters. Lucybelle did bring him a few times, taking breaks to let him out of the backseat and walk him on the road, but Vera had shown little interest in knowing him.

L'Forte did not greet Vera now. Shrewd fellow that he was, he remained in the chair and appraised the visitor from a distance. He looked undecided.

"Say hello to him," Lucybelle instructed Vera.

"He's a handsome fellow." That was generous.

"You hear that, L'Forte? She thinks you're handsome."

He wagged his tail (though not vigorously), hopped off the chair, and trotted over to Lucybelle's side, announcing the possibility of approval and also his understanding that keeping a wide berth was a good idea. Lucybelle laughed and petted him. "His first impression is cautiously positive."

"You live like a Spartan," Vera said taking in the sparse contents of her studio apartment.

"True. No artifacts. But don't worry about dinner: I got it all from the deli. It'll be quite tasty. Martini?"

"The truth serum."

Lucybelle laughed. "I think we're past secrets."

"Too bad."

"I thought you hated secrecy."

"But I love revelation."

"I have stories. Do they count as revelation?"

"I'm thinking yours will."

This brief exchange left Lucybelle reeling. What did Vera mean by "revelation"? Why had Lucybelle offered "stories"? What had happened to Vera's walls? She retreated to the kitchen to make the drinks and regain her composure.

"So?" Vera asked as soon as they were seated in the living room with their martinis. "Stories."

"Can we have a little small talk first?"

"I hate small talk."

"I see."

"So do you."

This was essentially true, though Lucybelle was capable of making it, which apparently Vera was not. "Okay. So tell me what you know about the editors of *Science* and *Nature*. How likely do you think it is that they'll publish the papers?"

Vera shook her head.

"Unlikely?"

"That's small talk."

Lucybelle didn't quite agree. She really was interested, quite invested, in the outcome of all their work.

Vera raised her martini, followed by her eyebrows.

"What you want," Lucybelle tried to tease, "is gossip."

"If you're talking about yourself, it isn't gossip."

It wasn't the martini. She'd only had two sips. Everything, suddenly, was quite simple: Vera had accepted dinner, maybe even a date, but the terms were full disclosure. So they both lit cigarettes and she began.

She'd already told her a restrained version of Phyllis and had admitted to an affair with someone else's girlfriend, but relating just the outlines of those romances had left her feeling chagrined. Tonight, by filling in the details, by fleshing out the full human comedy of her romantic history, she shed the emotional discomfort. Most of all, she loved making Vera laugh. She told about finding Fred in her kitchen, taking L'Forte to sleep in her

New York office, four years later finding Phyllis and three-year-old Georgia on her doorstep in Evanston, and leaving her ex in possession of a second apartment. She heightened the humor of these stories with contrast, giving a full accounting of the unfunny moment on the Michigan Avenue Bridge, staring down into the dark passing river, and her despair. She told about meeting Stella there, about Wanda's baseball bat. Telling these stories was cathartic, so many memories freed, sent off in their own little leather caps of wild flight.

She laid out the pictures she'd taken of Stella a year ago, and Vera surprised her by enthusiastically admiring the Thunderbird convertible in the background. Lucybelle even explained why Stella had made the trip to New Hampshire. She watched Vera's face as she told about the nude photographs, how they were an expression of Stella's artistic vision but also a potent bond between them, and expected to see disapproval. She cared, didn't want to see even a hint of displeasure on Vera's face, but over the past few minutes, during her telling, she'd made a silent but vehement vow that not a single deception would slip between herself and Vera.

"May I see the pictures?"

"No!"

"You're the one who mixed and served the truth serum."

"And I'm telling you all the truths. But you don't get to examine the primary documents."

"You'd better get us some food," Vera said.

They ate at the coffee table because Lucybelle didn't have a kitchen table. She put out two plates, the heated up squares of lasagna, the container of coleslaw, and a bottle of wine.

Vera's laugh was surprisingly full-chested, and the more Lucybelle heard it, the more she wanted to hear it. She'd never talked so much in her life. While Vera ate with a robust appetite, she heard herself describing Clare and segueing right into how they'd stumbled into sex in a New York building's entryway. She thought she'd gone too far, blown everything with this bawdy story, but Vera's entire being seemed to slacken. She set down her plate, having scraped off all the tomato sauce, and just smiled at Lucybelle.

"I guess I'm shocking you."

"A bit."

"Well, you've heard it all now."

"Let me add," Vera said in her formal voice, as if the forthcoming admission cost her something, "I don't mind being shocked."

"Oh." Now it *was* the martini that allowed her to hold eye contact. "Is that right."

"It is."

"So. You've never done anything inappropriate?"

"Of course I have, but I'm rather guarded."

"You don't like to make mistakes."

"Who does?"

"Some people don't mind."

Vera laughed. "True."

"I bought a cake. Coffee?"

"I hardly want to leave the impression that I don't make mistakes. My relationship with Susan was far from healthy."

"It sounds like parts were. At first."

Vera gave that singular hard nod of hers. "She wasn't dishonest. Just afraid."

"So now you have your collections and your pond."

Vera didn't answer, and Lucybelle got up to snap on the lamp.

"You're saying that I'm only willing to be in a relationship with myself."

"Is that true?"

"I guess it is."

Lucybelle resisted the urge to comment sarcastically. Instead she went to make the coffee and fetch the cake. When she turned back around, Vera was standing before her bookshelf, bent at the waist, reading the titles. Lucybelle put down the cake and went back to get the coffeepot and cups. By the time she poured the coffee, she'd decided on a different interpretation of Vera's relationship with herself.

"You can't have a good relationship with anyone else without having a good one with yourself," she said.

Vera looked caught off guard, as if Lucybelle had stormed her fortress from a different direction. Unable to think of a rebuttal, she quietly said, "Agreed."

Lucybelle laughed. "You're such a scientist. If a statement is true, you force yourself to admit it, even when you don't want to."

"Well, there's not any data supporting your hypothesis."

"There might be. My friend Harry is a psychiatrist. I could ask him."

Vera waved a dismissing hand through the air. "No. It's true. People who aren't comfortable with themselves can do such damage to others."

"I know you don't read fiction," Lucybelle said. "But there's this line in a Willa Cather novel that I love." She paused, having thought only of the heart of the quote, but now she wanted to recite the entire bit. She grabbed the book off the shelf and flipped through the pages until she found it: "'Suddenly something flashed into her mind, so clear that it must have come from without, from the breathless quiet. What if—what if Life itself were the sweetheart? It was like a lover waiting for her in distant cities—across the sea; drawing her, enticing her, weaving a spell over her.'"

"Life itself," Vera said softly. "Yes."

## Sunday, August 30, 1964

Lucybelle dug in the hamper for dog-walking clothes, pulling out her yellow, sleeveless blouse, which had a coffee stain on the front, and her rumpled madras shorts. She tied on her Keds, forgoing socks. She'd shower when they got back from their walk. Her plan for the day was to work on her novel, which she'd put off during all those weekends working on Vera's papers. She placed the draft on her coffee table and was standing, arms folded, looking at it when the doorbell rang.

Assuming it was her landlady, Lucybelle pulled open the door. There stood Vera holding the borrowed copy of Cather's *Lucy Gayheart*. "Thank you. I read it last night."

"That was fast."

"I can't write, but I can read."

Lucybelle wanted to invite her in despite the coffee stain, the jarring blouse and shorts ensemble, the state of her hair. L'Forte pushed out the door and gave one friendly bark at Vera. She smiled at him! Then she bent and even petted him. That did it. Lucybelle opened the door wider and asked if she wanted to come in.

"No," Vera said coming in the door. "It's rude of me to stop by like this. But I was running errands and so I thought I'd just drop the book off."

She wasn't running errands. It was Sunday. Nothing was open.

"I liked the whole book." She set it down on Lucybelle's coffee table. "What's this?"

258

Unfortunately, there was no hiding the manuscript. The title page announcing "A Thin Bright Line" by Lucybelle Bledsoe sat on the top of the stack. Vera dropped onto the couch and flipped through the first couple of pages. "What's this?" she asked again.

"A novel."

"You didn't tell me you'd written a novel."

"It's not finished."

"I want to read it."

"You don't read fiction."

"I just read Willa Cather, didn't I?"

"Please. Leave it alone."

Recognizing the threat, L'Forte barked again, this time aggressively.

Vera looked at the dog as she said, "I'm leaving for Greenland on Wednesday. I'll be gone for three weeks."

"What? Why haven't you mentioned this until now?"

"It's a follow-up trip. A couple of years ago the division obtained conventional aerial photographs, as well as some infrared imagery, in the Gulf of St. Lawrence. Northwest of Greenland, a bunch of islands in the Canadian archipelago. They also shot most of the pack ice all the way up to the North Pole. So we're going to—"

"Very interesting," Lucybelle said impatiently. "What I meant was, why haven't you told me you're leaving on this trip?"

"I didn't think my fieldwork was apropos of anything having to do with you."

Lucybelle felt the sting of that dismissal.

"Until now," Vera added.

She waited for the punch line.

"It won't matter if you let me read your novel because you won't have to see me at all for a few weeks."

At least Vera understood the level of vulnerability involved. Lucybelle picked up L'Forte and sat on the other end of the couch with him in her lap. She stroked his ears. "Take it." She gestured at the manuscript. "And go."

That night, to keep from thinking of Vera reading her rough novel, Lucybelle imagined the two of them flying. They were in a two-seater, so far above earth that the rivers were veins, the farms little squares, and the mountains a green disturbance. Mostly all they saw was blue sky.

## Friday, September 18, 1964

The manuscript was on her desk when Lucybelle got to work on Monday morning. There was no note. Nor did she see Vera before she left for Greenland on Wednesday. If she came into the lab at all that week, besides early on Monday to dump off the manuscript, she managed to avoid any corridors where they might meet.

The silence, both before her departure and also about the novel, felt as scathing as a blade. Vera could fly a plane, hike in the Andes, socialize with black bears in her own backyard, but she was terrified of revealing her heart.

Or maybe she just hated the novel.

Three weeks later, on a Friday while Lucybelle was at lunch, her secretary, Vivian, left a note on her desk. "Dr. Prescott would like you to call her."

She picked up the telephone to dial about five times that afternoon and stopped herself each time. Dr. Prescott knew where to find her.

Which she eventually did. A few minutes before five o'clock, she appeared in Lucybelle's doorway, once again walking past Vivian, who trailed her, saying, "Can I help you, Dr. Prescott?"

"It's okay, Vivian," Lucybelle said. "It's five o'clock. Have a nice weekend."

Vera shut the door. She looked nervous.

"You're back."

"Yes."

"Good trip?"

"So-so."

Lucybelle wanted to say, well good thing you didn't discover anything extraordinary because you're not getting any help writing a paper this time.

"Come to dinner tomorrow."

Lucybelle couldn't manage a no, just barely managed to not say yes.

"Let's swim before dinner. Bring your bathing suit and come early."

"What's early?"

"Noon."

She didn't allow herself to smile. "On one condition."

"That being?"

"L'Forte can come too."

"I was going to invite him."

"You were not."

"I was. Have him bring his swimming trunks as well."

## Saturday, September 19, 1964

She felt shy in her bathing suit, her limbs thin and pale in the warm after-noon sunlight. But Vera barely looked at her. She splashed in and stroked out into the pond a good hundred yards before flipping around and calling out, "Come on!"

Lucybelle was a good swimmer. She and her brother had spent many a summer day swimming in the Black River, southeast of Pocahontas. Still, she felt self-conscious of her form; it wasn't anything like the strong wind-mills and vigorous kicks that Vera used. Everything was a pleasant blur with-out her glasses, and she gave herself over to the sensual cool balm of the lake water. L'Forte sat at water's edge to wait for her. He didn't bark once, as if he knew his continued participation was dependent on good behavior.

When she reached Vera, they tread water, grinning like kids.

"Watch," Lucybelle said. She showed Vera her curious buoyancy: when she lay on her back in the water, she barely sunk below the surface.

"Now you watch. You have to put your face under to see." Vera somer-saulted and dove, spearing her hands toward the bottom of the lake, pro-pelling herself with a frog kick. She descended several yards, into the murky depths, just the soft, white bottoms of her feet visible. A few seconds later she broke the surface, gasping for breath.

Dr. Prescott was showing off like a teenaged boy.

"I'm going to swim to the other side," Lucybelle said.

"That's too far."

She started swimming, showing off in her own way. She wasn't that strong, but her unusual buoyancy meant she couldn't sink. Vera passed her within moments and reached the far shore long before Lucybelle did. In fact, it was farther than she'd ever swum in her life. As she pulled herself out onto the grassy bank, she flopped down and said, "You might have to go get the car to take me back."

Vera laughed her deep laugh and said, "Really?"

"If I tried to swim back, I'm afraid you'd have to rescue me in a more difficult way."

Without her glasses, Lucybelle couldn't see the expression on Vera's face. Maybe she was considering, as she was, which form of rescue would be the most fun.

"Give me half an hour. You'll be okay here?"

"Yes. Bring L'Forte, will you? He's probably worried sick." She could just picture him sitting at water's edge, his black eyebrow spots bunched as he strained to see her on the far shore.

Vera did a running belly flop into the pond and swam hard toward its center. Lucybelle watched her progress, a splashy blur, and thought she'd never been happier. She lay back in the grass, the sunshine on her arms and legs, no wooden pen, just a warm breeze and the distant sound of Vera swimming.

Once they were back at the cabin, dried off and dressed in shorts and blouses, Vera started the grill. She handed Lucybelle a glass of champagne. The sparkling sweetness was delightful.

They sat in the Adirondack chairs and L'Forte lay down at their feet, quietly watching some ducks.

"He knows that if he doesn't behave he won't be invited back," Lucybelle said.

"He doesn't understand that much."

"He does."

Vera made a soft *hmpf* sound to indicate that while she wouldn't argue, she thought ascribing higher consciousness to L'Forte was poppycock.

"The truth of the matter is, he's getting old. He probably doesn't even want to chase ducks anymore."

"Your novel is beautiful."

Everything jolted a bit.

"I want to read it again."

"I'm kind of stunned. I figured since you left it on my desk without so much as a note or—"

"You know I can't write."

"You can't even write a note?"

"I'm sorry. Did you think I didn't like it?"

Lucybelle took a deep breath, trying to accustom herself as quickly as possible to this new worldview: Vera liked her novel.

"Well, I'm stupid," Vera said. "Of course you would have thought that I didn't like it. Who wouldn't think that? I liked it very, very much. I'm in awe of your ability to write those kinds of truths. It makes me feel like my adherence to facts is a weakness, or a great limitation."

Before Lucybelle could think of any kind of response to this, Vera got up and said, "I'll get the first course."

She brought out two cups of gazpacho, a cold tomato and cucumber soup she said people eat in Spain. Then she put the marinated chicken pieces on the grill. As they cooked, she set up a card table and two chairs and threw on a cotton tablecloth, patterned with bunches of purple grapes and green vines, which she'd gotten in Italy. She carried out a plate of sliced honeydew melon and a bowl of homegrown lettuce.

"Just lettuce," she said. "If it's fresh, I don't like to ruin a salad with any other vegetables. A little olive oil, salt, and pepper."

While they ate, they talked about Vera's Greenland trip and gossip from the lab. She'd made fresh berry tarts for dessert, and they took these back to the Adirondack chairs with their coffee. Each bite of the meal was more pleasurable than Lucybelle thought it possible for food to be. Vera was right: Lucybelle wasn't a fussy eater when *she* cooked.

Most of the leaves were still a dense green, but the autumn light was distinctly more saturated than it had been when they'd sat outside earlier in the summer. The surface of the pond was a glossy plum color by five o'clock. The air was still thick with warmth, but a coolness tinged the edges, a slight hardness that promised coming ice.

"I don't know," Vera said, as if a question had been asked aloud.

"Yes, you do."

"I'm forty-two."

"So? I'm forty-one."

"You agreed to be a widow."

"Is that it? Is that the problem?"

"I can't bear any more—"

"Lies and secrets. Neither can I. If you'd like, I'll put a banner across my doorway at the lab that says, 'Lucy is a single queer girl.' Would that help?"

"Maybe it would." She didn't even laugh. "But what if I wanted you to strike the word 'single'?"

Lucybelle rose from her chair and kneeled next to Vera's. "I love you. I'll skywrite it, if you want."

"Would you?"

"Yes. I would." She got to her feet and pulled Vera to hers. They stood facing one another, their hands joined. "Do you know now?"

"I'm afraid."

Lucybelle went weak in the knees at her plain honesty. "You'd be a fool not to be."

Vera smiled, and Lucybelle drew all four of their hands around her own waist and joined Vera's at her back. "We could die of cancer next year."

"A tree could fall on us in five minutes."

"Not your trees. They're healthy."

Vera kissed her.

## Tuesday, December 29, 1964

For the next three months, they made love and talked, pretty much non-stop, whenever Vera was in town. She traveled a lot, flying all over the world for her work. The separations were excruciating and they intensified the urgency to make a plan—but for what? In the meantime, Lucybelle had astronomical telephone bills.

A couple of weeks before Christmas, Vera surprised her by announcing that she was going home to Cutter Creek, Illinois, for the holiday.

"Home? I've never heard you use that word for Cutter Creek." Vera's family was even more religious than Lucybelle's, and she hadn't had an adoring father to compensate for the effects of all that severe biblical judgment.

"I haven't seen them in five years. They're getting old."

John Perry and Helen had invited Lucybelle to Portland for Christmas, and Mother would be there too. She ought to go. "Okay. But I won't do this again."

"Do what?"

"Separate Christmases."

The plural, as well as the implied future, alarmed Vera and she tried to change the subject by pointing out a particularly high snowdrift.

Lucybelle said, "It's kind of ironic, because I think it's you and me, what we have, that's giving you the courage to face them."

"Hardly. They've all but disowned me because of my lesbianism."

"I know that. But our relationship gives me strength. Maybe it does you too. Their feelings likely haven't changed, but they can't hurt you now."

"I like the theory."

A pilot's license, a PhD, natural history collections from all over the world, none of these can protect a woman from the havoc of family treachery. Not even new love could do that. But it would only be a week, and then they'd be reunited. Lucybelle bought gifts for her nephews and nieces, particularly pleased with a large stuffed mountain lion for seven-year-old Lucy, and flew to Portland with some apprehension.

She was right to have worried.

Lucybelle arrived back in New Hampshire on the twenty-eighth, and Vera flew in the next day. The plan had been for Lucybelle to pick her up at the airport, but Vera called late the night before and, citing Lucybelle's poor winter driving skills, told her she'd take the bus to Lyme and call her neighbor, Mr. Carter, to pick her up in his truck. They had their first argument. Vera prevailed.

Lucybelle waited all day to hear from her and grabbed the telephone when it finally rang in the early evening.

"I just wanted to let you know I've made it safely home."

"I'm coming over."

"The road is buried in three feet of snow."

"Mr. Carter got through."

"He has a truck. And he knows how to drive in this weather."

"It's perfectly clear out."

"Eighteen degrees. Icy."

It wasn't even so much the content of what Vera was saying, since that was actually quite reasonable, it was her tone. Her voice had a lot of shove in it.

"What happened in Cutter Creek?"

"Nothing happened in Cutter Creek, believe me. Nothing ever happens in Cutter Creek."

"I'm coming over."

"Damn it, I said no."

Lucybelle couldn't speak for the tears in her throat. She could actually hear Vera breathing, as if she were working up to saying something momentous, and she was.

"I'm sorry. I didn't mean to be harsh like that. But listen."

She listened.

"I need to concentrate more on my work."

She kept listening.

"I didn't expect things to develop as they have, with you and me."

"Don't do this."

"I told you from the very start that I want my independence."

"You let those people in Illinois hurt you."

"No. It's not that. I need to feel free. I travel all the time for work. I'm away more than I'm home. Missing someone feels restrictive. I'm sorry, it's just who I am."

"That's a lie, and you know it." Lucybelle picked up the pillow on her bed and threw it across the room. "You're afraid."

"I don't want to be tied down. Relationships are binding."

"God, was I ever tricked into thinking you were so courageous. You're a coward like everyone else. Oh, how easy to never be disappointed by a pile of bones and feathers, by an icy pond. They won't ever hurt you, will they? In fact, they won't even *talk*. You have it all figured out."

"It's better to end it now. Before we get too mired."

"Mired. Nice word. I'm not mired, Vera. I'm in love with you."

"I've really enjoyed these three months, but—"

Lucybelle hung up on her. She pulled on her warmest wool pants and sweater, grabbed her coat and car keys, and slammed the door to her studio on the way out. It was true that she wasn't a great snow driver, but the highway was plowed, with only a few icy patches, and she drove slowly, despite the fury pounding her heart. Once past Lyme, the road conditions worsened, but she made it to the turnoff for Post Pond without any mishaps. There the snow was indeed a couple of feet thick, but deep tire tracks— Mr. Carter's truck, no doubt—had been carved through the drifts. She turned left on the snow-blanketed dirt road at the back side of the pond and continued driving into the forest, beginning to consider all kinds of crazy possibilities. Vera hadn't left Cutter Creek at all, was mired, to use her word, in the family, stuck there forever. Or she'd met someone new, and this was her way of moving on. Or she was a cold, data-driven scientist who'd only wanted to see if she could seduce Lucybelle, and now, mission accomplished, had lost interest.

By the time her Bel Air slid into the snowbank, she was in a state. Furious, heartbroken, and confused. The driver's door was smashed right up against the wall of snow. She grunted aloud as she made her way across the seat, her overcoat bunching up and inhibiting movement, so she could get out of the passenger side. She realized that while she'd thought to put on warm pants, a sweater, and a coat, she was still wearing her canvas sneakers. She jumped out of the car anyway and started trudging. The brilliant skyful of stars didn't help. They only reminded her of how dreadfully cold it was, their radiance literally light-years away, nothing to keep her warm but her own pulsing blood. Twice she fell. The second time she floundered for so long in the deep snow, trying to gain enough purchase to stand, that she cried out in frustration. A crust of snow covered her wool coat. She walked on, mucus running from her nose and tears freezing on her cheeks. She didn't have a hat. She got very cold.

She pushed open Vera's door and stood there on the threshold.

"Jesus," Vera said.

"On the telephone. You tried to break up with me on the telephone."

Vera pulled her inside the cabin. "Where's your car?"

"Down the road in a goddamn snowbank."

Vera wrapped her in a blanket and put on a kettle. She kept saying, "Jesus."

"You pick that Jesus bit up in Cutter Creek?"

Vera may as well have been a snowshoe hare with her foot caught in a steel trap, so visible was her emotional struggle.

"No," she said. "Are you hungry?"

Lucybelle had eaten toast this morning but couldn't remember anything since then.

"I'll heat up some soup."

"I don't want soup. I want you to kiss me."

"But you're so angry."

"You'll have to weather that."

Vera knelt down and took off Lucybelle's wet socks and sneakers. She stayed on her knees, warming the toes in her hands.

"Let's go to bed. I'd like to remind you of a thing or two."

"Jesus," Vera said again.

"No Jesus. And no more Illinois." She pulled Vera into the bedroom. "I'm hypothermic. Warm me up."

"Apparently," Vera said a few minutes later, "you were already warmed up."

"No talking. I'm still angry at you."

"I know. So I may as well tell you the rest."

"I want to make love again."

"God," Vera said.

"Please."

So they did, but then, afterward, Vera said, "You need to hear what I have to say."

"I don't think I do."

"They want to transfer me to Washington."

That was all? Lucybelle felt relieved. "Well, that's crazy."

"It's my job."

"You'd never leave your pond."

"I need a job to go with my pond."

"You're not serious. You wouldn't move to Washington."

"I banked my entire life on my education. The blood and sweat that went into getting this job, you can't possibly know."

"Don't patronize me. I do know. But what about us?"

Vera flopped onto her back and remained silent.

Lucybelle got out of bed. She found her soggy clothes in a pile on the floor and started to pull them on. Nothing had ever felt so soddenly dreadful.

"Please come back to bed."

"Why? Why would I do that?"

"Because I love you."

"How many days until you leave me again?"

Her voice was way too small, nearly choked, but she did say, "I won't."

In the morning a loud knocking awakened them. Vera pulled on her robe and closed the bedroom door before answering the front one.

"Sorry to bother you," Mr. Carter's loud voice boomed out. "But I wondered if you know whose car that is, down the way about a mile?"

"A mile?" Vera said.

*Yes!* Lucybelle wanted to shout. *A mile!*

Later that morning, Mr. Carter helped the two women tow the Bel Air out of the snowbank. He followed Lucybelle back to the highway to make sure she made it safely.


## Thursday–Saturday, March 25–27, 1965

At the beginning of the year, Lorraine Hansberry died and Malcolm X was assassinated. The country seemed to be coming apart. Civil rights protesters in Alabama were beaten, hosed, and attacked by police dogs. Lucybelle watched the televised broadcasts, searching the faces, hoping to find Stella's. She knew she'd be there with her camera.

On Thursday, March 25, after so much bloodshed and heartbreak, twenty-five thousand peaceful protesters arrived at the Alabama state capitol. Governor George Wallace refused to meet Dr. Martin Luther King, but the reverend spoke to the nation from the steps. "I know some of you are asking today, 'How long will it take?' I come to say to you this afternoon however difficult the moment, however frustrating the hour, it will not be long, because truth pressed to the earth will rise again. How long? Not long, because no lie can live forever. How long? Not long, because you will reap what you sow. How long? Not long, because the arm of the moral universe is long but it bends toward justice."

Lucybelle wanted so badly for Vera to be with her then, witnessing that moment. So much was ending, and yet so much also seemed to be beginning. How long would it take? King's words opened up a great tender hopefulness. Not long.

Vera called her the next morning at work to say that she would be in Puerto Rico another two weeks.

"That's too long."

"How's your novel going?"

It was Vera's way of reminding her that their separations had an advantage for her as well. Lucybelle wanted to hear, I love you. She wanted to tell Vera about Reverend King's speech. They were on the CRREL line, though, and could only allow themselves one or two personal comments, and those had to be bloodless.

When Lucybelle hung up she felt raw. She ached, both for Vera and for the future that Reverend King had described, where truth pressed to the earth, where you could reap what you sowed. However difficult the moment, however frustrating the hour.

She jumped at the sound of her buzzer and pushed the intercom button to find out what Vivian wanted. "Dorothy Shipwright called while you were on the line just now. She'd like you to call her."

"Dorothy?"

"The librarian."

"Thank you. I'll call her back."

Of course she knew who Dorothy Shipwright was, but they'd had so little interaction in the past couple of years. When they did need to engage at work, they both pretended they'd never been more than casual friends. Every once in a while Lucybelle suffered a spasm of guilt, as if her happiness were at the expense of Dorothy's unhappiness, but that was silly. What did one have to do with the other?

Still agape with Reverend King's words of optimism and flayed open by the sound of Vera's voice, she picked up the phone and punched Dorothy's extension.

"Have dinner with me tomorrow night," Dorothy said, sounding like her old affable self. "We'll celebrate spring."

Celebrate spring! What a contrast to that day on the train coming home from New York, Dorothy announcing her remorse over what had happened between them. Or the day of Lucybelle's fortieth birthday, Dorothy crumpled and sobbing over Mary's impending marriage. Lucybelle was happy to hear her cheerfulness. Perhaps Dorothy was unfolding.

"I miss you," Dorothy carried on. "It's stupid. We used to be such good friends."

Lucybelle had no plans for tomorrow night. She accepted the invitation.

Dorothy still lived in the apartment Lucybelle had found for her and her mother, the same one where her mother had died, but now the place was a surprising mess, with books on the floor and magazines stacked unevenly on the side tables. There were even two piles of laundry in the front room. "I haven't gotten any neater," Dorothy said, kicking at one of the piles. "Why bother? It's just me. I'm making us martinis. Look, I got us some Booth's." She held up the bottle.

Lucybelle didn't really want a martini but she figured she could just sip it. Once the drink was in her hand, though, she was glad for its support.

"I hardly ever get a proper drink anymore," Dorothy said. "Pastor Lane is opposed to excess, and it's hard to make a case for alcohol being anything other than excess." Dorothy deepened her voice and seesawed her jaw, doing an imitation of her pastor commenting on alcohol.

Lucybelle laughed, happy to see that her old friend's sense of humor was still intact. "So how are you?" she asked, truly wanting to know.

"I'm fine. Wonderful! I know you never approved of Mary, but—"

"I've never even met Mary."

"I know. But my choice to leave the life behind. You were judgmental of that."

"I'm sorry." What else could she say?

Dorothy grinned, appeared to savor the apology, terse as it was.

270

God, she missed Vera. How she'd like to be with her now, in the cabin at the pond, talking about everything, looking at that lovely, complex face. Vera had promised to be home in time for the pussywillows, but now another two weeks in Puerto Rico.

"I'm nowhere near as brave as you," Dorothy carried on. "Anyway, I'm happier this way. Stephen is so kind to me. They're teaching the baby to call me 'Aunt Dot.' Isn't that sweet? She's pregnant again."

Lucybelle nodded, tried to smile, and finished her drink.

"And I love my church. Pastor Lane can be a little overbearing, but we make fun of him—not to his face, of course!—and he's a good man. I've joined the bowling team!" Dorothy laughed too hard and color rose into her cheeks. Lucybelle remembered her in that pirate outfit and must have glanced below her face, because Dorothy said, "I've gained fifteen pounds. There're cookies at every single church event. But who cares? I'm on my own, I don't need a figure." She stood up. "I'll make a couple more drinks."

By now Lucybelle wanted another one. "I miss the egg rolls and dipping sauce," she called toward the kitchen.

Dorothy laughed again and brought out the fresh drinks. "We had fun. But we were so young. We could risk everything."

"We're not that old yet."

"Speak for yourself."

Lucybelle's stomach growled as she took a gulp of the second martini. She wondered when dinner would be served.

"Tell me about you," Dorothy said. "Any new loves in your life?"

Lucybelle and Vera each lived far from the lab, and also far from one another. They assumed that their relationship had not been detected by anyone, but they didn't know for sure.

"I didn't think so," Dorothy said. "Where would you meet anyone up here?"

A disturbing thought occurred to Lucybelle: Dorothy was a story she hadn't told Vera. She hadn't withheld it on purpose, not exactly. It would have been unfair, she reasoned with herself now, even unkind, to expose Dorothy in that way. She clearly would not want to be revealed. They all worked together, after all. Lucybelle took a drink of her martini and admitted the other truth: the story about Clare in the entryway passed as funny, but just barely; an account of the New Year's Eve jamboree with Dorothy would not be well received.

"I'm sorry," Dorothy said. "About what happened between us."

"It's in the past now."

"I can see how you would have misinterpreted everything."

So this was the point of the evening: to make sure Lucybelle knew that she was the jilted one. She kept herself from asking what exactly she had misinterpreted. The sooner they moved on from this topic of conversation the better.

"I did it for your own sake."

This was getting more twisted by the second.

"It started just for fun." Dorothy laughed her big goofy laugh. "You know, with the books."

"The books?" Everything began to spin. "What are you talking about?"

"That was so much fun! You knew it was me, right?" She laughed even harder, as if they were sharing a very funny joke.

"No."

"Really? You didn't? Oh, you goof."

Lucybelle found herself forcing a smile. How silly of her to take the books as threats. How stupid of her to not see the joke.

"I sent the first one because I wanted to know if you were. You know, one of the girls."

"You mean a lesbian."

"Ew. I hate that word."

That's why she'd used it. Lucybelle finished off her martini. Of course this wasn't a joke at all. She wondered if she could stand up and just leave.

"Look, it's no secret I had feelings for you," Dorothy said. "I mean, obviously."

Lucybelle's head began swimming.

"I invited you tonight because I wanted to apologize. I know what I did was wrong. But I did it for you, not against you. When I realized you were involved with that Stella Robinson girl, I got worried."

"What are you saying?" The betrayal loomed so large, was so suffocating, that in that first moment she couldn't even see it. All she knew was that she couldn't breathe.

"Everyone makes mistakes. God knows I have. But she had a girlfriend the entire time you were together. And you knew about Wanda."

How did she know Wanda's name?

"I was trying to protect you," Dorothy said. "That's how it started, anyway. But I'm a librarian. I love research! So I admit, it became a game too."

"You." Lucybelle felt as if she'd disgorged, rather than spoken, the word.

"Don't look at me that way. I want you to understand."

"You pretended to be my friend."

"I *was* your friend! That's exactly what I'm trying to tell you. Even when they stopped paying me, I tried to help."

"Paying you?"

"Hardly much. That was the least of it. I mean, sure, I took the money, why not? But that's not why I did it."

"Who paid you?"

Dorothy laughed. "Oh, you know, they don't really tell you who they are. But the extra income was nice. I had my mother to take care of, you might recall. The best part though was that I could help you at the same time."

"You took money to inform on my activities?"

"That's funny. You make it sound like a spy novel. Believe me, they weren't all that interested in you, anyway. In fact, they stopped paying me after a while. But I kept going. Because of how much I cared about you. I don't expect you to understand that part. I know the feelings weren't mutual."

"What do you mean, you 'kept going'?"

"I went rogue!" That familiar nutty spark lit her eyes.

Lucybelle almost laughed with Dorothy.

"The point is, as long as I was the one gathering information, I could control what information was gathered and who got ahold of it. Better it was me. You were safe in my hands. I was like a pressure-release valve. If I quit, someone who could have really harmed you might have taken over."

"You already said they weren't interested in me."

"Oh, they were at first. That's my point. They might have continued caring if I hadn't led them off the track."

"You hardly led them off the track. You told them about Lorraine Hansberry's party. About my relationships with Phyllis and Stella. What exactly didn't you tell them?"

Dorothy stood and walked into the kitchen. When she returned, she had the bottle of gin. "Refill?" Apparently she intended to pour right from the bottle, no vermouth, no ice, no olive.

"No. I'm leaving."

"We haven't had dinner."

"I'm not hungry."

She poured gin into her own glass and sat down, this time right beside Lucybelle. "Don't worry. You're safe now. *We're* safe."

A deep shudder rocked Lucybelle from her esophagus to her kidneys. To think she'd slept with this woman.

Dorothy put a hand on her forearm. "I want you to understand. That's why I'm telling you all of this. I was protecting you. I was trying to keep you safe."

"You went to Stella and Wanda's house. You asked Stella about Camp Century."

"Aha! So you *had* told her. I suspected as much. You're naïve, Lucy. You're so trusting. Thank god I intervened."

Lucybelle found no words to answer the enormity of what she was hearing. She felt as if Dorothy's revelations were vaporizing her. Her entire being puffing into a gas, disappearing into the atmosphere. She couldn't feel her legs enough to stand.

"I know my nature," Dorothy said, her voice deepening with feeling. "I know you think I don't. But I do. And here we are, in the boonies. Alone. We single girls need to stick together." Dorothy leaned forward and put her mouth on Lucybelle's. The press of her lips aroused a kind of terror, and for the briefest moment Lucybelle kissed her back, the warp of shame gravitational in its attraction.

Then, like a visitation from a god she didn't even believe in, sensations of salvation came to her rescue. The camera capturing light and defying fear. The reverberating voice of Reverend King: no lie can live forever. The messages in Bader's falling snowflakes.

She stood abruptly, their mouths sliding apart, grabbed her coat, and ran.


## Monday, March 29, 1965

On Monday morning, Lucybelle received a sealed envelope via the internal CRREL mail system. Inside, on a piece of lined notebook paper, were ten words: "Seriously. Think about it. You and me. It would work."

## Monday, October 18, 1965

A package addressed with the familiar blocky lettering, and bearing no information about the sender, arrived in her 9 Placid Square Street home mailbox. Inside was a new novel, *Mrs. Stevens Hears the Mermaids Singing*, by a May Sarton.

A note taped to the front of the book read, "You're right to have left that night. And to have ignored my note the following Monday. And to have steered clear of me ever since. Absolutely right. Please accept my full apologies."

Of course she hadn't signed the note.

It had been six months since Dorothy's divulgence, and still Lucybelle felt dizzy with the disorientation of deception. They'd shared so much laughter. Pocahontas and her mother. That night of joyous, yes it had been joyous, sex. Sure, they'd drifted apart; Dorothy's newfound piety had slid like an avalanche between them; and yet somehow Lucybelle had trusted, had believed in Dorothy's basic goodness. She still did. Despite the betrayal. The woman was doing ever so much more damage to herself than to anyone else. Every time Lucybelle wondered if she ought to tell Bader, she realized that there would be no point. He would probably just laugh; he'd had no idea who'd fed the goons their information. She thought of telling Phyllis and Ruthie too, but why upset them? Dorothy had been a mere cog, and now she was a discarded one.

Lucybelle dropped both the book and the note into her metal waste-paper bin. She set the bin on the kitchen floor and lit a match. She dropped the match into the bin. Flames leapt up the sides of the cylinder, as if the contents were especially incendiary. But she couldn't bear to burn a book. In fact, she wanted the book; what she didn't want was a gift from Dorothy. She reached in and pulled out the novel. She put it on the floor and stomped on the page edges that were already alight, putting out the fire. Her thumb, she realized, was badly burned.

## Winter 1965–66

Lucybelle and Vera could talk about anything. Willa Cather and Greenland, the ice cores and infrared imaging, the homophile rights movements burgeoning in New York and San Francisco, their families and religious upbringings.

Anything except the impending move to Washington, D.C.

Lucybelle tried. "What about your pond?"

"I'm never here anyway."

She couldn't bring herself to ask, again, "What about me?"

A tangled paradox rooted their very relationship. They'd fallen in love with each other's intelligence and independence, so that the harder they loved—love being an irrational expression that involved driving into snowbanks, talking all night when one should be working, crying out in physical ecstasy—the more it weakened their bond. They were both women who'd chosen lives of the mind, who'd always believed that they could not have both intellectual and emotional fulfillment. If Vera's life of the mind was taking her to Washington, then by the very terms of their personal identities and even relationship, that meant the end.

In the meantime, whenever Vera was out of town, which was often, Lucybelle missed her acutely. She dreaded the day when CRREL would announce that they were ready to move the Photographic Interpretation Research Division. The authorities hadn't yet named a date. Maybe, the colonel said, next fall.

So they had time. A few months. Maybe even a year. They proceeded as if that were their allotment, all they would get, as if the time were a surprising gift, but not something they should count on.

Sometimes the future looked like a bleak white place. A blank.

Still, they immersed themselves in work and each other, and the months slid by in days of revelatory euphoria followed, sometimes, by painful distances. They didn't bother much with arguing after the first year. What was the point? They loved each other too much to separate until they had to separate.

At times the problem seemed almost mathematical. Lucybelle thought there ought be a formula she could use to work it out. Once, quite spontaneously, she confessed her love for Vera to the most unlikely person in the lab, Russell Woo, maybe because of his extraordinary understanding of the laws of the universe. He accepted the news with a nod, as he might accept a new finding in the lab. She told Vera she'd told him, that she hadn't known why she had done so, and Vera smiled and said, "I like Russell."

Lucybelle tried looking for answers in other couples. Beverly and Ruthie managed, having recovered from the State Department scandal, but they persevered like alpine trees, twisted and stunted as they survived the rarified air and lack of nutrients. Stella and Wanda, though, they were living out in front of the line. Lucybelle wished she could call Stella, ask her how they did it. Courage, certainly. But there had to be other ingredients, a set of helpful instructions. There had to be a way.

The best Lucybelle could come up with was a nearly hallucinatory fantasy. She and Vera would go up in an airplane and disappear forever, like Amelia Earhart, crash-landing on a tropical island where they'd drink coconut milk and spear fish, swim in the warm surf and build a cabin of driftwood.

She made the mistake of telling this fantasy to Vera, she who hewed to the strictest interpretation of reality.

"Lovely," Vera sniped. "Has Dr. Leary fed you some psilocybin?"

## Saturday–Sunday, March 19–20, 1966

Then Lucybelle had an epiphany. Perhaps the mention of Dr. Leary's psilocybin did trigger a shift in her worldview. Or maybe it was just the lemons.

Vera had received a shipment of lemons from her friends in California that week. The day was cold and gray, and so she made drinks of whiskey, honey, lemon, and hot water. They sat outside, sharing one Adirondack chair, Lucybelle in Vera's lap, both wrapped in a wool blanket.

Lucybelle took a sip of the lemony tonic and spoke the idea the second it came into her mind. "We can grow our own lemon tree."

"I can barely grow lettuce here. You need lots of sun for lemons."

"I mean, let's move to California."

Vera hugged her harder. Sweet, daft Lucy.

"No, I mean it."

The idea was so good, so obvious and simple, that it was irrefutable. She felt lit up; her epiphany had to be contagious. "You'd be so happy. There are so many mountains out there," she said. "Bigger ones. Bears. Forests."

"I'm thinking," Vera said, "that when you sell your novel, you can move to D.C."

It was the first time she'd ever indicated that she too was trying to work out their lives together. Lucybelle kissed her. "I love you. And I couldn't bear D.C. Neither could you."

Vera sighed and Lucybelle knew she'd won a huge point.

"You could teach in California. I could get a job editing something."

"Teach where?"

Another point! "Berkeley. UCLA. Mills College. Pomona. There are endless excellent universities. They'd beg to hire you."

"I don't know."

It was the same thing she'd said, a year and a half ago, at the start of their relationship, right there in that very chair. Lucybelle said, "Yes, you do," just as she'd said then.

Vera looked scared, shook her head, but didn't speak. This was where Lucybelle wanted her, in the place before language. No words, no logic. So they made love, in the violet dusk, right in the Adirondack chair.

Then, in the morning, she backpedaled. Lucybelle knew it was coming because Vera hadn't spoken a word since she awoke. She showered and dressed silently, a slight scowl on her face. Lucybelle held her tongue, waited for whatever form the withdrawal would come in. If she gave Vera room, she usually got the most direct response, and that was the case that morning.

"My pond doesn't fail me. Nor do the veeries."

"If you go to Washington, you'll be leaving your pond anyway. And the veeries." Lucybelle let that sink in, but Vera just scowled harder, and so she spoke more directly to the point. "I can't promise to not fail you."

Vera turned her back to pour another cup of coffee.

"Listen to me."

But Vera wouldn't, not yet. Lucybelle put her forehead against the windowpane and looked out at the silvery skin of the pond, beyond to the fluffy treetops, and up to the blue sky that looked, even this hard morning, like the essence of hope. Her grouchy scientist lover be damned. Love has no mass or density; it's immeasurable. It might even be illusory. It's the purest risk.

She turned around quickly and caught Vera looking at her. Lucybelle said, "On our way to California, we could go to the Grand Canyon. And to New Mexico. No, first we'll fly to Paris!"

"Ha!" she cried a moment later because Vera was smiling. More! She was laughing with involuntary acquiescence.

## Thursday, July 28, 1966

"It's Dr. Bader," Vivian told her. "He says he's calling from Greenland. Do you want me to put him through?"

"Yes! Thank you."

"Sugar!"

"How's it going?"

"We did it." Were those tears thickening his voice? "Bedrock."

"Henri." Deeply moved, she set down her pencil and pushed back her chair.

"The entire ice core. 1,387 meters."

"The new drill worked!"

"Yeah," he said, still husky. "Yeah. You're my first call. You know the whole story better than anyone, sugar. The boys, their eyeballs are so pinned to their microscopes, even they don't get the significance of this core, the *big* picture, the epic we're about to reveal."

She knew this wasn't exactly true. It had been her job to write, translate, interpret, edit, sometimes advocate, and always make accessible the years of science leading to this moment. But the real reason Bader called her first was because she would listen, because with her he could be the little boy making an extraordinary discovery. Later, when he talked to the scientists and all the managers, he'd have to curtail his enthusiasm, his well-earned feelings of glory, his full-blooded emotional response.

"Congratulations."

"That's it? Congratulations?"

She felt sorry for Adele. No one would ever be a fraction of what this man needed. There weren't words or actions big enough to meet him.

"I need you to do a hell of a lot better than that. I need you to articulate what this means." He was nearly shouting. "Starting right now. As soon as I make the call to the fellows, I need you to be as clear as the proverbial fucking bell: we have just revealed 120,000 years of earth's climate history. The implications are unprecedented, stupendous."

"I'm on it, boss." Never mind that technically she was no longer in his line of command.

For the next few seconds she heard only heavy breathing, as if he were waiting for her to begin composing, out loud, on the telephone right then. She looked at the white walls of her office and projected onto them the glowing translucence of Greenland's ice.

From that massive depth, they'd extracted a complete core, just over nine centimeters in diameter, from the surface down to the rock.

It was ten years ago that Bader had ambushed her in Morningside Park, promised her an editorial team of her own, announced his hopes for the International Geophysical Year, threatened her with personal exposure. Since then she'd loved and left Phyllis, loved and left Stella, weathered the friendships of Beverly, Ruthie, and Dorothy. She'd written her novel. She'd found Vera.

Now this: Bader's vision realized.

She knew the ice core was already on its way, via refrigerated airplanes and trucks, to the Hanover lab. Where the language of ice would be deciphered. Where the reading of the ice core's stories would begin. Where she herself would write the first drafts of those stories.

As was his custom, Bader hung up without saying good-bye.

## Tuesday, August 9, 1966

A week and a half later, he appeared in her doorjamb at CRREL.

"Have Hauser and Woo given you the data yet?"

You'd think he would have gotten a haircut and a shave for this auspicious moment, especially given his hanging-by-a-thread relationship with CRREL and their lack of commitment to his research. She thought about suggesting it, maybe even a sports jacket and new shirt.

"When do you meet with the colonel?" she asked. "And by the way, hello, it's nice to see you. Long time."

"You're looking lovely, sugar. But this is no time for niceties. What have you got so far?"

"Nothing. I haven't received any raw copy."

"What the fuck is holding them up? Prepare yourself. Your workload is going to be huge in the next few months. I have a shitload of data I need you to write up."

"It's good to see you," she tried again. "How are you holding up?"

"This place makes me feel claustrophobic. The overabundance of greenery alone, it could choke a man. Then there're all these Army guys running around with their severe faces. A goddamn cultural desert. I mean—"

"Your excitement about the ice core is making you a bit dramatic. Also, you're contradicting yourself. Overabundant greenery or severe desert, which is it?"

They grinned at each other.

"That's your job," Bader said. "Prune my purple prose and fix my contradictions. Party on Friday afternoon. Two o'clock in the field across the street. Everyone gets the afternoon off."

"Did the colonel sign off on that?" Surely he hadn't.

"Which means I want the first press release finished by then. How hard can that be? How long is a press release? Three pages?"

She nodded and pushed the papers in the center of her desk to the edges, hoping to calm him down by showing him she was on it. Chances were he'd redline the entire first draft, so she might as well get the ball rolling. A moment later she heard his voice down the hall, too loud, becoming vituperative.

She walked over to the lab and found Peter Hauser hunched over a microscope.

"Give me everything you have on the Camp Century ice core," she said.

"Okay. How about Thursday afternoon?"

"Bader's here."

"He's *here*? In Hanover?"

"In the lab."

"Shit."

"We need to just do this."

"We have weeks of work to do before we're ready to publish."

"Just a press release. That we've reached bedrock."

Hauser sighed. He'd been with Bader from the start and wouldn't let him down. Still standing next to the microscope but staring up at the ceiling, he began while Lucybelle scribbled. "On July—Jesus, I don't even know the exact date. Ask Bader. Anyway, on July something, 1966, a team of glaciologists pulled a complete ice core from the surface of the earth. Be sure you say *all the way down to bedrock.* A total 1,387 meters. Got that? *One thousand, three hundred, eighty-seven meters.*"

Lucybelle nodded. "What's it tell us?"

"What's it *tell* us? Are you crazy? It's the most amazing—"

"Of course. I know. But I need to write this in a way that helps the public understand the significance."

Peter took another excited gulp of air and continued. "This gives us data from well before the last ice age, the Wisconsin, and into the pre-Wisconsin interglacial warm period known as the Eemian—"

"For the public, Peter. For the public."

"The isotope values will give us the first continuous record of earth's climate going back more than 100,000 years."

"Better. What else?"

Lucybelle neglected to ask Bader where he was staying but found him in the second motel she called. She drove the press release over and stood by while he scribbled corrections and scratched out entire sentences. She folded the draft into her purse.

"I need that tonight."

"You said by Friday."

"The *party* is Friday." Word at CRREL was that the colonel had nixed the party idea, but she didn't contradict Bader. "I want the press release in the hands of the media by then."

"You going to be here later tonight?"

"Where the hell would I go in this godawful backwater?"

Lucybelle went home and typed up a new draft of the press release, making the changes he wanted, and a few more of her own. She drove the fresh copy back to the motel, and after reading it, Bader smiled. "Nicely done. Good girl." He took a pencil to several sentences and handed it back to her. By midnight she'd made four round trips between her apartment and his motel, but the press release was finished.

He poured Jack Daniels into a motel bathroom glass and handed it to her. She sat on the edge of his bed.

"How are you?" he asked, and then before she had a chance to answer, he said, "I keep meaning to congratulate you."

282

"Congratulate me?"

"She's formidable."

She wished she couldn't guess his meaning.

"I thought it might work," he said.

"What might?"

"Don't play coy with me. You forget: I know all your secrets."

"No, you don't."

"So it's good?"

She remembered how he'd insisted that she and Vera work together, how he'd told Vera that she was single, and Vera's comments about him being meddlesome. "You set us up, didn't you?"

He roared with laughter, looking more like a wolf-man than ever before. Then, "I thought it was a good idea."

"But—"

"Who'd've thunk I'd have a new calling as a matchmaker?" He sounded truly pleased with himself.

"But—"

"I'm listening, sugar." He kept chuckling, downright voyeuristic now.

"You made it a condition of my employment that I have no intimate relationships."

"Only ones with women," he corrected, still grinning. "But I never expected you to take me literally." He paused. "And you didn't, did you?" More roaring at the sight of her face. "Thank god. I'd feel so guilty if I thought I'd somehow sentenced you to a sexless life."

Lucybelle pitched to her feet, the whiskey sloshing in her glass. This man who lived so loudly, so publicly, so vehemently, who knew the properties of every rock and ice crystal, had no idea about the insidious and deadly properties of secrets. Taken him literally? Of course she had. She considered slapping him, but her small hand would only bounce off that bony, whiskery face.

Bader reared back, mockingly. "Easy now, sugar."

"You pretty much blackmailed me to get me to come to New Hampshire."

He appeared to give that some thought. Then he asked, "Remember when we had dinner at the Drake Hotel?"

"Of course. What about it?"

"You told me then that you can't blackmail a person who isn't afraid or ashamed." Bader's face softened in a way that maybe only Adele ever saw. Affection graveled his voice. "You're neither. Not anymore."

That was true.

"You came to New Hampshire for your own reasons."

"I'll grant you that. But are you still getting reports from the goons?"

"No. Not since the move to New Hampshire."

"So how did you know?"

He raised his eyebrows, suppressed a smile, played dumb, pleased to have a path back to the sporting approach. "About what?"

"About me and Vera."

"Amanda Woo told Emily Hauser who told Adele. I don't know how Amanda knew."

So plain old gossip. That was refreshing. Lucybelle was strangely pleased that Russell had cared enough to tell his wife.

"Not that I was surprised in the least, since I'm the one who put the thing together. I refuse to fail at my efforts. Once I have a good idea, I know it'll bear fruit, sooner or later. Sorry for the pun."

"You can't take credit for Vera."

He tipped his head back and forth. "I think I can. It wasn't easy getting the two of you to agree to work together. But sure, after I accomplished that, you—or she?—did the footwork." He raised his eyebrows, formulating a joke.

"Don't."

He laughed and softened again. "Okay. In any case, I'm happy for you." He looked genuinely moved. "I truly am, sugar."

His sincerity dissolved what remained of her pique. Lucybelle touched her palm to his cheek. "Thank you."


### Friday, August 12, 1966

The colonel refused to sanction the party, so they started the celebration at five o'clock. The old guard was in high spirits, and even the more recently hired staff showed up for the baseball, beer, and food. Everyone except for Vera, who said she had too much work to do. Lucybelle was disappointed but hadn't pressed.

It was a hot summery day, the sun heavy in the west, the air muggy. Bader had loaded a keg of beer in the bed of a pickup and backed the truck right up to the edge of the baseball diamond that, earlier in the summer, the fellows had mowed and scraped out of the vacant lot across the street from CRREL. Even Bader gave himself over to what he considered a frivolous and time-wasting game on this celebratory afternoon. He flipped down the tailgate and positioned the keg for easy dispensing.

Lucybelle wore her White Sox baseball cap as she warmed up her arm with Peter Hauser. She was terrible at the game, could barely throw the distance between the pitcher's mound and home plate, and struck out nine times out of ten, but she'd joined a few games that summer. It was fun, and the dusty lightheartedness of the play distracted her during Vera's absences. The fellows humored her and gave her credit for being a good sport.

"Right here," Peter said smacking his fist into his mitt. "Aim here."

"I *am* aiming there."

He jumped to catch another ball flying three feet above his head. "Someone bring Lucy a beer," he shouted. "She plays better when she's fortified."

Bader ran over with a cup of beer and held it to her lips as if she were a child. Laughing along with everyone, Lucybelle shoved him away.

Peter's next toss came straight at her chest, but faster than usual, and so she jumped out of the way rather than trying to catch it. By the time she'd chased it down, Peter had made his way over to the keg, so she joined him, pouring herself a cupful. The cold bitter brew tasted wonderful on that hot and humid late afternoon. Bader was shouting out names, drawing up teams, and that's when she saw Dorothy—who hadn't shown up for anything not specifically required by her job for a very long time—organizing plates of food on the folding table.

She felt sorry for her. Despite her claim of contentment with her church and status as "Aunt Dot," and despite her sinister confessions and horrific acts of betrayal, Dorothy was a woman in the clutches of her own loneliness and shame. As she watched her fussing with the food, trying to not make eye contact, Lucybelle's sympathies won out.

"Dorothy!" she called out. "Be on my team! I don't want to be the only female playing."

"That puts two girls on the same team," Russell Woo objected. "We should separate them."

"Ha! You can handle us." She turned to Dorothy. "Right? They can handle us."

The look on Dorothy's face was a strange mix of longing and anger. She wanted to be on Lucybelle's team and she resented the suggestion that she might be on Lucybelle's team. "I'm not playing," she said, tenting the front of her paisley shift between her thumb and forefinger and kicking out a foot clad in a white sandal, showing she wasn't dressed for baseball.

"I'll trade you," Amanda Woo said. "I'll wear your sandals and you can wear my sneakers."

"No. But thank you." Dorothy forced a big smile and continued arranging the bowls of chips and plates of fried chicken.

Lucybelle's sympathy withered. It irked her the way Dorothy insisted on unhappiness.

"Sunlight!" Lucybelle heard herself announce. The declaration was both factual and corrective, if ridiculous.

"What about it?" Dorothy asked.

"Sunlight is . . . beautiful. It's a lovely day."

Dorothy kept looking at her, understandably confused, but somehow expectant.

Unable to make sense of her own observation, Lucybelle put out her cigarette and ran to take up her position in right field.

Bader threw the first pitch, and everyone cheered when it crossed the plate as a strike. Peter Hauser hit the next pitch at Lucybelle, who stood in right field enjoying the late sunshine, wondering why in the world she'd tried to get Dorothy to feel the life-giving, revelatory power of that star. She ran to meet the lackadaisical grounder, scooped it up to the sounds of cheering from everyone on both teams, and tried to decide where to toss it. Peter was already rounding second base, and she couldn't throw anywhere near as far as third base, and so she ran the ball to the infield. As Peter headed for home, she threw the baseball, as hard as she could, toward home plate.

Except that the ball flew out of her hand before she meant to release it. Everyone watched it sail in a high arc toward the women gathered around the food tables. At the exact moment Lucybelle saw that Vera had come to the party after all and was standing talking to Amanda Woo, the baseball hit her lover on the shoulder. Stunned, Vera dropped her plate of food.

"I'm so sorry! I'm so sorry!" Lucybelle cried running off the field, but Vera hadn't been hurt by the slow-moving baseball and she was the first to burst out laughing. Lucybelle hugged her, right there in front of everyone, and they bent at the waists, holding onto one another, laughing so hard the tears were streaming.

The moment was cathartic. So much had been freed. Bedrock! Vera! But it wasn't just her, all the scientists and support staff held their knees as they laughed, gulping air, the incident somehow releasing years of humor, irony, and love. Amanda and Emily gripped the food table, hiccuping their laughter. Even Beverly and Ruthie allowed themselves a bit of mirth.

After everyone recovered, they all drank down more cups of cold beer, and the game resumed. On her first at bat, Lucybelle hit the ball! Russell Woo, at shortstop, made a big show of getting under the pop-up fly, positioning himself to catch it, and then letting it drop a few feet over his head. Raucous cheering accompanied her run to first base. Foot securely on the white bag, Lucybelle grinned over at Vera, who was enjoying spectating.

Sunlight! Lucybelle thought. Golden sunlight.

When the next batter hit a drive down the line, the third baseman threw her out at second, which meant she could go stand with Vera, who fixed her a heaping plate of food. As Lucybelle took the plate, her hands covered Vera's for several long moments, and they smiled at one another. She sat in one of the folding chairs, suddenly ravenous, as she seemed to be whenever Vera prepared her food. She requested a sub for the next inning, which the fellows gladly provided. As they'd become sweatier, and a little drunker, their competitiveness had kicked in and her team was happy to replace their weak link. Lucybelle and Vera sat on the sidelines and joked with the other women.

She saw Dorothy leave, even turned for a second to watch her walk alone toward the highway, and entertained a fleeting thought that she ought to call her back, at least shout good-bye. But she didn't. Someone cracked another joke and she forgot all about Dorothy.

By dusk everyone was stuffed with food and beer and gritty from the clouds of baseball dust. The keg was empty. Bader was organzing plans to head over to Lander's Restaurant to continue drinking, and the women began stacking the dirty plates, bowls, and paper cups.

"I'm going home," Vera said. "You want to come?"

She spoke neither quietly nor loudly. Lucybelle refrained from looking about to see who was within earshot. She nodded yes. The men all left while Amanda, Emily, Beverly, Ruthie, Vera, and Lucybelle stayed with a handful of other women to finish the cleanup. The air was spongy with the last of the sunshine, warm beer, and August heat. Lucybelle let the pleasure of her friends' voices fall on her ears without listening to the meanings. Bedrock. Vera. She was so happy.

Dorothy's white Rambler barreled onto the field. She slammed the brakes, threw the transmission into reverse, turned the car around, and then backed the fender right up to the card tables, scattering the women who were covering the remaining leftovers with waxed paper.

"What in the world?" Beverly said.

"Whoa!" Amanda shouted.

Dorothy popped out of the driver's seat and stood behind the car door as if it were a shield. "Cleanup crew has arrived," she said too loudly, the background of the field making her big eyes look cowlike. "It's my specialty!"

"Dorothy, honey," Emily Hauser said, speaking calmly as you would to someone with a gun. Dorothy swiped at Emily's outstretched hand.

"Isn't that right, Lucy? Make a mess and I'll take care of it. Have a free night? I'll fill in. Need a babysitter? Same call."

"Do something," Beverly said under her breath to Lucybelle.

Emily reached again for Dorothy's elbow. "Let me have your keys, honey. I'll drive you home."

"How much has she had to drink?" Amanda asked. "She's upset."

"I'll say."

"Second that."

Dorothy huffed in outrage at being spoken about in the third person to her face. She wrenched her elbow free from Emily's grip and charged the card tables. She grabbed two Pyrex casseroles, one gummy with residual macaroni and cheese and the other glistening with the last bits of lime Jell-O, and tossed these into the trunk of her car, the second one cracking and breaking against the first one. She followed this up with Tupperware lids and containers, scraps of food flying.

The other women backed up, beginning to be frightened.

"What in the world triggered this?" Emily asked.

"She's having a nervous breakdown," Amanda diagnosed.

Dorothy kicked down the legs of a card table and shoved this into her trunk too. When she tried to slam the lid shut, it bounced back.

Lucybelle couldn't look at Vera. She knew this was her mess, whether she deserved it or not, and she probably did deserve it. She'd made so many mistakes.

Dorothy shoved and jimmied the card table until it cleared the trunk latch and then thunked the lid shut. She spun around and faced Lucybelle. "I know everything. I could ruin you."

"What's she talking about?" Amanda asked.

"Get her out of here," Beverly spoke in a low, hot voice.

"I'll talk to her," Lucybelle said. "The rest of you should go."

"Damn tootin'," Beverly said. She and Ruthie began hoofing back to the highway, where their cars—they still drove to work separately—were parked.

Emily directed the other women to fill their arms with what remained of the picnic debris, and then she cast an apologetic look at Lucybelle, who nodded, meaning to communicate, it's okay, please do leave. The small crowd of women hustled away.

Lucybelle now forced herself to look at Vera, who stood with her arms firmly crossed on her chest, a look of disbelief in her eyes. Lucybelle glanced back at Dorothy, a fiery comet hurtling toward the planet of her life. There was no point in asking Vera to leave too.

"I could ruin you," Dorothy said again, but quietly this time. She looked only at Lucybelle, as if she were afraid of Vera.

"Why would you want to do that?"

"Because you're a liar and you disgust me." She held onto the fin of her Rambler as if she were dizzy. "Rusty told me about the photographs. She said she could get me copies."

"What's she talking about?" Vera asked.

"Maybe Dr. Prescott would like to see the pictures," Dorothy said.

Lucybelle felt a sudden pressure behind her eyeballs, as if someone were inflating a balloon in her head.

"What's this about, Lucy?" Vera spoke in her authoritative PhD voice, the one that demanded exact answers. Lucybelle thought she had about three seconds to provide them or Vera would never again ask her another question.

"It's about Stella and . . . those pictures." Weak, way too weak.

"Why does the librarian know about those pictures?"

"The librarian," Dorothy said. "That's a good one. I'm a lot more than the librarian, Dr. Prescott."

"Maybe you should go home," Lucybelle told Vera. "I'll explain everything later."

"Or I could explain everything now," Dorothy said.

"I'm leaving," Vera said and the words sounded more final than any she'd ever spoken.

Lucybelle and Dorothy both watched Vera walk the fifty yards to the highway, her figure a diminishing dark weariness in the weakening light. They heard her shut her car door and start the engine. Lucybelle stood in the weedy field, encapsulated by the still hot evening air, watching the red taillights of Vera's car fade in the twilight.

"Why are you doing this?" she asked when every last vestige of Vera was gone.

"I trusted you," Dorothy said. "You didn't tell me about you and that hideous woman."

A hatchet of anger jerked up in her chest. "It's none of your business."

Dorothy forced out a strangled laugh. "None of my business? You took me home to your mother. You seduced me on New Year's Eve."

"That was five years ago."

"Yeah, well, and you kissed me just a few months ago. I told you I'm not interested and still you—"

"No," Lucybelle said. Clarifying that she had not initiated, had in fact aborted, the kiss would only unleash more of the shame, fuel the firestorm.

"Oh, I know what you tell yourself. You got up and left. But you kissed me. You were right there. I felt everything."

"I'm in love with Vera."

Dorothy exhaled as if she'd been literally socked in the stomach. "My mother is dead," she said. "I never even loved Geneviève. Or Mary. I loved *you*. I've loved you for years."

Lucybelle wanted to believe the tears were fake, but they weren't. They were real, salty streams flowing down Dorothy's cheeks. She couldn't afford sympathy, though. "I'm just convenient. You haven't really loved me. You don't even know me."

"I do love you. I do know you." Her intonation made the words "love" and "know" sound like "hate."

The red sun set over Dorothy's shoulder, giving her an inflamed aura, as if she were about to sizzle away in its heat. "I could get those pictures in a fast second," she said. "I could share them with Bader. With the colonel. I could send them to your mother."

"The first two don't want to see me naked. The latter already has."

"The disgrace of posing for that girl." Dorothy sat down in the grass, as if the weight of her threat collapsed her. She picked through a patch of clover, maybe looking for a four-leafed one. "I could send them to Dr. Prescott."

"Why don't you write a letter to Vassar, while you're at it. Make sure you get revenge on Geneviève, as well."

"That's what you think? This is revenge?"

"I think it's terror. Terror you're turning on yourself and on others. On me."

"You've got to be kidding. I have nothing to be afraid of."

"I know you're an intelligent woman. I also know you have a heart."

"Now you're the Wizard of Oz, are you?"

"Can we talk about how you know Rusty?" When Dorothy didn't answer, Lucybelle postulated, "You called Acme Transport and asked for a ride. Maybe you hoped for another interview with Stella. You lucked into Rusty as your driver. The two of you had a little heyday talking about me."

As Dorothy struggled to her feet, her shift hiked up to the tops of her thighs. She pulled it back down, cutting her eyes at Lucybelle. "Probably grass-stained," she said, as if that too were Lucybelle's fault, and walked slowly to her car, brushing off the back of her dress. She started the engine and drove forward.

Lucybelle stood directly in the path of the Rambler, and a hot fear shot adrenaline to the tips of her fingers and toes. She jogged off to the side, but Dorothy turned the wheel and drove slowly toward her. The sky was dusky and opaque, too early for stars. An occasional car passed on the highway, but otherwise the evening was silent, hot, heavy. She couldn't outrun a car, so Lucybelle just stopped and waited for whatever was going to happen next.

Dorothy drew up alongside her and rolled down the window. "Do you really think I'd run you over? How many times do I have to tell you? I love you."


## Saturday, August 13, 1966

Lucybelle managed to sleep for about an hour and a half that night. She got up and dressed twice, intending to drive out to Vera's. But without the right words, she stood to lose everything, if she hadn't already. In fact, she had no words at all. At three in the morning, she called Acme Transport and Wanda answered. She pictured her at the phone in a nightgown, Stella

291

sleeping through the call, the gorgeous dispatcher with the lilting voice already flipping through her list of drivers, choosing who she'd awaken to pick up this fare. Lucybelle cleared her throat and hung up the telephone.

At dawn Lucybelle drove to the airport. She caught the first flight to Chicago and called Acme Transport from O'Hare International. Maybe Rusty had legions of riders who asked for her specifically; in any case, Wanda didn't miss a beat, said she'd have Rusty at the airport in half an hour. It was more like an hour—an hour bloated with foreboding—before Lucybelle slid into the taxicab's backseat.

"What the hell?" Rusty said, recognizing her.

"I want to talk to you." Success in this mission depended on her keeping the upper hand, and that meant pretending confidence.

"Get out of my cab. I don't know you."

"Of course you know me, and we need to talk."

Rusty lifted the dispatch mic and said, "Wanda?"

"You don't want to do that," Lucybelle warned.

"Yeah, Rusty. What is it?" Wanda's voice sounded silky even over the dispatch intercom.

"Seriously," Lucybelle said quietly. "You'd be wise to hang up."

"Got the O'Hare fare," Rusty said, looking over her shoulder at Lucybelle, who shook her head and pointed a finger at the mic hook.

"Well, that's fine, Rusty. Now drive. What're you calling me for?"

Rusty signed off, turned around, and said, "Get out of my car."

"It's Stella's car. I'd rather talk to you than to her. But if you refuse to talk to me, I'll be forced to resolve this thing with her."

A cop slid slowly by and leveled an unpleasant gander at Rusty.

"I know all about you," Rusty tried.

"Good. Then we won't have to waste time on me. I want to talk about you. Let's go somewhere quiet."

"I said, get out."

"Your big mouth caused the raid of Stella's home and darkroom." Lucybelle watched the threat lodge in Rusty's consciousness.

"What are you talking about?" she asked, her quavering voice confirming some level of guilt.

"Let's go somewhere we can talk before that policeman bothers us."

Rusty pulled away from the curb and drove carefully, nervously checking and rechecking her side and rearview mirrors. Lucybelle leaned back in the seat and felt the swamp of exhaustion clog her brain. Was she doing the right thing? What was the alternative? Wait and see what might detonate? Less than twenty-four hours ago, she had been basking in the achievements of the last ten years and her hopes for the future. Sunlight and laughter.

Dorothy had lurched into her idyll like a Frankenstein.

Rusty pulled into an expansive and empty parking lot, a graveyard of cement and chain-link fencing. The closest building was a warehouse on the far side of the lot.

"I don't like it here. Take me to the lake. In Evanston." An urge to see the brink of water and sky, that crisp convergence, spoke the words for her.

"That's too far. You want to talk? Talk."

"The lake. Evanston."

Rusty reached under the car seat. But she didn't have anything there. The ridiculous bluff revealed her desperation.

"Come on, Rusty. The lake. Now. Or I'll call Stella."

Rusty parked facing the water. A brisk wind frothed the lake, freshening the hot August day. People walked along the shore in their shirtsleeves, smiling as if the world were a happy and benevolent place. Lucybelle opened the door and stepped out into the sunlight, intending to get into the front seat so she and Rusty could talk face to face, but when she reached for the handle, the cab shot backward, nearly hitting a pedestrian, who yelled and banged her fist on the side of the car. Rusty spun the steering wheel and took off forward, leaving Lucybelle standing by the lake.

Then, before she even had time to consider what to do, Rusty put the cab in reverse and gunned back toward her again, causing yet another pedestrian to shout and leap. Rusty reparked the car and stared straight ahead at the lake.

Lucybelle opened the front passenger door and got in. "I guess you changed your mind."

"I got a wife now," Rusty said, still refusing to look at Lucybelle. "We got a kid."

"So you need to keep your job."

"What do you want?"

"You hate me because I interfered with your family. That's fair enough. It's probably what caused you to talk to Dorothy about me."

"I don't know a Dorothy."

"Dorothy Shipwright."

"I don't know her."

Either Rusty was lying or Dorothy used an alias. That was almost funny, picturing Dorothy who was good at imitations, taking on a fake persona.

"Maybe she used another name. But she told you things about me, probably a mix of true and otherwise. You bit. You went right for her bait."

Rusty's freckles darkened and her knuckles lightened as she gripped the steering wheel. Her labored breathing caused her nostrils to flare.

"Did she pay you?"

"Hell, no!" The second the words were out of her mouth, Rusty closed her eyes and rested her forehead on the top of the steering wheel, realizing she'd just admitted to talking.

"I'm not going to do anything to hurt you or your family."

"As if you could." Mumbling now, her face still pressed to the steering wheel.

"I'm not going to tell Stella that you talked to Dorothy, or whatever she called herself. She'll never have to know that you caused the raid."

"Stupid white bitch," Rusty said, jerking upright in the seat, emboldened by a new wave of anger. "They raided her darkroom because her pictures show those racists for who they are. She's a brilliant photographer. Her pictures are total indictments."

Lucybelle didn't like being called a stupid white bitch, but she did like Rusty's hot pride in Stella's achievements. She was right: the raid might well have been based solely on Stella's journalistic photographs; it might not have had anything to do with Dorothy. She would never know for sure. "The point is, you shouldn't be telling stories to people you don't know."

"Let me know when you're done, because I need to get on to my next fare."

"You told Dorothy about those photographs. The ones of me."

Rusty swallowed. She put her hand on the key in the ignition, and Lucybelle saw that the hand was trembling. Rusty said, "That was just talk."

"You can imagine how that talk makes me feel."

"I don't care how you feel."

"You say you have a wife and child."

"Just leave me alone!" There were tears in her voice now and she looked Lucybelle in the eye for the first time. "Get out of the cab!"

"Okay. I'll leave you alone. Get me those two photographs and you'll never see me again."

"I can't."

"You can't what?" Lucybelle tried to calm her own voice.

"Get you the photographs."

"You told Dorothy you could get them for her."

"I burned those pictures years ago. Wanda asked me to."

Lucybelle sat back in the plush car seat. She smelled smoke and saw fire. *Whisper Their Love* ablaze in the wastepaper basket at SIPRE, reduced to embers. The tar pots at CRREL, fire truck sirens screaming. May Sarton's novel, the one she rescued, in her own wastepaper basket at home.

She reached over and put a hand on Rusty's shoulder.

"Don't touch me."

She didn't remove her hand. "Are you telling the truth?"

"Hell, yes. No one wants those pictures."

Lucybelle believed her. The disclosure blazed away the last of her fear, and she withdrew her hand. "Take me back to the airport."

## Sunday, August 14, 1966

The relief was biblical. Without the photographs as props, Dorothy could talk all she wanted to whomever she wanted. No one would listen. The accusations—of what? Perversion? Love? Refusal to love *her*?—would only expose Dorothy's own misery. Lucybelle slept for nearly twelve hours. Then, in the morning, she took L'Forte and drove out to the pond.

"Good," Vera said. "Let's just get this over with."

"You can't break up with me. It's my birthday on Tuesday."

"If you're trying to be funny—"

"Also, L'Forte couldn't handle it. He's almost fourteen, you know."

"This is too much work."

"Spoken by a woman who lives for work."

Vera pressed the butts of her palms into her eyes and then lowered her hands. She was crying. "What am I supposed to say?"

"Nothing. I'd like you to listen."

"I don't want to hear some tawdry story about you and that librarian."

It shouldn't have been funny, but it made Lucybelle laugh, which in turn made Vera suppress a smile, despite the tears.

"It sort of *is* tawdry," she said, "but that's not the embarrassing part."

She waited until Vera said, "Okay. What's the embarrassing part?"

"Just how stupid and ordinary the story is."

Vera leveled her gray, basaltic gaze, first out the window at her beloved pond, and then directly at Lucybelle, who added, "With a few unpleasant twists."

"You're trying to make me laugh."

"As hard as I can."

"Did you sleep with her?"

"Sort of."

No one could make a face of exasperation better than Vera, but she let the shoddy language pass and moved on to, "When?"

"Five years ago on New Year's Eve. Once."

Vera's expression slackened in relief.

"She sort of hasn't let go, though."

This time the exasperation, at the repeated use of "sort of," was combined with another suppressed smile.

"And I wasn't careful with her feelings. I should have been ever so clear from the moment I realized how she felt."

"When was that?"

"That's part of the problem. I never quite paid enough attention. I knew she was lonely. I occasionally noticed she fixated on me. But she fixated on other people too."

Vera still looked unsure, about everything.

"So you want the whole story?"

"I really don't."

"What's the alternative? You leaving me?"

Vera looked back out at her pond. At least she didn't say yes.

"I'll tell you everything," Lucybelle said lighting a cigarette, which she handed to Vera before lighting another one for herself. "Then you can decide."

More tears filled Vera's eyes and while she hated hurting her, Lucybelle was deliriously happy to see the tears, to know that Vera wouldn't, couldn't, leave her. The terms of their relationship, from the beginning, had been full disclosure and she knew she had to be quick and precise, like performing surgery, but rather than taking something out, she was adding information in. She told the stories of Dorothy, of Rusty, and of her trip to Chicago the previous day.

When she finished, she put the manila envelope on the kitchen table.

"What's that?"

"The pictures."

"Jesus."

"You once wanted to see them."

"That was before. I hardly knew you then."

"That doesn't make any sense. When it comes to emotions, logic fails you."

"That would be true of everyone."

"But especially of you."

Vera sat down at the kitchen table and picked up the manila envelope. She held it up to the light for a moment, as if she could cheat and look at the pictures through the veil of the orange enclosure. Then she cut her eyes at Lucybelle, who tried to make a funny face. Vera shook her head, no-nonsense, and undid the clasp. She slid out the shiny eight-by-tens.

Lucybelle knew the pictures by heart. The one where the light cuts her in half. The one where her hair resembles a burning bush. The pale glow of her skin in all of them, the contrast with the shadows, the way she's moving into the patches of sun, almost slinking, but head up as if she senses the radiance just beyond her reach. The experience of having that afternoon from eight years ago now in Vera's hands was surprisingly soothing, her life becoming one organic whole, her loves overlapping, touching.

Vera looked at each picture for a long time. Her shoulders loosened. She sighed repeatedly. She handled them gently, setting each one face down when she was done. Then she went through them again, looking for an even longer period of time, becoming absorbed, maybe seeing beyond the image of naked Lucybelle to the art that Stella had made. Or maybe just looking at naked Lucybelle.

Finally she said, "Do I ever get to meet her?"

"I hope so."


## Thursday, September 29, 1966

The bird screams pulled Lucybelle away from her typewriter and over to the west-facing window of her studio apartment. The full moon backlit the huge elm tree, silhouetting the murder of crows sitting in its canopy. There had to be at least a dozen of them, twitching and turning circles on their respective branches, their scaly little feet nimbly negotiating the rotations, all cawing some urgent story.

Lucybelle had left L'Forte at the pond a week and a half ago, on Saturday morning, and Vera said neither she nor the dog would see Lucybelle until she mailed the manuscript. Vera, who hadn't allowed him out of the car in the beginning, now claimed that L'Forte was happiest where he could sniff tree bark and watch ducks. He was too old to chase anything. In fact, Lucybelle feared more for his life than she did for that of the wildlife living near Post Pond. An elderly dachshund might make a nice snack for a bobcat, for instance. Vera promised to keep him safe.

Lucybelle finished typing the final draft shortly after midnight, her hands aching from the hours of pecking. She put the manuscript in the box she'd bought for that purpose, along with its cover letter, and set it on the end table that had been with her since Pocahontas. Harry knew an agent in New York who'd agreed to read the novel. Tomorrow she'd take it to the post office.

Lucybelle stood eyeing the packaged manuscript, feeling a bit scared, tentative, doubtful. As long as her novel was in her own head, or at the very most on pages under the bed, it held a potency, a promise. Now it seemed like nothing more than a stack of paper, 454 pages to be exact, stamped with words. Still. There it was. Finished. Remembering that she hadn't yet read the day's mail, and that there had been an envelope addressed with a childish nine-year-old scrawl, Lucybelle scooped up the letter and dropped into her wingback chair.

*Dear Aunt Lucybelle,*

*I started fourth grade two weeks ago. Mr. Ellison is my first man teacher. Shannon and I talk too much and so he made me stay after school yesterday. She didn't get caught and I didn't tell on her. He made me write, "Ask not what your classroom can do for you— ask what you can do for your classroom," a hundred times on the chalkboard. My hand still hurts.*

*Did you have a nice summer? I did. We went camping in the Wallowas, next to a lake, and we got to rent horses to ride. Mine was named No Name. I also went to Camp Namanu. My favorite counselor was Miss Jo. She wasn't my counselor, but I liked sitting*

*at her table in the dining hall. She sang the loudest of all the counselors.*
*Mom let me cut my hair short-short like Miss Jo's and I also got to buy*
*Converse high-tops. The Campfire Girls slogan is WoHeLo. That stands*
*for Work, Health, and Love.*

*Have you read Silver Chief? It's a really good book about a dog*
*who is half wolf. He lives on his own in the Arctic. I was trying to*
*finish it last night, but Dad caught me under the covers with my*
*flashlight.*

*Please write soon.*

*Love,*
*Lucy*

Ask not. What a ridiculous thing to have a child write. So much of her life she'd believed that getting what she wanted was impossible. So often she'd asked not. For god's sake, *Ask! Ask!*

She pulled an ice cube tray out of the freezer and dropped three cubes in a glass. She poured in a healthy measure of gin. She drank and smoked, listening to the crows in her elm tree and thinking of the ones that had circled high in the white hot sky above her healing pen in Pocahontas. They'd been her first glimpse of the beyond. She'd envied their shiny black-winged escape.

Now it was her turn.

The very day after she and Vera had given notice, the colonel announced the closure of Camp Century. The Greenland ice sheet moved like a great beast across the top of that landmass, and no amount of manmade engineering could stop it from pulling away the ceilings and tearing down the walls of the city under the ice. Camp Century was collapsing and needed to be evacuated. Project Iceworm had fizzled. No missiles were ever launched or even brought on site. The ice cores had, in the end, won the day. Lucybelle poured more gin on the withered ice cubes and lit a fresh cigarette. She raised her glass to the crows: good riddance to the whole idea of hiding in defense, fearing what might come flying over the pole. No more.

They wouldn't sell the cabin at the pond yet. They'd leave one of their cars there while they took the trip out West. The Grand Canyon! Taos and Albuquerque! Vera insisted that they would camp, but Lucybelle planned on taking lots of cash, hoping for the occasional motor court. They'd stay with Vera's friends in California, the ones with the lemon tree, who were already scouting jobs for both of them. They'd fly back and share the remaining car until they were ready to leave New Hampshire for good. The rest was still unknown, but they'd definitely go to Paris in the spring. Or, if one or both of them already had a job by then, they'd go in the summer. They would go, though, that much they'd agreed was not negotiable. They would go to New Mexico and Paris.

The anticipation of that train she was about to ride into the future of her happiness was almost impossible to endure. She got up and took down Willa Cather's *Shadow on the Rock*. She had two more days off, plus the weekend. She'd reread the Cather in preparation for their trip. Maybe Vera would want to read it aloud together. She also took down *Shakespeare: The Complete Works*, Daddy's gift to her so many years ago. Inside *Hamlet* she found the notes she'd taken about her Halloween taxicab ride with Stella, and inside *The Merchant of Venice* she found an old letter from Phyllis. She hadn't heard from her in years. Georgia would be nine years old, the same age as her niece Lucy.

As she started to push the thick Shakespeare volume back onto the shelf, she noticed that paperback, *Whisper Their Love*, which she'd hidden in the dark recess at the back of the bookshelf. She withdrew the book and placed it on her coffee table.

Tomorrow she'd see Vera and L'Forte. They'd make dinner and then make love. They'd stay up too late, go into work sleepy, and it wouldn't matter, not much.

She poured herself another gin.

# Postscript

**Berkeley, California, 2016**

Early that morning of September 29, 1966, a fire consumed much of Lucybelle's apartment. According to her death certificate, she died of carbon monoxide poisoning. Our lives overlapped for only nine years. I remember adoring her; she was kind, funny, and elusive.

The call came long before dawn, too early to be a neighbor or a friend. I heard my parents' voices, speaking not in hushed morning tones but agitated ones, followed by my father's footsteps plodding down the hall and into the bathroom. Then came the awful sounds of a grown man who doesn't cry, crying. My mother hustled to the kitchen to make coffee and eggs, attempting to hold our household of seven together in the face of crisis. We sat and ate. She told us the news.

I remember the strange light in the days that followed, as if even the air had been hollowed out and left for dead. And yet it wasn't one of *us* who had died, so the absence was this dark place lurking just outside the circle of my immediate family. A single woman, well past the marrying age, my namesake, suddenly gone. With one exception, we didn't talk about her death again until I started writing this book. We barely talked about her *life*, though I listened avidly for stories, pulling the tidbits close: her alleged sickliness as a child and the sunshine pen built by my grandfather; she and him being the only two who ever checked out *The History of the Decline and Fall of the Roman Empire* from the Randolph County Library; her passing the bar exam without going to law school; her unusual buoyancy in water. What I've learned in researching and writing this book is that her family didn't know anything about her life past those Arkansas years.

Lucybelle's fire has blazed in my imagination ever since that early morning phone call. So often I've considered the dreadful details: Was she awake or asleep when she died? Did she struggle to get out a window or door? Was she in bed, and if so, did her bed burn? Was she in bed alone? Is there anything left of her life? How could I not imagine the flames?

I did try to find out more, especially after I came out at the age of eighteen, just ten years after her death, and it occurred to me that she too might have been gay. That's when my older sister said she vaguely remembered a companion named Vera. Everyone in the family remembered a dachshund. When I asked my mother to tell me more about Lucybelle, she replied that she was "extremely bright and extremely independent," that she wouldn't let men hold doors open for her, and that "if you're asking if she was . . . like you . . . she probably was, though I'm sure she never acted on it."

My mother also told me that Lucybelle started the fire herself by falling asleep with a cigarette in her hand, and that my grandmother did not believe that story. My grandmother had claimed at the time that this was impossible: Lucybelle didn't smoke. Her boss had replied that he couldn't recall ever seeing her without a cigarette in her hand. Apparently, she was an amazing keeper of secrets. She would stay with us for days at a time and never smoked. She must have been miserable, jonesing for a cigarette the entire visit. Neither she nor her clothes ever smelled of smoke. Had she really been a smoker?

I've considered so many scenarios, including that the fire that killed Lucybelle wasn't an accident. It seems nearly absurd that, as an adult, she would have hidden her smoking from us. It also strikes me as assertively unkind that her boss would have been so aggressive in telling the family what a "chimney" she had been. There are many other details in her story, especially surrounding her death, that just don't make sense. I remain open to other interpretations of her death, and yet, in the end, my judgment falls to the accident version. I still ache to know the full truth.

There is so very much we don't know, can't know, in doing historical research. Emma Donoghue writes, in the afterword of her collection *Astray*, "When you work in the hybrid form of historical fiction, there will be Seven-League-Boot moments: crucial facts joyfully uncovered in dusty archives and online databases, as well as great leaps of insight and imagination. But you will also be haunted by a looming absence: the shadowy mass of all that's been lost, that can never be recovered."

What broke my heart most as the years went by was the possibility of there being someone out there, a woman perhaps, who mourned Lucybelle. Someone I could know, someone who would tell me who she had been.

As it turned out, there was. By the time I found her, she too was already dead.

In the meantime, my occasional bouts of questions to my father yielded no further information. And so, decades passed and I resigned myself to never knowing the real person who was my namesake.

Then came the walk at the Berkeley marina with my friend Carol Seajay. I was telling her the scant story of Lucybelle because in helping my parents move into a retirement home, I'd found that intriguing photograph of her.

She's sitting on the giant aboveground, horizontal root of a tree, wearing trousers, her elbows resting on her spread-apart knees. In her hands is an apple. She's looking at the camera with what appears to be defiance. Someone—Lucybelle?—had written the word "showdown" on the back of the photo.

Carol said, "Google her."

And I thought, computers were invented in roughly 1945, the Internet in the late 1980s, a good twenty years after Lucybelle's death. Why would there be anything online about this thin, smart, kind, and funny midcentury woman who grew up on a farm in Arkansas? So far as I knew, she'd been born and, forty-three years later, been sucked back into the ether.

Still, as soon as I got home that night, I typed "Lucybelle Bledsoe" into my browser. Up popped an article about her that had been published in a recent Routledge volume called *The Biographical Dictionary of Women in Science: Pioneering Lives from Ancient Times to the Mid-20th Century*. I was completely floored that she'd done work important enough to merit a full-page entry in such a book. Moreover, I had not had any idea that she had made her living as a science writer, as do I. She'd worked for a government agency called the Snow, Ice and Permafrost Research Establishment, which in 1961 became the Cold Regions Research and Engineering Laboratory, organizations intrinsically linked to today's Division of Polar Programs, which had sent me to Antarctica two times. I would eventually discover that some of her work contacts know my work contacts.

The second and only other Internet entry I found about Lucybelle was an obituary in the *Journal of Glaciology*. The fact alone that she *had* an obituary in that journal took my breath away. I had just two years earlier published a book called *The Ice Cave: A Woman's Adventures from the Mojave to the Antarctic* about my own obsession with ice and its properties. I was currently immersed in writing my very icy novel, *The Big Bang Symphony: A Novel of Antarctica*, subsequently published in 2010. I am deeply interested in the polar regions, have visited both ends of the earth several times. These ice caps, so profoundly linked with my own imagination, apparently comprised Lucybelle's lifework as well.

Her obituary in the *Journal of Glaciology* states:

During the period of time she was associated with SIPRE and CRREL, she personally edited almost every report printed in both the internal

305

report series and outside journal-publications. In developing a style and setting the standards for these reports, she was the unlisted co-author of hundreds of reports and informal teacher of many scientists.

Her editorial work extended far beyond grammatical corrections and adherence to style. She could spot incorrect equations, slipshod terms and desultory sentences. One of her unique talents was her ability to recognize faulty logic even on very technical matters. Many researchers (both young and old) have seen their raw, sometimes confused manuscripts transformed into beautifully simple, well-presented reports. She was always willing to be of service to others with no thought for personal prestige.

It also says, "Too often we, as authors of scientific reports, take for granted the careful work of good technical editors and seldom do we give them the proper credit which they so rightly deserve. So it was with Lucybelle Bledsoe. Although you will not find her name listed as author or co-author of any research papers, she has been a full-time worker in the field of glaciology for the last ten years. We believe that she contributed a great deal to the field of glaciology."

So began my research in earnest.

First I tried to find James Bender, the coworker who'd written the obituary. I found twenty-two age-appropriate James Benders in Zabasearch and sent off my queries to each and every one. I began receiving responses, by e-mail and by postal mail, all of them kind, some wishing me well, none being the right James Bender. Once I received an empty, unsealed envelope, addressed in my own hand to myself. It was haunting. I never did find James Bender; perhaps he is dead.

I went back to my elderly father. I pressed my questions once again, now armed with her employment history. He was as surprised as I was about her entry in *The Biographical Dictionary of Women in Science*. He remembered "some foreign guy with an accent" that he had met in her apartment once, a man with "a big and irascible personality," a man who figured large in her work and who "demanded they get all the attention." Thankfully, I wrote down every word my father said because his incomplete sentences and thoughts often seemed meaningless. Later, through interviews with Lucybelle's coworkers, and after finding articles on the history of polar ice cores, I learned that the irascible man was Swiss-born Henri Bader, a civilian scientist who refused to salute his military bosses and who is credited with pulling the first-ever ice cores from both Greenland and Antarctica, the beginning of climate change research.

After the 1966 success in Greenland, Bader and his team moved on to Antarctica where in January 1968 they reached the bottom of the ice and withdrew a 2,164-meter core. These ice cores reveal a complete profile of the late-Pleistocene and Holocene climate cycle, showing all the climate events, their frequency, and the changing environmental conditions up to the present day, including new and precise information about the concentration levels of greenhouse gases. Bader's achievements are considered highly significant both because of his technical accomplishment in figuring out a way to drill through the shifting glacial ice caps, and for the major scientific score of obtaining for the first time ever a continuous ice core, representing more than 120,000 years of climatic history. Because of his work, the vast databases of earth's history contained in the northern and southern ice caps became accessible to human investigation. The data stored in these cores are still being studied today.

Henri Bader was also the conceptual father of the International Geophysical Year, a multinational project of cooperative science, the effects of which are still rippling throughout scientific knowledge. I'm fond of the fact that my birth, in 1957, coincided with the International Geophysical Year.

I also asked my father, yet again, about Lucybelle's personal life. He told me the story of her giving up her New York apartment to a roommate who was getting married, and how that had infuriated their father because she'd found the apartment in the first place. Why would she just walk away? my father and grandfather wanted to know. I suspected a love drama.

My father also told me that Lucybelle had been writing a novel, maybe together with her roommate, he wasn't quite sure. Nothing came of it, he thought. I quietly wondered how he would know if anything came of it, any more than my mother would know if she had "acted on" her lesbianism. The "maybe together with her roommate" intrigued me.

Then, warmed up, my father offered a final provocative yet tenebrous story. "A few years ago," he couldn't remember exactly how many but I'm guessing *quite* a few years ago, a man called him. The man said he was the ex-husband of Phyllis, Lucybelle's New York roommate, and that he was in trouble. My father's words: "Her friend's husband was in the CIA.

Husband of Lucybelle's roommate and she was very bitter. Case of a sex problem, discovered he was gay. A little bit off his rocker. He was scared someone hated him and that someone might hurt him." He asked if my father would help him, and Dad said that he would. He never heard from the man again.

Who knows what is significant, if anything, in this story, but what it made me think about was how homosexual men and women often married in the fifties and sixties, in the attempt to make a workable life. I used these stories in inventing my character Fred.

The actual story is quite strange. How did this man get my father's phone number in Portland, Oregon? And why would he call the brother of his ex-wife's former roommate (or lover)? What did his fear about being gay, being possibly blackmailed, have to do with Lucybelle? Not to succumb to conspiracy theories, but I do occasionally at three in the morning ask myself if this incident is in any way related to Lucybelle's death. My father is not a teller of tales: every detail he related would have been exactly as it came to him. Unfortunately, the above quote is the sum total of his remembered knowledge on the matter.

For the record, I made several attempts at getting Lucybelle's Freedom of Information Act files but was told there was nothing to get. Actually, they did send me a few sheets of paper: my own letters, ones I'd written recently to various individuals and agencies, inquiring about her work and fluency in Russian.

I read lots of McCarthy Era history, including everything I could find on Camp Century. To the best of my knowledge, Project Iceworm never developed, no missiles were ever kept in Camp Century or anywhere else under the Greenland ice cap. Camp Century itself, situated 140 miles northeast of Thule Air Base, closed in 1966 because it was being destroyed by the movement of the glacial ice. Today the relics of that experiment are buried deep in the snowcap, which is rapidly melting. Perhaps one day in the future, artifacts from that great experiment—books, aluminum tubes, the barber's scissors, reels of film—will begin emerging from their frozen time capsule.

Meanwhile, once I knew where Lucybelle had worked, I began contacting everyone I could find who had worked with her. My letters and e-mails startled some of her contemporaries; after all, from their points of view, it seemed as if they were receiving correspondence from someone they thought fifty years dead. On my end, the experience of receiving letters about my aunt, finally after years and years of longing to know her, was one of the most gratifying experiences of my life. Every single person I talked to told me three things about her personality: that she was intensely private, never shared details about her personal life; that she was a particularly warm and kind person; that she had a wonderfully dry sense of humor. When I asked who her friends were, they told me the office manager, the office manager's friend who was a secretary, and the librarian, all single women "who usually ate lunch together." The office manager, according to one of my interviewees, was "a real martinet." I had to look the word up: a rigid disciplinarian; one who demands absolute adherence to forms and rules. My contact said she "ran a tight ship," for which they were all grateful. His tone and his choice of words brought another word to mind: bulldyke.

When I asked if they thought Lucybelle was gay, the youngest of the bunch answered, "She sure wasn't the type to go home to cook dinner for the hubby and kids." Most said, "I wouldn't know anything about that." At least three said, "You should speak to Marge Gow." Unfortunately, Marge Gow, who was married to one of the scientists, Tony Gow, did not answer my e-mails or phone calls. (Let me say now that neither Marge nor Tony figures as a character in this novel; my two scientists, Russell Woo and Peter Hauser, and their wives Amanda and Emily, are entirely fictional.)

I read all the gay and lesbian history I could find. An essay by Estelle B. Freedman of Stanford University, "The Burning of Letters Continues," published in her collection of essays, *Feminism, Sexuality, and Politics*, was exceedingly instrumental in helping me get to the heart of Lucybelle's story. And I do mean "heart." As I interviewed people, I felt more than a little sheepish being so interested in her intimate life, especially when talking with the scientists. It felt frivolous, as in, what does it matter whom she loved or if she was gay?

But the more I thought about it, the more I came to believe that nothing is more important than who and how we love. Why is that the part of history that gets dropped or trivialized? Most of us make a great number, maybe the majority or even all, of our decisions based on whom we love. Love may well move history forward with greater intensity and motivation than any other force (except, sadly, for hate). I wanted to tell a love story:

mine for my aunt, my aunt's for her lovers. I wanted to re-create the emotional fullness that might have existed in packets of burned letters. I wanted to give Lucybelle a love life that felt erased by my mother's declaration that she "never acted on it."

However, I was also concerned with the possibility that I might be projecting my own wishes for Lucybelle onto her life, that I was letting the lens through which I look at the world color this story. Or perhaps I should say, color *too deeply*, because of course we can only see the world and interpret events through our own particular lenses.

That's where Estelle Freedman's essay saved my project. She points out that many lesbians in the past did not keep their letters. They burned them. They spent their lives hiding the evidence. This means that when researching lesbians in history, so much has to be gleaned from conjecture and inference, and that this is *valid*. The hard evidence, in many cases, simply does not exist. In fact, its very absence is a clue.

That essay gave me the confidence to make not just assumptions, but reasoning deductions: Would a woman who was very intelligent, said by all to be particularly warm and possessing a wicked sense of humor, seriously live her life without any intimate relationships? Couple that with her extreme independence, the fact that she shot off the farm in Arkansas at her first opportunity and headed straight for Greenwich Village, my sister's memories of a companion, her coworkers' coded (and in a couple of cases explicit) ways of telling me that her good friends at work were lesbians. Then too there is everyone's assertion that she was extremely private about her personal life, meaning she kept secrets, a kind of pre-burning of letters. None of this is proof, I know that, but it adds up to pretty damn good evidence.

How could my mother be so sure about Lucybelle's intimate life? Neither she nor my father knew a single one of Lucybelle's friends. They didn't know she smoked, let alone chain-smoked. Freedman's article gave me the courage to value my suspicions, based on evidence, and to keep digging.

I headed off to New York, where I spent hours reading in the Lesbian Herstory Archives, and Chicago, where I visited the Gerber Hart Archives. I read all the issues of the first lesbian newsletters, *Vice Versa*, published in the forties, and *The Ladder*, published by the Daughters of Bilitis in the fifties. I called up lesbian seniors in both cities, with introductions from friends, and asked them if they knew Lucybelle. I loved this part of the research. These lesbian octogenarians went right to work, publishing notices in their newsletters and calling their friends to see if anyone had heard of my aunt. Several made sure to tell me what I already knew: the vast majority of lesbians in the forties, fifties, and sixties did not go to bars, were not public about their intimate lives, usually had small groups of close friends and socialized privately at house parties. No one knew her.

Then I talked again with Chet Langway, a scientist who worked closely with Henri Bader on the ice cores. He remembered going out to "some pond" a few times and having drinks with Lucybelle and the woman who lived at the pond. She was the first female scientist CRREL had hired, and while he remembered that she worked for the Photographic Interpretation Research Division, he couldn't think of her name. A few days later he e-mailed me, "Her name just popped out of me last night: Vera Prescott." This corroborated my sister's memory of a companion named Vera.

Off I went to New Hampshire to see the Cold Regions Research and Engineering Laboratory, and also Lucybelle's apartment, which had been rebuilt after the fire on top of the same garage in Lebanon, New Hampshire. Maps showed me that there were a number of ponds in the area, and I hoped to figure out which one was Vera's. While I was in New Hampshire, I screwed up my courage and called a couple of people I'd already spoken with by phone. I made a lunch date with Lucybelle's secretary, Donna Valliere, a character who does not figure in the preceding novel.

What a difference interviewing in person makes! I suppose when you're face to face with someone, it's much easier to judge whether she, the interviewer, is reasonable, well-meaning, and trustworthy. My contacts opened up. Also, it had not occurred to me to come out to these contemporaries of Lucybelle's when I wrote or called them. Maybe it just seemed silly to write, "By the way, I'm a lesbian." But that was a big mistake. I now made a point of coming out to my interviewees, which in turn made it safe for them to tell me what they knew about Lucybelle's homosexuality. In fact, when I talked about this with her secretary, Donna, she explained that they didn't want to spill the beans about their friend and colleague to some stranger calling from California, even if she was her niece. That made perfect sense. They were protecting my aunt! I was touched.

Donna was nineteen years old when Lucybelle hired her. This was just six months before the fire. Donna's boyfriend happened to live across the street from Lucybelle, and so she had some pertinent details about the fire. She told me that the office manager and secretary were "a known couple," though "nothing was ever said out loud." She said she'd heard that Lucybelle "had women in her life."

I took a deep breath, hating to be a bother, but there I was in New Hampshire, so I called Marge Gow again. She answered the phone. When I told her who I was, she said, "I've been expecting your call." Several of my interviewees told me they'd talked among themselves about my being in town and doing this research. Later I would realize that Marge hadn't been avoiding me; many older people simply don't do e-mail (even if they have accounts) or even return long-distance phone calls. Marge suggested lunch at Applebee's the following day.

I was actually shaking as I sat waiting in the booth. In came Marge and her husband, Tony, and before she even sat down, she said, "I knew your aunt and her partner well. They were so kind to me when Tony was in the field." The Gows, in turn, were so kind to me that afternoon, sharing everything they could remember about both Lucybelle and Vera. The Gows knew which pond, and I visited it that afternoon.

Marge, who had lived next door to Lucybelle when the lab first moved to New Hampshire, before Lucybelle moved to the apartment over the garage at 9 Placid Square Street, also told me that all she did in her spare time was write. She said she could hear the typewriter going for hours. Marge sometimes asked how the novel was coming along and Lucybelle would say either well or not well. This fiction-writing pursuit was corroborated by my father's story, by her degree in literature, and also by an interview I did with her best childhood friend, who now lives in a nursing home in New Mexico. When I asked the childhood friend, "Did she ever talk as a young girl about what she was going to do when she grew up?" the answer came back, "Write. No question. Absolutely, she was going to write novels, that was all there was for her." If she ever published a novel, perhaps under a pen name, I have not been able to find it.

This childhood friend from so many years ago, who was in tears half the time we talked, also told me about the harshness of Lucybelle's religious upbringing, her outsized sense of humor, and her pranks as a girl. In grammar school, Lucybelle apparently arranged what would now be considered flash-mob performances, in which she organized her classmates to stand up in the middle of lessons and spontaneously recite funny

312

poems. My father, too, remembered these school-wide jokes that Lucybelle orchestrated.

As I dug and dug, I came up with many "crucial facts joyfully uncovered" but was also "haunted by a looming absence: the shadowy mass of all that's been lost, that can never be recovered," to quote Emma Donoghue again. Thinking about the erasure of women's lives from the historical record, and how I wanted to handle this erasure in writing this story, brought to mind a quote by Monique Wittig: "There was a time when you were not a slave, remember that. You walked alone, full of laughter, you bathed bare-bellied. You say you have lost all recollection of it, remember. . . . You say there are no words to describe this time, you say it does not exist. But remember. Make an effort to remember. Or, failing that, invent."

And that is exactly what I've done with this book. I've made every possible effort to remember. I've asked dozens of others to also try to remember. Where memory has failed, I've invented.

How much of the story is true and how much is invented? A lot of it is true. Nearly but not all of the characters existed, but for most of them I have only the smallest amount of information about their personalities. I extrapolated wildly from these bits. I've made up all the dialogue, and most of the emotional content of Lucybelle's relationships.

In the end, I used every scrap of information I had about Lucybelle's life. I didn't necessarily intend to use this flotsam and jetsam so thoroughly, but the bits kept finding their ways into the narrative. Joseph Wood Krutch was indeed her graduate school advisor; she was at Columbia during the time Allen Ginsberg was, although I have no evidence that they ever met or spoke; she did become fluent enough in Russian, presumably so that she could read what the Russians were doing in their ice research, to tell my father that reading Turgenev in his native tongue was easier than reading Tolstoy; Tiny Davis and Ruby Lucas, who both played in the famed International Sweethearts of Rhythm band and were a couple for forty years, did have a lesbian club, Tiny and Ruby's Gay Spot, at 2711 South Wentworth Avenue in Chicago, which got torn down in 1958 to make way for a freeway; all the lesbian pulp novels and their authors are real; Mayor Daley did set off the air-raid sirens when the White Sox took the pennant in 1959, terrifying much of the city's population who did indeed believe the Russians were invading; a contact at WGN provided me with the White Sox announcer's exact wording for the baseball game broadcasts; Camp

Century was a real place, existing in the location and with the amenities and for the purposes I describe in the novel; I have a photograph of Lucybelle accepting some award from military brass, although I have no idea what the award is for; the CRREL lab did cancel its opening-day party due to President Kennedy's assassination the previous day; the CRREL scientists did make a baseball diamond in the field across the highway from the lab and Lucybelle loved baseball; she did send me a stuffed mountain lion, which I treasured; she was indeed extraordinarily buoyant in fresh water; all the fires in the novel did occur, including the one in Lucybelle's kitchen wastepaper basket; the office manager and secretary at the lab were in fact a couple, according to several sources, though I know nothing more about their lives. This is just a bit of the factual detritus that found its way into my story.

I sent away for Lucybelle's death certificate and was shocked to see that it listed her marital status as "widowed." I'm quite sure she never married. Why would she have married and kept the husband secret? An employee of New Hampshire's Division of Vital Records Administration kindly dug through her file and was able to tell me that this information about her marital status came not from the family but from her employer, the Army Corps of Engineers. This bit led me to invent the McCarthy Era story of Henri Bader asking her to claim she was widowed.

Lucybelle and Vera did have a dachshund named L'Forte. I don't know where he was the night of the fire, but I saved him in this story because I couldn't bear another loss. To the end of her long life, Vera continued to have dachshunds.

As anyone who has done historical research knows, the process is far from scientific and the answers are at best approximations. I asked everyone what Lucybelle went by. I heard everything from, "Just Lucy, so far as I know," to "Absolutely, always Lucybelle. I never heard it shortened." So for the novel I chose to have most of her contemporaries refer to her as Lucy, but to have her think of herself as Lucybelle, as she was known by the family.

As for accounts of her death, the factual record slides around even more. My father told me she died trying to get out a window. His story leaves me with a particularly anguishing image. The fire marshal's report, written by someone who was not at the scene, said she died crouched under a table. Several of her coworkers told me that they'd heard, from the local firefighters who were at the scene, that Lucybelle had tried to get out of the apartment but the carbon monoxide had so poisoned her brain that she confusedly walked into the closet, rather than out the door, and died there. This last story is also the version told by the people who lived across the street from her.

How much of this story is true? If forced into an answer, I'd say about fifty percent. I'd also say I've never written a truer story. I have changed the names of all the characters except for my aunt's and Henri Bader's. I've done this because what I've written is a novel based on a framework of facts, but it is not a factual account of anyone's life, including my aunt's. I've kept Bader's name because of his historical importance, and while I did hear a few firsthand accounts of his personality and accomplishments, I know nothing about his nonscientific actions or conversations or marriage (though he did have a wife named Adele). I've invented dialogue, actions, and emotions for Henry Bader, as I have for all of the other characters. I have a bit more information about Vera, as described above and below, but nowhere near enough to call this a biography.

To this day, I have only a handful of primary documents: Lucybelle's death certificate, both the fire department's and the fire marshal's reports, the telegram my father sent to her upon my birth (though why this last was returned to my father and stored in my baby book, I don't know), a couple of letters Vera wrote to her mother, and some photographs. There are no extant letters written by Lucybelle, not a single one that I know of, and no journals. From the telegram I learned her Evanston address and from the death certificate I learned her last New Hampshire address.

For several years I'd been plagued by my inability to find an address for her in New York, where she lived from 1944 to 1956. I spent hours in the New York Public Library scrolling through microfiche of the telephone directories, year by year, finding nothing. Not everyone had a phone in those days; sometimes all the residents of a building shared one line. The phone could have been in a roommate's name. I knew where she worked, at the Geological Society of America, which was housed in a building that has since been consumed by Columbia University, but the GSA no longer has records dating back to Lucybelle's time. A friend of a friend who lives near Columbia showed me his apartment, and I considered putting her up there, near her job. But I wanted her to live in the Village, and so I spent about three afternoons wandering around, considering addresses for her.

Because I'd named Willa Cather the godmother to this novel, I decided to put Lucybelle at 1 Bank Street, in the building that now stands in the same location of the building where Willa Cather had lived with Edith Lewis. I liked thinking of Lucybelle in Cather's space.

On a recent trip to New York that had nothing to do with this novel—I'd already begun writing and had completed a draft and a half—I found myself with a free afternoon on my hands. My partner, Pat, suggested we go back to the New York Public Library and look again for Lucybelle's address. "We might find a really good librarian," she said.

We found two. First, Sarah, who worked in the basement of the Jefferson Market branch, sent us to the genealogy and local history room of what she called the Lions Library, the central one on Fifth Avenue. I'd already spent hours there squinting at microfiche, but she said to tell the librarian she'd sent us. So I told Mr. A. Rubenstein (as his nametag read) of the Milstein Division that Sarah had sent me, and I also told him what I was looking for. He searched a number of different ways, and eventually showed me a new historical database with a city directory.

Gold. Lucybelle Bledsoe had lived at 277 West 12th Street, in the heart of the Village. What's more, the address I had given her already, 1 Bank Street, is exactly one short block away. I sat there in front of the NYPL computer, next to Mr. Rubenstein, and wept.

Throughout doing this research and writing this story, I've wanted to believe that Lucybelle had a good life. This crucial piece of the puzzle, that when she'd left the Arkansas farm she'd gone straight to Greenwich Village, told me she sure was trying, if not succeeding, at having a good time with her years.

The part of this story that haunted me in the beginning haunts me still. I could have known Vera. Once I had her full name (which, again, I've changed for this book), I found her obituaries. She died in 2002, thirty-six years after Lucybelle's death and just six years before I started this research. I learned from her obituaries that she had been an environmental activist, had been very active in the Sierra Club, and that the Michigan chapter has named an award for her. She knew both David Brower and Ansel Adams. She also had indeed been a pilot, a fellow of the American Academy of Sciences, and a member of the Association of Women Geographers. She loved to travel and had been all over the world. From the obituaries I got the names of an arts organization and a Unitarian church in the foothills of

Georgia's Appalachian Mountains, where she spent her last years. I wrote the director of the arts organization and the pastor at the church. A wonderful woman, a member of the church's small congregation, wrote me back.

Leah and her husband were good friends with Vera at the end of her life. They got to know her through the church that Vera founded with a small group of old lesbians. When Vera was dying, it was Leah and her husband who cared for her, helped her get her house and papers in order, and notified her family. Leah said that Vera was fairly private and didn't talk openly about her relationships with women. When I asked Leah how she knew Vera was a lesbian, she answered, "It was sort of obvious."

Vera did leave CRREL after Lucybelle's death and taught in a couple of universities before she retired. She settled in Monterey, California, with a dachshund named Adam, where she lived for many years. I was a short couple of hours away in Oakland and Berkeley. I like to think it's possible, although I realize highly unlikely, that Vera read some of my published work. If she had, wouldn't she have contacted me? Not necessarily. In fact, probably not.

When she was seventy years old, Vera bought a small camper truck and set out, with another dachshund, Ulysses, to travel around the country for an undecided amount of time. According to her nephew, she said she'd let people know where she decided to live when she figured it out. Seven months later, she settled in the Georgia mountains.

Leah told me that Vera always wore Birkenstocks, with rag wool socks in the wintertime, and sweatshirts with "sayings" on them. She loved discussing philosophy and religion with Leah's husband. Leah said that "if Lucybelle was anything like Vera, they would have been a tremendous pair."

Vera's family disapproved of her lifestyle and, according to Leah, she had a difficult relationship with them. When she was dying, Leah wrote to Vera's brother and told him that he should come if he wanted to see her. He didn't make it in time to say good-bye, but he and his son arrived in time for the funeral. The son, a seventeen-year-old boy, stood up at Vera's service and announced that she would be going to hell. Presumably, according to Leah, because she was gay.

I wrote to this brother of Vera's, asking for information about her and also about Lucybelle, and he did send me some letters Vera had written to their mother. These let me know that Vera wrote about Lucybelle, about her having a cold or her car being in the shop, in her letters home. Their dachshund, L'Forte, is mentioned often. I'm heartened that despite her family's disapproval, Vera persisted in at least not erasing the everyday parts of her life with Lucybelle from the record.

Leah told me about another nephew, the son of Vera's sister, who had spent significant time at Post Pond during at least two summers. She said that this nephew "was a real favorite." I wrote him and he wrote back saying, "The letter I just received was somewhat of a heartthrob when I recognized the name on the return label." He said Vera had been heartbroken at Lucybelle's death. He also told me that Vera quit smoking as a result of the fire. The two women had been kind to him as a boy. Unfortunately, he found corresponding with me difficult, whether because of the content or his communication skills, I don't know, but he did not want to continue. He said he'd been very young when he knew Lucybelle and Vera and that he'd told me everything he remembered.

It torments me that I didn't find Vera before she died. I can only imagine the wealth of information about my namesake I could have had. I try to find comfort in realizing that while it wouldn't have been impossible to find her, it was nearly so. Until Routledge published the article about Lucybelle in *The Biographical Dictionary of Women in Science* in 2000, I had no clues for beginning a search. Even after finding the article, it took me a few years to follow the trail, put together the hints and evidence, which eventually led me to Vera.

This story about one decade in my aunt's life covers a vital period in American history, including the McCarthy Era and the Cold War. It was a time of foment, the launching decade of great change. In May 1966, just a few months before Lucybelle's death, Stokely Carmichael rose to power and the Black Panther Movement was formed. In June of that same year, the Third National Conference of Commissions on the Status of Women convened. Twenty or so women met in Betty Friedan's hotel room and again over lunch the last day of the conference. The National Organization for Women (NOW) was conceived. National conversations about racism and sexism were in full bloom.

However, conversations about the history of climate, and the future of climate, not to mention the related weather disasters, were still decades away from public purview. The important stories found in the ice cores would not reach a widespread audience for another fifty years. But the work of Henri Bader, his scientists, and Lucybelle was vibrant and present in their day. *They* knew they were seeing something vitally important. Such is the pace of societal consciousness.

I wrote this book to give Lucybelle love; but I also wrote it to express my gratitude for those women, especially her, who wrote the true books that didn't get published, who did the science without getting a scrap of credit, who lived independently and loved freely, who dreamed about the Arctic and the Antarctic, who, in short, made my world and all the things I care most about possible. My namesake Lucybelle and I share so much: writing fiction, loving women, polar dreams.

How do you change shame into inheritance? How do you change secrets into living history? My heroine dies and so this is a tragedy. I don't believe the saying that "everything happens for a reason." Sometimes a great tear happens in a life, a ripping apart, a random violence to the spirit. Lucybelle Bledsoe—like Lorraine Hansberry, like Rachel Carson, and so many others—died far too early. And yet she came a very long way from the farm in Pocahontas, Arkansas, to Greenwich Village to Chicago and finally to Lebanon, New Hampshire. I hope she found at least as much love as I've granted her in this novel.

Vera's ashes are spread in Lake Superior's Isle Royale National Park, where they have enriched the soil trod by an abundance of wolves and moose, far from civilization. Lucybelle is buried in Pocahontas, Arkansas.

# Acknowledgments

Thank you to the extraordinary librarians and archivists who spent hours of their valuable time helping me uncover Lucybelle's story: Jocelyn K. Wilk at the Rare Book and Manuscript Library at Columbia University; Jeanette Hammann, director of publications at the Geological Society of America; Patrick Leary at the Wilmette Historical Museum; Steve Bailey and Sean Fleming at the Lebanon Public Library; CRREL librarian Elisabeth Smallidge; CRREL public affairs specialist Marie Darling; George Pappas of WGN-TV, who offered not only some crucial details about the history of television and baseball but also provided me with the exact audio for the television broadcast of the 1959 American League pennant game between the Chicago White Sox and the Cleveland Indians; and especially Asa Rubenstein of the Milstein Division of the New York Public Library, who found Lucybelle's Greenwich Village address, a detail that confirmed a hunch I held dear. Joan Nestle, one of my heroines, is the genius behind the Lesbian Herstory Archives in Brooklyn; her work has rescued thousands of remarkable women from obscurity. She also helped me personally in pointing out a wealth of research directions for this project. Deb Teddy and Dee Johnson, also of the Lesbian Herstory Archives, were helpful as well. I am also grateful for the Gerber/Hart Library and Archives in Chicago.

Thank you to many stellar historians. Without the groundbreaking work of Marilyn Ogilvie and Joy Harvey, who researched and published *The Biographical Dictionary of Women in Science: Pioneering Lives from Ancient Times to the Mid-20th Century*, I would not have begun this project. John D'Emilio, a University of Illinois at Chicago post–WWII historian, with special expertise in women's and gender studies, was generous with his time, and his books were essential to my understanding of the era. Estelle Freedman, trailblazing historian of Stanford University, generously read the entire manuscript. And, as described in my postscript, her published work on lesbian history opened doors for this project and gave me the courage to continue researching.

Thank you to Lucybelle's contemporaries and coworkers who talked to me on the phone, via e-mail, and in person, in some cases many times: Lisa Davis, Marie Kuda, Sarah Huber, Mark Baden, Lark Hutto, Wynne Ewing, Chet Langway, David Minsk, Willy Weeks, Jerry Brown, Herbert Ueda, Jim Bender (posthumously through his revelatory obituary), Steve Bowen, Sandy Smith, Donna Valliere, Marge and Tony Gow. Their memories and stories are the heart of my novel.

Thank you to friends who read early drafts of *A Thin Bright Line*: Pat Mullan, Martha Garcia, Suzanne Case, Robin Ellett, Dorothy Hearst, Elizabeth Stark, Alison Bechdel, and Carol Seajay, who prompted me to Google my aunt in the first place. Thank you as well to WOMBA, Word of Mouth Bay Area, an extraordinary group of women writers who provide a backbone of daily support.

Thank you to friends who pointed me in the direction of crucial tidbits: Barb Johnson, Jim Van Buskirk, Lance Brady, Francisca Goldsmith, Don Weise, and Ian River Hoffmann. Guy Guthridge, formerly of the National Science Foundation's Artists and Writers program, is a font of knowledge about people in ice research. Anne Laughlin, a novelist and real estate broker, managed to get me interior pictures of Lucybelle's Evanston apartment, which in turn helped me to imagine her life there.

A number of government officials provided records that shed light on my aunt's life: the New Hampshire State Fire Marshal's Office, which is part of the State of New Hampshire Department of Safety; Christian A. Simon of the Lebanon Fire Department; and Yvette, certification supervisor at the New Hampshire Department of State, Division of Vital Records Administration.

My extraordinary agent, Reiko Davis, has worked brilliantly and tirelessly on behalf of my work. I cannot thank her enough.

My parents, John Perry Bledsoe and Helen W. Bledsoe, welcomed Lucybelle into our home when I was a child and later told me everything they could remember about her. My father loved hearing my discoveries about his sister in the last few years of his life.

I'm thrilled to be working once again with the University of Wisconsin Press and want to thank Dennis Lloyd, Amber Rose, Andrea Christofferson, Sheila Leary, Carla Marolt, Adam Mehring, and especially Raphael Kadushin, who for so many years has been a leading light in publishing LGBT stories.

Thank you, most of all, to my partner, Pat Mullan, who understands better than anyone how much this book means to me. Thank you for listening to every detail, multiple times, for so many years.